CLEATS *in* CLAY

JACKSON CORDD

Dreamspinner Press

Published by
Dreamspinner Press
5032 Capital Circle SW
Ste 2, PMB# 279
Tallahassee, FL 32305-7886
USA
http://www.dreamspinnerpress.com/

Cleats in Clay

Cover Art by L.C. Chase
http://www.lcchase.com

ISBN: 978-1-62380-287-5
Digital ISBN: 978-1-62380-288-2

Printed in the United States of America
First Edition
January 2013

I dedicate this novel to Granny, a real salt-of-the-earth Okie, who told me often: "Keep your feet in the clay, but don't forget to reach for the stars. Your arms are longer than you think."

I try to remember her wisdom every day and keep my dreams big.

CHAPTER
One

FOLLOWING the directions from Gertie at the bed and breakfast, Bobby Lane turned off the crisp concrete highway onto less-traveled asphalt. The GPS in his rental car indicated the directions pointed southwest, moving him farther from the outskirts of the tiny town of Brungess.

The land around Bobby looked like what he would expect of the western panhandle of Texas. A few scrawny mesquite trees and scrubby grass clumps stood across the gentle roll of ground. The drier conditions of the area seemed more suited for cattle than farming, maybe. Or it might not be worth anything at all. This was starting to feel like a bad idea.

The GPS voice announced another turn, which put Bobby onto an even less-used gravel-packed road. He had to pull over nearly into the ditch and slow to a crawl when a tan SUV passed from the opposite direction. The vehicle didn't have any markings, but the array of antennas and doodads adorning the SUV screamed out like a neon sign, announcing "cop car." The older man in a sheriff's fedora glared at Bobby suspiciously as he drove by, as if he was trying to gauge his level of criminality while passing.

Once Bobby accelerated onto the road again and proceeded west, the surroundings looked even more desolate. He wouldn't even be doing this if it weren't for Nate, but he tried not to think about that. Even six months after—

Look at the speedometer, look at the road, look out the rearview, Bobby directed himself, trying to distract his thoughts.

Bobby drove the Chevy rental about three more miles before the GPS sang a gentle tone and a soft feminine voice announced, "Destination reached."

Looking around, Bobby found himself in the middle of the road, in the middle of nowhere, but Gertie had warned him to expect this. The farm roads and drives hadn't made it into the GPS database. He could see a turnoff to the left about nine yards ahead, just as Gertie predicted. Bobby pulled up and took the turn.

It hardly seemed to qualify as a road, but the hard dirt was fairly smooth and free of vegetation, as if it had been recently plowed and scraped clean. Bobby glanced at the written directions and drove farther south. He fought the subtle urge to turn around. Bobby was usually up for one of Nate's adventures, but this seemed more like a fool's errand.

Two more turns put him on a bare-rutted trail. Only two worn grooves vaguely indicated the direction of travel. Now Bobby truly was out in the middle of nowhere.

He followed the tire tracks and eventually reached an old iron cattle gate. Bobby parked in front of the gate and peered around. He could see the aged fencing stretched out in either direction, cordoning off a square of land roughly three acres or so in size. Most of the fence seemed to be of the banded-wire style, but one sagging stretch along the backside was of the old horizontal planks common with horse ranches. Along the top of the gate, in runic-looking letters, was the name Vorleik.

Other than a cluster of conifers in the southwest corner, only a small shed sat on the empty expanse of wooly weeds.

This couldn't be the right place.

Bobby had expected to find a house or maybe a warehouse sculptor's studio or something. The small shed looked barely large enough to hold a lawn mower. Certainly no one lived or worked in that tiny building.

Then he noticed the small shiny box mounted on the pole next to the gate. The newness of the box contrasted so boldly with the rusty gate pole, Bobby should have spotted it right away. He turned off the car, grabbed the purchase receipt left behind by Nathan, then climbed out of the rental.

It was some sort of buzzer call box, with no visible speaker, though. Bobby pushed in on the bar-shaped button, but nothing happened.

What has Nate gotten me into now? Bobby wondered as he waited.

Maybe the button was broken.

Bobby looked out into the land again but saw nothing.

He turned and started back toward the car when movement caught his attention. He looked over to see a huge war hound bounding across the scrubby expanse, heading straight for him.

Well, maybe not a war hound. When the dog stopped in a flanking position on the inside of the gate, Bobby could see the beast's color markings, stance, and high triangular ears looked much like a German shepherd's. But the dog's large size, squared shoulders, and muzzle weren't typical of that breed.

The dog let out one low, quick gruff, sort of an "I got my eye on you" warning, indeed, watching with intelligent eyes as it stood in a defensive stance.

"Hey there, girl," Bobby said after glancing down to verify the sex. It felt strangely rude not to say *something* to the expectant beast.

The dog didn't reply.

The dog's ears twitched slightly and swiveled to the side, as if she'd heard something from behind.

Bobby looked up and saw a blond man wearing only loose jeans, pull-on shoes, and an oversized T-shirt jog-walking toward the gate. Just like the dog, the man seemed to have appeared out of nowhere.

As the man approached, Bobby noticed right away how short he was. Bobby had never been considered tall himself, only five foot ten while wearing shoes, but he felt very tall now. The other man was at least five inches shorter.

"Down, Heim." The man spoke in a strong tenor voice. The dog immediately sat on her rear and dangled a huge square tongue out the side of her mouth.

"Truck break down?" the little blond man asked, looking over the obviously athletic tourist with sudden suspicion.

"Truck?"

"Take it you're not Fed Ex," the man concluded. "Why you botherin' me, then?"

Bobby walked to the gate and displayed the page in his hand. "I've got a receipt."

The man just stared at him as if he'd spoken in ancient Greek.

"Gertie sent me. I've got a purchase receipt," Bobby repeated.

"Gertie?" The man seemed to spit out her name. "What's she gone a-doin' now?"

A gust of the late March winds blew through, pulling the heat out of Bobby. He looked back at the warmth of the car. "Never mind." Bobby slumped. "This is obviously some kind of mistake."

The man rubbed his hands along his bare arms in the chill of the wind. "Now hold on, there. If'n ya come all this way…." The man looked Bobby over again. "Scootch out, Heim, let the man in," he said to the dog before pushing a button on the inside of the gate post. Like a giant pocket door, the gate retracted along the edge of the fence as the dog moved over to the side of the drive and sat again.

Bobby climbed back into the car and started it. For one brief second, he did have the thought to just turn around and flee back to civilization, but he gripped the wheel and drove through the open gate far enough for the man to close it again.

After the man punched a button, he and the dog jogged ahead. Bobby drove the car slowly along beside them. Getting farther into the property, he could see some kind of space hollowed out of the flat ground ahead. Then he noticed part of the flat expanse of land was actually the roof of an underground house.

As he got closer, Bobby realized that a trick of the distance and the shed's proportions made it appear smaller from the road. The building was actually much larger, more the size of a one-and-a-half-car garage. He parked in front of the garage when the man motioned him to stop.

After grabbing his jean jacket and slipping it on, Bobby left the car again. "I'm Bobby Lane," he introduced as he followed the man toward the dug-out area.

"Name's Odis, if'n Gertie didn't already tell ya that, and this here's Heimdalla."

"Heimdalla?"

Odis stopped. "You makin' fun of my heritage, boy?"

"Oh, uh, no," Bobby stammered. "It's just an unusual name." He looked down at Odis again. He had used the word "boy" the way an elderly man would, but Odis didn't seem that old. He had that "over thirty" appearance, with a full head of dark-blond hair only showing the beginnings of hairline recession. He certainly didn't *look* like an old man.

Odis walked toward a set of steps that descended into the area carved from the ground. "Don't know your Nordic mythology? Guardian of Asgard?"

Bobby just shook his head. In school, athletics had been his strength. "What breed is she?"

"Shep-weiler," Odis replied. "Though ya hear the name rott-herd thrown around too. Never liked that one. Sounds too much like somethin' nasty you'd throw outta the fridge."

Bobby looked down at Heim as she followed them down the steps. Her large square frame definitely hinted at rottweiler parentage. She trotted ahead to a sliding glass door and looked back.

On the south side, a grassy patio area had been hollowed out of the ground. On the north, a curving bank of glass wall stood open to the spring equinox sun. The unique house hugged into the earth like a grand sculpture, probably designed by Odis himself.

Odis slid open the door and motioned to a wrought iron patio-style table and chairs by the windows. Heim trotted in behind them. She claimed a spot by the glass to warm in the sun but still kept an alert watch on Bobby.

Bobby sat and studied Odis. He could see around his eyes and brow traces of wrinkles that hinted at "maybe forty," but nothing to indicate why Odis would act like such an old man.

"Now, then," Odis sighed as he sat at the table. "What's this nonsense about a receipt? Can't deliver on somethin' I ordered?" Odis asked, glancing over at him. He thought Bobby had the appearance of a thirtyish gym rat and seemed barely as smart as one too. This boy looked like a brick, and something about him just seemed like trouble. Maybe Odis should have left his ass out in the cold.

"No." Bobby put the printed-out page on the table for Odis to look at. "It's something that was ordered *from* you. Last year. I'm here to pick it up."

"A commission?" Odis grumbled at his fool sister again. He'd told Gertie to quit messing with the Internet. Obviously she didn't listen to him. And Gertie hadn't bothered to tell him about it, or maybe she did? Sometimes things could be a little fuzzy.

"Prepaid." Bobby pointed to a spot on the receipt. "And a hefty amount too. For delivery this week."

"This is made out to a Nathan Price." Odis looked up. "You said your name was Bobby."

He nodded. "Nate's… no longer here. That's why I'm picking it up."

Odis started to ask for further explanation, but the expression of bereavement he saw befall Bobby's features said more than any words could. "I see, then."

Bobby looked around the interior of the house, trying to distract himself. It was an open-floor-plan kind of design, like a studio loft apartment carved from concrete. The curves of various sizes that portioned out the rooms clung against each other in graceful arcs. He couldn't see a straight line in the place, which gave the house a quiet, artful beauty.

Odis cleared his throat. "Why'd Gertie send ya out here?"

"She didn't have any pieces left in your shop at the B and B in town. Sent the last one to a gallery months ago, she said. Thought you might have one here."

"Well, then, suppose we should have a look-see."

Odis walked to the sliding glass door and waited for Bobby. They went back out into the March wind, Heim trotting behind. Odis followed the banked curve of glass toward the east side and opened another sliding door. The glass here faced the west to catch the afternoon sun.

Heim sat outside near the door as though she had no interest in entering this room.

Once inside the studio, Bobby noticed a slight stale tinge to the air, like the inside of a closet that hadn't been opened in many months. Another vague familiar smell also hid in the room, but Bobby couldn't put his finger on what it was.

A large beat-up wooden table stood in the middle of the room. On the table by a stool, something, probably a work in progress, was covered by a large gray towel.

Odis motioned to a side wall covered with mostly naked shelves. Bobby saw only two pieces there: a small statue of a bird that looked to be preening itself, and an animal. Stepping closer, Bobby saw the small animal was an armadillo, crouching over like it was preparing to roll up into a ball. While detailed, the two pieces fashioned of clay looked rather small and common, more like the kind of kitschy thing for sale on one of those shopping channels. They certainly didn't look worth the hefty payment Nate had made.

Bobby turned to the table. That hidden statue or carving, whatever it was, looked to be about four or five times the size of the other works. Maybe it would be more valuable. "What's that one?"

"Nothing," Odis said flatly.

Bobby raised an eyebrow. The work in progress certainly looked like something; some mysterious shape hid under that towel.

Odis motioned back to the shelves. "What about those?"

As Odis waved toward the shelves, Bobby noticed he had large hands, maybe a little oversized. He also saw that Odis's knuckles looked a little enlarged. "Well, they're nice. Kinda small."

"Won't do ya, huh?"

Bobby shook his head. "If you don't mind my saying, they seem kind of ordinary."

"Hm." Odis nodded curtly. "Never pegged you to have an eye." He threw a slight smile at Bobby.

"Is this all you have?"

"Yep, 'fraid so."

"Then maybe I should just get a refund."

"Can't help with that. Gertie does all my business stuff. I just do the art."

Bobby glanced back to the worktable. "What about—"

"You don't want that one, trust me," Odis said as he quickly moved back to the sliding door and opened it.

Bobby followed Odis back to the house door. Heim padded along. Once inside, Bobby noticed that while it looked beautiful, the place had the same utilitarian feel as the studio. Nothing in the living space seemed warm or homey.

Bobby paused inside the door. There was nothing for him here. He should just make his exit. Yet something about Odis made him hesitate. After all, he had driven out *this* far. It wouldn't hurt to stay a minute.

An awkward silence hung between them.

Odis motioned back to the wrought iron patio table. "Grab a chair, then."

Bobby walked over and sat.

"So," Odis said over his shoulder as he moved to the kitchen area and got a pitcher from the refrigerator. "Tell me somethin' about yourself. Inspire me for this commission."

"I'm Bobby Lane."

Odis returned with two iced teas, with one large square cube in each glass. "You done said that, and ya look too young to be president, so I'm failin' to see why it's so important."

Bobby studied him again. "Baseball player. World Series. You really don't know?"

"I don't cotton much for sports. Must not be as good at it as ya think ya are."

"Playing isn't exactly what I'm famous for." Bobby struggled. He'd never had to explain it to anybody before; most people just knew. The news had made such a big splash. "Game two of the series? I ditched my team?"

Odis appraised him carefully. "Don't seem like the flighty flake type. Must be more to the story than that."

Bobby stewed. "There is…." It would be easy enough to just get up and leave, make some excuse and head out the door. But Odis was waiting. Those kind blue eyes of his seemed to deserve an answer.

Odis watched him.

"I… Nathan had to stay late, didn't fly in until the first afternoon. In the cab on the way to the hotel, he went into convulsions and the cabbie took him to the hospital. I played part of the first series game, pissed off that Nate hadn't shown. It wasn't 'til that night, back at the hotel, I found out he was in a coma."

"So he was your lover?"

"Husband," Bobby corrected strongly. "We had a ceremony and everything in Boston four years ago. Had to keep it quiet, though. Management was too worried about a scandal."

As Odis got up and left the room, Bobby watched, shocked by the reaction. *How dare he just get up and—*

Odis returned and handed something to him. Without thinking, Bobby took the items. He looked down at the pipe and lighter. It was one of those old-fashioned corncob pipes like he'd seen in some hillbilly movie once. And it didn't smell at all like tobacco. Bobby realized it was the same faint lingering smell he had noticed in the studio. Marijuana.

"Go ahead," Odis urged as he sat in the chair next to Bobby. "You're a man who needs a toke if I've ever seen one."

Bobby looked down at the pipe. He'd had weed before, of course, back in college. He'd always been too worried about his career to have any kind of drugs since going professional. It was one of the things Nate used to tease him about sometimes. A glass of bubbly at New Year's was about all he did. Athletics, his body, were too important and kept him wary of such temptations. He'd seen too many other players crash their careers with booze and drugs.

"Light up, dude," Odis urged, echoing the voice of Nathan in his head. That voice of Nathan was also nagging him to loosen up.

Bobby brought the pipe to his mouth and struck the lighter. He inhaled a little and held the breath, struggling not to cough as he fought the spicy burning tingle in his throat. He coughed anyway.

Odis took the pipe from him as he exhaled slowly. Odis took his own hit.

Bobby was a bit surprised at himself for taking the smoke. He watched Odis put the pipe and lighter on the table.

"Now then, baseball."

"Baseball," Bobby echoed.

"You played a long time?"

Bobby chuckled. "Since I was old enough to hold up a bat, seems like."

"Nice for a man to have a passion." Odis nodded.

Bobby looked at the corncob pipe. *Go ahead, one more*, the voice of Nathan urged.

Odis followed his gaze, then picked up the pipe and lighter and put them in Bobby's hands.

Bobby inhaled deeply this time, letting the intoxicating smoke dance in his nose and throat as he held the breath in.

"You got a touch of twang, but it's not Texas. Where ya from?"

"North Carolina, but Dad's from Ohio. Spent a lot of time there growin' up." Bobby felt something stirring in his mind, like the fingers of that tight stranglehold of control he always felt were loosening slightly.

Odis watched him put the pipe back on the table. "They fired you? When you went to the hospital?"

Bobby shook his head. "Not then. They told me to show for the second game, but I refused. I wasn't gonna leave Nate."

"Then?" Odis encouraged.

"When I didn't come in for the third game, someone leaked it to the media where I was. *That's* when it turned into a three-ring freak show."

Odis picked up the pipe, but this time when he handed it to over, he cradled Bobby's hand in his own a few seconds before letting go.

Bobby inhaled another huge lungful, then slowly released it. "He died that night."

Odis gently took hold of Bobby's hand. Then he slid the pipe from Bobby's fingers with his other hand and put it back on the table.

As his mind's strangling fingers loosened more, Bobby felt suppressed anger emerging. "If it had been one of the other players, a player's wife, there'd'a been memorials... people woulda written songs...." He felt his face hardening. "Sympathy of the media woulda been—"

Bobby clenched his fists. "Instead, *I* get the clusterfuck freak show." He leaned forward against the table as he scowled. "*I'm* some kind of villain for not supporting the team." He took a deep breath and slapped his palm on the table. "*Never mind* Nathan's fuckin' dead, there's a World Series to win!"

All of Bobby's strength poured out with his words. He slumped back down into his seat.

Scooting his chair closer, Odis reached out and gently touched Bobby's drooped chin, pulling Bobby's head up to look into his face. "I hope the fuckers lost."

"Yep, they did."

Odis gazed at Bobby with sympathetic blue eyes. "Maybe"—Odis took his hand and pulled Bobby to his feet—"maybe you *should* see it."

He led Bobby by the hand back to the studio. "It was a work commissioned by the Equestrian Society," Odis explained as he guided Bobby around the worktable. "I struggled with it over a week, not getting anywhere before...." Odis pulled the towel away from his work.

The emotional impact of the piece hit Bobby like a punch. He clutched at his stomach as he stared at the horse.

The clay sculpture was about twenty-four inches tall, and only the animal's front section was visible. Its rear legs and rump appeared to be inside the table, trapped in a quagmire of muck. The horse's eyes were wide with panic, a terror visible in its straining muscles as it fought to liberate itself from the puddle of thick mud, its right hoof cracked and split from the effort of trying to pull itself free.

Bobby slumped back against the cabinet. "Shit," he moaned, not able to take his eyes from the raw clay. It felt as though all his suppressed emotional pain sprang to life in front of him. He felt himself sinking to the floor as the fingers of control in his mind completely released their grip.

"Whoa, dude," Odis said, reaching out to hold Bobby upright before he slid down to the floor. "I didn't expect to knock ya off your feet."

"It's, it's very… powerful." Bobby dropped his gaze to the floor, fighting the chaos spiraling inside. Odis's hand on his arm felt so firm. The room seemed to be getting warm. His thoughts felt jumbled. The room got hotter. He couldn't seem to pull them—his thoughts—together.

Bobby thought he saw a blurring streak across the front of the glass as a strange buzzing noise filled his ears momentarily.

Odis put his other hand on Bobby's chest and pulled him up to his feet. "Oops."

"Oops?" Bobby asked, the word making a funny echo in his head.

"Maybe my sister." Odis leaned toward him.

It seemed like Odis was going to kiss him. Bobby shook his head, trying to clear the fuzzy jumble of tangled thoughts. "Maybe?"

Odis pushed him back to lean upright against the cabinet. "I said, it may be my sister."

Bobby saw Heimdalla appear in front of the glass windows. He watched the large dog bouncing and jumping in an excited way.

Gertie strolled up and marched right through the sliding glass door— or maybe she opened the door first, Bobby couldn't remember. "There you are. You don't ever answer your damn phone."

Bobby gave her a friendly wave. "Heya."

Gertie started to say something else, but her eyes drifted over to the clay horse on the worktable. "Odis." She sucked in a breath. "That thing is hideous!"

"That's why I backed out of the equestrian job. Unless you think maybe they'd want it?"

"Lord have mercy, no! That thing needs destroyed!"

"No!" Bobby yelled out, surprised by the sound of his own voice. "It's Art. Can't destroy Art." He almost giggled from the way his voice gave *art* a capital letter.

Maybe he did giggle.

He glanced over and Odis was grinning at him. He could feel the heat of Odis's handprint still on his arm.

Gertie looked over at Bobby. "Odis!" She clucked her tongue. "Honestly, I send you a client and you get him stoned out of his gourd."

"Just a couple of tokes to help the man relax."

"You sure it wasn't a couple of bongs?"

Bobby giggled at the way the word "bong" seemed to keep echoing in his head. *Bong. Bong.* He looked over at Odis again. He was still talking to "his sister," to Gertie, but their words were boring and he didn't pay any attention. Bobby just looked at Odis's face as he talked. The way his dark-pink lips moved to form words. The way his Viking nose sat boldly on his face, strong and straight. The way the tiny lines around Odis's eyes seemed to flicker and dance as he spoke.

Odis had a very handsome face.

Bobby gazed lower. Odis had a nice body. Odis had big feet.

"Mr. Lane!" Gertie's voice said again.

Bobby looked over at Gertie. "Me?"

"Yes, you. I'm glad you found the place. I would offer to have you follow me back to the B and B and I'd give you a room, but you're obviously in no condition to drive. So there's a free room at the B and B when you sober up enough to make it back to town."

"In town, the B and B in town."

Gertie smiled tightly. "Right. Free room."

"Free room, okey dokey."

Bobby looked up again at the door, but Gertie had disappeared.

Odis put his hand on Bobby's back. "Right, then, let's get you back in the house."

The hand on his back felt so large and warm. Bobby took careful steps as the hand gently pushed him forward. The floor didn't seem to be exactly where it was supposed to be.

CHAPTER
Two

AFTER some walking, Bobby was back at the patio table. Odis said something about a drink.

Heim came over and sat next to him, putting her chin on his knee. Bobby reached down and touched her head. Her fur felt so soft, like warm melted chocolate. Heimdalla looked up at him with kind eyes as he rubbed and patted her head.

Odis set a mug of coffee on the table in front of him.

Bobby sat up and took the mug. He carefully took a sip. It wasn't coffee at all. It was sweet and chocolaty with just a tiny hint of bitter. The warm flavor danced on his tongue and in his throat. This was the best chocolate he had ever tasted.

Bobby looked up when he heard a chuckle. Odis was smiling at him. "You seem to be enjoying that mocha."

Bobby smiled. "Yep. It's good."

Odis laughed. "You're stoned," he teased.

Bobby just grinned without replying and took another sip. He gazed up at Odis over his mug.

"So," Odis said. "You keep lookin' at me."

"You keep lookin' at me," Bobby warmly echoed back.

"I asked you first."

Words. Bobby didn't want words. Words got in the way. After all the friendly touching in the studio, Bobby wanted action. "Just kiss me."

Odis looked surprised. "And what makes ya think I'd be inclined to do that?"

"You keep lookin' at me."

"Really, now?" As he tilted his head, Odis grew a crooked grin. "But what if I'm mostly straight?"

"Mostly? That leaves a *bunch* a wiggle room."

Odis chuckled. "And what exactly are you looking to wiggle?"

Bobby sat forward. The buzz was thinning out, but he still felt strangely comfortable. "What do you mean by 'mostly straight'?"

"Like most artists, I don't have a lot of hard and fast rules about what's interesting or attractive."

"Oh." Bobby took another sip.

"Bein' such a shrimp, though, it's hard enough catching a woman's eye, and men are even more difficult."

"So you've never been with a man."

"Never said that." Odis smiled. "Yer puttin' words in my mouth now, boy."

"Sorry. So tell me about them."

Odis sipped from his own mug a moment as if he was trying to decide if he should answer. "It was only one guy, actually. I thought it might be a mistake. He seemed to be reluctant about his desires. But I was curious and went along. We fooled around a little. As soon as he got off, though, which was way quick, he couldn't get out the door fast enough."

"Ouch, that sucks."

"So what about you? What was your first time like?"

Bobby drained his mug and held it out to Odis. "If you can get me some more, I'll tell you the whole long gruesome story."

Odis took his empty mug. "Sure thing, stud," he said with a wink.

Bobby watched Odis putter around in the kitchen area. He filled the mug with some brewed coffee, then spooned in some sort of powder to give it the chocolate flavoring. Bobby noticed how large his knuckles looked as he stirred the coffee. Odis seemed to move slowly, almost gingerly, when he reached up into the cabinet to put away the flavor container.

When Odis returned with the drink, Bobby looked him in the eye. "I'm just curious—how old are you?"

Odis sat in the chair next to him. He started to come back with something quippy, but seeing the honesty in Bobby's eyes, he simply said, "Forty-seven."

"I didn't think you were *that* old. Is that why you act so elderly, then?"

"Humph. And what's an elderly man *act* like?"

"Saying things like 'humph' and 'boy' and moving slow sometimes."

Odis took a sip. "The language prob'ly comes from hangin' around my grandpa too much. The other stuff you see is prob'ly the arth-a-ritis. I got stuck with it early, before I was even thirty-five."

"Oh, sorry." Bobby felt strangely embarrassed for bringing it up.

Odis smiled back at him. "I though you was gonna tell me a story?"

"Right. Well, I knew about myself in high school, about being gay and all, but I decided to keep up appearances and date girls. I was biding my time until college.

"So, I start college, and I'm just itching to get with a guy, but I don't have any clue how to go about it. But I notice one of the assistant coaches for the baseball team, Mitch, keeps looking me over. He wasn't too much older, maybe twenty-five, so when he asks me to go fishing up at his cabin one weekend, I jumped right on it."

"Old man of twenty-five." Odis chuckled.

"As you can guess, we didn't actually get any fishing done. It was a great weekend. I thought I might be falling in love. How sappy is that?"

"You were young."

"Then the next week at school, he was kind of distant. Which I halfway expected, since I'm sure that kind of fraternizing would have been more than just frowned upon. It wasn't until I found out he'd invited another player up to the cabin that next weekend...."

"You were just another notch in his bedpost," Odis offered.

"Yep, and that fuckin' hurt."

"So how did you meet Nathan?"

"Ouch, ya just go straight for the jugular, huh?"

"You don't have to—"

"No, I will." Bobby took a big sip. "Just give me a sec."

"I didn't mean to put you on the spot," Odis said with a tone of concern.

"It's fine." Bobby took another sip. "We actually met that first summer after freshman year. I didn't wanna go back and deal with my parents, so I hooked in with five other guys and we shared a crappy two-bedroom apartment. I got a summer job with a landscaping company to pay my part of the rent. And I met Nathan that first day after work, when we took the equipment back to the warehouse for the night. He was on another crew."

"What did you say to him?"

"Me? I didn't say a word to him. I noticed him right away, of course—he was so hunkalicious I couldn't *not* notice. Nathan recognized *me*, though, and came over. Turns out he was a big baseball nut and had seen me playing for the college team."

"You went out on a date?"

"Oh no, we just hung out. I'm sure he was throwing out signals left and right, but I was so green I wouldn't have noticed. It wasn't until Fourth of July…."

Odis waited, then urged him on. "What happened then?"

"We were sitting out in the dark, watching the fireworks over campus, and Nathan turned to me and said, 'Am I just wasting my time, or are you ever gonna kiss me?'"

Odis chuckled. "So I'm guessing you did."

"Oh yeah, we had our own personal firework show that night."

"I'll bet you did," Odis teased with a wide grin.

"So what about you? How long have you been living alone here?"

Odis glanced around the space. "That obvious, huh? Well, Tina moved out about three years ago. I think she was a closet gold digger waiting for me to strike it rich in the art community. Guess she got tired of waiting. Last I heard she's in Dallas with some famous painter."

"And you haven't had anybody since?"

"Nope. Once you get past forty, it's hard enough to meet people if you're six foot tall and ruggedly handsome. Somebody like me, though, it's pretty much a write-off."

"You shouldn't put yourself down like that. You're still handsome, even if ya are *old*," Bobby said with a wink.

"Are you flirtin' with me again?"

"Maybe...."

"Humph." Odis sat up and put his mug on the table. "I don't know what I can promise. Never really went down that road before."

"I'm not asking for promises. I'm not exactly in the shape to be making any myself."

Odis leaned forward in his chair, hesitating as he got close to Bobby. "Then what do we do?"

Bobby chuckled. "It's not like there's some queer manual we have to follow. Just do whatever you want to. I'll let you know if I don't like it."

"You sure about that? I'm an artist, don't forget. I might have some strange notions."

"I'll try to tolerate it," Bobby teased.

Odis reached out his hand as Bobby sat up and put his mug on the table.

Odis rubbed Bobby's head and traced along the top of Bobby's ear with his thumb.

Bobby sighed and moved his head closer to Odis's open palm. It seemed like it had been forever since someone had touched him like that.

Odis hooked his fingers into Bobby's chestnut locks and gently pulled him closer to his face. He took in the fragrance of Bobby's hair. The soft scent of lemongrass and faint masculine musk excited his nose.

Bobby looked up and raised his finger to trace along Odis's stubbly jaw.

Odis peered into his eyes, appreciating every detail of the smoky cigar-brown color. Then Odis turned his attention to Bobby's raised arm. He put his hand out and grasped Bobby's bicep, squeezing Bobby's solid muscles with his fingers. "Take your jacket off?" he asked.

With his heart now racing and feeling the stir in his groin, Bobby removed the jean jacket and dropped it on the floor, revealing the plain green T-shirt underneath.

Odis moved his mouth to the crook of Bobby's elbow to explore it with his lips and tongue. He dragged his mouth farther up the arm, gently suckling at the solid bicep. He placed his nose near the armpit, hesitated briefly, then brought his mouth to the jaw below Bobby's ear and licked and suckled at the stubbly hairs.

"Dear Lord," Bobby moaned.

Odis traced his tongue along Bobby's jaw, hesitating when he got to the chin and near Bobby's mouth. Then he worked his way down to the center of Bobby's chest and traced the collarbone with his tongue back toward Bobby's armpit. Odis hesitated again, then raised his mouth to kiss and lick at Bobby's Adam's apple.

Bobby moaned again, enjoying this unusual attention. Odis seemed to be targeting the things that made him male. Bobby had to reach down and adjust himself—the denim of his jeans had quickly turned into a tight prison for his dick.

Odis rose and gazed into his face.

Bobby gazed back. "You can go to the armpit, it won't gross me out."

Odis chuckled. "I didn't think it would, but it stinks of deodorant."

Bobby laughed. "Never had anybody tell me deodorant stinks before."

"It does when I want to smell *you*." Odis leaned in and sealed his lips around Bobby's mouth before he could reply. The kiss was light and curious.

Bobby raised his hands and put them on Odis's back. He was going to pull him in closer, but Odis broke the kiss and stood up. "Sorry, all that coffee. I'll be right back."

Bobby stood and watched him go into the bathroom and close the door. He looked over at the bed. He thought about going over there, but Odis was being hesitant and he didn't want to appear presumptuous. With another thought, Bobby pulled off his T-shirt and scrubbed the jersey material inside his armpits, hoping to remove some of the offensive deodorant. He dropped the T-shirt on top of his jacket when he heard the door open again.

Odis returned from the bathroom. "Sorry," he said. "I can't...." His eyes zeroed in on the tattoo above Bobby's left nipple.

"No promises, remember? It's cool."

Odis approached Bobby, holding his hand out toward the hummingbird tattoo. He hovered his hand above the skin art briefly before pulling it away. "No, I mean, I'm a shit, I have to apologize."

"For what?"

"Earlier, your name really didn't ring any bells." Odis sat at the table and grabbed his mug. "After you started your story about the Series, though, I *did* remember. And I didn't stop you. I made you tell me the whole thing."

Bobby sat down. "Hey, it's not like you forced me or anything." He smiled when he saw Odis's gaze. The man couldn't keep his eyes off the hummingbird. "It's okay. I'd never had to say it out loud like that before. It was kind of... liberating."

"Cathartic?"

"Show-off. Pullin' out those five-dollar words on me," Bobby teased.

"You're not a brick. Don't even try to pull that off."

"A brick?"

"Most men are like bricks, solid and hard and *dense*. You're not a brick, Bobby Lane."

"Oh." Bobby looked in his empty mug. "Seeing's how I'm not a brick, then, maybe we could get some food?"

"*Feed* you? Lord, you're just all *kinds* of trouble, boy," Odis teased as he went to the kitchen. He browsed around in the fridge. "I'm not exactly set up for hosting. How about a bologna sandwich?"

"Bologna? What are you, twelve?"

"Don't make fun of the fixins or I'll stick you with peanut butter and jelly."

"That's a thought." Bobby smiled. "I haven't had peanut butter and jelly in a long time."

"All right, then, classic grape or strawberry banana?"

Bobby stood with his empty mug. He also grabbed Odis's mug from the table and went into the kitchen. "Strawberry banana? I don't think I've ever seen that flavor in the store."

"Prob'ly not. It's one Gertie makes for the B and B."

Bobby filled the two mugs with coffee and got the flavoring powder from the cabinet. "Let's go with *that* one, then." He stirred in the flavor and took the mugs back to the table.

"All right," Odis agreed, getting out the bread.

"Be right back," Bobby said, excusing himself.

Bobby entered the bathroom. It was a small, compact space much like he expected, except for the huge shower. It took up one whole curving wall, a space large enough to house four people comfortably, maybe eight people if they were really friendly. At least a dozen chrome heads protruded from various locations of the polished lava-rock interior.

He chuckled to himself as he peed. It didn't look like a shower—it looked like a religious experience.

Bobby had to fight the urge to just strip off his jeans and climb in. Then he noticed the yellow washcloth hanging on the rod near the shower door. The washcloth was still damp, so he used it to scrub his armpits, then along the treasure trail of hair where he liked to spray his cologne. Bobby always tried to be optimistic.

He returned to the lounge area and saw the sandwich, neatly cut into two rectangular halves, waiting in front of his chair. Odis was sitting at the table with his own plate. Bobby looked down as he sat. "Toasted?"

"Well, of course. The peanut butter rips up the bread if you don't toast it first."

"You artists, just can't do anything normal." Bobby chuckled before taking a bite. The bread was very lightly seared, just enough to give a slight crunch but leaving the bread soft in the middle. Bobby decided he liked the sandwich that way.

They ate quietly, each taking momentary glances at the other.

Odis gazed at Bobby's bare chest. He still had a muscular look, but the muscles appeared slightly softer, as if Bobby hadn't been faithful with his workouts of late. Odis thought it was a nice look, more natural somehow. His eyes kept drifting back to the deep blue ink. "You do realize what a big fat tease you are." He smirked. "Sitting there all shirtless and all."

"Oh, is that a complaint? 'Cause I can put the shirt back on."

"No, merely an observation."

"You seem to like my tattoo," Bobby said with a grin. "Just making my own observation."

"I do. I'm surprised sometimes with the high degree of art some tattooists are capable of."

"I'd think they would *hafta* be great artists. If people are permanently applying something to their skin, they don't wanna get stuck with some half-assed scribble."

Odis laughed. "Point made. Never thought of it that way." He waited until they finished their food and then walked over to Bobby. He leaned down for a closer look at the hummingbird. The inking was quite impressive; the rich blue and highlighting green-and-yellow colors shimmered with the iridescence of the real thing. "It's extremely unique, I hope you realize. How much did you shell out for it?"

"A hundred bucks, all together."

"No, you're shittin' me…."

"I'm not. Nate and I both got one right after that first Independence Day. Back then, twenty years ago, getting married wasn't even a dream yet, so we thought up the idea of matching tattoos. For fifty bucks each, we both got one over our hearts."

Odis pushed in on the skin with his finger, watching the iridescent shimmer. "I've never even heard of tattoo ink like that."

"It wasn't 'til years later we even realized how special it was. She was a huge biker dyke who lived right off campus. When we told her the reason for the tattoos, she got all mushy and just did an outline, told us to come back. She spent two weeks altogether on the tats. I have no idea where she found that special ink."

"So you're thirty-eight?"

"I'll be forty April 1."

Odis snickered. "Then you'll be an old man like me," he teased. He lightly put his palm on Bobby's chest and rubbed his fingertips along the tiny words inscribed along the bottom of the tattoo. "Why hummingbirds?"

"When we got to her place, we hadn't really decided on anything. Nathan had suggested a pink rose, but that seemed kind of girly to me, just a huge invitation for locker-room teasing. So she showed us her scrapbook, and one of the pictures was of a work she did with some roses and a hummingbird."

"And it caught your eye."

"Yeah, it seemed so playful and flirty and kind of romantic."

"And the hummingbird didn't seem girly?"

"Well," Bobby said with a shrug. "It's mostly blue. That's a boy's color."

"What's the 'nip and ripple' mean?"

"That's our initials pronounced out—*N*, *I*, *P* and *R*, *P*, *L*."

"Oh, so you're Robert, then."

"Robert Petri Lane, and before you even ask, yes, my mom was a huge Dick Van Dyke fan."

Odis sat back on his heels. "Wait, Robert Petri?" He got up and went into the bedroom area and started rifling through some kind of filing cabinet. "I remember that name, kinda sticks out."

"What are you looking for?"

Odis searched in another drawer and then yanked out a folded printout. "Here it is." He brought the paper back to the table. It was the original order sheet Nathan had filled out online. Odis put his hand over the bottom section of the page to hide it as he showed the printout to Bobby. "That's why Bobby Lane didn't register with me. He'd made it out as a gift for Robert Petri."

"I kinda use that name as an alias sometimes."

Before Bobby could look at the page too closely, Odis whisked the printout away and put it back in the filing cabinet.

Odis returned and hesitated briefly before he leaned down and kissed Bobby. He sank down to his knees as Bobby opened his mouth. This quick kiss tingled with more heat than the previous effort.

Odis lowered his mouth to the hummingbird and licked at the colored ink on Bobby's skin. He turned his head, his nose pointing towards Bobby's armpit. Bobby put his hand on the back of Odis's head and gently pushed him toward the hairy space under his arm.

He didn't hesitate this time. Odis buried his nose and mouth in the space, reveling in the masculine smell and taste of Bobby.

Bobby moaned in reply as his groin twitched.

Odis rose back up and kissed the end of Bobby's nose before gazing briefly into his eyes. "Okay, stud. I've got my inspiration. Time to go."

"Go?" Bobby frowned. "You're kicking me out?"

"Yes." Odis nodded. "You're a huge distraction. Can't get any work done if you're here. Get over to the B and B. Gertie can get you some real food and a bed while I work."

"Work?" He groaned. "What a shit. Get my engine all revved, then throw me out."

"I'm sorry. Only for a bit. Let me get this outta my head, and I'll call ya back."

Bobby fished up his shirt from the floor.

"I'm not trying to be mean, I'm sorry. I just… I just need to focus on work."

"Fine," Bobby conceded as he pulled on his jean jacket. "You better call me."

Odis smiled. "Oh, *that* I can promise. I'm not done with you yet."

"Better not be." Bobby tried to look mean but didn't feel as if he quite pulled it off, and his disappointment showed through. "I guess I'll go…."

"Green button opens the gate, red one closes it." Odis watched as Bobby went through the door, then climbed the steps. Damn if he didn't have a gorgeous man's butt.

Odis went to his kitchen. He opened the cabinet door and looked at the prescription bottles. He hadn't taken any of the arthritis pills for the day yet, but he closed the cabinet without getting any. The stupid pills made him so fuzzy and clouded that working was difficult. Instead, Odis opened one of the drawers and loaded his pipe from his pot stash. Toking didn't make the pain go away, but it helped him not care about it so much.

Bringing the pipe, Odis walked over to the studio. He took a deep toke while looking at the equestrian piece. After Bobby's defense of the horse, Odis opened the kiln and put the raw clay sculpture inside for firing.

Once the piece was situated and the kiln turned on, Odis gathered up his carving tools and brought out some bricks of wet clay, then threw it all onto the worktable. His fingers hurt and complained, but he took another toke and ignored them. Odis then set to work on the clay, starting the slow task of teasing and shaping the sticky material to copy the image in his head.

CHAPTER
Three

BOBBY made it back to Hasting's Bed and Breakfast just before dark. He parked and entered the vestibule area of the Victorian-style home and pushed the buzzer.

A portly man breezed in and greeted him with a vibrant handshake soon after. "Bobby Lane? I'm John Hasting. Good to meet you."

"Hello."

John ushered him into the hallway. "I couldn't believe it when Gertie told me you'd been by here earlier. What brings ya out to our neck of the woods?"

"Just dropped by to see Odis about a sculpture."

"Did you find what yer looking for?"

"Don't know yet," Bobby answered honestly.

John pulled him conspiratorially close. "Just so ya know, I thought that was a real crappy deal ya got. I hope yer suing the pants off the bastards. Don't care what side your bread is buttered on, nobody deserves to get treated like that. Enough to turn a man from watching baseball altogether."

Bobby just shrugged. "Thanks for the support. I was planning to retire after the season anyway, though."

"Don't matter. The way they got the media all stoked, they deserve to have it turn around and bite 'em in the ass."

"There's some legal action in the works. Shouldn't really discuss it, though."

"A'course not. Keep your hat on tight."

Gertie stepped in from the dining room. "Howdy again, Mr. Lane. I see ya made it back in one piece. Just settin' the table for some dinner. Come on in. Don't suppose my brother fed ya."

"Thank you," Bobby said as John led him into the dining room. "And we had some peanut butter and jelly sandwiches."

"Honestly, he eats like he's still in junior high. Miracle the man survives out there," Gertie thought aloud as they all sat down to the table with a dish of pot roast and vegetables. "Not a vegetarian, I hope? Guess I shoulda asked earlier."

"No, ma'am. Man's gotta have meat, as far as I'm concerned."

Gertie chuckled. "Just call me Gertie. Dig in, boys."

They each filled their plates with food and sampled a few bites before Gertie looked over at Bobby. "So, other than the wacky weed, what were you boys up to out there?"

At her frankness, Bobby nearly choked on his roasted potato. "Not much, just had some sandwiches and talked. Then he said he was inspired and kicked me out."

John smirked. "Damn lucky dawg. I bet he shared his good shit too."

Gertie nearly dropped her fork as she studied Bobby more closely. "He said 'inspired'?"

"Yeah, that's what he said."

"Guess I shouldn't be surprised." Gertie appraised Bobby as she took another bite. "A fine looker like you's prob'ly turned more than one straight man's head. At least he's working again. I don't think he's stepped foot in that studio in over a year."

"How bad *is* the arthritis?"

"Prob'ly worse than he complains about, I'm sure. But it's not just that. He kinda lost his fire when Tina left. Hasn't done a real show in over four years."

John toasted the air with his glass. "Good riddance too. Never liked that bitch."

"Now, now," Gertie scolded her husband. "Be nice."

John looked over at Bobby when he finally clued in to the previous conversation. "You mean, you and Odis?"

"Just talked, mostly. Not a big deal."

"Oh," John disagreed, "it *is* a big deal. Odis is buttoned up tighter than a nun. With Marsha, he wouldn't even hold hands in public after they'd been married five years."

Bobby just ate, trying not to dwell on it, but he remembered how Odis had held his hand as he took him back to the studio.

"Hm, never thought I'd have a *brother*-in-law."

Gertie swatted John's hand. "Don't be so presumptuous." Then she turned to Bobby. "But John's right. My brother doesn't jump into relationships lightly."

Bobby was starting to feel a bit on the spot and decided to change the subject. "So, what was that you were saying about his 'good shit'?"

John nodded. "When he started smoking regularly about ten years ago, he never trusted buying it off the street, so he started growing his own. Just a couple of plants, for personal use. Won't ever sell any, no matter how much people beg."

"Other people know about it?"

Gertie nodded. "Small town, ya know. Everybody knows everything. Wouldn't be surprised if people start dropping in here just to see a celebrity. But I haven't told anybody other than John."

"I kept it quiet too. Figured the last thing you need is more gawkers."

"I appreciate that."

Gertie put down her silverware. "We'll see if the quiet lasts. How long ya in town for?"

"Hadn't planned to stay at all—was just going to pop in and out. But Odis said give him a couple of days, so I'll hang around a few, I guess."

"Well, we don't have people standing in line for rooms, so I'll set you up with one, like I promised."

"I'm not a freeloader. I'll pay the normal rates."

"But—"

"No buts. Like you said, there's not exactly a line, so I'm paying my share."

"All right, then." Gertie didn't argue more. "There's a clothing store down the road to the south, mostly western stuff, but if you didn't bring any luggage, ya may want to pop over. They're open 'til eight."

"Appreciate it." Bobby stood and grinned at Gertie. "And thank you for the excellent meal."

"No trouble."

John loaded up another helping. "See ya later."

Bobby made his way back to the car and headed for the clothing store. He turned up the radio but couldn't stop thinking about Odis. The man Bobby had spent the day with and the man Gertie and John had described at dinner just seemed like two totally different people. Maybe Gertie just didn't know her brother as well as she thought she did.

Yet there had been that hesitancy. Bobby had assumed it was from being with another man, but maybe it was actually from Odis just being intimate, period. It left Bobby with much to ponder.

He found the tiny clothing store, and as Gertie described, it was mostly western wear. Bobby got another pair of jeans, some socks and underwear, and picked out three of the plainer-looking shirts.

With the radio loud, Bobby drove back to the B and B.

He walked upstairs to the small but cozy room Gertie had assigned him. He put the purchases away in the dresser before taking out his phone. He should call Sharon before it got too late.

"Hey," Sharon answered. "You on your way back?"

"Not yet, got a room for the night. Things turned out a bit more...." Bobby paused, unsure how much to tell his friend. Should he bring up what happened with Odis? "A bit more complicated than I expected."

"Oh?"

"The work wasn't done yet, so I'm waiting for the artist to finish."

"What's going on, Bob? I know you're not telling me everything. You didn't want to make the trip in the first place. I practically had to shove you onto the plane. Now you're staying the night?"

"I don't know, Shar. It's complicated. Can we just leave it at that for now?"

Sharon sighed into the phone. "Just watch your back. Don't let any of those Texan gunslingers sneak up on you," she said with a laugh.

Bobby laughed along. "You watch too many of those cheesy westerns. I'm gonna get some sleep and call ya later."

"All right, then, and I expect details next time. G'night."

"Good night."

AFTER hanging up, Bobby lay on the bed in his room, flipping absently through channels on the TV. This seemed like so many other wasted nights in his life. He couldn't count how many evenings he'd spent in hotel rooms, waiting for the next day's game.

But this night was so different from those. Instead of feeling the pregame excitement and chatting on the phone with Nate, he was feeling a bit of guilt and stewing over Odis. Mentally, he knew the cheating guilt was ridiculous, yet he couldn't seem to completely shake it off. Even though Nate was gone, Bobby had been unswervingly faithful to the man for over twenty years, and convincing his heart not to feel any adulterous blame was a challenge.

Odis. He sighed again at the thought of the little man.

Odis took him by surprise. So soon after Nathan's death, Bobby certainly hadn't planned on flying to Texas and making out with some guy, but he had. Getting that postcard and those peculiar instructions had set off this strange chain of events, a chain to the receipt in Nate's desk that pointed him here. In some improbable way, it was almost as though Nate had planned for his little tryst with Odis to happen.

Bobby flipped through more channels. He still couldn't wrap his mind around that exploratory session he had shared with Odis. In the moment, that sharing had felt so natural, so desirous, but now he questioned why he'd allowed it to happen. Was it just the weed and the loneliness spurring him forward?

No, it was Odis. Like some leprechaun, Odis enthralled him with a hidden power to have his way.

Bobby had to chuckle at his own thought. No, from what Gertie and John described at dinner, he *knew* Odis wasn't some kind of player. Those explorative urges must have been just as unexpected for him as well, especially considering he was exploring the uncharted territories of another man.

Now that Odis was inspired—which had seemed like such a surprise to Gertie—did that mean Odis was done with him? Bobby hoped not. Those explorations had such an unusual mix of tenderness and heat, they left Bobby hungry to explore more of Odis's attention. Odis had also said he wanted more, but would he still feel that way in the sober light of a new day?

Allowing a noisy yawn, Bobby turned off the TV and settled under the covers. Hopefully, Odis wouldn't keep him waiting here long. Though he'd seen the work of the struggling and hurting horse, he was curious about what kind of sculpture the man would come up with. But maybe Bobby should be concerned. What if this new sculpted work also came from such a dark place?

Bobby pushed that thought aside as he fell into sleep.

THE next morning, Bobby awoke with the dawn. He had planned to just sleep in, but his body clicked into the old habit of rising early for game days.

He rolled over. The scent of coffee teased at his nostrils. The thought of it roused Bobby from the bed.

After getting dressed into a new shirt and his old jeans, which still looked acceptably clean after only one day's use, Bobby wandered downstairs. He found Gertie in the dining room.

"Mornin'," she said with a curt nod.

"Morning, Gertie."

"Up kinda early…."

"Old habit." Bobby smiled at her, thinking she didn't seem like a morning person.

"Have a seat, just fixin' to scramble some eggs. I'll bring ya some in a minute," she said, handing him a mug of coffee. "Sugar, cream, whatnot's on the table."

"Thanks."

Bobby sat at the table and grabbed a sugar packet as she went into the kitchen.

Gertie returned a few minutes later with two large serving platters covered in scrambled eggs, bacon, toast, and a few muffins. She disappeared again and returned with plates and silverware, and she handed a set to Bobby before sitting down. "Dig in."

"Thank you." Bobby loaded up a plate as John stumbled in and muttered something on his way to the kitchen.

John returned with a mug of coffee and sat down, still looking bleary-eyed.

"Good morning to ya," Bobby said.

"Yeah," John replied, nursing his coffee.

Gertie just took a piece of toast. "Sleep well?"

"Yes, you have very nice rooms here."

Gertie nodded. "Even bein' right on Main Street, everybody says it's always quiet."

"It is," Bobby agreed. "Is there a gym nearby where I could squeeze in a workout this morning?"

"No. Town doesn't really have one. Different people talked about startin' some kind of health club from time to time, but it hasn't ever happened."

"Oh well, just a thought."

"Your best bet might be Odis. He has a whole setup over at his place. Hot tub and all," she said with a wink.

John just grunted and shook his head. "Still too early in the mornin' to wrap my head around that one."

"Around what, honey?"

"Odis… and a man."

"Not for us to worry about," she told John. She turned to Bobby. "Although, I was thinkin' last night, after the divorce from Marsha, Odis did seem a bit infatuated with Tucker for a time."

Bobby nodded. "He said I wasn't the first guy to ever catch his eye."

"Well." She looked directly at Bobby. "I'm not one to meddle— much, anyway—in my younger brother's business. But he hasn't had an easy time of things lately, so don't go jerking him around."

"Certainly not," he reassured her. "I'm not that kind of guy."

"Didn't think you were, or we'd be having an *entirely* different conversation," she said strongly.

"Point taken." Bobby nodded firmly.

"Now, then, Brungess doesn't have much in the way of things to do. Not much of a tourist town or anything. I'll see if we can't come up with something, though. Hate the idea of ya just sitting in your room at loose ends."

"How about a library? Can always find some reading to catch up on."

"Great idea. I'll call over later and set it up. You can take my card and check out a few books, I'm sure."

"Sounds like a plan."

TWO cups of coffee later, Bobby followed Gertie's directions to the library and returned with some fiction books to read. He stretched out on his bed upstairs and dug into a recent action novel.

He was only starting chapter three when he heard the beep noise from the hotel phone on his bedside table, indicating an incoming call.

He placed a bookmark and picked up the receiver. "Hello?"

A tired voice on the other line said, "Hey, stud. I finished."

"Hi, Odis. You did?"

"Why don't you grab some fried chicken and beer, then come on back?"

"All right. What did you make?"

"Nope, nope, don't spoil the surprise. Just get over here, stud."

"All right. See ya in a bit."

AFTER consulting with Gertie about where to get the chicken and beer, Bobby picked up the supplies and drove back out to Odis's place. He left the car and pushed the gate button on the back of the box. Before the gate was completely open, Heimdalla raced up and bounced around at his feet. As soon as Bobby opened the car door, she jumped into the backseat and sat, her square tongue hanging out of a doggy-smile face.

"Guess you're coming along, huh?"

Bobby pulled the car into the property, got out, and closed the gate. Heim just watched him from the backseat, happy as a clam.

He pulled the car up in front of the shed and turned off the engine. When Bobby reached in for the bags of food and beer, Heim jumped out and bounced around his feet again. After Bobby retrieved the items and closed the door, Heim raced down the stairs and waited for him at the house door.

Arriving at the bottom of the steps, Bobby saw Odis through the glass. He was sitting at the patio table, looking frightfully like a mad scientist. His hair was all frizzed out, a pair of reading glasses barely clutched to the edge of his nose. The lenses magnified the dark circles under his eyes in a gruesome way. As Bobby approached with the parcels, he could see Odis's hands were clean, but traces of red clay still clung stubbornly under his fingernails. Odis looked up.

Then Bobby saw the huge grin on Odis's face and thought he might be one of the sexiest men he'd ever seen.

"Hey, stud, ya made it," Odis said as he moved to the kitchen, put his eyeglasses on the counter, then fetched some plates.

"Was beginning to wonder if you were gonna call." Bobby glanced over his disheveled appearance again. "How much sleep did you get?"

"Sleep? I was busy. Just finished a bit ago."

The men filled up their plates and opened their beers. Bobby sat at the table.

Odis put his plate on the table. "First things first," he said, and he leaned over Bobby and captured his mouth with a warm kiss. Odis's tongue tasted spicy and peppery from the weed still lingering on his breath.

"Well, hello to you too," Bobby sighed when Odis pulled back.

Odis grinned as he took his seat and started eating. He dug into the food as if he hadn't eaten in days.

Bobby doubted he'd had anything since the sandwich yesterday. "So—"

"Patience," Odis said between bites. "Let a man get some food first."

"All right."

Odis took a swig from the beer bottle, then held it out to look at the label. "What kind is this?"

"One of the local brews I got hooked on in Boston. Was surprised to see it at the liquor store. Hope it's okay?"

Odis smiled. "It's a lot better than that piss water out at the convenience store. It's *very* okay." He took another swig and, with a smile, savored the heavy taste of the hops.

Heim sat down next to Bobby, then put her head on his knee.

Odis clucked his tongue. "Scootch on, Heim. Don't be beggin'. He ain't gonna give ya none either."

"Aah, but she looks like she's starving," Bobby teased.

Odis clucked his tongue again. "Damn dog ain't starvin'. Prob'ly eats more than I do."

"You heard him," Bobby said, looking down at the pitiful dog. "Move along."

Heim pulled her head off of his knee and scooted over about a foot before lying down on the floor and exhaling a pitiful sigh.

After devouring about half the food on his plate, Odis pushed it away. "Now, then." He took another huge swig of beer, then let out a burp.

Bobby finished off his biscuit. "I get to see it now?"

"Wouldn't mind gettin' to some other business, but I can tell your curiosity will eat ya alive if I don't let ya see it first." Odis stood and took his hand, then led him out to the studio.

The piece was covered with a damp towel. This work looked even larger than the horse, thirty, maybe even thirty-six inches tall.

"Now, no touching, it's still wet," Odis warned as he carefully removed the towel.

Done in various hues of red and gray clay stood a huge weeping willow. Bobby was instantly drawn into the strange beauty of the figure. The branches and thin tassely leaves of the proudly standing tree leaned to one side, blown by a phantom breeze.

As Bobby looked closer, he noticed more details. On the ground by the tree's trunk lay a scattering of tiny chipped and discarded-looking bricks, and a tiny broken fishing pole lay atop them. In the upper branches of the tree, two tiny hummingbirds hovered as they faced each other. Carved into the bark of the trunk, a tiny heart framed the monogram "nip + rpl."

Odis put his hand on Bobby's shoulder as he admired the work. "Told ya you weren't a brick."

Bobby noticed the words "Happy 40th" inscribed along the face of the work's base. "This is *me*?" he asked, trying to keep his voice from cracking.

"Kinda how I see ya, tall and strong, but branches soft enough to bend in the wind without breaking."

Bobby couldn't keep his eyes from watering as he gazed over the sculpture. "And this is what Nate asked for?"

Odis chuckled. "Not specifically." He picked up the moist towel and carefully placed it back over the clay piece. "He just asked for something strong and joyful with that inscription. I kinda filled in the rest."

"Why are you covering it? It's way too beautiful to keep hidden." Bobby wiped at his cheek.

Odis rolled his eyes. "Not hiding it. Hafta let it dry slowly or the clay cracks. Just leave me to my job."

Bobby distracted himself from his tearful eyes by looking around the studio. He noticed another covered work on the counter and various carving supplies near it. "You started another one?"

"Kinda need to talk to you about that." Odis took Bobby's hand and led him back to the house.

Bobby looked down at his hand in Odis's. It seemed like such an intimate thing to do, but Odis didn't even seem to think about it when he took his hand. Bobby wiped at his cheek again, hoping Odis didn't think he was some kind of limp pansy.

CHAPTER
Four

WHEN they got back inside the house, Bobby helped Odis move the mess from the patio table to the kitchen counter. Odis rinsed off the dishes and left them draining in the sink, then put away the leftover chicken in the fridge while Bobby got two fresh beers.

Feeling more composed, Bobby followed Odis back to the table.

Odis took a swig of beer. "Now, then, I need to ask a question that's prob'ly gonna be painful as fuck for ya to answer, but I do have a reason for asking."

Bobby took two big swallows of his beer. "All right, then, ask."

"How exactly did Nathan die?"

Bobby winced. "Aneurism." He took two more big swallows.

Odis watched him, waiting for the whole story.

"He'd hidden it from me the whole time I knew him. I knew many of his extended family had already died young from something, but he never told me any details, only that it was a genetic thing. Because he seemed so—no, he *was* healthy. So I always assumed he didn't have whatever affliction it was. I suppose the lies were as much my fault for never asking point-blank for some real details."

"So he *knew* he had that aneurism," Odis said.

"I found out in the hospital, when his doctor flew up, that Nate had put off a new surgery the doctor wanted to try. His scan in August had the doctor worried—oh." Bobby stopped himself. "For about the last decade he'd been having brain scans every six months, I found out. He was basically a walking time bomb."

They sipped their beers.

"Anyway, doctors had this stint thing they wanted to try, but Nate pushed it off until November. Doctors gave him a whole list of things to avoid, one of which was flying. Damn bastard."

Bobby sat and tried to breathe. "The aneurism burst when he was in the cab leaving the airport, and all the bleeding pretty much scrambled his brain. You can guess the rest."

Odis got up and returned from the kitchen with two more beers. "Nathan seems pretty noble to me," he said as he handed one to Bobby.

"*Noble*? How the fuck do you get that? He lied to me for twenty-two years. Even in August, he didn't say one word about the doctor or the surgery. He *could* have told me about it all then, at least."

"And if he had told ya, in August, what would you have done?"

"Made him get the surgery."

Odis frowned as he sat back down. "*Made* him?"

"No. You know."

"You would have nagged him about it. And you would have worried about it. It would have put you off your game. If Nathan knew it was your last season, he wouldn't have wanted to take that away from you."

"Yeah, he knew I was retiring."

"Of course he did. And he was being altruistic, letting you have the last of your career before droppin' all of *his* shit on you. Or trying to, anyway. He knew the Series wouldn't be over until November."

Bobby scowled at him.

"Go ahead and get pissed at me, if it helps. But you know I'm right. I'm sure Nathan felt that he was on borrowed time for those last ten years and didn't want to waste a second of it with fretting or what-ifs."

Bobby just stewed in his chair.

Odis left him alone for a few minutes before continuing. "I told you I had a reason for asking."

"And what would that be?" Bobby said, trying to hide the hard edge in his tone.

"Nathan's work order was actually for two commissions. One for April 1, which was for your birthday. The other... well, it seems a bit macabre to me, but it's not my call in the long run."

"What *is* the other one?" Bobby asked.

"He attached CAT and X-ray scans of himself for me to make a bust that he wanted delivered to your address on July 3."

"He wanted me to get his *head* for our anniversary? *After* he died? That twisted fuck."

"Well, I don't know if that's true or not, but I hafta wonder, since the order was filled out October 16."

"That's… that was the day before the first game of the Series."

"So, hafta wonder." Odis shrugged. "Seems Nathan knew the risk he was taking by getting on that plane and wanted to leave you something, just in case."

Bobby just shook his head and slumped further into the chair. "Now I'm just confused. What the hell was he up to?"

"I certainly can't say, I didn't really know the man. But you see the macabre element I was talkin' about. I thought maybe there was some point to it I didn't see."

"None that I'm aware of, either." As he pondered it, though, it seemed maybe Nate had more future surprises in store. Bobby sat up and finished off the rest of his beer. "I mean, a bust might be nice down the road sometime, but I'm glad I found out now instead of having it just show up out of the blue in July. That's just too soon. Opening a box with his head in it would have been *utterly* creepy."

"Can't argue with that," Odis agreed as he drained his beer.

Bobby looked over at Odis. The man looked exhausted, like he needed about twelve hours of sleep. The darkened circles under his eyes drooped almost as much as his eyelids. "I should go. You need some rest."

"Yeah, the beer's crashing me."

Bobby stood and stretched, feeling his back pop. "Oh, Gertie said I should ask you about working out here."

"On the west side, across the patio just past the stairs, is a little gym room. You're welcome to it." Odis glanced over at Bobby's jeans. "Do you have some workout clothes? Very doubtful any of mine would fit you."

"No, I didn't really plan on staying around, so I didn't pack anything."

"There's a Walmart over by Hutchinson, about twenty minutes from town. If ya think it's worth the trouble."

"All right."

Odis stood up and walked over to Bobby. He rubbed his hand across Bobby's chest. "I had hoped to pick up where we left off yesterday—"

"You look like you're about to pass out, though. Better just get your butt in bed. I'll see if I can find that Walmart and come back later."

Odis gave his bicep a squeeze as Bobby turned to the door. "Come back later, then."

"Sleep tight," Bobby said as he left the house.

BOBBY eventually found the Walmart. Along with a duffel bag, some jogging shorts, and a few plain T-shirts, he also got some toiletries and an electric grooming razor. He realized it had been a while since he'd done any manscaping.

When he got back to the B and B, he spotted Gertie in the living room folding some towels as she watched TV. He gave her a wave.

"Howdy, Bobby. You been back over to Odis's?" she asked, noticing the Walmart bags in his hands.

"Yeah, we ate and he showed me the sculpture he did. He was up all night working on it, though, so wanted to get some sleep."

"He finished already? What is it?"

"Just saying it's a weeping willow tree doesn't begin to describe it."

Gertie smiled. "That's usually the way his work is. It's never 'just a' something. Did you like it, though?"

"Like? Love? Admire? I don't even know which words to use," Bobby admitted.

Gertie chuckled. "I look forward to seeing it, then." She glanced at the shopping bags again. "You plannin' on staying longer?"

"Odis said I could use his weight room. Then I realized I didn't have any workout clothes, so he suggested the Walmart. Do you have any scissors I could borrow to open some packages?"

"Should be some in the top dresser drawer in your room with the sewing kit. And I'm sorry. I thought about Walmart last night but reckoned it might be too far out of the way. I *should* have mentioned it."

Bobby shook his head. "Don't even worry about it."

"Oh, you gonna be around for dinner?"

"Don't think so. I'll head back out to Odis's in a bit and may stay awhile."

Gertie smiled. "Well, then, you two enjoy yourselves. Gotta get back to the laundry."

Bobby went up the stairs and into his room, where he dumped the shopping bag contents onto the bed. Since he had toiletries now, the need for a shower suddenly seemed pressing, but he decided to call Sharon first. He pulled out his phone and dialed.

"Hey, Bob," she answered.

"Hey, Shar," he said, slumping back onto the bed.

"So, you're staying another night, aren't you? I can hear it in your voice."

"How could you hear that? I only said two words."

"Exactly. You always get terse when there's something you're afraid to tell me."

Bobby sighed. "Yeah, one more night."

"Spill already," Sharon urged.

"Well, it's kinda the artist. I... I don't know."

"Don't know what?"

"Well, he's kinda attractive."

The phone was dead quiet for a moment. "I'm not gonna do this, Bobby," Sharon declared. "I'm not gonna be your shoulder to cry on. You know I loved Nathan to death, and I miss him like shit, but Nate was the one who died. Not you."

"What?" Bobby sat up in shock.

"Where are you staying?"

"Hasting's B and B in Brungess."

"All right. If you're having some kind of feelings for this artist, you know Nathan would be the first one to tell you to quit pining and get off your whiney butt. Go do something about it. If you don't, I'm gonna fly out there and kick your ass. I've got your address now," she threatened.

Bobby hesitated.

"Quit being a dumb jock and go."

Bobby just shook his head. "When did you get to be such a hard-assed bitch?"

"The minute you needed it. Now get off the phone and get moving. Go see that artist or just come home. Either way, I don't want to hear any more about it."

"Yes, ma'am."

"Try to have some fun too, while you're at it," Sharon said before hanging up.

Bobby picked up the electric razor, opened the package with the scissors, and then headed to the bathroom. Since he was going to work out first, he decided to just trim up a bit and do a quick rinse. Besides, he couldn't get the thought of using Odis's shower out of his head.

After getting back to his room, Bobby packed up the toiletries, jogging shorts, and a change of clothes in the duffel bag he'd bought and headed back to the rental car.

BOBBY pulled up to the gate and hadn't even gotten out of the car when Heimdalla showed up to greet him. She enjoyed her car ride back to the house. She bounded ahead to the house door, but she crooked her head curiously when Bobby turned right at the bottom of the stairs. She tagged along behind him to the exercise room.

When Bobby opened the french-style doors, he breathed in the inviting familiar gym smell of hot tub chemicals and old sweat. He was surprised to see so much equipment as he glanced around the room. Besides the Bowflex in the corner, he also saw a cycling bike, a stair-step machine, and a treadmill. In the other corner, the hot tub bubbled away, its gurgling sounds muffled by the padded cover.

Heimdalla hesitated at the doorway.

"I'll be all right. Go stay with Odis," Bobby told the dog.

She gave him a once-over glance, then headed across the patio to the main house.

Bobby stripped off his jeans and pulled on the jogging shorts, only then realizing he'd forgotten to bring a towel.

He decided to start with the treadmill.

As Bobby jogged along, Sharon's words from their last phone call kept echoing in his head. *"Quit pining and get off your whiney butt"* seemed to be the favored phrase. But didn't he have every right to pine? *It's only been 162 days since Nathan died. Not even a full six months have passed. Aren't people supposed to grieve for a year or something?*

With his heart rate up comfortably, Bobby went and examined the wall-mounted instruction chart for the Bowflex. He set up the machine to do some chest exercises by hooking a pull-down bar to two steel cables that dangled from an upper support bar.

He lay down on the bench, trying to clear his mind and focus on the task at hand. He counted his reps aloud. "Pull, two, three, four. Two, two, three, four. Three, two, three, four."

He stopped, suddenly aware of someone watching him. The french doors opened and Odis stepped in. "Don't stop. Just had to see what had Heim all bugged out." Odis gazed at Bobby's athletic body. His bare thighs and calves looked so solid, not at all overbuilt.

"Four, two, three, four." Bobby could still feel Odis's observing eyes study him. "That's kinda distracting."

Odis motioned to the cabinet by the hot tub. "There's towels and stuff in there, and the tub should be primed if ya wanna use it after."

Bobby stopped and sat up. "What was that about Heim?"

"She was in a tizzy about something, thought maybe somebody was at the gate. But she pointed over here when I got outside."

"She sure is a friendly dog," Bobby said.

"Friendly?" Odis crinkled his brow. "Wouldn't call her that. She's kinda aloof, except for Gertie."

"She's friendly to me. Always runs out to the gate and wants to ride in the car." Bobby moved his right knee, spreading his legs open a bit farther as he readjusted on the bench.

"I'll be damned." Odis glanced hungrily over Bobby once more. "I'll clear out and let ya get back to it. Just come in the house when you're done. I might be layin' down, but just come on in anyway."

"All right." Bobby lay back down on the bench.

Damn. Bobby forgot how many reps he'd done. He started over. "Pull, two three, four."

Odis turned back. "Why do you count that way?"

Bobby stopped again and glanced over. "Best technique."

Odis looked confused.

"First stroke is force, then hold it for one count, and release slower over two counts. Maximizes the workout if you double the resistance."

"Never heard of that. Is it something new?"

Bobby sat up as he thought back. "Don't think so, been doing it awhile. We got workout critiques every year at spring training, so don't remember when exactly." Bobby could practically feel the caress of Odis's eyes as he studied his body again. Something in Bobby's shorts twitched.

"Oh." Odis hesitated.

Bobby took his hands off the bar and watched Odis.

Odis couldn't take his eyes off those legs—or the basket of his shorts. "Maybe you could show me sometime."

"I'd be happy to…." Bobby smiled as he noticed where Odis's gaze had landed. "Maybe right now. If you'd like."

Odis licked his lips. "Sure. If you'd like." He took a step forward.

With a mischievous grin, Bobby raised his arms and put his hands back on the bar. Odis brought his eyes up and saw the lines of Bobby's tightened pectorals under the snug T-shirt. Odis took another step closer.

Bobby tightened his grip on the bar and flexed his pecs, his nipples shrinking in excitement as his chest muscles bulged under the tight fabric. Odis seemed mesmerized by the demonstration as he took another step forward.

"Pull." Bobby pulled down on the bar, the muscles of his arms and shoulders bunching with the effort. "Two," he said while holding the bar down right in front of his navel.

Odis's gaze flitted from the bulging arms to the tightened shoulders and back to the squeezing pectorals. He didn't know where to look.

Shifting on the bench, Bobby opened his thighs farther apart, providing more room for his swelling erection. Odis followed the movement and watched Bobby's growing basket. Odis stepped up next to the bench and then looked into Bobby's face.

"Three," Bobby said as he slowly raised the bar up level with his nipples. As his eyes locked with Odis's, Bobby's grin softened at the enchantment he saw in those blue eyes.

Odis breathed in the musky, working scent of Bobby as he stood so close. Unconsciously, Odis reached a hand down to adjust his own swelling jeans.

"Four." Bobby raised the bar the remaining distance.

Odis put a hand on each of Bobby's shoulders and then squeezed slightly, feeling the strong muscles as he leaned in for a kiss.

Their lips touched, and they both felt a new passion and desire in the contact. Bobby took his hands from the bar and surrounded Odis in his arms, pulling him in as he opened his mouth.

Odis put his fingers behind Bobby's ears and gently caressed the flaps of cartilage with his thumbs as he explored Bobby's mouth in a tentative french kiss. He lifted his leg and straddled the bench as Bobby moaned.

Bobby spread his legs and pulled Odis closer. He slid his hands down Odis's back.

Odis widened his legs as Bobby pulled on his lower back, bringing him so near that their swelling groins nearly touched.

Bobby started leaning back, pulling Odis down with him.

Odis's forehead bashed into the pull-down bar as he leaned forward. "Ow."

Bobby broke the kiss as they both chuckled. "Sorry."

Odis stood up and raised the pull-down bar so it rested on the two hooks at the top of the machine.

Bobby stared at the swollen groin in front of his face, taunting him. It was so close, he could stick out his tongue and lick it.

Odis was suddenly aware of Bobby's warm breath on his crotch. Odis looked down as Bobby examined the denim-sealed package in front of him. Odis felt the crotch of his jeans tighten even more.

Bobby raised his hands and placed one on each of Odis's thighs right at the lower brief line. He gently held the tight muscles, pushing in with his thumbs slightly as he slid his thumbs up the inside, tracing the seam of the jeans to the bottom of the denim bulge.

"Oh," Odis moaned as he stood frozen, hype-aware of the strong masculine hands grasping him.

Bobby leaned in, opening his mouth wide and sealing it on top of the bulge before exhaling a large breath.

"Jeez-us," Odis moaned as every nerve in his dick suddenly lit afire in the hot blast of air.

Bobby chuckled at the exclamation, sending twitches through Odis's legs with each pulse of his laughing breath. He pulled back and slid his hands around the outside of Odis's legs and raised his hands to his hips. The denim package twitched, beckoning for his attention. But something besides lust seemed to be fueling Bobby. He lifted his gaze to Odis's face and tugged slowly on his hips, pulling him down to sit on the bench again.

Odis wore an expression of disappointment.

Bobby kissed him again and erased it.

They shared a deeper kiss and hugged each other closer as their tongues danced with each other.

Bobby ran his hands down Odis's back, then moved them inside his untucked shirt and slid them along his bare skin.

Odis moaned at the sensation of Bobby's strong, roughened palms and fingers on his skin. This wasn't the soft and delicate grasp of a woman.

Bobby pushed his fingers in tighter, rubbing the muscles under his skin.

No mistaking—these were the hands of a *man* pulling Odis forward.

Odis curled his fingers into the short hair at the back of Bobby's head and opened his mouth even wider. He tried to pull Bobby nearer, but he couldn't seem to get close enough.

Bobby slid his mouth away from Odis's lips and over to the corner of Odis's jaw, right under his ear. Bobby nibbled and sucked at it.

"Oh jeez," Odis moaned as his fingers tightened against the back of Bobby's head. These were the strong teeth of a man chewing under his ear.

Odis wanted to see the manliest part of Bobby. He moved his hands under Bobby's armpits and then stood, pulling Bobby up to his feet with him. He leaned in, feeling the bulge of Bobby's swollen groin rubbing up against his stomach.

Bobby bent down and lowered his mouth to the base of Odis's neck so he could nibble his upper shoulder.

Odis dropped his hands to Bobby's lower back, pulling him closer and moaning as Bobby's manhood pressed into his stomach.

Odis couldn't wait anymore. He had to see inside Bobby's shorts. Right now, before he lost his nerve.

Bobby turned Odis's head and pulled Odis's ear to his mouth so he could lick at the sensitive cartilage surrounding the orifice.

"Jeez-us, what are you doing to me?" Odis moaned while lowering his hands. He hooked his thumbs into the waistband of Bobby's shorts and started pushing them down.

Two quick sharp barks echoed in the hollowed-out courtyard outside as a buzzing doorbell noise echoed in the room.

"Damn," Odis said as he pulled away. "Someone's at the gate."

Bobby breathed heavily, watching Odis will himself away and turn to the door. "Is it Gertie?"

"No, Heim doesn't bark when Gertie comes. It's a vehicle she doesn't recognize," Odis explained as he went to the french doors and left.

Bobby looked around the gym. *So much for getting a workout,* he thought as he gathered up all his things and put them in the duffel bag. He took the bag and went into the main house.

CHAPTER
Five

As Bobby stood by the dining table, he watched through the house's glass wall as Odis carried some kind of cardboard delivery box and took it into his studio.

Odis returned to the house a moment later, empty-handed. "Sorry about that, just a delivery." He smiled at Bobby. "Where were we?" Odis asked as he stepped closer.

Bobby reached down and took hold of his T-shirt to slip it off.

"No." Odis reached out to stop him. "Keep your shirt on," he told Bobby. Odis didn't want to see the tattoo. He didn't want to see that mark of Nathan on Bobby's heart.

With a flirty smile, Bobby reached out, grabbed the bottom of Odis's shirt, and yanked it over his head before Odis had a chance to protest.

Bobby grinned at the vision of Odis's bare chest. His muscles weren't bulked up at all, just nicely solid and toned on his thinner frame. And those nipples. As large as half-dollar coins, Odis's pink areolas tightened as Bobby reached out a hand to the nearly hairless chest. Odis's untanned pinkish-beige skin looked like some sort of rare and exotic balsa wood. "You never go out in the sun?"

"Not much." Odis swallowed as Bobby's masculine hand rubbed over one of his nipples. Bobby's thumb wasn't even large enough to completely cover the areola. "Always mean to lay out but just never get around to it."

"Then don't." Bobby reached out his other hand and caressed it very lightly above the waistband of Odis's jeans, tickling the sparse hairs along Odis's flinching bare stomach. "Your skin is so beautiful the way it is."

Odis panted as he looked into Bobby's eyes. "Are you just gonna tease me? Or can we get in the bed now?"

"Bed?" Bobby toyed lightly with a finger at Odis's stomach, following the golden-haired treasure trail up to Odis's navel. "I really should grab a shower first...."

Odis looked up at Bobby. A shower did sound good—very nice, actually—but the height difference concerned him. Odis was afraid it might make things awkward if they were standing. He feared things would get clumsy enough once they got naked—there was no point in adding extra complications. He would rather be able to lie on the bed.

Bobby couldn't understand Odis's hesitancy. "I promise I'll keep my hands to myself, mostly."

But Odis didn't want Bobby to keep his hands to himself. He knew he was reaching a point of no return. Naked in bed was better. Odis leaned forward and made a show of inhaling through his nose. "You don't need a shower... yet," he told Bobby as he nudged him in the direction of the sleeping area.

Bobby took a step backward toward the bed. "You sure?"

"I'm sure," Odis said, toeing off his shoes and kicking them behind himself. The shoes plop-plopped onto the concrete floor somewhere in the dining area.

Bobby reached down and untied the strings on his sneakers. He toed them off and left them behind as Odis nudged him further. "In a hurry?"

"Yes." Odis reached out and lightly fondled the swollen package in front of him.

When Bobby was just inches from the bed, Odis hooked his thumbs into the waistband of Bobby's shorts and slid them down to his knees, finally revealing Bobby's dick.

Odis marveled at the circumcised member that stood out proudly, welcoming his attention, but he was unsure what to do about it. He reached out his hand and stroked along the length. Bobby's dick twitched and swelled even more.

"Now who's teasing?" Bobby asked.

Putting his left hand on Bobby's shoulder, Odis nudged him to sit on the bed as he undid the buttons of his own jeans with his right hand. He then leaned down and yanked the shorts off Bobby before tossing them aside. He nudged forward, pushing Bobby backward to recline on the bed.

Odis looked down at Bobby's dick, which stood straight up like a tall, fleshy fireplug.

Bobby watched the look of wonder and hesitation on Odis's face as he studied his cock. It was as if he'd never seen a man's erection up close and personal. "I thought you'd done this before?" Bobby asked with a hint of concern.

Odis stroked one finger along the side of Bobby's dick, pushing it over and watching it spring back up. "Yeah. It was a long time ago, though, and we were only thirteen. Not exactly… mature yet."

Leaning up, Bobby gently took hold of Odis's hand. "No promises, remember. We can stop if—"

"I don't want to stop," Odis said firmly. "At least you're not bigger than me. I was kinda worried about that."

Bobby almost laughed. He knew he had an above-average endowment and thought maybe Odis was joking, but then he looked again at Odis's large hand, his large nose, recalled his large feet, and of course those large nipples…. *How much is this little man packing?* "I don't want you to worry," he said, wondering if maybe *he* should be the worried one. "You set the pace. Whatever and whenever you want."

"Okay," Odis agreed, running his finger through the pubic hair around the base of Bobby's dick. "Your hair is so short down here."

"I trimmed. Manscaping?"

"Oh. I've never done that. I'm just 'au naturel', I guess you'd say." Odis reached his hand down to rub on Bobby's balls. They seemed almost bald with their shortly clipped hair.

Bobby moaned from the pleasure of the gentle touch as his curiosity ratcheted up another notch. "Take off your jeans?"

"Oh, sure," Odis agreed. He was so taken with the sight of Bobby he had forgotten to remove them. He stood and slid the denim down his legs before tossing the clothing aside.

Bobby leaned up to take in the view. He could see why Odis didn't trim. The faint dusting of fine blond hairs looked naturally short and tidy. The dark-gold pubes nicely framed Odis's uncircumcised cock, not at all like the unruly mess Bobby's pubes liked to grow into. "Is it really bigger?"

Odis climbed onto the bed, sat on Bobby's thighs, and put his cock right up against Bobby's. Odis was definitely longer, almost an inch more, but his shaft was much thinner, not much bigger around than a broomstick.

"You have a *very* nice cock," Bobby complimented, itching to feel it inside him. It looked like it would be a glorious ride.

"I like yours." Odis gently squeezed their dicks together. "It's all plump and juicy."

"Aaah," Bobby sighed as Odis rubbed their cocks together.

Odis looked up at the pleasure on Bobby's face. He grasped a little firmer and stroked their dicks again, watching Bobby's bliss. *What is this man doing to me?*

Bobby saw the questioning expression. "What do you want?"

Odis didn't know how to answer the question. He wanted everything all at once. He looked into Bobby's eyes. Odis wanted to—he felt a need to....

Sensing the hesitation, Bobby asked, "Can I taste you?"

Odis released their dicks and slid his hands along the T-shirt Bobby still wore. He rose to his knees and moved forward, hovering over Bobby's chest and putting himself right in front of Bobby's mouth.

Bobby stuck out his tongue and licked, tasting the sample drop from the tip of Odis's cock. The tantalizing flavor reminded him of raw oysters with a bump of lime zest. Odis didn't have the gritty bitterness that Nathan'd had.

Bobby ran his tongue across the tip again, pushing against the foreskin fold and exposing a little more of the head. He licked again. He felt the shiver in Odis's legs. Bobby found the flavor quite appealing. A tiny hint like Roquefort hid in the masculine musk. He manipulated the foreskin with his tongue again and another shake vibrated through Odis's legs.

"What are you doin' to me, boy?" Odis replied as he gazed down. The look of satisfaction on Bobby's face seemed to ignite Odis's core even more. That new itch he felt became more demanding.

"Are you complaining?" Bobby teased before he used his tongue again.

Odis gazed down at Bobby and said, "Nope." Desire lessened his fear as he contemplated his new itch. He didn't see any animal hunger or hints of aggression there in Bobby's face, just a playful desire. Odis hadn't seen any indication that Bobby wasn't gentle. Maybe he could trust him.

Bobby nearly whimpered when Odis scooted back, removing his cock from reach. He wanted to latch on to that cock with his mouth and feel Odis squirm above him as he sucked it dry. But Bobby restrained himself, letting Odis set the pace. "Where you going?" he asked, trying not to sound disappointed.

"Not far." Odis nudged farther back until he was sitting on Bobby's hips and feeling Bobby's dick pushing against the cleft of his ass. He raised the bottom of Bobby's T-shirt to reveal his stomach before leaning forward and pushing his dick into the newly clipped hairs of Bobby's stomach. He winced. "Ow, kinda stubbly."

"Maybe I shouldn't have trimmed," Bobby apologized.

Odis shifted his attention. He widened his legs a little bit, opening the cleft of his ass and leaning back, trapping Bobby's dick within the fleshy vise. He looked at Bobby again while feeling that demanding itch in his core.

Bobby wore a look of concern. He sensed where Odis was heading. If this was Odis's first time, they would need some preparation. "No, you shouldn't—"

"Yes, I should," Odis declared as he reached his hands back and spread his cheeks wider, trapping Bobby's dick tighter. He bent forward slightly and raised his rear, stroking Bobby's clenched dick.

"Aaah," Bobby moaned. This was an unusual sensation, with only the sides and top of his cock feeling the pressure and movement of Odis's flesh. The more sensitive lower side and cockhead felt exposed and unused as Odis worked slowly up and down.

Odis leaned a bit more and took hold of Bobby's hands as he stroked a little faster with his ass. He wanted to give in to what he'd long denied himself and feel Bobby inside him.

Bobby moaned again. The pressure was still only on the sides of his cock. The underside and head of his cock grew desperate for attention. He could almost feel the nerves getting more sensitive, reaching out for any sensations. "No, you shouldn't," he tried to argue again.

Odis continued the stroking motion. He reveled in the novelty of a swollen dick so near his itching opening. Maybe he shouldn't, but he was going to anyway.

Bobby felt his cock going into a frenzy. The exposed areas were screaming for attention now in an almost painful way. The nerves struggled to find any touch, any sensation. Bobby tried to raise his hands, but Odis kept them pinned down. "Please, no...."

"Yes," Odis replied, lost in some blissful place and not really aware of Bobby's struggle. He arched his back and angled forward.

"Don't," Bobby said more forcefully. He certainly had no objections if Odis wanted to bottom, but he didn't want the man to hurt himself. Lacking in experience, Odis would need a better position, good lubrication, some stretching, and guiding instruction.

Odis raised his right hand and spit into it before closing his eyes.

"No!" Bobby gasped as he wiggled under Odis, trying to change the position and move his cock away from Odis and his intentions. Saliva was *not* the best lubricant, especially not for a virgin.

With his eyes closed, Odis moved the moistened hand toward his ass, reaching for Bobby's dick.

"Stop, now," Bobby barked.

Odis rubbed his wet hand along the exposed underside of Bobby's dick.

The hungry nerves of Bobby's cock responded to the touch with an overwhelming wave of sensual contact. Bobby felt the starting edge of an orgasm. He could fight it, tamp it down and save himself for later, but Odis was still lost in some strange bliss and ignoring him.

Maybe if he came now, he could stop this impending train wreck. So Bobby let the sensual waves grow, let his balls tighten as Odis stroked his moist fingers along the now sensitive head of his cock. "Aah, jeez-us," Bobby hissed as his body stiffened.

His eyes still closed, Odis felt Bobby tensing. He felt Bobby's cock swell and twitch and spurt. He felt the hot moisture of Bobby's semen splash onto his back and dribble along his ass. The wonderful sensations of Bobby's orgasm made him want to pleasure himself. He shifted forward, taking his weight from Bobby's hips, and reached his hand down to his ass.

Bobby hissed again when Odis dragged his hand along his sensitive head to gather up some semen. Bobby rose and pushed Odis to one side, rolling him off.

Odis threw his eyes open. "What—?" He saw the pained expression on Bobby's face.

Bobby sat up and glared at him. He started to say something but clenched his mouth closed.

"What?" Odis asked again in frustrated confusion as his dick softened.

Bobby took a deep breath and tried to compose himself.

Odis frowned. "You didn't enjoy that?"

"Hell no."

Odis looked confused.

Bobby's face softened as he lost his anger. "Do you not understand the words 'no' and 'stop'?"

"But...?" Odis seemed too flustered to form words.

Bobby sighed. "Unless some other safety word's been set up ahead of time, then no means no. You didn't listen to me."

Odis reached over to the nightstand and got a tissue to wipe his hand. "You're right," he said, not looking Bobby in the eye. "I got carried away. I just wanted...."

"I know what you want." Bobby softened more. "And I'm totally on board with that, but I don't want to hurt you, or let you hurt yourself."

Odis looked chagrined as he stared down at his feet. "I was being stupid."

"No." Bobby smiled slightly. "More like naïvely enthusiastic." He reached out to Odis's chin and pulled his face up to meet his gaze. "I get it, I do. Just listen to me, though."

"Okay." Odis smiled meekly. "Guess I kinda killed the mood."

Bobby smirked. "Pretty much."

Odis sat up and turned a little so he could face Bobby better. "Okay, I'm listening now. Tell me what I was doing wrong."

"Well, first off, we need a better lube. What kind do you have? Water or oil based?"

"Lube?"

"Lubricant. Slick." Bobby sighed. "From the lost look on your face, I'm guessing you don't have any."

"Um, shampoo?"

Bobby chuckled. "Jeez-us, are you trying to kill yourself? Soap products burn, and they dry out *really* fast. Don't try that until you're very experienced and want some kink."

"Oh." Odis sighed. "I guess it's more complicated than I thought."

"Not really, but you just didn't think, period."

"All right, I get it. You don't hafta keep rubbing it in."

Bobby dropped his gaze. "Sorry, not trying to."

Odis reached out and took hold of Bobby's hand. "Okay, lubricant. There's a drugstore in town, but they're small. Don't know if they'd have any."

"A specialty-type store would be best. Like an adult store?"

"Not really any nearby. Prob'ly have to get up to Amarillo for that."

"Well, Walmart should have something, anyway." Bobby looked at him with a serious face. "And there's another topic we should discuss too."

"Oh?" Odis asked, not liking the serious tone. "And that is?"

"Condoms."

"I'm not really worried about getting pregnant," Odis joked, trying to lighten the tone a little. "And I've been celibate for three years and always wore condoms before then. Tina said she was on the Pill, but I didn't trust there wouldn't be some kind of 'accident'."

"And you're just gonna trust me? Not even ask?"

"I know you were committed."

"How do you know I haven't since then?"

"Aside from the fact you couldn't even kiss me yesterday without looking guilty?" He pointed to the circumferential dimple around Bobby's naked ring finger. The slight shrinkage revealed continuous years of wearing a ring. "That fades in just a few days. So when did you take the wedding ring off? Yesterday? Day before?"

"Yesterday, before leaving for the airport." Bobby sighed. "I guess you artists notice things."

"As bad as detectives. Also, when you were drinking your coffee, you kept reaching your thumb over to that finger, like you expected to find the ring there." Odis looked Bobby in the eye. "I do have some condoms. If it will make you feel better."

"This isn't about me. I can agree, though, in this circumstance. But this is an exception. Please, if you ever get with another man in the future, you have a full FBI background check and five years' worth of negative tests before you consider not using a condom."

Odis looked hurt.

"What?"

"We haven't even screwed yet, and you're already dumping me." Odis suddenly seemed aware of his nakedness. He gathered the loose bedsheets around him and pulled a handful up over his lap.

"I'm not—" Bobby tensed up. "What exactly are you expecting here? I do have to get back on a plane and go home at some point."

"I thought… never mind. You should just go get on that plane now, if that's what you're going to do."

Bobby stiffened. "You're kicking me out again?"

"At least you got off this time, first."

"Not really. I was too worried about the situation to enjoy that. And that's beside the point. You still haven't answered my question."

"What question?"

"What are you expecting? What do you want, Odis?"

"I don't know. I hadn't thought up any great plans for the future. But I hate how this is starting to feel like a one-night stand." Odis scrutinized Bobby. "I… do you really just wanna get back on a plane and leave?"

Bobby shifted on the bed, turning slightly away from Odis. "That's not—" He couldn't look at Odis. "That's what I have to do."

"Is that just an excuse? 'Cause you don't *hafta* do anything."

Bobby shifted again.

"Seriously." Odis turned and scooted over to get in front of Bobby. "When was the last time you did anything just for you? Something that wasn't motivated by what others needed or what would look best for the team's PR?"

Bobby turned his gaze to the bathroom door, unable to answer.

Odis got up from the bed. He went to his laundry basket and yanked out a pair of baggy blue boxers and slipped them on. Then he went into the kitchen.

Bobby turned around to watch him.

Odis returned a minute later with the corncob pipe and lighter.

"I don't want that."

"Didn't ask you." Odis sat on the edge of the bed. "But I think maybe you need some. You need something, anyway." Odis took a big hit from the pipe.

Bobby shifted on the bed, turning around to watch Odis. He nonchalantly glanced around the floor for his gym shorts but didn't see them.

Odis exhaled. "I'm sorry I said that, about kickin' you out. I just get defensive sometimes." He held the pipe and lighter tightly by his lap, as if he had no intention of sharing.

"All right."

Staring down at his hands, Odis rubbed his fingers on the roughened corncob, making a faint scratching noise. "If I asked you something, could you truly think about it and answer honestly?"

Bobby started to say something flippant, but he glanced over at Odis and saw the serious look on his face. "Well, I guess it depends on the question."

"Oh." Odis sighed in disappointment.

"Not that I don't want to be honest, but it may be something I don't have an answer for."

Odis looked up at Bobby.

Bobby glanced down to the pipe in Odis's hands. Nathan had always accused him of being a control freak. Maybe Nate and Odis were right. Maybe he did need something. He reached out for Odis's hands.

Odis relinquished the pipe and lighter.

Bobby put the stem in his mouth and took what he thought would be about a medium-sized hit. That warm, spicy flavor danced in his mouth and nose. He handed the pipe back to Odis.

Odis watched Bobby's face. "You don't do this very often," he commented, holding up the pipe in gesture.

"No, don't really do much of anything. Am I that obvious of a lightweight?"

"Yes."

"Damn. I thought I had that party-boy image nailed," he teased.

Odis chuckled and waited. He wanted Bobby to hit that mellow glow.

Bobby looked at the pipe again. "John said something about you grow your own?"

"Yeah." Bobby reached out for the pipe again, but Odis clutched it close. "No, I don't want you getting silly on me again."

"Silly?" Bobby sat back. "Not me."

"Like a teenage girl, you were," Odis said, sounding strangely like Yoda.

Bobby lay back on the bed. His mind… it was hard to define. It was like it was getting warmer somehow.

Odis smiled. "Now, back to that question."

"There's been lots of questions." Bobby rubbed his face with his hand. "Which one?"

"What's waiting for you back home?"

"Oh. There's the house… then there's lots of legal details, and…."

"That's it? Just a house and a bunch of lawyers?"

"Oh! Sharon's there too."

"Who's Sharon?"

"She's a friend. Well, more Nate's friend. She's my friend too, though, I guess."

Odis pulled his knee onto the bed and turned to face Bobby. "Anything else? Anyone else?"

Bobby shook his head in a vaguely negative way.

"What about your family?"

"Family sucks," Bobby declared. "And they're in Ohio anyway."

Odis paused. He was definitely curious about those family details, but he'd save that for a later conversation. "Okay, let me lay this out and make sure I got it all."

Bobby nodded as he stroked his hand across his face. "Okay."

"So what you have waitin' for you is a friend of Nathan's that's your friend by proxy, a big and empty house full of Nathan's memories, and legal proceedings having to do with Nathan's illness and death."

Bobby scowled under his hand. "Bastard."

"Did I leave anything out?"

"No, that's just a nasty way to put it."

"Is it not the truth?" Odis studied Bobby, waiting for an argument. "That's the bottom line, though, right? There's nothin' there that isn't tied to Nathan somehow."

Bobby sighed.

"Then why are you in such an all-fired hurry to get back there?" Odis asked bluntly.

"Because...." Bobby shook his head. "I don't know. 'Cause it's home?"

"Maybe it *used* to be home."

Bobby sat up and looked at Odis. "It *is* still home."

Odis just met his glance without saying anything.

"It *is*," Bobby defended. "What's your point in bringin' all this up, anyway?"

"No point, exactly. I just wanted ya to think it through instead of falling back on instinct."

Bobby could feel his buzz fading. He looked over at the pipe in Odis's hands. "Okay, I thought about it."

Odis offered the pipe again. "Just don't get carried away."

Bobby took another medium-sized hit. As he held the breath, he noticed a familiar lime zest flavor among the spiciness. It was a faint taste he remembered from Odis's precome. He handed the pipe back to Odis and lay back on the bed again.

Odis took another hit, then put the pipe on the nightstand.

Bobby felt that warmth in his mind again, encouraging him to relax.

Odis stretched out on the bed beside him.

They looked up at the ceiling in blissed-out silence.

CHAPTER
Six

BOBBY closed his eyes as he lay next to Odis on the bed. Like he had some new superpower, he could sense the warmth of Odis's body lying so close.

Strange echoes from their conversation kept popping into Bobby's head. Odis was right. Nothing but Nathan's memories waited for him back there. Bobby had no pressing reason to hop back on a plane, if any reason at all, really. Well, except the legal shit. But probably most of that stuff could be done with fax and computer video and e-mail. Unless he had some kind of court date.

Bobby reached up his left hand and absently scratched on one of his right ribs. He felt the jersey material of the shirt under his fingers. Keeping his eyes closed, he turned his head toward that warm spot of Odis. "Why did you make me leave the T-shirt on? You have an athletic fetish or something?"

"Not really, although you do look pretty fuckin' hot in those tight jogging shorts."

"They were out of large and extra large. Had to get a medium size."

"Maybe you should always get mediums. They make your ass look so—"

Bobby resisted the topic change again. "You didn't answer my question, though."

"Do you want me to?"

"Of course. You sure get evasive sometimes."

"I wanted you to keep the shirt on so I wouldn't have to look at the tattoo."

"I thought you liked my tattoo?" Bobby asked.

"I do, but I didn't want the reminder of why it's there."

"Oh?" Bobby asked.

"I can't help thinking, sometimes, it's really Nathan's tattoo."

"Oh." Bobby sighed. "I know what you mean. Sometimes when I see it in the mirror, I wish it could be like the wedding ring, and I could just take it off." Bobby felt the warm patch next to him moving.

Odis kissed his forehead. "It's too much a part of you, though. You'd hate yourself later if you had it removed."

Bobby sighed in agreement.

"I met him," Odis confessed suddenly. "Nathan, I mean. I remember from his picture."

Bobby sat up. "When?"

"About ten years ago, I think. At my art show in Key West."

Bobby reclined again. "Oh yeah, that must have been the year he and Sharon came down to Florida with me when I started spring training. They had kinda a mini-vacay before they went back." Bobby rubbed his hand along his chest, unconsciously massaging the hummingbird tattoo. "And you remember him?"

"Yeah. Like you said, too hunkalicious not to notice him. And he spent almost an hour chatting me up about the different works. He seemed honestly interested too, not like one of the snobby farts just tryin' to score art points."

Bobby made a strange sigh, trying not to remember Nathan.

Odis leaned over and kissed his forehead again.

Bobby scratched absently at his nose. "Why do you want to keep me here?"

"*What?* It's not like you're a prisoner or anything."

"You got awfully upset about me leaving earlier."

"I suppose I did. I don't know."

"Being evasive again," Bobby warned.

Odis took a deep breath. "I'm—" He took another breath. "Well, I don't know how to articulate it, and even if I did...." Odis hesitated. "I'd just sound like a silly old fool."

"Articulate what?"

"Don't you *feel* anything?"

Bobby opened his eyes. "You mean besides horny?"

"So this is just you being horny?"

"Honestly, I don't know." Bobby rolled on his side to face Odis. "With Mitch, it was the newness of it all. Nate and I had basically dated over a month before anything… and I already had some serious feelings by then."

"You were already in love with him?"

"Yeah, I guess I was."

"And now?"

Bobby looked into Odis's face. "Dammit, I—" Bobby sighed. "I wish I had more experience. Some kind of comparison, you know. Maybe if I'd played around a little, I'd know."

Odis just nodded.

"And you?"

"Well, I'm kinda struggling for a frame of reference myself. I *can* tell you I haven't felt anything quite like…. But is it just the novelty of being with a man? I can't say," Odis admitted.

"So, we both need to go out and find some other guy to fuck, just to see?"

"Oh?"

"Is that what you want?" Bobby asked.

"Is it what *you* want?"

Bobby brought his hands up and rubbed on his face. "Dammit… not really."

"Then let's not do that."

"All right." Bobby noticed his butt was starting to feel cold. "Do you know where my shorts went?"

Odis sat up and rooted around in the sheets at the foot of the bed until he found them. "I'm kinda glad you don't want to find another guy. I don't know if I could." He handed the gym shorts to Bobby.

Bobby pulled them on. "Why not?" He lay back on the bed, closer to Odis.

"In my whole life, you're only the fourth guy I've even had any kind of attraction for. I don't think I could just find some random guy in a bar or anything."

"I prob'ly could. I went to bars when the team was on the road. Definitely saw a few hotties along the way."

"If you were faithful, why go?"

Bobby laughed. "Believe me, after about a week of nonstop macho bullshit, I needed the gayest place I could find for some cultural detox."

"I never thought about that. I didn't realize you'd be on the road that much."

"Kinda made me wish I was better at football. Those guys only have one game a week, usually. Depending on the schedule, we'd have at least five games in a week, plus travel time. In the old days, we could be on the road three weeks at a stretch. But with more plane usage and computer scheduling, it's been a lot better the last few years." Bobby frowned. "It *was*. I keep forgetting it's over."

Odis reached out and rubbed his finger along the furrows in Bobby's forehead. "I'm sorry."

"What are you apologizing for?"

"I keep bringing up all these bad topics."

"It's not your fault they're... I don't know." He looked into Odis's face. "I don't really mind talking about it." He reached out and took hold of Odis's other hand. "I don't mind at all."

"I just feel like I'm pouring salt in the wounds, sometimes."

"You're not." Bobby gently squeezed Odis's hand.

Odis noticed Bobby's face still looked tense and decided to try distracting him. "I just don't know what you're doing to me. You're kind of a problem." He pulled Bobby's hand down to his boxers.

Bobby looked down and saw the tenting of the fabric. "So this is just a lust thing," he teased. "I guess one of us will have to go find that Walmart."

Odis gazed into Bobby's eyes. "Guess so."

Bobby grinned devilishly. "Of course, there are other ways to deal with these kinds of problems."

"Oh?" Odis tried to look innocent. "What are these other ways?"

"I can do what I wanted to do a while ago...."

"Well, then, you can just talk me through, whatever."

Bobby scooted down and freed Odis's cock through the large fly of his boxers. "Who says I'll be able to talk?" he asked before licking along the foreskin fold.

"Oh," Odis moaned. "In that case—oh... I'll just shut up—oh damn."

Bobby reached his hand into the fly opening and massaged Odis's slightly fuzzy balls as he continued to work on Odis's swelling cockhead with his tongue.

"Oh shit," Odis moaned louder.

Bobby chuckled and pulled back. "I thought you said you were going to shut up?" he teased as he gently rubbed Odis's balls.

"I meant I would stop trying for coherent conversation."

Bobby put his other hand around Odis's cock and pulled back a little, sliding the skin and exposing more of Odis's cockhead before placing it in his mouth.

"Oh holy shit," Odis moaned as his eyes rolled back into his head. He panted heavier as Bobby worked with his tongue and sucked Odis's cock deeper into his mouth. "Oh holy. What the fuck are you...." Odis had trouble calming his breathing as he looked down and saw Bobby's grin. "...doin' down there?"

Bobby pulled back, showing that playful grin as Odis breathed heavily. "I guess I'm doing it right? I never played with an uncut cock before."

"You're definitely on the fast train to a protein snack."

Bobby lightly squeezed his cock.

"About a three-minute arrival time, if you keep that up."

"Huh, and I thought old men were supposed to take a long time." Bobby slid back more of Odis's foreskin and inhaled his cock into his mouth again.

"Who you callin'—oh holy fuckin' shit...."

Bobby had planned to stretch out the oral play a bit more but got carried away by the wonderful taste and feel of Odis in his mouth. He pulled back the rest of the foreskin and worked his tongue at the base of Odis's cockhead.

"Oh, fuckin' fuck, fuck," Odis yelled as he went into orgasm.

Bobby pulled his mouth back a little as Odis gushered semen onto his tongue. He applied more suction and swallowed, loving that unique flavor of Odis.

"Oh fu—stop, stop, stop," Odis hissed.

Bobby removed his mouth and scooted up to kiss Odis. He had to back off, though—Odis was panting hard and couldn't seem to catch his breath. Bobby chuckled. "I thought you said it would take three minutes."

"Shut up" was all Odis could seem to mutter.

Bobby hugged him and stroked his hair as Odis recovered.

"That...." Odis looked into Bobby's eyes.

"That was good?"

Odis smirked. "More like, over the moon."

"You never had a girl give you head?"

"Not like that." Odis smiled. "They always went about it like they were doing the laundry or something. I guess that was part of what made it so hot, seeing how much you enjoyed doing it."

"I guess I like making you squirm and get all incoherent."

Odis kissed him deeply, rubbing his fingernails up Bobby's sides and feeling him shiver. The passion of the kiss was like a warm, fuzzy blanket that surrounded them with comforting bliss.

Odis pulled back. "So I'm your first with a foreskin?"

"Well, it's not like I've never seen one, and I've seen some in porn."

"You watch porn?" Odis smacked himself in the head. "Oh duh, on the road...."

"Yeah, spent a lot of nights in hotel rooms with porn for company."

"That...," Odis said as he shook his head. "It must have been lonely."

"Part of the job, I guess."

Odis nestled in against Bobby's chest. "So what kind of work are you going to do now?"

"I don't know. I could take over the landscaping business, but that was always more Nate's shtick. He left it to me, but...." Bobby shrugged. "I'm not sure how his mom would feel about me taking over."

"His mom? Why would she care if it was Nate's business?"

"Well, it was the family business. Nate took it over after his dad died."

Odis looked confused.

"Oh, I didn't mention? I found out when I went to Nate's for the family Labor Day barbecue that his dad was my boss."

"You were with Nate all summer and he didn't bother to tell you it was his dad's landscaping company?"

"Well, I'm sure at first, he was worried about me taking advantage. Then we got… distracted and just never got around to talking about it."

"Humph. And you want to give it back to his mom?"

"I don't know, maybe? I'll have to figure something out this month, though. It's about time to start gearing up since winter's over."

"That's part of the legal stuff you were talking about?"

"Yeah, and some lawyers are pressuring me to file suit."

"You don't want to?"

"It'll just start up the circus again."

"I'm sure it will." Odis kissed his forehead. "But won't it help set a precedent for other gay players? And not just baseball…."

"I know."

They cuddled on the bed together, enjoying the feel of each other.

Odis broke the silence after a few minutes. "Guess it's time for that shower now."

"All right," Bobby agreed.

Odis stood up and stripped off his boxers and dropped them on the bed, then pulled Bobby to his feet. He slipped the gym shorts off Bobby before trying to lift off Bobby's shirt. He wasn't tall enough and had to step onto the bed to pull the shirt over Bobby's head.

Bobby smirked. "This is kinda weird."

Odis took his hand and led him to the bathroom. "How so?"

Bobby glanced down at his hand in Odis's, remembering what John had said about Odis's ex-wife. Odis certainly didn't seem to have a problem holding *his* hand. "I'm usually the shortest guy in the room, seems like. You make me feel tall, though."

"Shut up right there. Don't even use the *C*-word or I'll smack you." Odis noticed Bobby still had his socks on. He guided Bobby to sit on the toilet and slid the tube socks from his feet.

"All right, but what's the *C*-word? Just so I won't use it accidentally."

Odis rolled his eyes as he pulled Bobby into the shower. "I'm talking about the 'cute' word."

"Oh?" He watched Odis punch a few buttons on the space-station-looking panel. Eight jets of water streamed out around them.

"I'm not a kitten or a puppy or a Valentine's card. It's kind of insulting to call a grown man 'cute'."

"Oh." Bobby watched Odis push in on a rounded rock by the middle jet, and a thick stream of gooey soap squirted from the wall. "This has got to be the fanciest shower I have ever seen."

Odis lathered up the soap in his hands and then started rubbing it all over Bobby's back. "Thanks. Designed it myself. Had to fire three plumbers before I found one that could see my vision."

Bobby couldn't stifle himself, and a pleasured moan escaped as Odis worked his hands firmly along his back. He was already sprouting wood when Odis moved his hands to his ribs and chest.

Odis tried to ignore Bobby's growing dick, without success. His own began growing in response. Or maybe it was the feel of Bobby's chest muscles under his hands that got him excited again. He rubbed his soaped hand on top of the hummingbird tattoo and tried not to think about the ink too much.

After feeling along the wall, Bobby found the soap dispenser spot and lathered up his own hands. He started rubbing the soap onto Odis's shoulders. He dug his fingers a little deeper to work the tight muscles along Odis's neck and upper spine.

"Yeah." Odis sighed. "That's the spot. Always get kinked up there."

Using a tight grasp, Bobby massaged up the base of Odis's neck. "The word I thought of a while ago wasn't the *C*-word, but it might be just as insulting."

"What word?" Odis asked with open curiosity.

Bobby leaned down to Odis's ear. "You're like a leprechaun," Bobby whispered.

Odis laughed warmly as he got more soap. "Well, wrong culture, but hafta admit it is a bit original."

"Wrong culture?"

"I'm not Irish, boy. But don't really have anything similar in Nordic mythos, though." Odis lifted his hands to Bobby's neck and ran his thumbs along Bobby's lower jaw. "Attitude-wise, Loki would kinda fit, but he wasn't short."

"Well." Bobby grinned. "I'm half-Irish, so does that count?"

"In that case—" Odis pulled Bobby's head down for a quick kiss. "—I could get used to it."

Bobby wrapped his arms around Odis's shoulders and raised him up for another kiss. "How about if you're just *my* leprechaun?"

"I could definitely get used to that," Odis said with a huge grin. He draped around Bobby, letting one hand drift down to Bobby's ass. He grabbed at it with his slippery hand. Odis enjoyed the solid feel of the manly flesh in his grasp.

"You trying to get me all cranked up again?" Bobby asked, pulling Odis up against his hard cock.

"I just love your butt. I never thought a *man's* butt could be so interesting."

Bobby lowered his hands down Odis's back. "I like yours too," he admitted with a grin as he rubbed his wet hands over Odis's tight little rear end.

Odis slid his hands up to Bobby's back and yanked him into a tight hug, burying his face against Bobby's chest.

Sensing a shift in mood, Bobby looked down at him. "What?"

"I know you hafta, but I don't want ya to leave." Odis felt the water getting colder but didn't want to move to turn it off. "I want you to stay in my island."

After rinsing off his hands, Bobby maneuvered them away from the cold jets. "I'm not leaving, not right away. Just don't think about that 'til we have to." Bobby looked over the control panel, failing to see how to turn off the chilling water. "Is there a manual for these shower controls?" he teased.

Odis chuckled and released his grip to punch the button to turn off the water. "Green one is 'on' or 'off', depending." He looked up at Bobby.

"Island?" Bobby asked.

Odis got towels from the little cabinet by the shower door and handed one to Bobby. "Oh, well, the art world is kind of a circus in its own way. When I built this place, I thought of it as my own private island, away from it all."

"Well, it's a nice island," Bobby said as they dried off. It seemed kind of lame, but that was all he could think of to say. He followed Odis back toward the bed.

"Sorry the water got cold so fast. It's only a thirty-gallon tank. With that many jets running, it doesn't stay warm long." He took Bobby's towel and threw both of them into the laundry basket. "Was planning to put in one of those on-demand-type heaters, just haven't done it yet."

Bobby stretched out on the bed. "Well, you should put that on your to-do list." He hugged Odis when he lay down next to him. "I can imagine all kinds of interesting things with a lot of hot water."

Odis smiled. "I bet you can." He ran his fingers through Bobby's wet hair, watching how the short chestnut-colored locks wanted to curl around his fingers. "You ever grow your hair out longer?"

Bobby grinned playfully. "Trying to imagine me as a woman now?"

"No, of course not," Odis defended. "If I wanted a woman, *you* wouldn't be here in my bed." He leaned in and lightly kissed Bobby's lips.

Bobby pulled him closer, opening his mouth and going deeper. They enjoyed the taste of each other and that fuzzy-blanket feeling a moment before separating. "I don't let it grow longer. It turns into an unruly mess like a dirty old mop."

"I doubt it. That sounds like something a mom would say...."

Bobby dropped his gaze. "Anyway, I keep it short."

Watching Bobby's face, Odis prodded, "Tell me about your momma." He saw a brief hint of pain before Bobby pulled on a poker face.

"Nothing much to tell."

Odis studied him, knowing that was far from the truth. But Bobby still wouldn't meet his gaze, so he let it drop.

Without looking up, Bobby asked, "Roll over?"

Odis rolled onto his back. "Like this?"

Bobby put his hand on Odis's hip and nudged him to keep rolling. Odis rolled over onto his other side. Bobby spooned in behind him, sighing as he wrapped his arm around Odis and clutched at his chest.

Odis settled in against Bobby. He'd never been on the inside of a spoon and found it strangely comforting. He could feel Bobby's knees right behind his, his butt fit right into the fold of Bobby's lap, and he could feel Bobby's breath right behind his ear. Odis was surprised at how well they seemed to fit together. He relaxed into the embrace.

"This feels so great," Bobby whispered sleepily in Odis's ear.

"Yeah, it sure does." Odis felt the drowsiness and didn't fight it. He let Bobby's slow breathing rhythm lull him into sleep.

CHAPTER
Seven

AS BOBBY slowly awoke, he was aware of lying on his back sandwiched between two warm bodies. *Wait*, he thought. *Two bodies*? He opened his eyes and tried to rise, but a weight on the sheet kept him pinned down. On his left was Odis, curled up next to him. On his right, a dark mass of fur snored away. Heimdalla was on top of the sheet, effectively trapping him. After managing to wriggle his arm out of the bedcovers, he reached down and patted her. "Morning."

She replied with a slurp from her square tongue across his upper forearm and then lay back down.

Not thinking of anything better to do, Bobby settled back in and watched Odis sleep.

Bobby wasn't even sure what time it was when he heard his cell phone ringing. "Shit," he groaned, trying to sit up. "Where's my pants?"

Heim looked up at him, then jumped off the bed and rooted around on the floor. As Bobby crawled to the edge of the bed, she ran back and dropped a pair of blue boxers in his lap just as the phone stopped ringing.

Bobby chuckled. "Thanks, but I meant *my* pants, not Odis's." He gave her a pat on the head for trying to be helpful.

She disappeared again, then brought back Bobby's jogging shorts as he stood up.

"Much better," Bobby praised her with a smile, taking the shorts and patting her head again. He slipped on the shorts as he tried to remember where he left the duffel bag that held his jeans and cell phone. He recalled leaving the duffel by the dining table and started that way. The phone call was probably from Sharon, so he wasn't in a hurry.

He dug the phone out of the bag to check the messages. She'd probably just leave a terse note about calling her back. But the missed call wasn't Sharon's number, and the caller didn't leave a voice mail.

Bobby was debating whether to do a star-callback, when the phone rang in his hand. "Hello?"

A professional female voice pattered in his ear. "I'm with Schmitt and Murdock, and I'm trying to reach Robert Lane. Is this Robert I am speaking with?"

"Yeah, I'm Robert—"

"Glad to finally reach you, Mr. Lane. I'm calling in regards to the settlement offer. A conference meeting has been slotted for 2:00 p.m. at our Boston satellite office."

"Wait, what settlement? Two o'clock today? I can't make that."

She clicked her tongue in his ear. "You haven't been informed of the commission's settlement arrangements?"

"No, I've been traveling. I'm actually in Texas right now."

"I see," she said very crisply. "Hold one moment, please."

Bobby held the phone away from his ear, not wanting to listen to the supposedly soothing John Lennon remix. He glanced over at the phone and saw it showed 7:02 a.m.

A strong baritone male voice ended the awful music. "Mr. Lane?"

"Yes."

"This is Ted Humphrey from the law offices of Schmitt and Murdock. We're representing the commission, and they are reaching out to offer a settlement. You weren't apprised of this?"

"No. And I can't do anything today. I'm out of town."

Bobby heard the rustling of papers. "No, I don't see in your file a record of initial contact. So, Mr. Lane, consider *this* your initial contact. You have seventy-two hours to secure legal representation, then we can make our settlement offer. I'll pencil it in for...." More papers rustled. "Thursday 11:00 a.m. Our office will contact you Wednesday to confirm. This is the cell phone number we are speaking on?"

"Yes. What kind of settlement is this?"

"I'm not allowed to divulge that information at this time, Mr. Lane. We will go over everything in recorded session on Thursday."

"Okay, I guess Thursday will work."

"Fine. Have a good day."

The phone went dead in Bobby's ear.

So much for hanging out awhile in Texas.

Odis got up, pulled on his boxers, and then crossed the room to him. "G'mornin'. Who's that?"

"Oh, a law office. The commission wants to give me a settlement. They wanted me there at two o'clock this afternoon."

"Yeah, I kinda heard most of it. Let's get some food in ya, stud. PBJ sandwich?"

Bobby laughed. "I suppose that's fine."

Odis chuckled as he walked to the kitchen area. "I hate to cook, if ya hadn't noticed."

"I did sorta notice that."

"So," Odis said as he started the coffee maker, "you should prob'ly head back today, then."

"You're kicking me out again?" Bobby tried to sound teasing. "I don't have to be there until Thursday."

Odis looked hurt, and then glared at him as he put the bread in the toaster and gathered up sandwich supplies. "Please stop saying that. I'm not 'kicking you out', and ya should know that. But you'll need time to get your corn in a row a'fore you go in that meetin'."

"What corn?" Bobby chuckled at the strange expression.

"Get your own lawyer and shit, is what I mean. Those people on the phone aren't on *your* side. You go in there without your own lawyer, they'll eat ya alive."

Bobby watched Odis make the sandwiches. "But what if I just wanna take the settlement and get this all over with?" Bobby followed as Odis took the plates of sandwiches to the patio table.

"Well, that is one way to go...."

They sat and bit their sandwiches. "What would *you* do?"

"First off, kinda depends on exactly what the offer is. I'm guessing, though, they'll just throw a lot of money at ya, maybe even add some kind of gag order so it'll all quietly go away."

"Okay. If I don't take it, though, what would be the point?"

"You mean, what are you fighting for? A public apology? Maybe. Reinstatement? But I know that doesn't mean much since you wanted to retire anyway...."

They ate in silence until the coffeemaker beeped. Bobby got up and filled the mugs Odis had already set aside, and brought back the two coffees. "I can't see any real point to that, though. It'll just stir up the circus again."

"That it would. But it would show 'em that the gays have teeth. Maybe make 'em think twice about pullin' this kinda shit again."

Bobby just nodded as they ate.

"Not that my advice is worth much, but since you're askin'... I'd say, unless it's something completely insulting, take their offer, but throw in a condition that they name something after Nathan. You know, like the Nathan Price Memorial Stadium or something, just so they'll see his name every day and be reminded."

Bobby chuckled. "I kinda like that. Who knew you were such a vindictive bitch?"

Odis curled the corner of his lip up. "Never been called a bitch before. Don't know as I like it...."

"It's a compliment, trust me."

"Okay, stud," Odis said with a wink, then laughed.

They sat and gazed at each other over the empty plates, trying to ignore the impending good-bye.

Odis cleared his throat and broke the silence. "Something I've been wondering about," he dangled in the air.

"Oh? What?"

"Why'd you get on a plane and come out here in the first place? You coulda just used the phone and shit, ya know."

"Well...." Bobby clutched at his coffee mug. "It's Nate's fault."

Odis got up and filled his mug, then brought the carafe over and topped off Bobby's. "How?" he asked when he got back from returning the carafe to the warmer.

Bobby took in a deep breath. "It all started when I got a postcard in the mail. From Nate."

"When was this?"

"About two weeks ago. Surprised the fuck out of me at first, but it was sort of his thing. I was always at spring training during my birthday every year, so Nate would send me little notes and cards, kinda hinting about my present, so he could give it to me in person when training broke and I came home. He liked being there when I opened it, thought it was too impersonal just to ship something down."

"Okay, sounds like a fun guy." Odis waited but had to prompt Bobby again. "What did the postcard say?"

"To pull out the silverware drawer in the kitchen and check underneath. I did and found a key taped under it."

"Oh, cool." Odis grinned. "A scavenger hunt."

"Yeah, I guess. Didn't know what the key was for until the next postcard came. It told me to check in the upstairs linen closet. And I found a small lockbox that the key fit. Inside was a pawn ticket."

"This is sounding very elaborate. Who was sending the cards?"

"Never found out. At first I thought it might be Sharon, but she was at a business thing in Baltimore, and the cards were postmarked from New York. I asked her about it, but she didn't know. She seemed as surprised as I was, but agreed it was *exactly* the kind of thing Nate would do."

"So, the pawn ticket?"

"Was for a book, *Woke Up In a Strange Place*. I found a note stuck between pages thirty-eight and thirty-nine."

"Ah, your age. I admire his cleverness. But I never heard of that book. What's the story about?"

"It's about a gay guy who wakes up in the afterlife and the journey he goes through to reconcile with the life he lived."

"Oh. Well, fuck. That's almost a kick in the nuts."

"Exactly." Bobby drained his mug. "Although it was a *great* book. I sat and read it all that night."

Odis kept trying to catch Bobby's gaze, but the other man's eyes stayed aimed at the table as he sipped his mug.

"Had to go through several more steps before I found your receipt, with a plane ticket and a note to come out here and pick up the sculpture."

"Humph." Odis got up and brought the carafe over to fill Bobby's mug. He set the empty carafe down on the table after topping off his own.

"Yeah, humph. Not only did he set all of *that* up, there's the thing with preordering the bust too."

"I'm sorry," Odis apologized. "Knowing all that now, I might have screwed up another surprise of his. He prob'ly set up another little thing for the anniversary."

"Well, I'm through with surprises. I'm trying to get past all this, move on, ya know. But Nathan keeps showing up and yanking me back down, it feels like."

"Humph," Odis replied. It seemed more like Nathan was kicking Bobby in the butt to get him moving again. It was kind of a harsh thought, though, so he didn't say it aloud.

Bobby gazed over at him. "We're out of coffee," he said, pointing to the table.

Odis stood up and started gathering dishes. "Suppose we should get ya on that plane, then."

Bobby started to say something about getting kicked out but clamped his mouth. "Can we at least cuddle first?"

"Cuddle? Or do ya just mean that as a starting place?"

Bobby laughed. "Caught me."

"Well, call Gertie and set up a flight. We'll see how much time there is 'til you hafta get to the airport."

"Why Gertie?"

"She has connections with workin' the B and B. Plus she loves doin' that kinda stuff."

"Shit, the B and B. I've still got stuff over there."

"Is it anything you need?"

"Not really, just some clothes and toiletries."

"Then don't worry about that. I can fetch it over here next time I'm in town." Odis pointed at the wall phone by the kitchen area. "Pound key then one will speed-dial Gertie."

Bobby picked up the phone as Odis disappeared into the bathroom. He updated Gertie on the situation, and she promised to call right back with details.

Odis returned from the bathroom, carrying Bobby's dirty socks.

"She'll call back in a few minutes when she's done."

Odis walked up to Bobby and gave him the socks and a warm kiss. Bobby thought it tasted too much like minty toothpaste but enjoyed the kiss anyway. Odis pulled away. "You know I don't want ya to go, right?"

"I know. But you're right. I've been putting this stuff off, and it's time to deal with it. Once I get it out of the way, we can see where things are...."

Odis's eyes hardened. "What do you mean? That sounds like a maybe."

"But...." Bobby looked away. "I'm just—after I'm gone a few days, you might decide this was just a fun, inspiring fling."

Struggling with a sudden surge of anger, Odis resisted punching him. "You don't believe me? I'm not some childish flake. I... fuck you." He spit out the words and turned away, immediately regretting the outburst as he walked into the bedroom area to find the rest of Bobby's clothes.

Bobby tried to ignore the sting. "You said yourself that you don't have a frame of reference. How can—"

The phone ringing interrupted him. Bobby answered it immediately. "Hello?"

Odis tidied up the bed area and tried to calm himself as Bobby got his travel details from Gertie.

Bobby hung up the phone. "Flight in three hours."

"That doesn't leave any time, since ya hafta drive back to Amarillo first." Odis searched around the bed and gathered up the rest of his dirty clothes as Bobby went into the bathroom to get ready.

He returned a few minutes later in his clean jeans. "Sorry," Bobby apologized. "I don't want to start a fight. I just want to make sure you know what you want." He sat at the table and pulled on the clean socks.

"I just hate bein' called a liar."

Bobby put on his shoes and tied them up. "That's not at all what I said."

"Not in so many words, but maybe I'm just bein' defensive again. I want ya to come back." Odis went to the kitchen and got a business card from one of the drawers as Bobby pulled on the clean shirt. "This has all my numbers on it," he said, handing the card to Bobby. "Call me, but keep tryin' if I don't answer right away, I might be busy."

"Busy? With what?" Bobby asked as he slipped on the jean jacket.

"I actually feel like working. I might be in the studio awhile." Odis gave him a tentative hug.

Bobby squeezed back and kissed his forehead. "All right. I'll call and keep you updated." He released Odis, picked up the duffel, then walked out the door before he let himself get distracted by the thought of Odis still wearing nothing but his boxers.

Odis watched him leave, feeling a heavy pit in his gut. At least Bobby said he would call.

CHAPTER
Eight

AFTER tidying up the house and checking his supply inventory in the studio, Odis thought about heading to the B and B. This bold new vision he had in his head, if he really wanted to pull it off right, involved the use of some new materials. He could use Gertie's computer to research and order the necessary supplies—or, more likely, watch over Gertie's shoulder as she worked the computer—and he could also grab Bobby's things, since he'd be there anyway.

It only took a few minutes to open up the garage and untarp his jet-black El Camino, but the car's refusal to start left him stranded. Upon finding the battery dead, Odis chided himself for not driving the car more often as he hooked up the charger and waited the required two hours for the battery to build up enough juice to work.

After returning to the house, Odis changed the sheets on the bed but regretted the task as soon as he threw them in the washer. The fabric still held faint traces of Bobby's aroma. Maybe he should have left them. *But that's just silly*, Odis scolded himself. *Grown men shouldn't run around smelling each other. Although that might make sporting events more interesting.* He chuckled aloud at the thought.

Odis dawdled around with other house chores, checking the garage occasionally until the charger's green light finally came on. He reached into the car and turned the key. The car roared to life after a sputtering cough.

Heimdalla looked in the car, then back toward the house when Odis opened the car door wider for her. After a studying glance up at Odis, she trotted back to the house.

"Damn dog. Just stay here, then," he grumbled at Heim as he crawled into the rumbling El Camino. Odis smiled as he backed the vehicle out of the garage and drove to the gate. Even after all this time, the car's feel and power still gave him a rush. He'd gotten it brand new back in 1987, paid cash for it from the earnings of his first big art show. He patted the steering wheel as he waited for the gate to open. *They just don't make cars like this anymore.*

GERTIE gazed up with shocked eyes as Odis walked into the B and B. She jumped up off the couch. "Odie?"

"Hey, sis," he threw out as he walked toward the office. "Is that computer thingy of yours turned on?"

"Most likely." She rushed up behind and followed him into the office. "Everything okay? Did Bobby make his flight?"

"Oh, sure, he done left hours ago. Just wanted to grab his stuff and check on orderin' some supplies." He sat down at the desk and fiddled with the mouse, trying to figure out where that damn cursor doodad was hiding.

Gertie nudged him aside. "Let me, before you break something. What kind of supplies?" she asked as she opened the web browser and scrolled through the art supply bookmarks folder.

Odis explained what kind of materials he needed as Gertie hopped from one website to another.

Gertie checked another site, still not finding what they were looking for. "Why don't ya head upstairs? Bobby was in the yellow room. You can grab his stuff while I dig around a bit."

"Okee." Odis left, grateful for the exit. All those flashing boxes and things on the computer screen just made his eyes hurt.

"There's some paper bags in Granny's buffet. Left side."

"Gotcha," he said as he walked into the dining room. He grabbed one bag, then decided he might need two. Odis trotted up the stairs.

Other than a neat pile of used clothes on one of the wing-back chairs, the room hardly looked occupied. As he walked toward the chair, Odis caught a whiff of Bobby's aroma from the dirty clothes. He put the clothes in one of the bags, scolding himself for being a weirdo as he tried to ignore the wonderful musky scent.

What was up with him? He'd never really given a second thought to the way any women smelled, unless they were covered with noxious perfumes he wanted to avoid. Why this sudden obsession with Bobby's scent?

As he checked the dresser drawers and collected more of Bobby's items, he thought he heard a new guest arrive downstairs. He checked the nightstand and closet and found a few more things, then searched the bathroom before departing.

When only partway down the stairs, he heard a booming cop voice.

"Odie, you little shit," Tucker Krickson growled at him from the lower hallway.

"Hey, Tuck." Odis avoided his eyes. He always thought Tucker had the aura of a honey badger, especially when he had his ire up. His yellowy-brown hair had much more gray in it now, making him even more ruggedly handsome. That muddy-brown sheriff's uniform seemed to make Tuck's eyes look vividly greener. Damn him, Tuck would have to show up in that foxy uniform. Odis held the bags in front of his crotch.

"What's this I hear about Bobby Lane?" Tuck growled as Odis walked down the stairs. "He was in town? At yer house? And ya can't even bother to pick up a fuckin' phone to call your friend?"

"Who said we were friends?" Odis teased—mostly. "When was the last time ya even came by my place?" Odis tried not to look directly at him. Tuck sure was aging well, for a man who was older than he was, by a few months, anyway. He watched Tuck dangle the ranger's hat he held by the brim in front of his waist. The little tassely things on the front band thumped against the lower brim as he fidgeted.

Tucker clenched his jaw angrily, which deepened the crease lines along his brow and made him look mean, but Odis could see the shadow of hurt in his eyes. "I've been busy... and you weren't 'zackly all warm and friendly last time I popped over."

Odis stopped on the second step so he could be at Tucker's eye level. "Well." He paused. He couldn't even remember what it was they'd been fussing over in the first place. Odis frowned and let out a big sigh. "Let's just wipe the slate, okay?" He tried to smile warmly but was afraid it looked lecherous.

Tucker nodded. "Agreed."

"What'cha doin' here?"

"Saw the Camino, bonehead." Tucker dropped his gaze. "Was on my way over anyway, though," he added quickly. "Pearl over't the liquor store said we had a strange football player or somethin' in town, and I headed over to check. Found out from Gertie it was Bobby Lane."

"Oh, yep."

"*And* he was out at your place." He seemed to scrutinize Odis. "So what's up, Odie?"

Odis glanced self-consciously at the office doorway. "Ya still on duty?"

"Just 'til three. Why?"

"Then run over to Pearl's, grab some of that Boston beer, and come out ta the place when ya get done. We can chat about it there."

Tucker followed Odis's gaze to the office door, then looked back with a suspicious smile. "*Boston* beer? All righty, then. I'll drop by." He looked right into Odis's eyes and grinned briefly. "I think somebody's been—"

Gertie came into the hall. "You boys quit yer fussin'. Get in here, Odis. I think I found it but want ya to check it over." She turned to Tuck. "Ya stayin', Tucker? Or are ya going back to work?" she hinted.

Tuck nodded with a slight bow. "On my way out now, Gertie." He glanced back up at Odis. "And I'll be there." He turned and walked out through the foyer.

Odis watched him through the door's glass, trying not to stare at his still shapely bubble-butt. Tuck put on his hat, squared it, then moved away to his tan SUV, which was sitting in the parking lot.

Odis followed his sister into the office and got all the supplies squared away. Since it was an unfamiliar material, he ordered about four times more of it than he anticipated actually needing. That would leave plenty to experiment with if he made mistakes.

"So what *is* up with you and Bobby?" Gertie suddenly blindsided him with the question.

"Who says anything's up?"

Gertie gave him a scrutinizing glare. "Don't try and pull that innocent act on me. That man was under my roof and ate at my table. I can see and hear things, ya know."

Odis folded under his sister's stare. "I don't know. Honestly, Gertie. I'm just takin' things one day at a time." He went to the door before she started grilling him more.

"Go on, then. Patch things up with Tuck. I'm tired of him hangin' around here all the time."

Odis raised an eyebrow. "I didn't know he was."

"Oh yeah, makin' a regular pest of himself. Always tryin' to nose into family business. Your business, mostly."

"Oh. Okay. I'll have a chat with him about that, then. Thanks for the help with those orders."

"Go on." Gertie waved him off and turned back to the computer.

IT WARMED into a nice sunny afternoon, so Odis paced around the outdoor patio area. Bobby hadn't called yet, but he had to make plane transfers, so it might be a few more hours before Odis heard from him.

He studied the yard, trying to decide if he should maybe plant some flowers or something to liven up the boring grassy space. He got distracted, though—his thoughts kept drifting to Tuck. Odis hadn't known he was hanging around the B and B.

Heim jumped up from her sunning spot and barked once before she ran up the stairs. *Must be after three o'clock.* Odis went into the house to wait.

He watched Tucker coming down the stairs carrying a huge paper bag. Being out of uniform didn't reduce his attractiveness. The tight black denim jeans and green western shirt he now wore seemed to show off his body even more. Odis jogged over and opened the sliding door for him. "Hey, Tuck."

Tuck walked in and set the bag on the patio table before adjusting his Texas Rangers baseball cap. "Really, Odie? This iron table is still here? I helped ya drag that off the patio almost four years ago."

Odis just shrugged. "What's in the bag?"

"The beer ya asked for, bonehead." He reached in and pulled out four different six-packs of brew. "Ya didn't say an exact brand, so I got anything that said 'Boston' on it."

"Oh," Odis said, picking up the maroon-colored pack. "This is the one. Guess it never hurts to have extra beer around." He grabbed another of the six-packs and took them to the refrigerator.

Tuck chuckled as he picked up the other two packs. "Nope, never does." He looked around the house as he followed Odis to the kitchen. "What in Valhalla, Odie? Ya could've at least got another dining table. I don't know why ya even let Tina clean ya out that way."

"It's just stuff. Wasn't worth fightin' her over." Odis got out the last two cold beers and handed one to Tuck.

They opened their bottles and stood in the kitchen, trying not to look at each other. Odis finally glanced up and saw the worry on his friend's face. He motioned toward the dining area. "Let's sit down."

They took seats on opposite sides of the table. Odis looked up at Tuck again. "Okay, I'm sorry. I'm a total dick."

Tuck just nodded. Then he waited, watching Odis with his examining cop stare.

"I shouldn't'a picked a fight like that. I was more mad at myself than you anyway." Odis took a swig of the bottle. "Quit staring at me like that."

"Fine. But what were you angry about? I never did understand that."

"Oh, anger's not quite the right word. I...."

Following a suspicion, Tuck cocked his head to one side and smiled slightly. "This is tied in to Bobby, isn't it?" Tuck said, making it sound more like a statement than a question.

Odis nodded and took another swallow of beer.

Tuck kept studying him. Then his green eyes suddenly flared. "You little shit! You fucked him."

Odis dropped his head, knowing there wasn't any way to hide his blushing. "Not exactly."

"Well then, what exactly *did* happen?" Tuck peered over at him intently, waiting for the answer.

"We... um... fooled around a little. Then he slept here." Odis glanced up, completely surprised by the hurt look he saw in Tucker's eyes before he pulled on a stoic mask.

"Shit." Tuck sighed heavily. "Just fuck it all."

"So, go ahead, then. Start in on the fag jokes."

Tucker shook his head as he leaned back into his chair and stared at the ceiling. "You know, for such a smart and sensitive guy, you sure can be blind and stupid."

"What'cha mean by that?"

Tuck made a flourish over himself with his hands. "Look at me, you idiot." Tucker sat up again and caught Odis's eyes. "Really *look* at me for a second."

Odis studied Tucker. He noticed the cut of his graying honey-brown hair looked a bit stylish for a sheriff. He saw the slight dimple of an ear piercing in his left earlobe. Then he recognized the look of desire in Tucker's eyes. "Oh. Well, shit."

"Yeah." Tucker nodded when he saw the dawning of Odis's realization. "You bonehead."

"God dammit all." Odis turned his eyes from Tucker's gaze. "So that off-and-on thing you had goin' on in Hutchinson, that was a guy?"

"Yep, a mechanic at the Walmart." Tuck watched his face as Odis mentally realigned his world. Odis finally looked back at him.

Tucker nodded firmly. "So, now tell me the truth, what was all that shit about after Tina left?"

Odis squirmed. "Well, after she left, it seemed all I could think about was you. And having you hanging around was just too aggravatin'. So I chased you off. It never crossed my mind you might want me too."

Tucker finished off his beer. "After you divorced Marsha, I almost came out to you."

"Oh?" Odis finished off his own beer.

"Yeah, that night after we went bowling, and that chick, what was her name?"

Odis shook his head.

"Anyway, that chick kept throwing herself at ya every time I was up, and I got so jealous. It was almost enough for me to tell ya."

"Oh, that's the night you wanted to hang around in the parking lot forever and talk. I always thought that was kinda weird." Odis got up and reached out for Tucker's empty beer bottle. He headed back to the kitchen.

"That was the night."

Odis checked in the refrigerator. "May still be warm."

"I don't care, get me one anyway."

Odis brought back two bottles. "Maybe I should shake it up first, just to check?"

"Don't be an ass. Just gimme." He took the bottle and opened it carefully. It felt cold enough.

Odis dropped down in the chair next to Tucker. "I wish you *had* told me. I kinda had the hots for you then too."

"Well, I was kinda on again at the time, so prob'ly wouldn't have done anything about it anyway."

Odis suddenly chuckled. "Look at us, a perfect pair of boneheads." He gazed over at Tucker.

Tucker gazed back. Now that Odis wasn't trying to hide it, his desire made his blue eyes glow. Tucker leaned over and put his lips on Odis's.

Odis yanked back. "Hey, um… wait."

Tucker blinked at him. "What's wrong now? I thought we had this shit settled?" He saw the shadow of guilt lingering over Odis's eyes. "Loki's nuts," he spat. "You fell in love with him," he almost whined.

Odis shrugged. "Maybe. I don't know."

"Damn cock was only here two days. Just *two days*." His head drooped in sad resignation. "Well, fuck me up."

Odis reached out and rubbed his hand along Tuck's shoulder. "I'm sorry. Dammit. I didn't think you would care so much."

"Didn't think I would care? Are you *really* that dense?" Tuck shook his head. "I've had a crush on you since high school, ya idiot bonehead."

"High school?"

"Yes, high school. Remember the prom?"

"Other than Marsha throwing up all over Gramps's truck? Not much."

"After that, when you took her home and came back to the gym. Why *did* you come back to the gym?"

"Oh, it was still so early, and you and your date…."

"Karla."

"Yeah, you and Karla were still there. Didn't want to just ditch out."

"Uh-huh," Tuck said in a knowing tone.

"Speaking of which, whatever happened to Karla? She kinda disappeared after graduation."

"She's in Amarillo with her girlfriend of ten years. But quit changin' the subject. What happened after you came back?"

"Oh, you know." Odis gazed up at the ceiling, trying to remember. "We were goofing off back sorta behind the bleachers."

"And...?"

"Karla was teasing me, saying I didn't have a girl to kiss, so I leaned in to kiss her." Then Odis's eyes suddenly lit up. "Fuck. *You* leaned down and kissed me instead." Odis laughed. "God, how could I forget *that*?"

"Well, I tried to play it off as a joke, said I didn't want another guy kissing my date. She thought that was so funny 'cause she didn't want to kiss a guy anyway."

"Dammit. I feel like such an idiot now." Odis looked over at Tuck. "All this time we mighta...."

"Just forget that, Odie. You said earlier today 'clean slate', so let's start with here and now." Tucker looked back at Odis, questioning. "So. What about Bobby?"

Odis sighed. "He's coming back so we can figure this out."

"Bobby's coming back?" A cold jealousy sank into Tucker's gut. He couldn't even look at Odis as he pushed himself away from the table and stood. "Fine, then." He paused, not even looking in Odis's direction. He felt so wounded he didn't trust himself to speak, so he turned and walked out.

Odis watched him walk up the stairs with heavy steps. "God dammit all," he hissed under his breath. He was getting tired of the sight of guys' asses leaving him.

CHAPTER
Nine

BOBBY maneuvered around the stack of mail on the floor as he stepped into the foyer and turned the alarm off. He should be happy about getting home, but the empty house provided no comfort. After dropping the duffel bag into the wing-back chair, he scooped up the mail. He sorted through it and found nothing important. He tossed the mail onto the side table before stepping into the living room.

Without Nathan's presence to liven it up, the huge house around him felt so vacant and dead. Bobby ignored the upper floor and went around the dining room to the side stairs. He started down the treads that led into the basement den.

Vaguely, he could smell it as he reached the bottom step; that stuffy odor of stale habitation hung heavily in the air. He looked around at the messy room that had been his refuge for the last few months. Obviously the maid hadn't come down here. Probably not since the early days, after he scolded her for running the vacuum cleaner while he was watching a movie.

Blaring away, the wide-screen TV he'd forgotten to turn off eerily illuminated the room. The coffee table was still littered with wrappers and half-eaten bags of long-stale chips. Lying sideways on the floor, an empty tumbler glass flanked the front of the couch. The white pillow he had dragged from the bedroom now looked all beigey and stained. Its matching comforter didn't look much better. At the side of the couch, the large trash can overflowed with TV dinner plates and a Bushmills bottle. Even though the liquor had lasted more than a month, the empty whiskey bottle seemed to tease him, telling him what a shit he was. Bobby felt disgusted at the sight. He immediately turned and nearly ran back upstairs.

He stopped in the kitchen. The blinking light on the answering machine advertised seven waiting messages, but he ignored that for now. He headed to the cleaning closet and grabbed some of the large trash bags. If he didn't get back down there and start cleaning now, he'd lose the gumption to return. He also grabbed a can of scented room deodorizer and entered the doorway to the smelly den.

He sprayed a scenty trail down the stairs and sent a few shots into the room before gathering up all the litter into the trash bags. He turned the TV off when he uncovered the remote amongst the archive of refuse on the coffee table. Once the bags were full, he dragged them back upstairs and tossed them into the city bin outside.

After another trip downstairs to tidy and clean, Bobby deemed the room finally acceptable and returned to the kitchen. He glanced around the huge cooking space. Bobby hated this house now, he decided. He never did *really* like it—the place had always been one of Nathan's dreams. Nate had been the one to want the big suburban house full of bouncing children.

That should have been a huge red flag that things were terribly wrong, Bobby realized. A decade ago, when Nate suddenly backed off the idea of getting kids, he should have paid more attention. If he'd delved deeper, maybe Nate would have told him about the aneurism. *Or maybe not. Nate managed to keep his condition a secret for so long. Why would he suddenly spill it?*

Bobby shook his head. It didn't matter anymore. Time to call the Realtor. Well, tomorrow he would—it was too late in the evening to do it now.

The blinking light of the answering machine beckoned him. Bobby went over and hit the button to play the messages.

"Good morning, this is Schmidt and Murdock—" Delete.

"I'm with Schmitt and Murdock—" Delete.

"Schmitt and Murdock calling—" Delete.

"Bobby, call me," the female voice demanded in an almost angry tone. Lorainne hadn't bothered to identify herself, but of course she didn't have to. She knew Bobby would recognize the voice of Nathan's mother. *Shithead*, he cursed himself. He hadn't called her back when she left a message last month. Or the month before.

"I'm with Schmitt and Murdock—" Delete.

Dial tone. Delete.

"Schmitt and Murdock call—" Delete.

"No more messages," the machine announced.

Drumming his fingers on the counter, Bobby tried to decide who to call first. He'd promised Odis he'd call him as soon as he got home, and he'd already neglected that. Yet Lorainne had sounded so pissed. Maybe he better call her before it got too late. He nodded as he dragged out the phone list. *Call Lorainne first. Texas is in a different time zone anyway; that can wait longer.*

He dialed the number. "Hello?" her terse voice answered.

"Hi, Lorainne. You left a message?"

"Yes I did, Bobby," she answered sharply. "Many messages. Many, many messages."

"Okay, sorry, I'm calling back now—"

"Lunch tomorrow. You be here. Noon," she told him crisply.

"Okay, I will," Bobby agreed, hoping nothing else came up in the meantime.

She hung up without saying good-bye.

Bobby felt stunned. Lorainne had every right to be mad at him, since he *had* been kind of ducking her. Hopefully he could smooth things out over lunch.

Time to call Odis. Bobby didn't want to do it standing in the kitchen, so he went to the refrigerator and grabbed a beer. Before the door closed, he grabbed a second one. Then he went upstairs.

He stood in the doorway of the master bedroom a moment. That room just seemed haunted, though, so he went farther down the hall to a spare room. Sitting down on the bed, he fished out Odis's business card and stared at it. The thoughts that kept plaguing him on the airplane resurfaced. Odis had turned so clingy right before Bobby left, which kind of worried him. He kept having doubts. *Maybe those feelings in Texas were just a drug-induced euphoria? Or was it more?*

He finally dialed Odis's house phone.

Bobby opened a beer and took two big swallows while the phone rang in his ear.

"Hello?"

"Hey, Odis, it's Bobby."

"Heya, stud," he almost cheered. "Made it home finally?"

"Yeah."

"You don't sound happy about it."

"Well, you're *so* right, you know. I just feel like I'm an invader camping out in Nathan's house. I'm calling a Realtor tomorrow."

"Good first step."

"And I'm having lunch with Nate's mother tomorrow."

"Prob'ly a good thing too."

"So what about you? Anything exciting happen after I left?"

"Um, well, sorta…." Odis hesitated. He wasn't sure how much he should tell Bobby about Tuck's confession. Or the kiss.

"What? What happened?"

"Well, I ran into Tuck when I went back to the B and B to get your stuff. He ended up coming over here and hanging out a bit."

"Oh, Tucker? The other guy you had a crush on?" Bobby felt a strange pang of jealousy at the thought.

"Yeah. He was kinda hoppin' mad, though, that I didn't call him while ya was here."

"I wouldn't mind meeting him. Well, hope you got everything smoothed over."

"I think so. He didn't seem mad when he left." *Just hurt as all fuck.* But Odis didn't say that.

"What about the studio? Get anything done today?"

"Just piddled around a little, ordered more supplies. Prob'ly get on it tomorrow."

"That's good." Bobby stifled a yawn. "Sorry, Odis, I'm kinda beat. Maybe I should go to bed and call you tomorrow."

"Oh, okay," he said, trying not to sound disappointed.

Bobby heard the tone, though. "What?"

"Well, that just sounded kinda impersonal…."

"And what were you expecting, phone sex?"

"Oh Lordy, no. I don't think I'd even know how ta do that."

"Then what?"

"I don't know, stud. Just say g'night and go to bed."

"Okay, good night and go to bed," Bobby teased.

Odis chuckled. "G'night."

Bobby put the phone back on the cradle as another yawn crept up on him. He didn't even bother to take off his clothes. After turning off the nightstand lamp, he stretched out on the bed and fell asleep.

BRIGHT sunlight burned Bobby's face and rudely woke him up. He sat up, noticing he had forgotten to close the window drapes the night before, and this room faced the east. *Oh well, got things to do anyway.* He crawled off the bed and stumbled to the bathroom while his mind hashed over the to-do list for the day.

After his first cup of coffee, he called the Realtor. Not knowing what Lorainne might have planned for the little lunch visit, he set up a late appointment at four thirty. Next, he called the lawyer's office that had been hounding him about suing the commission. He explained about the settlement offer, and they agreed to meet with him the next morning to square up details.

Then his cell phone beeped the "low battery" tone. Bobby went upstairs to the master bedroom. For some reason, he felt like an intruder as he walked very gingerly through the room to the dresser, with a silly fear of stirring up ghosts. He could almost feel Nathan's dead presence hovering around the room and the thought made his skin crawl. He found the charger, yanked the power cord from the wall, and nearly ran out the door and back to the spare bedroom he had staked out the night before. He set up the charger on the nightstand and plugged in the cell phone. He grabbed the empty beer bottle and the one still unopened before wandering downstairs again.

After eating a toaster waffle and downing another cup of coffee, Bobby stretched and felt more human. *Maybe I should go to the sun room and get a workout before the lunch date.*

AS HE stepped onto the Prices' porch just a hair before noon, Bobby tried to shake the sense of nervousness that suddenly inhabited his intestines. *Chill out, it's just Lorainne*, he kept telling himself as he pushed the doorbell button and waited. He was afraid she would chew him out royally, and of course he deserved every word of it.

Lorainne Price opened the door and just stood in the threshold as she closed her house robe more tightly with the belt.

Bobby couldn't believe how worn-out she appeared. Her skeletal face looked withered away. At least twenty pounds had fallen off her, and those lost pounds showed so dramatically on her thin and once healthy frame. Dingy gray hair sagged from her head and clung like limp seaweed around her face. "Lorainne?"

"Come in, then, since you actually showed up," she said in a resigned tone as she moved aside and allowed Bobby entrance. She clutched the robe closer to her.

Stepping inside, Bobby caught the whiff of a familiar odor, the same stale smell from the basement. He suddenly felt like such a dipshit. He should have known Lorainne would be hurting as much as he was; he was just too stupid to think. He followed her into the living room. "I'm sorry. I should have called sooner."

"Might have been nice," she said while dropping onto the couch and retrieving a bar glass half-full of pale yellow liquid from the side table.

Bobby sat farther down the couch. He looked over the robe she wore. "We aren't going out for lunch?"

"This is it," she announced, offering up her glass. "Bar's over there. Get your own."

"Maybe later." Bobby felt completely lost for words as he glanced over. He couldn't think of a single thing to say that might offer comfort for this woman.

She looked over at him. "You should sell that fucking business."

"Oh?" Bobby replied, taken aback by her harshness. "I was going to talk to you about that, thought maybe you might want it—"

"*Why* the fuck would I want it? After it killed my husband *and* my son? Dump the shitty thing."

Oh, fuck me. Bobby's guts wrenched with ten times more guilt. He'd forgotten about Frank. Well, not forgotten, exactly—he was never really close to Nathan's dad—but of course Lorraine…. *Oh, fuck me with a splintery stick.*

"That foreman guy, Jacob, Jason, whatever… Nate was always bragging on him doing such a good job. Sell it to him."

"Well, he prob'ly won't have the cash for that."

Lorraine looked over at him with a sneer. "*Prob'ly*? When did you turn into a hick?"

"Oh, well, I just got back from Texas."

"Don't worry about Jameson. I'll give him the money. He can take a big raise and pay me back over time." She downed the remaining liquid and placed the empty glass against her cheek. "What the *hell* were you doing in Texas?"

"Um…." Bobby wasn't sure how to answer that. He didn't want to say anything that might provoke Lorraine more. "Well, I've been getting postcards," he started.

Lorraine stiffened. "You too? I thought *you* were behind it somehow. What kind of sick shit is this?"

"I didn't know you got some too."

"Yes. From some asshole in New York."

"That's where mine were postmarked from."

"Well, find out who the fuck is sending them and stop it. I don't find it *at all* amusing."

Bobby shook his head. "I tried to track it down, never did find out."

"Well, try *harder*." She wobbled a bit as she pulled herself to her feet. "And send that Johnson guy over here. We'll sell him the business."

"Okay," Bobby agreed as he stood up also. "I'm sorry."

"It is what it is." She walked toward the bar. "You can let yourself out."

"You sure you don't want to, maybe, go out for some food?"

Lorraine turned and glared with him, a don't-fuck-with-me look smoldering in her eyes. "Just let yourself out."

Once he reached the hall, Bobby almost ran back to the front door, but the weight of guilt in his guts kept him moving slow. She obviously needed some help, but he doubted anything he or anybody else did would actually do any good. Not until Lorraine herself decided it was time to move on. He hoped that would happen soon.

THERE'S no time like the present, Bobby thought as he crawled back into his Prius. He drove over to the Lawn Gnome Landscaping office. They might still be out at lunch, but he could hang around and wait since he didn't meet with the Realtor until four thirty.

Stepping inside the kitschy A-frame building, he looked around for Gerald, the general manager, as he walked to young and perky Ivette's desk. Technically she was just the secretary, but everybody knew she was the grease that kept the office running. Bobby almost laughed when he saw her. She'd shorn off her hair on the left side, leaving a strange hanging bang on the right. At least it wasn't electric purple anymore. The lemonade yellow looked more like a potentially legitimate hair color.

"Hello, Mr. Lane," she said with a warm smile. "Haven't seen you around in a while."

"Hi, Ivette. Where's Gerald?"

"Out looking at some new tillers. Heard about a deal on some." She sort of stood up from her desk. "Anything I can help you with?"

He looked at the map of greater New England displayed on the wall behind her and had a sudden inspiration. "We wouldn't happen to have any contacts in New York, would we?"

Ivette's face sort of closed in, as if maybe she had something to hide. "New York? Why would you be asking about that?"

Bobby looked her in the eye. "Postcards."

"Oh." Ivette sat down quickly.

"Know anything about them?"

She nodded slightly, swallowing hard. "Nate asked me to."

Bobby went around the side and sat in the "interrogation" chair flanking the metal desk. They'd nicknamed it that years ago when Nathan said it looked like how they set up the police stations in the cop TV shows. "When was that?"

"Last September." Ivette studied Bobby up and down as she hesitated. "You know he was psychic. Said none of his paths made it to Thanksgiving. So he set up the cards with me, for after."

Bobby flinched. *Psychic? What the fuck?* Psychic? What the hell else had Nathan kept secret?

"You didn't know…." Ivette watched him process the new information. Then she leaned over toward him. "I have dreams sometimes," she admitted to him. "That's how we started talking about the whole paranormal thing."

Bobby still had that stunned look on his face. "Psychic?" he finally managed to voice aloud.

Ivette nodded again. "Yes, Mr. Lane."

"Did *you* know about the aneurism?"

"Not exactly. I knew there was something, but he never gave me any details."

"Well, shit. *Psychic?*"

"Yes…." She reached out and patted his hand. "He tried to explain it to me once, what it was like."

Bobby looked over at her. "What did he say?"

"He said it was like the world was a spiderweb, and he could see the threads. The threads between people and the paths they could lead to."

Bobby just shook his head.

"He said it was mostly a confusing mess he tried to ignore, but every once in a while, he'd see something really clearly."

"Well… shit." Bobby frowned. "I don't even know how to wrap my head around this. Why didn't he ever tell *me* about any of it?"

"You know I can't answer that," she said. "Maybe it was too frustrating for him to try and explain it. I *do* know it took a while for him to talk about it with me."

Bobby shook his head and brought his thoughts back to the task at hand. "I just left Mrs. Price. She wants the postcards to stop."

"Oh." She looked earnestly at him. "Are you sure? There's only two left, and they seem kinda important." Her hand wandered to the handle of the second desk drawer.

"Just two? How many are left for me?"

"Just one. I'm supposed to mail it June 15."

Bobby exhaled. "You *sure* they're important? They're really wigging her out."

"Yes."

"What about mine?"

Ivette hesitated, then slid open the drawer and handed him a postcard. "This is your last one."

Bobby looked down at the card. He saw the sketch of a skinny dog and one phrase: *Unlock your cupid's heart.*

Ivette looked at him and saw his confusion. "I was hoping it made sense to you… I have no idea."

"No fuckin' clue." Bobby groaned. "He's really pissing me off with all this."

"Maybe that's what he wanted. Or part of it."

"*What?*"

"You know, if you got pissed, maybe you wouldn't wallow so much."

"I'm not wallowing."

"Really?" She gave him a stabbing look. "And when was the last time you even stepped foot in here? How long did you hide in that house without *anybody* seeing you?"

Bobby hung his head. "All right. Maybe a little."

"A little." Ivette smiled tightly. "Right."

Bobby thought about the earlier conversation. "What was that about Thanksgiving?"

"Nate said none of his paths would make it to Thanksgiving. He said he had only about a month, month and a half left, depending on the *exactity* of how things rolled out. That was the word he used."

"Why didn't he tell *me* that?"

"He was so excited about you guys getting into the Series. Said it was only a one-in-three-hundred chance from what he could see, but you guys made it. He said it was about 90 percent certain you'd win it too. *If you didn't get distracted.*" She sighed supportively. "So he was doing his best not to distract you."

This seemed so much like the conversation he'd had with Odis almost forty-eight hours before that he nearly chuckled aloud. Then he remembered the time zone difference. It *was* exactly forty-eight hours. *Well, shit on a shingle.*

Ivette smiled at him. "Nate could be so noble sometimes."

Oh, fuck me.

She dropped her smile when she saw his pained expression. "You don't think?"

"Maybe. Just reminded me of something somebody else said."

"Oh." Ivette looked back down at the drawer. "What about the other postcards?"

Bobby wobbled his head. "If you think they're important, then just keep with the plan. Don't suppose it could do the woman any worse. Maybe it *will* help her."

She closed the drawer sharply as someone walked in. "Okay, then."

They both looked up to see Gerald walking through the door.

Gerald nodded as he walked up. "Hello, Mr. Lane. Turned into a nice day out there."

"That it did." Bobby stood and shook his hand.

"What brings you out here? Everything okay?"

"Well, I was just out at Mrs. Price's. We have a proposition for you."

BOBBY left the Lawn Gnome Landscaping office with just enough time to grab a burger on his way back to meet with the Realtor. Gerald was more than thrilled with the idea of buying out the business, and they spent the early afternoon hashing out details.

Waiting in line at the drive-through, Bobby let his thoughts wander back to the postcard still resting on the passenger seat where he'd tossed it. *Unlock your cupid's heart.* He pondered the phrase, but it just seemed so vague and meaningless. He glanced down at the sketch of the dog. *A skinny dog. A... greyhound? A greyhound! Cupid!* His face broke out in a huge grin as he solved the puzzle. *Of course. Two years ago on Valentine's Day, we went to the dog races and won a few bucks. Afterwards, down at the pier for lunch, we ended up spending the winnings on that silly crystal decanter. Where is that decanter now?*

Ah, shit! Bobby squinted as other little bits and pieces started clicking into place. Details of Nathan and his trips to the racetrack. How he *always* wanted to wander the pens first, see the dogs or horses in person and pet them when he could get away with it. How *Nate* always picked the bets. And now that Bobby thought about it, he could not remember a single time they lost. *How did I not see that then? God, it's so obvious. It's like Nate had inside information.*

Nate had never been greedy about it, though. They shared just a few small winnings, making an occasional happy afternoon of it.

Other details started falling in, clicking into the mosaic in such a blur Bobby was fighting a headache. He kept remembering strange little things Nate had said here and there throughout their relationship. Nate's offhand suggestions now felt like little prenudges before something came up.

He yanked up his head and focused on the world again when the car behind him honked. Bobby moved the car forward, taking his place at the window. His food was already waiting; he merely had to pay and then collect his bags. He drove back to the house, his mind an agitated jumble.

CHAPTER
Ten

ONCE the Realtor had been dealt with, Bobby looked once again at the postcard. The *unlock* and *heart* were still a little confusing since the crystal decanter was oval shaped. The *heart* word could just belong to the cupid phrase, merely another part of the reference to Valentine's Day.

As for the *unlock* part, the decanter just had a simple lid that rested atop the jar. *What could the unlock be referring to?* he pondered as he went upstairs, recalling that the decanter was in the master suite.

Bobby froze in the doorway of the bedroom, scolding himself for being so silly. This room was *not* haunted. He spotted the decanter on the dressing bureau. *Just walk in and open it.*

He started across the room, his walk turning into a jog. Instead of just opening it, which seemed like a long waste of time to spend in the bedroom, he grabbed the decanter and hurried back out the door. He exhaled finally as he looked down at the container he clutched in his hands. Bobby took it downstairs to the kitchen before he opened it.

Inside, he found only one item. He removed the dully glinting brass key and examined it closely. It was a smaller skeleton-key sort of shape, with a fancy scroll design at the head of it. The unfamiliar image looked like the blending of a fleur-de-lis and a Celtic knot. Definitely unusual and distinctive. Bobby would remember if he'd ever seen it or saw it again. Maybe that was the point. *So now the unlock part makes sense. But* what *do you unlock?*

His cell phone rang. He fished it out of his pocket and looked at the screen. A call from Sharon.

"Hey, Shar, s'up?"

"You still in Texas?"

"Nope, darlin', moseyed on back hereabouts yestee-day."

"Gawd, Bobby, you were only there two days. They hickafied you that fast?"

Bobby laughed. "What are you up to?"

"Just got home from work, checking to see if you need a butt-kicking."

"Don't think so. Had a busy day. Saw Lorainne."

"Ah, shit, is she doing better?"

"I didn't see her before, so can't judge if it's better or worse, but she's pretty bad."

"I know, poor woman. Husband and son in less than five years. That's gotta suck a big green donkey one."

"I know." Bobby looked down at the key. "Hey, I got another postcard too. This one led to a brass key."

"*Brass* key? What kind of key?"

"One of the smaller old-fashioned ones, like maybe for a jewelry box or something. Has a weird Celtic-knot thing on it."

Sharon paused. "Looks sorta like a French fleur-de-lis?"

"Yes, sorta looks like it."

"I have the box. I'm off work tomorrow. How about I bring it by then?"

"Sharon, what're *you* doing with it? And *really*? You wanna wait until tomorrow?"

Sharon laughed. "Of course not, bitch, just wanted to freak on you a bit. I'm dying to know what's in it too. I'll be there in twenty."

"Okay, see ya."

"Later."

WHEN Sharon arrived, they ended up sitting on the barstools at the kitchen bar. She set the brass heart-shaped box on the counter. On the top lid, Bobby saw a larger version of the unusual fleur-Celtic knot. "Nate gave this box to me, like, ten years ago. Wanted me to hold on to it. He said I'd know when to give it back."

"Ten years ago…." He looked Sharon in the face. "So, did you know anything about him being psychic and all?"

She didn't seem surprised by the question. "What did you hear?"

Bobby studied her. "I talked to Ivette today. She mentioned a few things about it."

"Like what?"

"God, Shar, why are you still covering for him?" He sighed exasperatedly. "Just tell me…."

Sharon looked down at the box. "Let's open it first. Then we can talk about it."

Bobby sighed again and picked up the key. "Okay. But you better spill."

He inserted the key and unlocked the box. The lid stuttered open on stiff hinges as they both leaned down to peek inside. Only a folded sheet of paper took up the space.

Bobby took out the page and unfolded it. He and Sharon puzzled over the strange computer printout they saw.

$A+C=$ *typical :(*
$B+A=$ *rich?*
$B+C=$ *intense?*
$B+A+C=$ *jackpot*

Bobby glanced at Sharon, who stared back. "What the fuck?" they both asked at once. Then they laughed nervously.

Sharon looked down at the note again. "That fuckin' shithead. I was hoping the box might explain some things. *This* is just nuts."

"Well." He frowned over the message. "Maybe it just doesn't make sense *yet*. Ivette was the one sending the postcards. I wasn't supposed to get this last one until the end of June."

Sharon smirked. "I think we could wait 'til hell freezes over and *this* shit *still* won't make any sense." She went to the chiller and grabbed one of the bottles of wine. She snagged two glasses on the way back.

Bobby got the corkscrew from the drawer and handed it to her. "Okay, spill."

"He had some weird vision thing," she said as she opened the wine. "Nate said he could see how things were connected and how they *might be* connected. He really didn't tell me much more than that."

"Why'd he keep it a secret from me?" he asked as she handed him a glass of wine.

"He was afraid it would screw with your relationship. That if you knew he saw things sometimes, you'd be tempted to ask, and he'd be tempted to tell you. Since your career was a game of chance, he worried about consequences. It was easier not telling you at all than having to tell you 'no' all the time."

"But," Bobby started to argue. Then he frowned. "The temptation *would* have been there, I guess. I would have respected him, though."

"Most of the time, maybe, but the *tension* would have still been there. Even if you didn't ask aloud, you'd wonder. You'd examine every little thing he said, looking for extra meanings. I know I did sometimes."

"True. I guess." He held up his glass to toast. "To Nate and his fucking secrets."

Sharon clinked his glass. "He sure loved 'em." She snickered. "Even his fricking name. Took me eight years before he told me what his middle name was."

"Oh." Bobby chuckled. "I only held out a year before I snooped in his papers and found his birth certificate."

Sharon laughed. "Wish I'd had that option. I don't know why he was so embarrassed about Ichabod."

"Well, does bring to mind that silly Halloween story."

Sharon swirled her wineglass. "Now your turn. Tell me about that artist."

Bobby took a big swallow of wine and then sat back on the stool. "You might have met him, I think."

"*What*?" Sharon leaned forward. "Who is he? When?"

"In Key West, do you remember meeting a sculptor?"

"Oh, the little midget guy, Opie or something."

Bobby scowled. "Geez, Shar, could ya be any more offensive?"

"Sorry." She flinched back. "That's the guy? The sculptor?"

"Yeah. He's not a midget, just, shorter. And his name's Odis. Named after a god or something."

"Oh." Sharon poured some more wine into her glass. "I remember him, but I didn't really talk to him. Nate did, though, spent a long time chatting him up." Sharon swirled her glass with a puzzled look on her face. "And he's the guy Nate sent you to."

"You say that like there's something wrong with him."

"No. Like I said, I hardly talked to him." Sharon waited a minute, but Bobby just kept staring off thoughtfully. "So, tell me. What happened in Texas?"

Bobby shook his head. "I honestly don't know. We made out that first day."

Sharon smiled as she eyed him. "Mr. Lane," she teased. "You just walk in and start kissing a strange man?"

"No, we smoked some pot first."

Sharon's eyes popped open. "And what magic spell did he put on you to make *that* happen?"

Bobby smiled sheepishly. "No spell. He didn't know who I was, so we started talking about Nate and everything. Then he gave me his pipe."

"Well, then, I won't argue."

"Argue?" Bobby puzzled aloud.

"With Nate. If it took sending you to Texas to pull you out of… whatever, and get you talking, then I'm not going to argue with Nathan's methods."

"I'm sure he's happy to know he has your approval." Bobby looked over at the brass box. "So, did Nate get that box in Key West?"

Sharon just shook her head, but her eyes widened when she caught Bobby's train of thought. "Oh no, we got it in Savannah, Georgia, where we stopped for the night on the way back."

Bobby nodded. "He got the box and gave it to you *right after* Key West." He smoothed out the enigmatic note and studied it again. "Then this *must* have something to do with Odis."

"Beats me." Sharon looked down at the note.

"The timing of the box right after meeting him sure points to it."

"Maybe." Sharon glanced at Bobby again. "Okay, after getting stoned and making out the first day, what happened the second day?"

"The piece Nate ordered was for my birthday, so Odis stayed up all night finishing it while I was at the B and B. He showed it to me the next day, then took a nap while I worked out. We sorta ended up in bed after that."

"Bobby Lane, you slut," she teased with a silly grin. "What was the sculpture?"

"A huge weeping willow tree, with hummingbirds and other stuff."

"Wow, sounds great. I can't wait to see that."

"Oh, it is great," Bobby said, his face lighting up. "It's all strong and soft, both at the same time. And lots of personal stuff too, like he carved *n.i.p. plus r.p.l.* inside a heart on the trunk of the tree, you know, like a lover's stamp... lots of stuff."

She peered at him over her wineglass. "And when did you fall in love with him?" she asked very quietly and innocently.

"The second day was when—" Bobby suddenly jerked up and stared at her. "Who said I fell in love?"

"*You* just did, dear," she answered with a knowing smile.

"Shit." He scowled. "He... I don't know, Shar. I keep trying to convince myself I was just feeling weird shit from the weed, but it's not working." He dropped his head. "I think I did."

She topped off his glass with the last of the wine. "It's all right, Bobby. I'm sure Nathan's trying to prove with all his theatrics that he wants you to move on. You should."

Bobby swirled his glass, watching the circular movement of the wine.

"When are you going back?" Sharon asked.

"Once the commission stuff is done. Maybe Friday, if we close it up fast. I'm meeting with some lawyers in the morning."

"Then I shouldn't keep you up late." Sharon patted his hand. "I'll miss you, you know."

"I'll only be gone for the weekend."

Sharon gave him a studied look. "If you say so. But if there *is* something there, you should pursue it. Nate might just crawl out of the grave and drag you there himself if you don't."

Bobby scowled at the zombie movie image that formed in his head. "From what I've been learning about him, he just might."

"Then don't piss him off." Sharon stood up and took one last glance at the note. "I'm off, then. Good luck with the lawyers."

"Thanks." Bobby escorted her to the door and locked it behind her. He set the security alarm and cleaned up the kitchen. After putting the cryptic note back into the brass box, he snatched it up and went upstairs, where he left it on the nightstand in the spare bedroom. He studied that strange design as he stripped out of his clothes and got ready for bed.

The thought of calling Odis did enter his mind as he crawled under the covers, but drowsiness from the wine dragged him into sleep before he could sit up again.

MORNING sun rudely invaded his room again. Bobby had once again forgotten to close the blinds the previous night. He got up, dressed conservatively, then went to the early morning legal meeting, which turned into a long day of "hurry up and wait."

After a brief greeting from a prim lady named Ms. Gentry when he first arrived at the legal office, Bobby was left sitting in the lobby for nearly twenty minutes until a young man, hardly more than a kid, pranced up to collect him. "We're in conference room two," he said over his shoulder as he quickly led Bobby down the hall.

Inside the conference room waited Ms. Gentry and another presumed lawyer, who jumped to his feet and introduced himself. "I'm Mike Horbath; we spoke on the phone yesterday. Please grab some coffee or snacks from the buffet and have a seat," he said while motioning to the table of donuts and croissants near the corner.

After getting a croissant and sitting at the table, Bobby exhaled sharply. "I don't want this to turn into another big thing. I've decided to just take their settlement."

"If that's what you want," Mike said while trying to hide his disappointment. "We'll respect your wishes not to chase it. Let's start by you explaining what they've offered so far."

Bobby described the previous phone calls from the commission and some of the ideas he'd spoken with Odis about. The lawyers got very excited when he mentioned the Monday-morning phone call he got while in Texas. Mike jotted down a few quick details and rushed from the room with Ms. Gentry, leaving Bobby feeling abandoned and a touch nervous.

"Don't worry," the kid said when he saw the concern on Bobby's face. "You're in good hands here."

"Why do you say that?"

"Our firm is part of the Lambda Legal Group. We take LGBT issues *very* seriously." When his phone buzzed, the kid glanced down at it briefly. "I need to step out for a minute. Anything you need or that I can get…?" he asked with a tiny hopeful glint in his eye.

"No, I'm fine," Bobby told him.

The kid got up and nearly ran out of the room while fiddling with his phone, leaving Bobby to sit alone.

He was beginning to feel lost and forgotten until Ms. Gentry poked her head in the door. "Apologies for the wait. We're still on the phone. I can send Kyle back in if you need anything?"

"No, I'm doing okay," Bobby told her as he got up and returned to the buffet for another cup of coffee.

He started to get a bit aggravated after another hour passed. He glanced up when the door opened again. Kyle breezed in with a handful of bags and deftly yanked out containers of food. "I thought you might want some lunch."

Bobby took one of the Styrofoam containers, smelling the bread and meat. He opened it to find a club sandwich fashioned from flatbread, with a helping of turkey and a container of mayo on the side.

"Wasn't sure if you're veggie, so had 'em put that stuff on the side."

Bobby loaded the meat and mayo into the sandwich. "I'm not." He took a big bite.

Kyle smiled as he took a bite from his own sandwich. "Seems like so many people are nowadays. Always have to think ahead."

"Thank you for the lunch. What's taking so long, do you know?"

"Oh, you know how these things are." Kyle shrugged. "I'm sorry, maybe you don't. This is the arguing-back-and-forth-until-somebody-blinks stage," he said cheerfully.

Bobby glanced over at the twinky-looking Kyle. "How long have you worked here?"

"Oh, I'm still on internship. I hope I get to stay, though. I really like kicking ass for the cause, you know."

Bobby chuckled. "I don't know much about this legal stuff. Do you know why they got so excited when I mentioned that phone call Monday?"

"Dude," Kyle said with a hand flourish. "That's, like, so far into the gray side of ethical, trying to railroad you into a quickie meeting and all." Kyle grinned. "I'm sure they're making the most out of that leverage."

"Humph," Bobby said, then almost chuckled at himself. "If I'd been in town, though, I probably would have just gone to the meeting."

"So glad you didn't." Kyle finished inhaling his sandwich. "I'm the one that's been pestering them to get your case. I'm a big baseball fan, and I want to make sure you're taken care of."

Bobby glanced over at him again. "You play?"

"Shortstop. Started with T-ball way back forever ago and played all the way up through high school. Decided to focus on studies in college, so I didn't play any ball at Harvard."

Bobby thought about the kid's quick reflexes and agility. "I bet you did well with that."

"Passable. My batting always sucked, though, so didn't consider getting serious." Kyle gazed over at him. "I play for the Rainbow League now. You ever thought about joining us?"

Bobby shook his head. "It wouldn't seem fair, being a pro and all."

Kyle gazed at him with his cutest smile. "I'd love to have you… join the League, I mean."

Bobby smiled back politely. He appreciated the flirting, but even without Odis in the picture, such a young kid didn't arouse his interest. "I'm just too old for that now," he said gently, trying not to squelch Kyle too forcefully.

"Damn shame." Kyle sighed. "I bet you've got *plenty* of miles left in that gas tank of yours."

"Well, even if I don't play, it might be nice to go to some of the games."

"That would be awesome. Just look us up on the Internet. You can find all the schedules and stuff there. It would mean a lot to the players if you *did* visit."

"Then I'll definitely look into it."

Kyle started to say something else, but the door opening interrupted him. Mike and Ms. Gentry scurried back in, both wearing huge grins. "I think you'll be happy," Mike told Bobby.

"What happened?"

Mike tried to look more serious. "First off, if you accept this, then it's a done deal. You just need to drop by here in the morning for some paperwork to officialize everything."

"What was the offer?" Kyle cut in.

Ms. Gentry spoke up as she passed a sheet of paper to Bobby. "Besides the substantial cash settlement, we got a section of box seats in the stadium to be renamed the Nathan Price Box, in which you have the first row of eight seats permanently reserved. They have also agreed to add sensitivity seminars as part of spring training. For management too, not just the players."

Bobby's eyes bugged out when he saw all the zeros in the settlement number. "This...," he said while shaking his head.

"Dude," Kyle said, "I'm sure they could get more, but you said you didn't want a big fight."

"No. I mean, this is *too much*. I don't need all of this." Bobby shook his head. "What the hell am I gonna do with so much money?"

Kyle smiled. "Is there anything else you *do* want?"

"No. The box seats are a nice touch."

"Thanks." Mike beamed. "That was my idea."

Kyle took the paper from Bobby. "If you don't want anything else, then take the offer."

Bobby glanced around at the expectant faces. "Okay," he said while nodding slightly.

"Let's get it set in stone, then," Mike cheered as he and Ms. Gentry left the room again.

Kyle scooted his chair closer to Bobby. He smiled hesitantly. "I'm almost afraid to bring this up now. I don't want you to think I'm just a shark smelling blood in the water."

"What?" Bobby asked softly.

"If you don't want this money, the idea of charity is bound to cross your mind. I'd like to give you something to think about in that regard."

"Okay."

"Let me tell you what the Rainbow League is *really* all about. Sure, we have lots of fun playing baseball with mostly gay and lesbian players, but everybody covers their own costs for uniforms and such. The real goal for the League is that all profits from the gate and concessions go to support the Rainbow Camp."

"Rainbow Camp?"

"It's kind of a summer camp social experiment. We aim for LGBT and urban kids to have two weeks at a facility together in the

Appalachians. We try, especially for the urban kids, to get as many scholarships as we can, so they can come at no cost."

"Queer and urban kids together? How do you keep it from turning ugly?"

Kyle smiled. "That's where the experiment part comes in. Most of the LGBT kids are fourteen to eighteen, since they don't usually come out sooner than that, but we try and get the urban kids as young as four or five. We're hoping that by reaching out to them that young, the urban kids can see the greater opportunities and options they might not see otherwise. Those options could help keep them off that ugly road of drugs and gangs they'll be confronted with later in life. And the LGBT kids get the self-esteem of being mentors for the younger ones."

"Wow," Bobby said with a grin. "And that really works?"

"This will be our sixth summer. And it's going great so far. We had to turn away about twelve kids last year because the place we rented wasn't big enough. I actually sponsored three of the kids out of my own pocket."

"That's definitely something to think about."

Kyle patted him on the shoulder. "Then go look up our website—there's lots more info there—and give it some consideration. And not just for the money, either. We can also use counselors and supervisors, especially ones with sports backgrounds. *Your* story could be very inspiring for the kids."

"I don't know about that," Bobby said with a shrug.

Kyle patted Bobby's shoulder again as he stood. "Just something to think about." He started toward the door. "Let me check if they need you anymore. Back in a sec."

Bobby grabbed the paper off the table again and stared at what seemed like an incredibly, gigantically huge number.

Kyle returned. "You're done. Come by about ten o'clock tomorrow and we'll finish it up."

"Thanks." Bobby shook Kyle's hand as he approached the door. "And I'll look over that website too."

Kyle smiled. "Oh, and happy birthday," he yelled as Bobby headed down the hall.

CHAPTER
Eleven

BOBBY passed through the flimsy boarding tunnel and entered the Amarillo airport in the early evening on Friday. Gaining an extra hour as they flew across the country made the flight seem pleasantly shorter. Clutching his duffel bag close, he glanced around the open hallway past the boarding area at the overhead signs, looking for the arrows pointing to baggage claim. This time he'd decided to pack—maybe too much, he'd thought while dragging the stuffed suitcase into the Boston airport hours before, but he didn't want to be caught short again.

Following the signs, Bobby made his way downstairs to the carousel. The long-sleeved western shirt seemed a bit warm now that he was in Texas, and he hoped he wasn't sweating too much as he and the other passengers formed a tired arc of bodies around the empty curve, waiting for the luggage to arrive. The belt started with a lurch, and the bags soon appeared one after the other.

Bobby spotted his garment bag right away and claimed it. He was focusing on the revolving belt, watching for his blue Samsonite, when someone tapped him on the shoulder. "Mr. Lane?"

Putting on his public smile, Bobby turned slightly, still trying to keep his eyes on the luggage parade. It wasn't unusual for him to be recognized in public. Many people who weren't baseball fans remembered him from the series of silly and humorous commercials he did for his watch company sponsor over the years. "Yes. That's me."

"Sorry." The low baritone voice of his audience nearly cooed with his Texas drawl. "Don't mean to be distractin' ya. I'll wait 'til ya fetch yer bags."

"Thanks." Bobby nodded, turning his attention away from the uniformed man and back to the belt. It was a brief wait before he spotted his blue suitcase. He walked over and grabbed it off the carousel.

"Let me," the baritone man said from behind, taking the Samsonite from Bobby's grasp and lifting the suitcase away as easily as though it weighed a mere pound. "Any more?"

Bobby bristled and puffed out his chest as he looked up at the big man who had just stolen his bag. He relaxed a bit when he saw the *Bruien County Sheriff Department* patch on the arm of the brown uniform. He glanced up at the face of the tall officer and for a brief second thought he recognized him. But of course he couldn't have—he'd never met this graying-blond man before. "No, that's the only suitcase," Bobby said, maybe a little harshly. "Can I have it back now?"

"Hell, I'm sorry," the officer said as he set the case on the floor next to Bobby. "I'm bein' a rude-ass." He put out his hand. "I'm Tucker Krickson. A friend of Odie's."

Bobby took his hand and shook it. "Tuck, right? Odis and Gertie did mention you." Bobby tried to ignore that warm little zing he felt as he held Tuck's hand. He smiled slightly as he released the handshake. The demeanor of this handsome and mature man pushed the needle of his gaydar alarm high into the suspicious zone. "What brings you to the airport?"

"Came up to give ya a lift to save ya getting a rental car."

Bobby picked up his suitcase and started looking for signs leading to the rental car area. "You didn't need to do that," he said over his shoulder as he moved west toward where the signs pointed. "I already have a car reserved."

"No point in wastin' your money." Tuck hurried around and got in front of him. "I ain't takin' no for an answer," he said, bearing down on Bobby with his commanding cop stare. "I'll drive you. I didn't get to meet you last time you's in town."

"Fine." Bobby wilted. He was just too tired to argue with this formidable man.

Tuck snatched the suitcase handle from Bobby's hand. Bobby again noticed that warm tingle in his fingers when Tuck's hand brushed up against his. "This way."

Bobby followed Tuck into the parking lot. He recognized the doodad-adorned tan SUV as they approached it. Bobby let out a chuckle. "We *did* meet last time I was here. Well, you glared at me, anyway."

Tuck opened the SUV's back door and stowed the luggage. "When was this?"

"When I was driving out to Odis's the first day. I was in the Chevy you passed on the gravel road." Bobby walked around to the passenger door. Tuck had already unlocked it with his electronic key ring, so Bobby climbed in. The tantalizing smells of musky man, leather, and coffee wafting in the warm air teased his nose as he buckled in. He inhaled the pleasant scents as he set the duffel on the floor in front of his feet.

Tuck jumped into the driver's seat and put on his seat belt. "Sorry. Didn't mean to glare, if I did. I was rankled with myself." Tuck started the SUV and pulled out of the lot.

"Why?"

"I'd been too busy fiddlin' with the radio to notice ya on the road and only happened to glance up at the last second. Almost ran ya over."

"No harm done."

"I almost stopped to jump out and apologize to ya. If I'd known who was drivin', I woulda."

Tuck navigated the streets and soon had them cruising down the interstate highway. Because he hadn't said anything else, Bobby glanced over at Tuck. "Where's your hat?"

"Only wear it when I'm on duty. If I have it on too long, it gives me bad hat hair," Tuck replied with a smirky scowl.

Ding, ding, ding went the gaydar. Bobby smiled as he gazed out the windshield.

As they drove in silence again, the tension seemed to grow more pronounced. Bobby couldn't interpret the expression he saw on Tuck's face the few times he chanced another long glance at the man.

The silence seemed to almost solidify around them the farther they drove. Bobby finally had to say something to try to break the tension. "So, you've been friends with Odis a long time?"

Laughing maybe a little nervously, Tuck smiled warmly. "Yeah, ya could say that."

Bobby waited, but Tuck never elaborated. He finally asked, "How long?"

"I'm only three months older than Odie, so since we's in diapers, most likely. We grew up in the same grades, same Boy Scouts, same Sunday school... just forever."

"Almost like a brother?" Bobby asked.

Tuck's face tightened. "Don't go sayin' a thing like that. We ain't never been brothers."

"Oh," Bobby replied, taken aback at Tuck's strong reaction. He couldn't understand why Tuck bristled so negatively at the analogy.

They continued another five miles, the strained silence settling between them again. Bobby noticed Tuck glancing over at him more frequently, but he still couldn't read his expression. As the tension level ratcheted higher and grew more uncomfortable, Bobby began to regret agreeing to this ride. *Maybe Tucker is just intimidated by my celebrity status?*

Bobby finally blurted out, "You wanted to meet me, Tuck, so talk. I don't wanna keep going like this for the next hour."

"I don't either," Tuck agreed. "It's...." He hesitated, never finishing the sentence.

After waiting, Bobby got more irritated. "It's *what?*"

Tuck looked over at him with a lingering glance and then whispered, "Fuck it all." He punched in the accelerator when they approached the road sign indicating a rest stop farther ahead. Tuck sped to the next exit. He pulled off into the rest area, barely slowing as they took the curve. He drove past the little restroom building and continued toward the far end, jumped the SUV up over the curb, and drove into a tangle of budding pecan trees.

Bobby was quite sure this was illegal, but who would argue with a sheriff's car? "What the hell? Have you lost your mind?"

"Maybe," Tuck grunted as he reached across the seat gap, placed a large hand behind Bobby's head, and pulled him forward.

Bobby raised his hands to Tuck's chest with the intention of pushing him away, but when Tucker's lips touched his, an electric sensation short-circuited his resistance. Bobby leaned into the crackling fizz of the kiss. He wilted into Tucker as he opened his mouth, and imaginary sparks warmed his face and sent a tingle through his whole body.

Tuck pulled away much too soon. He stared with a gaping expression. "Gawds of Valhalla," he whined.

Paralyzed and overwhelmed, Bobby stared at him, watching as he opened the car door just enough to slink out. The door closed softly when Tuck slumped back against it. Bobby stared at his hunched back through the window. He tried to ignore the kiss but fought against the impossible. That was, by far, the most passionately charged kiss he had ever felt in his life. If he hadn't been there to see Odis, there was no doubt he would kiss Tucker again. *What a fucking mess.*

Bobby tried to compose himself as he watched Tuck. He was still leaning back against the SUV and hadn't moved a muscle since crawling out. Bobby unbuckled his seat belt and exited before walking around the car to face him.

Tuck slouched against the vehicle in a deflated daze. He glanced up when Bobby approached, then dropped his gaze to the ground. "This is just all kinds of fucked up."

Bobby nodded. "You know I'm on my way to see Odis, so you wanna explain to me why you did that?"

"I did it so you wouldn't be mad at Odie."

"*What*? In what universe does that even make any sense?"

Tuck exhaled heavily. "I know Odie's an honorable guy. He'd feel the need to tell ya I kissed him the other day. I thought… if I kissed you too, you couldn't get mad at him for it. Which ya shouldn't, 'cause it was my fault anyway." Tuck shook his head. "But Gawds almighty, I *never* expected a kiss like that."

"Like what?" Bobby asked, wanting to hear his side of it.

"Like. Some kinda live wire. Just about bust open my britches."

Bobby hated the way the man looked so defeated. "Can we talk in the car? We still got a ways to drive."

"Prob'ly right." Tucker nodded and got back into the SUV.

Bobby crawled into the other side. Tuck started up and slowly reversed out to the asphalt before Bobby even had his door closed.

They returned to the interstate in a hushed silence. Bobby finally spoke again. "Okay, Tucker, so why did you kiss Odis?"

"Please don't call me that. Everybody calls me Tuck except my Pa."

"Okay, Tuck. Why'd you kiss Odis?"

Tuck wobbled his head. "Maybe we shouldn't talk about that."

"Really?" Bobby stared at him. "This mess is already plopped between us like a smelly dead horse. I think we should."

"Fine." Tuck glanced over at him. "I've been in love with him forever, and when I found out he might be into guys, I took a chance. But he pushed me off, sayin' he was waitin' for you."

"Okay." Bobby sat a moment to take it in. "And why'd you find it so important to come pick me up at the airport?"

"You just wanna beat this to death, don'cha."

"It's already dead. I'm trying to beat out the smell of it."

"Fine." Tuck inhaled slowly. "I was hopin', when I picked ya up, that maybe you'd be a bad guy. Then I could tell Odie how terrible ya were. But a'course, that's all shot to hell, since ya ain't a bad guy."

"I'm not such a good guy now." Bobby turned and stared out the window.

"Why ya say that?"

"Because the only thing keeping me from telling you to drive us straight to your place is Odis. And after that kiss, it's a bit of a fight, let me tell you."

Tuck glanced over at him. "So you felt a little somethin' too?"

"More than just a little." Bobby watched the little green mile marker pass by and then turned back to Tuck. "So what do we do now?"

"*We?*" Tuck barked. "Fuck you."

"What?" Bobby defended. "Why you cussing at me?"

"There ain't no *we* to this. You already got Odie. I'm just left out in the cold."

Bobby stared back out at the road as another mile marker passed. He didn't speak again until he saw the next mile marker. "It's all *your* fault, you know. It was your brilliant idea to kiss me."

"Shut the fuck up," Tuck whimpered.

Bobby waited quietly until another marker whizzed by. He glanced over and Tuck still looked all deflated. "How'd you know I was gonna be at the airport? Did Odis tell you?"

"Nah, found out from Gertie. Odie hasn't talked to me since…."

"Right," Bobby said. After another mile or so, he decided to steer the conversation to a totally different track. "How did you get into law enforcement?"

"Always wanted to be a Texas Ranger, you know, all good and honorable and do the right thing. After the academy, though, they didn't have any openings, and I ended up in the sheriff's department in Hutchinson. When they had an openin' in Brungess the next year, I grabbed it. Been there ever since."

"Are you out? With the sheriffs?"

"No. Been thinkin' about it a lot, though. Attitudes are a bit different than they were when I first started twenty years ago, and I've earned my stars over the years. I think maybe I could come out and not cause any coronaries."

Bobby nodded. "It's kinda incredible, you know, to think how much things have changed in twenty years. When Nate and I first got together, the idea of getting married was so far beyond even being a dream that it never even crossed our minds. We went from that to actually having a legal ceremony on our seventeenth anniversary."

Tuck squared his shoulders and sat up a little straighter. "Tell me about Nate. Was he in baseball too?"

"No, landscaping. Had a real artistic eye with lawns and plants."

"And you were together twenty years?"

"Yes, a long-assed time that went by in a blink."

They sat in silence. Bobby counted three mile markers before Tuck spoke again. "I'm sorry, Bobby."

"What're you apologizing for?"

"I'm bein' such a rude-ass, buttin' in where I don't belong."

"I don't mind talking about Nate."

"That's not what I'm talkin' about. Gettin' between you and Odie. I may be a little jealous about it all."

"*May* be?" Bobby chuckled. "I think you're *way* past maybe."

"Fine," Tuck snarled at him. "I'm tryin' to be nice and you're just gonna pick on me some more."

"I wasn't picking. I was teasing you, Tuck."

Another mile marker passed by.

"So," Bobby said as he fidgeted with opening and closing the top snap of his shirt. "Did you tell Odis? That you loved him?"

"Yeah, right before…." Tuck's shoulders slumped. "Dammit all ta hell. Why'd ya even come to town, anyway?"

"Now you're saying this is *my* fault?"

"Kinda is, ain't it?"

Bobby looked over and watched Tuck. "But if I hadn't come to town, you and Odis would have stayed in whatever kind of stasis loop you've been in for, for however long. So yeah, I guess you could say it's my fault the gravity got changed."

Tuck sort of nodded contemplatively. "So yer sayin' your comin' here was a good thing?"

"Would you rather have just had more of the same? For another twenty, thirty years? Then maybe some deathbed confession about your feelings at the end?"

"Nope, sure wouldn't want that." Tuck sat up straighter. "I guess that woulda been it, though, or pretty likely."

"Right, but now everything's shook up because of Nate. And there's a chance for something different."

"Nate? What's he gotta do with it?"

Bobby laughed, and the chuckles tapped into his frustration and took him over, tumbling out maniacally. His uncontrollable barks of laughter came out almost like hiccups. His eyes watered as he forced himself to calm. "What is there that Nate *doesn't* have anything to do with?" he finally coughed out, fighting against laughing more.

Tuck stared over at Bobby as he came unhinged, trying to remember where he put his Taser gun, just in case. He watched until Bobby seemed to recover his composure. "Okay, wanna try explainin' that again?"

Bobby looked over at him and took a deep breath as he dabbed a stray tear from his cheek. "I just found out when I went back that Nathan kept a huge-assed secret from me the whole time. He was some kind of psychic. Nate was the one who left the plane ticket for me to come visit Odis in the first place. Among other things."

Tuck sat expressionless as another mile marker passed.

Bobby watched him. "Didn't mean to totally freak your shit over there."

Shaking his head, Tuck stiffened his shoulders. "My granny had *the touch*. That's what we called it, the psychic shit. She would have dreams sometimes."

After a few minutes of silence, Tuck cleared his throat. "So what exactly did Nate do? With the ticket and all?"

"Well, he arranged to have postcards mailed out at certain times, kinda set up a scavenger hunt thing. It eventually led to a receipt from an order he made with Odis, and a plane ticket to pick it up."

"He practically dropped you into Odie's lap, then," Tuck said with a frown.

Bobby nodded. "I guess he did."

"You the only one that got postcards?"

"No, he had some for his mother too. I think they got her to talk me into selling the landscaping business. Guess he was afraid I'd fuck it up."

Tuck shook his head. "I doubt that. Prob'ly wanted to free you up from it." After a brief silence, the next marker zipped by. "You know he's working again—Odie, I mean—since you showed up."

"He told me over the phone. Said he was trying something new."

"You didn't know Odie before, so ya prob'ly can't appreciate how important that is."

"I've heard talk from Gertie. I get it." Bobby looked over at Tuck's green eyes. "If you love him so much, why didn't you make a move before now?"

Tuck winced. "Fear, mostly, I guess. Even when I got the occasional signal from Odie, I was afraid to take the risk. I didn't wanna destroy what we *did* have. And the timing was never quite right either. If he wasn't in a relationship, then I was."

"That sucks."

"Well, it is what it is."

Bobby almost shivered when he once again heard the words Lorainne had spoken. "I know it probably doesn't mean shit, but I am sorry."

"For what?"

"Stirring up all this and making a mess. It feels like that's all I've managed to accomplish."

"No, what you said before was right. Something had to change the gravity around here. It's not just me and Odie. Seems like the whole town has kinda gone into a pause mode. About time we shake things up."

"But like you said, it kinda leaves you out in the cold."

"Then I'll buy a fuckin' coat, I guess. Quit worryin' about me. You just make this thing with Odie work, or so help me, I *will* kick your ass for causing all this shit."

Bobby laughed. "I bet you would too."

"Damn straight."

Another mile marker passed by before Bobby saw the road sign declaring "Brungess 15 miles." He looked over at Tuck. "So, what does Brungess mean in Viking?"

"Nothin'. It was a mistake back when they created the town. Was supposed to have been Brun*gress*, which is Norwegian for 'brown grass'. But some typo or somethin' got screwed up and the last *r* got left off. By the time everybody noticed, the state wouldn't change it, said we'd have to reincorporate again. They didn't think it was worth the extra cost and hassle, so they left the name that way."

"That sucks." Bobby glanced over at Tuck again. He'd mentioned having past relationships, so Bobby wondered if they failed because he'd been pining after Odis the whole time. Or maybe it was his job that got in the way? "Was it hard dating while being an officer?"

"Well, yeah, I guess ya could say that. Not the dating part, actually. Finding guys *to* date is the hard part. Bruien County isn't exactly a homo hotbed, ya know. And the sheriff thing means I had to be *extra* careful even looking."

"But you did find dates, or was it more the one-night stand kinda thing?"

"Mostly just one guy. It was tough going. He was more in the closet than I was, but on a personal level, though. I never had any doubts about myself, just had to keep on the down-low for the job. He didn't have that excuse, really." Tuck paused a moment in thought. "Spent more time broke up than together over the years. I finally just gave up on it."

"Sorry," Bobby said, wondering at the strange kind of sympathy he felt. His own story had nothing in common with Tuck's. If anything, it was almost the opposite. So why should he care?

"It is what it is," Tuck said with a shrug.

Bobby watched out the window as the sun finally dropped behind the horizon and the dusk slowly took hold. The night, so full of dark secrets and mystery, had never been his favorite; he'd rather have the shining light of day. Which seemed so ironic now, after spending all those years with Nathan, the greatest mystery of them all. He almost chuckled aloud at the thought.

"What's on your mind?" Tuck asked, glancing over at him. "You seem kinda amused."

"Oh, just thinking about secrets and mysteries and Nate. Hard to believe you could live with someone forever and they keep such a huge thing from you. Worst part is, I'll never know. I'm just left with all these questions now... and the bastard's not even here to answer them."

Tuck nodded. "Kinda sucks. With all the trouble he went through with this other shit, you'd think he woulda done something that could give ya at least *some* of those answers."

"Tell me about it." Bobby sighed with frustration.

Tuck smiled over at him. "Let me put on my investigational hat, see if we can't get somewhere."

"Okay," Bobby agreed.

"From what I've heard of Nate, it doesn't seem like he'd just 'forget' to do something like that. There must be a *reason* he didn't say anything and isn't sayin' anything even now. Maybe try and figure out what that reason is." Tuck nodded as he thought it over. "That at least gives a startin' point for some investigatin'."

Bobby laughed. "Well, the reason is as much of a mystery as everything else. Doesn't exactly help, Tuck."

"Sorry, I tried."

"I know, and I appreciate it." The dimmed headlights softly illuminated the dusky gloom, so Bobby could barely make out the sign for the Brungess exit when it appeared.

Tuck slowed to take the exit. "You know, I wish I *could* hate you. It'd sure make this a little easier."

"Well, I'm glad you don't. And I disagree about the easier part. Unless you just want to cut Odis totally out of your life."

Shaking his head, Tuck turned onto the two-lane highway and aimed for Odis's place. "No, I don't want that, either."

Tuck drove them farther into the country, both men hushed in quiet contemplation.

CHAPTER
Twelve

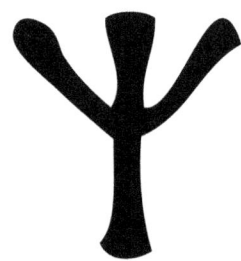

Algiz Rune

THEY drove in a calm silence until finally reaching the Vorleik gate. Bobby unclasped his seat belt and grabbed the duffel bag as they approached. "I'll get it," he told Tuck and waited for the SUV to stop. He got out and pushed the gate control button, then waited until the SUV pulled inside.

Bobby nearly fell over when Heimdalla jumped on him and tried to lick his face. He'd forgotten about her and hadn't been watching for her arrival. "Ooph, down, Heim." Bobby punched the gate control button to close it as Heim danced around his feet. "Yes, I'm happy to see you too." Bobby reached down to pet her head before she bounded off to greet Tuck as he exited the SUV.

Bobby jogged up to the vehicle as Tuck removed his bags from the back. They made their way downstairs, and Odis greeted them at the sliding door. He glanced up at Tuck as he pulled it open. "Tuck? Wha'cha doin' here?"

"Gave Bobby a ride from the airport, bonehead." Tuck set the suitcase down inside the door and glanced around for someplace to hang the garment bag.

Odis pointed to the bathroom door. "There's a hook on the outside," he said before turning to Bobby. "How are ya, stud? Hope the trip wasn't *too* unpleasant," he said while glaring back at Tuck as he hung up the bag.

"It was okay. Managed to clear the air a bit, I think."

Tuck rushed back over. "Don't get all riled up, Odie. I just had to say my piece and give ya an apology. I'm headin' out right now."

Odis looked up. "Apology for what?"

"For all that shit the other day. Let's not let it get in the way. Please?" Tuck grabbed Bobby's hand and shook it firmly. "Nice meetin' ya finally," he said with a smile as he left through the sliding door.

Bobby still felt a lingering tingle in his hand as he watched Tuck climb the stairs. "So, from what Tuck was saying in the car, some serious confessions went on after I left."

Odis pointed to the wrought iron table, then hurried into the kitchen and prepared two of the mocha mugs while Bobby took a seat. Odis brought the drinks back and gave one to Bobby. "Yeah, some intense shit. What all did he tell you?"

Bobby glanced at Odis as he sat down. Hoping he had his most charming smile on, Bobby said, "Before or after he kissed me?"

"He *kissed* you? That bonehead," Odis said with a smirk. "Then I guess he told ya he kissed me too."

"Yeah, he did." Bobby stood up. "Speaking of kiss," he said as he walked around the table and pulled Odis to his feet. "We never said hello." Bobby leaned down, and the two embraced and brought their lips together. Just as before, the warmth of the kiss surrounded them like a fuzzy fleece blanket.

Bobby nearly sighed as he shared his mouth with Odis. Being with this man felt so nice and comforting. But his thoughts soon turned to his kiss with Tuck. Bobby pulled away from Odis, trying to forget that sparking fizz of earlier in the evening.

"Hello, stud," Odis said as he hugged him close. "This just isn't the same as a phone call."

"No." Bobby squeezed Odis tighter. They stood for a moment, neither wanting to break the embrace.

Bobby looked down. "I kinda feel bad for him, though."

"Who, Tuck? Why?"

"He feels kinda left out. Like I bested him somehow."

Odis chuckled. "I never reckoned he'd be jealous of ya, but I guess he would be."

After a final squeeze, Odis pulled away and sat back down with his drink. "So how was the trip? I got the feelin' there's some things you didn't wanna talk about on the phone."

Nodding, Bobby sat down and grabbed his mug. "Yeah, a few more surprises."

"Oh? Like what?"

"Found out Nate had a secret life as a psychic."

"*What*? Holy shit." Odis chuckled. "And just when ya thought it was all figured out. How'd ya find out about *that*?"

"Well, found out the secretary at the landscaping place was the one sending the postcards, and she gave me my last one, by the way. And she fessed up about Nate seeing threads or some shit. Then I found out Sharon already knew and was keeping it a secret too."

"Damnation." Odis took a sip. "And what about the last postcard?"

"Pointed me to a key that opened a box Sharon had been holding." Bobby fished in his jeans pocket and pulled out the key, then held it up.

Odis stared at the brass key. "Oh. What nationality did you say Nathan was?"

"I don't think I ever said. East Coast mutt like me. A lot of Scottish, I think. Why would you ask that?"

"Because." Odis took the key and set it on the table. "I was wondering why he'd pick a key with a Nordic rune on it. If maybe it meant something personal to him."

"*Nordic*? Oh fuck me," Bobby sighed. "Nathan? What the *fuck*?" he yelled.

Odis waited until he had Bobby's attention again. "This is algiz, one of the Elder Futhark rune alphabet. It originally represented an elk and was ascribed the meaning of 'unity'. But in later times it came to be thought of as the life rune, like the Egyptian ankh."

Odis retrieved his reading glasses from the kitchen and came back to the table before putting them on his nose. He turned the key in his hand and studied the brass rune closely. "This is exquisite detailing."

"Oh," Bobby said, jumping up to look for his suitcase. "You should see the box it fits. It has a bigger one on it." Bobby retrieved the heart-shaped brass box from his suitcase and brought it back to the table.

Odis glanced down at it. The larger lines and knots weren't fashioned from snakes like he had expected to see. Instead, the lines and curves appeared to be antlers intertwining. In the lower branch of the rune, the fretwork subtly formed an elk face. "Definitely elk, so it has the unity meaning." Odis looked up at Bobby. "What's *in* the box?"

"Just a bizarre-assed note. Some weird math shit. We couldn't make heads or tails of it."

"We?"

"Oh. Sharon was there when I opened it the first time." Bobby inserted the key and retrieved the note. "Have a look."

Odis unfolded the paper and gazed over it.

$$A+C= typical :($$
$$B+A= rich? $$
$$B+C= intense? $$
$$B+A+C= jackpot $$

Odis scrunched his brow as he puzzled over the strange equations.

"His final words," Bobby said. "And it's more cryptic garbage."

Odis sat back in his chair. "I don't know about *final* words."

"What do you mean?" Bobby asked as he got up to go pee.

"I told ya he wanted me to make that bust for July, but I never told ya the inscription he wanted on it."

Bobby glared at him as he leaned down onto the table. "Not you *too*. I'm tired of everybody keeping secrets." Bobby pushed away from the table and stomped to the bathroom, then closed the door firmly behind him.

Odis studied the printout again. He jumped up when a sudden inspiration hit him, and he compared the letters vertically. He headed to the kitchen as Bobby returned from the bathroom. Odis glanced over at him. "I think I found something," he said as he grabbed a pencil from the kitchen drawer and took it back to the table.

"Oh?"

Odis set the printout down and vertically circled the first three letters of each "answer," spelling out *TRI*. Then, next to the first *A*, he wrote *rtist*.

"I see," Bobby said as he watched Odis work.

Next to the first *B*, he wrote *obby*.

"Humph," Bobby grunted with a sort of agreement. "Then what about the *C*?"

Odis smiled. Beside the first *C* he wrote *op*.

Bobby stared down at the new scribbles. "No way." He shook his head. "No *fucking* way." He glanced up at Odis. "Nate can't be suggesting all *three* of us together?"

"Yep." Odis chuckled. "The man must'a had a huge ego to think it takes *two* of us to replace him."

"No." Bobby dropped down into his chair and grabbed his mug, then nearly drained it with a huge gulp. "How would that even fucking work?"

"I've heard of the hippies tryin' things like that. Don't know how many actually worked in the long run, though."

Bobby looked back at the printout. "But that's not the only option."

"No, but he's got that frowny face after the 'typical' configuration of me and Tuck. I'm guessing because that one doesn't benefit *you* any."

"But you and I would be 'rich', possibly? What does he mean by 'rich'? In a financial sense, or more metaphorical? God damn you, Nate. Why'd you hafta be so cryptic?"

"Maybe," Odis mused. "Maybe Nate was hoping to see more and leave a better note but never did, or didn't have a chance to." Odis went over and grabbed his mug. "What could he mean by 'intense' next to you and Tuck?"

Bobby chuckled. "Well, I might have a clue about that."

"Oh? Do tell."

"Well, the kiss, for one thing. It was, almost electric. Full of sparks. And all the other emotions in the car as we argued and joked and talked were, like, they didn't have a low setting on the volume, all cranked up."

Odis nodded. "And you don't feel anything when you kiss me?"

"Hell yes, I do. It's just totally different. It's all warm, like getting cuddled up in a fuzzy blanket."

"Humph," Odis said before chuckling. He stood and grabbed their empty mugs. "I feel the same thing. That warm blanket thing with you, and Tuck's kiss was all full of fireworks." He took the mugs into the kitchen for a refill before returning them to the table. "What did you argue about?"

"Oh, mostly about me coming to town and how he can't hate me."

"*Hate* you? That bonehead."

"Well, when you look at it from his perspective, if he hated me, it'd be easy for him to discount me and try to push me out. Or at least, he could feel like he *had* that option. I think he's prob'ly too honorable of a guy to actually do that kind of thing, though."

They both drank their mocha and quietly mused over the note on the table.

Odis nodded. "Right, then." He gazed up at Bobby. "I guess we should call Tuck."

"Are you sure we should drag him into this? I mean... I still don't see how such a thing could work."

"Tuck isn't really attractive to ya?"

"Oh, it's not that. The guy is *very* appealing. But I think you and I have something that could stand on its own."

Odis nodded. "I think so too. But now that *this*"—he motioned to the note—"is on the table, kinda can't get it outta my head."

Bobby just looked at him and sighed heavily.

Odis got up and leaned down in front of Bobby, wrapping his hands around his shoulders and pulling him into a soft, brief kiss. He pulled away and rested their foreheads together, peering into Bobby's eyes. "Okay, then, 'no' on Tuck."

Bobby gazed back but didn't think he could hide the traces of doubt lingering in his mind.

Odis stood. "I'm hungry as a racehorse. What say I grab my shoes and we run into town for some dinner?"

"Sure," Bobby said as he stood. He watched Odis as he got some socks from the dresser and pulled on his moccasins. "Those look almost like leather crocks."

"My elf shoes? I think they're comfy."

Bobby chuckled. "*Elf* shoes?"

"Well, that's what I always call 'em. Seems like somethin' the elves would wear in one of those Tolkien stories." Odis headed into the kitchen and retrieved the car keys from a kitchen drawer.

"If you say so."

"Ya makin' fun of my footwear, boy?" Odis asked as he took Bobby's arm and led him through the sliding glass doors.

"Nah, they seem kinda fun, old man."

As Odis led up the stairs, Heim trotted up and tagged along. "I'll hafta back out first. Won't be enough room for ya to squeeze in," he said as he slid open the barn-style door on the garage.

Bobby whistled when he saw the shiny black El Camino. Heim ran to his feet. "Nice car. Must be a classic now."

"It's an '87." Odis got in and backed the car up. When Bobby opened the passenger door, Heimdalla jumped in and claimed a spot in the middle. Bobby scooted in next to her.

Odis chuckled. "Goddamn dog."

Bobby hesitated before closing the door. "She's not allowed in the car?"

"Oh, I don't care. She just never wants to ride with me."

After Bobby pulled the door closed, Heim slurped him across the cheek with a wet tongue and lay down half across his lap. "She seems friendly to me."

"Well, *you* take her, then. She's never seemed to like *me* much. Tina took all the furniture and left the dumb dog."

Bobby jumped out to open the gate. As he waited for the car to pull through, he tried to avoid thinking about Tuck, yet his thoughts kept drifting back to that kiss they had shared in the SUV. He still couldn't really perceive the logistics of how a threesome would work, but like Odis said, once the possibility had been mentioned, the idea of it kept invading his thoughts. Bobby pushed the button to close the gate before getting back in the car. Heim claimed his lap again.

Odis started driving toward town. "What kinda music do ya prefer?"

"Don't really care," Bobby said. "Just no gangsta rap, please."

Odis fiddled with the stations and found a swinging rockabilly song. The female singer kept whining something about 3:00 a.m. Bobby tried not to think about Tuck and Odis in the same bed, waiting for him.

The next song was a male singer, crooning about three more days until he made it to Abeline. Bobby flipped off the sky, thinking, *Fuck you, Nate.*

Bobby rubbed at Heim's head and ears, trying to distract himself from the song lyrics. "Tell me about Tina," he almost yelled over at Odis.

"What about her?"

"Gertie, John, and Tuck didn't seem to like her much. There must have been something *you* saw in her."

"Don't rightly know. I never did see much in her, either. Guess the biggest thing was that *she* liked *me*."

"Did you love her?" Bobby asked, relieved that the next song from the radio was about honkey-tonkin' and didn't mention any threes.

Odis shook his head. "I tried ta convince myself I did, but no. Not really."

Bobby frowned as he looked down at Heim. "Is that what it's like with me? Just because I showed interest in you?"

"Oh *hell* no. I made the first move on *you*, if ya recall. I held your hands when I gave ya the pipe while you told me about the Series. I wanted to hug you too, but I left ya your space. You seemed to be having a moment, so I didn't wanna crowd ya."

"Sorry, I was kinda in my own head at the time, didn't really notice."

"It's okay." Odis grinned as he turned onto Main Street. "You flirted with me after, so it worked out." He reached out and patted Bobby's knuckles. "I felt closer to you talking to ya on the phone this week than I ever did with Tina when she was right in the dining room with me."

"Then why'd you stay with her?"

"Guess having half a something seemed better than having nothing at all," Odis said as he pulled into the restaurant parking lot. He steered into an empty slot near an alley before turning off the headlights.

Heim sat up when the car stopped and Odis rolled down the window about six inches before he opened his door.

Bobby patted her head. "We just leave her in the car?"

"It's a nice April evening. She'll be fine as long as we bring somethin' back."

Bobby followed Odis into the red brick uptown-style 1900s building, and they soon found a table. An older waitress carrying a nearly empty tea pitcher hurried over. "Evening, Odis. Who's your friend?"

"This here's Bobby."

"Hey, sugar. Ya boys want the blue plates?"

Odis nodded. "Two of 'em. And tea for me."

The waitress looked over at Bobby. "Sure, tea for me too."

As she wandered away to the next booth, Bobby glanced across the table. "What's the blue plate?"

"Catfish and fixins. Kinda their specialty."

Bobby nodded. "Sounds good."

Their waitress brought over two glasses of tea. "Just a few minutes, sugars."

Bobby reached over for the sugar packets on the table, and Odis put his hand on top Bobby's. "Taste it first. It comes sweet."

Bobby took a sip, glad for Odis's intervention when the syrupy tea oozed down his throat. "Wow, I'd say so."

Odis chuckled.

Bobby glanced around the restaurant. The renovations to the older building had been carefully done, maintaining the character of the previous space, which looked to have started out as an old feed-and-seed store. He spotted the back of a man wearing a sheriff's uniform sitting over at a corner table, but knew right away from the balding black hair that it wasn't Tuck.

Once again, the suggestion in Nate's note crossed his mind. Bobby found himself suddenly curious about what Tuck looked like underneath that uniform. The man seemed to be taking care of himself. He probably looked very good for a guy approaching fifty.

Odis cleared his throat. "Can't keep Tuck off your mind either, huh?"

Bobby smirked. "No. It's like having something caught between your teeth. Can't keep from picking at it." He gazed over at Odis. "Maybe if I could understand how such a thing works, I could give a more definite 'yes' or 'no' to the whole idea."

"Well, from what—"

The waitress brought over a big tray and set a blue plate down in front of Bobby first, then one in front of Odis. Bobby looked down at the small plastic plate with only two slices of fried catfish and a few french fries and pieces of okra. "Kinda skimpy on the portions," he said with a smirk.

Odis chuckled. "It's all ya can eat. She'll be by with more as soon as ya finish it."

Bobby took a bite of the fried catfish. It was so fresh from the fryer, the food nearly burned his tongue. He fanned the front of his open mouth and grabbed his tea.

Chuckling, Odis told him, "Careful, stud, it might still be hot."

Bobby flipped him the middle finger as he swallowed some tea.

"Anyway, as I's sayin', when the hippies did this sort of thing, they'd set up some ground rules ahead of time," Odis said as he took a bite of fish. "Just to kind of define what everybody could expect."

"So would it always have to be all three of us? Or would we break off into pairs?"

"That's part of what we'd figure out with the rules." Odis stabbed some of the okra with his fork. "Would ya be jealous if Tuck and I…?"

Bobby sort of shrugged as he chewed on a mouthful of french fries. "Would *you*, if Tuck and I?"

Odis thought as he ate some more fish. "Would kinda depend, I guess. If ya started makin' out right in front of me and shut me out, I would. But if I's busy and you two… prob'ly not then."

As Bobby put the last piece of his fish into his mouth, the waitress showed up with a big basket on a tray. Using metal tongs, she dropped more fries, okra, and two more pieces of steaming fish onto Bobby's plate. She moved around and did the same for Odis. "Anything else ya guys need, Odie?"

Odis glanced over at Bobby, who shook his head. "Not right now, Cin. Thanks, hon."

As the waitress scooted away, Bobby looked over at Odis. "And you knew some groups that made this kinda thing work?"

Odis nodded as he ate some more okra. "Knew one ménage à trois that was together over ten years last I heard from them, but that was a time ago. They were two girls and a guy. I don't know if that'd make a difference."

"How long ago?"

"Let's see, saw 'em last at my third art show? Or maybe fourth?" Odis ate another piece of fish. "So's prob'ly '92 or '94."

Bobby sort of nodded his head. "Any way you could get in touch with them now? Find out if they're still…?"

"S'pose I could try." Odis watched Bobby eat. "Would that— knowing that, I mean—make a difference?"

"Well," Bobby replied after finishing off his fries, "if they *are* still together, it would give me some hope that such a thing could really work and not just be a 'happy fun time' experiment."

Odis chuckled at his strange expression. "Happy fun time?"

Bobby gazed at Odis as he finished his last piece of fish. "You never watched *Ren and Stimpy*? 'Happy fun time' or 'happy happy joy joy'?"

Odis shook his head as the waitress appeared again. She moved slower this time, peering at Bobby as she loaded more fish and fixings onto his plate. She moved over to Odis's side of the table, still glancing at Bobby. After loading up Odis's plate, she looked at Bobby. "Sugar, Nick back at the grill said he thought you looked like Bobby Lane, that baseball guy?" she said, dropping her gaze to the table.

Not sure what her reaction might be, Bobby nodded apprehensively.

The waitress playfully slugged Odis in the arm. "Dang you, Odie, ya didn't say ya was bringin' in a celebrity." She went over to Bobby's side of the table, wiping her hand on her apron before extending it to him. "My name's Cindy, in case the goofus didn't tell ya. Welcome to the Catfish Store."

"Thanks," Bobby said as he shook her hand. "It's great catfish."

Cindy smiled down at him. "I won't let ya leave here 'til ya hafta unbutton yer pants," she said with a wink.

Bobby blushed at the strange innuendo.

"Oh, no, sugar," she said with a laugh. "I meant ya'll be so stuffed, it'll be like Thanksgiving." She patted Bobby on the shoulder, still chuckling as she moved away.

Odis smiled at Bobby's rosy-red face as he continued to eat. "So, what are your thoughts?"

"Well, it *is* an interesting idea. But like I said before, I think you and I kinda have something, and I'm a bit cautious to risk it trying something that might blow up in our faces. You know, since we could all end up with nothing in the end."

Grabbing more okra, Odis nodded. "Well—"

Cindy appeared again with a pitcher and filled up their tea glasses. She looked down at Bobby with a serious expression. "Nick was just fillin' me on that whole mess. I'm so sorry, Mr. Lane. Nobody deserves that kind of shit."

"It's okay, Cindy, you don't need to apologize for anything," he said with a kind smile.

"Oh, but you know." Her expression lightened. "I hope ya enjoy yerself here in Brungess. Take that rascal out and get him into some trouble. Make him take ya over to the Blue Barn. Lord knows when's the last time he had any fun," she playfully teased while looking at Odis.

Odis rolled his eyes at her. "Just behave yerself, Cin. Maybe he don't wanna go to no honky-tonk full of straight rednecks."

Cindy chuckled. "Maybe not, I guess." She looked over at Odis and noticed the warm smile he got when he glanced at Bobby. Her eyes suddenly got wider. "Odie?" Then she broke out into a wide grin. "Well, you two go on with yerselves, then," she said, nodding as she went to the next table.

Odis smirked. "So much for keepin' things quiet." He looked over at Bobby. "Cin's one of the biggest gossips in town."

"Oh, I see." Bobby ate another piece of fish. "You gonna be okay?"

"Sure. No point in tryin' ta keep secrets, I guess."

AFTER two more rounds, Odis and Bobby finished their meal and paid, then returned to the car with a small Styrofoam clamshell of food they'd smuggled out for Heimdalla. The dog bounced around in the El Camino when she saw them leave the restaurant. The guys crawled into the car, and Odis fed the bits to Heim.

Bobby watched her happily gobble up the fries and fish. "So what now?"

Odis sat back without starting the car. "Not that I'm tryin' to rush things, but if yer seriously considerin' this, I think we should call up Tuck sooner rather than later. I just have this feelin' it might be one of those window-of-opportunity kinda things."

Nodding, Bobby fished his cell phone from his pocket. "Well, let's go ahead and call him, then."

"You sure?"

"Not totally, to be honest. Still kinda scares me a little, about it blowing up. But...."

"I'm willin' to try." Odis pulled out his wallet and dug around for a ratty-looking business card. He handed it to Bobby. "Tuck's cell number's on the back."

After struggling to read the faded pencil marks, Bobby punched in Tuck's number. He glanced over at Odis as the line rang.

Odis started up the car. "Tell him to meet us at the house."

CHAPTER
Thirteen

As Tuck fluffed his pillow and turned down the blanket, his cell phone rang. Not knowing if it might be the department calling, he quickly reached to the nightstand and grabbed the phone. "Tuck."

"Hey, it's Bobby."

He relaxed a bit. "Hey." Tuck glanced at the clock and saw it was only 8:45 p.m. He hadn't realized it was still so early.

"Listen, we uh, kinda might have a situation," Bobby started. "Could you meet us at Odis's house?"

Tuck felt himself once again tense up as his cop instincts kicked in. "What kind of situation, exactly? Should I get backup?"

"Oh," Bobby chuckled. "Nothing like *that*. It's cool, we just wanna talk."

"*Talk?*" Tuck replied pointedly as the sense of threat faded. "You *are* on a freakin' phone. So talk."

"Really." Bobby's inflection sounded almost desperate. "It's... just come to Odis's, okay?"

Tuck reached in his closet for some shoes. "Fine. I hafta work early tomorrow, so no high jinks," he said as he slipped on his sneakers. "I'll be there in a bit."

"See ya." Bobby hung up.

As he moved to the living room, Tuck ran his fingers through his hair. One glance in the hall mirror as he grabbed his keys made him think his hair was a lost cause, so he grabbed his ball cap and slipped it on before heading out.

As Tuck drove farther from town, his mind kept wandering to dark places. He had already struggled with, and mostly won, the battle to set aside any desires for Odis or Bobby, so a touch of anger now began to boil at once again being reminded of what he couldn't have. *Can't these guys just leave me alone?*

Tuck wasn't even sure why he was driving out to Odis's. Hell, he still wasn't sure why he'd even gone to the airport to pick up Bobby earlier in the day. What *had* he been expecting? He shook his head as he turned onto the gravel road. He needed to get over this, get past whatever strange compulsion kept steering him toward these guys. This wasn't healthy behavior *at all*.

He thought again about Bobby's call. If it hadn't been for that desperation in his voice, Tuck wouldn't be bothering with this. It wasn't a fearful desperation—Valhalla knew he heard enough of that with his job. Bobby's voice had that yearning quality he'd heard in some of those late-night calls from Hutchinson. Or maybe he was just a boneheaded lovesick puppy hearing imaginary things. *Gods, hope I'm not* that *far gone.*

BOBBY and Odis followed Heimdalla down the steps and into the house. Odis hadn't even had time to offer Bobby a beer when Tuck came down the steps behind them. He entered the door, then bristled hesitantly just inside.

Odis chuckled at Tuck. "Nice of ya to dress up for us," he teased.

Bobby, fighting back a grin at seeing Tuck dressed in a pair of tight jogging pants, a faded sweatshirt, grubby-looking high-tops, and his beat-up Texas Rangers cap, motioned to the table. "Heya, Tuck. Come on in."

Odis headed for the kitchen. "I'll get some beers."

Tuck and Bobby sat down at the table. Tuck glanced between the other two men. "What's this all about?"

Bobby accepted a beer and watched Odis sit down after handing one to Tuck. Then Bobby took a deep breath. "It's... you remember I told you about Nathan being psychic and all?"

Tuck nodded as he twisted the top and took a sip from the bottle.

"Well," Bobby said, looking down at the note still sitting on the table. "This is the latest thing he left for me." He picked up the note and handed it to Tuck. "The pencil marks are what Odis deciphered of it."

Tuck studied the note in silence. He turned it over and found the back blank, then studied the front again.

Odis leaned forward. "And?"

Taking another swallow of his beer, Tuck remained expressionless as he glanced from Odis to Bobby, then back down at the note. "Is this some kind of April Fools' joke?"

Bobby shook his head. "No, that was yesterday. That's really what Nate left."

"And you're okay with this?" he asked, staring right at Bobby.

"I have some reservations, to be honest. But Odis said he knows of this kind of thing working."

"It was two girls and a guy, but same principle."

Tuck glanced unreadably between Odis and Bobby again. "Well, fuck a duck." He reached into his pocket and retrieved his cell phone. After punching some keys, he held the phone to his ear. "Hey, Josh, kinda had somethin' come up. You free to work the seven-to-three shift tomorrow?" He nodded while listening to the phone. "Yep, okay. See ya Sunday, then." Tuck closed his phone and set in on the table, then set the note next to it before he looked up at Odis. "Go grab yer pipe."

Odis went outside and around to his studio and returned a minute later with his corncob pipe. He went into the kitchen for a baggie of pot and brought everything to the table. "So," he said while loading the pipe with some of the dried weed, "I guess you're stayin'?"

"I don't know about *stayin'* stayin', but we should at least sort all this out." Tuck looked up at Odis when he handed him the pipe and lighter. "And *you're* surprisin' the fuck outta me. I find out in the same week you're into guys *and* threesomes?"

"I've never done a threesome," Odis said, shaking his head.

Tuck turned to Bobby. "Have you?" he asked before lighting up.

"No, never even really crossed my mind."

Exhaling the breath of pot smoke he held, Tuck set the pipe on the table, then leaned back into his chair. "So *none* of us knows what the fuck we're doin', but you wanna try this anyway?"

Odis and Bobby nodded silently.

Tuck reached down and adjusted the crotch of his sweatpants. "Loki's nuts," he muttered exasperatedly. "And ya guys don't mean this as just a one-time roll-in-the-hay thing either," he muttered aloud.

Bobby shook his head, trying not to look at the enlarging package in Tuck's sweatpants. "I don't think that's at all what Nate meant."

"Me neither," Odis said.

Tuck sat up and grabbed the pipe again. He kept staring at the note as he took a big hit and held the breath. He handed the pipe to Odis, but Bobby reached out and grabbed it instead.

"Careful, stud," Odis warned. "That's the one I named Orange Brain-Bash."

Tuck chuckled at the name, sending intermittent bursts of vapor out his nose like strange smoke signals.

Bobby inhaled a small drag and handed the pipe to Odis. Odis took a hit, then set the pipe and lighter on the table.

After exhaling, Bobby smiled sheepishly at Tuck. "Not exactly orthodox, I know."

"Nope," Tuck replied, leaning back into his chair.

Bobby glanced over and noticed the glint in Odis's eye as he admired the way the sweatshirt had tightened around Tuck's chest and accentuated the curves of his pecs. Odis cleared his throat. "So, what're yer thoughts?"

Tuck smirked. "This could either be totally fantastic or completely FUBAR. I can't really see any middle ground here." He sat up again, grabbed his beer, then drained it.

Bobby drained his own bottle and scurried to the fridge for a round of refills. As he put the empty beers in the trash, he noticed some orange plastic lying in the bin. Something about that particular shade of orange nagged at him, but Bobby shrugged it off and went to the refrigerator. He brought back the fresh beers and stood between Odis and Tuck as he gave each a bottle. Bobby thought the room seemed to be getting warmer. "Odis said something about rules…."

"Oh," Odis said, taking his eyes off of Tuck's chest. "Right. Ground rules."

Tuck nodded. "Like a contract. Prob'ly need sumthin' like that ta lay it all out. So what's the first rule?"

Bobby looked at Odis, who seemed to be drawing a blank, so Bobby spoke up. "First rule, prob'ly doesn't need to be said, but no outsiders. This would be a totally exclusive thing just with us three."

"Right," Odis agreed. He looked right at Tuck. "No diddlin' on the side."

"Hey." Tuck bristled. "Don't look at me. I haven't diddled in about nine months now."

"Oh?" Odis asked playfully.

Bobby looked over at Odis. "That's all I got. What other rules? What about pairing off?"

"Well, the way the Sunflowers did it, they'd have a threesome at least once a week, and then they had different 'date' nights to pair off with."

Tuck nodded at Odis. "So, like Monday night, you and me'd have a date, then Wednesday night, you and Bobby, then Friday, me and Bobby. And all of us together on Tuesday, Thursday, Saturday, and Sunday?"

Bobby chuckled. "That schedule seems a bit optimistic, but I kinda like the 'date' idea."

Tuck laughed. "Hey, if we can make up our own rules, why *not* be optimistic?"

Odis grinned. "I could go with that, except maybe Sunday. Should have a day off to get laundry and shit done." Odis scooted closer to Bobby and nudged him with his hip to get closer to Tuck. "I think a lot of it will depend on your work schedule, Tuck."

"Right." Tuck glanced between the men. "And does this mean we'd hafta live together? I don't think there's enough room for all of us here. Speaking of which," he said, looking up at Bobby. "Does this mean you'd be movin' out here? I can't see even *tryin'* sumthin' like this if yer not."

Odis ran over and started rifling through his filing cabinet while Tuck gazed at Bobby.

"Well." Bobby smiled. "There's absolutely nothing tying me there anymore, and I just got a fat check. The thought of moving *has* been on my mind." Bobby turned to glance back at Odis in the other room. "If you guys wanna try this, I'm game."

Tuck kept studying him. "What about work?"

"Haven't even thought about *that* yet," Bobby admitted with a frown.

Odis rushed back with a big tube of rolled paper and plopped it onto the table. Bobby grabbed an empty beer bottle out of the way and Odis unrolled the tube, revealing a huge set of blueprints.

Odis smiled over at the other guys. "Here's the rest of the house. This," he said, waving around in the air, "this part is just the starter module." He motioned behind himself to the bed. "That's supposed to be a living room. This module was designed ultimately for entertaining." On the drawings, he pointed with a finger to the opposite side of the dug-out patio. "*This* is where the master suite is supposed to go." He pointed to an area next to the studio. "And a spare bedroom here."

Tuck and Bobby glanced over the plans. Then Odis rolled up the top sheet to reveal a second page. "And this second circle goes on the other side of the garage, adding a huge craft studio, storage, and more bedrooms, possibly." He grinned up at Tuck. "All totaled up, it's about five thousand square feet. Is *that* big enough for ya?"

"Damn, Odie, why didn't ya ever finish it?" Tuck asked with a touch of concern in his voice.

"Didn't seem like much point when I's alone. And didn't feel like buildin' any damn shit for Tina." Odis rolled up the second sheet, showing a larger garage plan underneath. "And here's the extra two-car garage that goes with it."

Bobby glanced over the drawings. "How long would all this take to build?"

"Well, ya know the old saying, ya either spend your time or ya spend your money. So if ya got a lot of money to pay, could prob'ly get it done in sixty days." Odis patted Bobby on the shoulder. "No point in bleedin' out the nose, though. Reasonably priced, I'd say four months for the whole ball of wax. Less than thirty days for just the master suite."

Tuck sat up more squarely. "Okay. Sounds like we got some good options for the future, but we still don't know if it'll actually really work. With three of us, I mean. You two've already hooked up, and I'm assuming it was good...."

Odis released the papers, and they lazily rolled back into a tube shape. "We didn't really." Odis blushed. "Bobby just gave me a blow job."

Bobby stepped closer to Tuck and put his hand on the larger man's back to massage him lightly between his shoulder blades. "Then I guess I owe *you* one, to start."

Tuck gazed up at Odis with slight worry in his eyes. "You *really* sure about this, Odie?"

Odis walked around to the other side of Tuck's chair. He slid the ball cap off of Tuck's head, filling the air with Tuck's musky scent as he dropped the cap on the table. Odis placed a hand on each side of Tuck's face as he leaned down. "Yeah," he said as he moved closer for a kiss.

Tuck felt the warm sparkles of Odis's kiss as another set of hands reached around his shoulders and down to his chest, sensually rubbing and massaging his pecs through the sweatshirt. His pecker swelled to full mast in a mere instant.

Deepening the kiss, Odis pulled his right hand away from Tuck's face and moved it down to rub the swollen tent in Tuck's sweatpants. Bobby kneeled and licked Tuck's ear. As Odis kissed Tuck, Bobby slowly suckled farther down his neck as he scooted closer and pushed his swollen groin against Tuck's thigh.

Tuck pulled away from Odis's kiss. "Holy fuckin'...," he managed to mutter. "You guys are like a couple of incubuses."

Odis whispered, "Incubi," as he moved to the side and slid his hand into the neck opening of Tuck's sweatshirt to rub firmly at Tuck's sparsely haired pecs.

Bobby moved around to Tuck's mouth and kissed him with electric sparks. Tuck reached out and grasped Bobby's ass as he felt the waistband of his own sweatpants sliding slowly down to just below his hips. Bobby pulled away long enough to maneuver around and kneel between Tuck's legs. Bobby kissed Tuck again with the sparking fizz as he moved his hands under the hem of Tuck's sweatshirt and rubbed Tuck's slightly furry stomach.

Odis moved his mouth into the kiss, but it was too strained and physically awkward for all three sets of lips to fit together, so Bobby pulled away. Odis took over and kissed Tuck with warm fireworks as Bobby kneeled on the floor. Bobby slid the front of Tuck's waistband down to his thighs, revealing a cock even larger than Odis's. "Damn, Tuck," he exclaimed admiringly. "Are all you Vikings hung like this?"

Both chuckling, Odis and Tuck broke the kiss. Odis smiled down at the sight of Bobby kneeling in front of Tuck's erect, uncircumcised dick. He'd never seen Tuck with a full hard-on and thought it was definitely worth exclaiming over. "There is a legend," Odis said, "that Loki gave birth to a horse, and some of the Nords were descended from him."

After wrapping Tuck's cock gently in both hands, Bobby squeezed slightly, feeling the firmness of his flesh. "Well, *you* guys got some of that horse blood, that's for sure," Bobby said. Then he opened his mouth wide and engulfed the head of Tuck's cock.

A pleasant moan escaped Tuck.

Odis moved back and grabbed the hem of Tuck's sweatshirt, then slid the shirt off the frozen man. "You okay?" he whispered near Tuck's ear.

Eyes still closed, Tuck moaned. "Fuck yeah. Ooh. Just kinda busy," he managed to mutter. The glorious feeling of Bobby's hot mouth working his pecker seemed to be stealing all of his concentration.

Putting his hands gently on Tuck's shoulders, Odis leaned him back in the chair before bending down and licking at one of his nipples.

"Oh fuck me," Tuck nearly hissed as Odis reached up and gently tweaked at the cartilage of Tuck's ear while nibbling at his nipple.

Odis gently dragged his teeth up Tuck's torso and then moved his mouth near Tuck's ear, whispering, "This is the blow job part. We haven't got to the fucking yet." Gazing down to watch Bobby feed on Tuck's dick, Odis licked and suckled at Tuck's ear.

"No shit," Tuck teased back. Then Bobby did something with his tongue and Tuck clutched the arms of the chair, moaning, "Oh shit. What—?"

Bobby grasped him firmly and slid down more of the foreskin, working deeper with his tongue as Tuck's cockhead swelled larger.

"Oh fu—" Tuck gasped.

"That's it, stud," Odis urged Bobby on. "Worship that dick."

Bobby gazed up at Odis and nearly grinned as he did another tongue swirl.

Odis moved around to kiss Tuck, but when he saw Tuck panting heavily, he decided to move back down to his nipple.

"Oh!" Tuck nearly screamed. "Oh fuck me!" he moaned as his torso stiffened and he bucked his hips upward, ejaculating as Bobby pulled his mouth away.

As Tuck's legs shivered, Bobby grabbed hold of Odis's hand and pulled himself up to share a warm and fuzzy kiss.

As Bobby stood, Odis leaned closer to the still-panting Tuck. "Did *that* work?" he asked teasingly.

"Fuck yeah," Tuck agreed as he opened his eyes, gazing over at Bobby as he sat up. "Can we move to the bed, though? These iron chairs suck," he said as he tried to rub at the reddened indentation left behind by the hard chairback.

Odis lightly massaged at the mark across Tuck's shoulder blades. "Sorry. I'll hafta go buy a padded dining set."

Bobby took Tuck's hand and helped him out of the chair. He noticed the lacy impressions on Tuck's forearms as Tuck pulled up his pants. "No more metal chairs," Bobby agreed.

CHAPTER
Fourteen

WHILE Odis took a bathroom break, Bobby and Tuck walked over and sat on the double bed to remove their shoes. Bobby reached out and played with the tuft of graying blond hair in the center of Tuck's pecs. "You have a nice chest," Bobby complimented.

Tuck shrugged. "I try to keep up. Shoulda seen it twenty years ago."

"Don't be that way," Bobby said with a frown. "It's still tight," he said, rubbing the faint solid lines of Tuck's pectoral muscles for emphasis. "It's easy to have a nice body when you're young. Being older and *still* having a nice body is even more sexy, I think."

After grabbing the back of Bobby's head, Tuck pulled him close for a quick, sparking kiss. "Thank you, by the way. Yer one helluva sucker."

Bobby waggled his eyebrows. "I've got other talents too," he teased.

Tuck grabbed the collar of Bobby's western shirt and yanked firmly. All the snaps popped like the rapid spatter of firecrackers as he pulled open Bobby's shirt. Tuck gazed at the hummingbird tattoo as he slipped the cotton fabric over Bobby's shoulders. "And whatta we have here?" he asked in an admiring tone.

"Just some old ink," Bobby replied almost dismissively. He didn't want to bring up Nathan again. Not right now.

They heard the toilet flush before Odis emerged. As Tuck dropped the shirt on the floor, Odis moved over and sat on the other side of him.

Tuck gave Bobby another quick kiss, before he turned to Odis. "I think we need a bigger bed too, since you're goin' furniture shoppin' and all."

"Good idea," Odis agreed with a nod. He grinned over at Bobby and then glanced back to Tuck. "I think it's Bobby's turn now. He hasn't had a warm Texas welcome yet."

"For shame," Tuck nearly barked. "We'll hafta fix that right now," he said as he got to his feet and playfully pushed Bobby back onto the bed. Turning to Odis, he asked, "You want the head or the tail?"

"Um," Odis replied in confusion. "What's the difference?"

Tuck chuckled. "Do you want the ass end or the pecker?"

Bobby sat up. "Don't I get a say in this?"

"Of course, stud," Odis said. "Whatta ya want?"

"First off, we need supplies." Seeing the lost look on Odis's face, Bobby crawled off the bed. "Never made it to Walmart?"

Odis shook his head.

"Don't worry," Bobby replied as he crossed the room. "I brought some this time." He sat on the floor in front of his suitcase. As Bobby dug around in the bag, Heim left her spot in the kitchen and sidled up next to him to give him a slurp across the cheek. Bobby chuckled. "Hello to you too." Heim sat next to him and watched as he found and retrieved a zippered leather bag. He closed up the suitcase and brought the shaving kit back to the bed.

Tuck took the bag and unzipped it as Bobby sat on the bed again. He pulled out a ribbon of condoms. Tuck looked between Bobby and Odis. "Do we need these? I'm clean."

Odis glanced at Bobby, then said, "We talked about it before, and I am too."

Bobby played a look of mock shock on his face. "Wow, Tuck, an officer of the law condoning unsafe sex?"

"Yes or no?" Tuck barked.

"I'm clean," Bobby replied.

Grinning as he saw the other contents of the bag, Tuck put the condoms back and pulled out the bottle of lube. He zipped the kit closed before setting it on the floor next to the bed.

"So," Odis said as he slid up the bed next to Bobby, "you never did say what ya want."

Bobby glanced over at Odis as Tuck crawled up the other side next to him. "Maybe I'm just being a control freak. You guys do what you want," Bobby offered.

Tuck reached over and unbuttoned the top of Bobby's jeans. "Let's get these pants off first."

As Tuck leaned in and kissed Bobby, Odis undid the rest of the buttons on Bobby's jeans and slid them off to the floor.

Tuck moved down and nuzzled Bobby's ear, whispering, "You have *great* legs." He kissed Bobby as Odis removed the boxer briefs, leaving Bobby naked, his throbbing cock begging for attention. Tuck glanced down and then smiled. "*And* a great pecker," Tuck told Bobby before another kiss. Tuck looked over at Odis. "Ya got on a lot of clothes over there," he teased.

Odis pulled off his T-shirt and jeans, revealing that his stiffened dick was ready for action. He looked to Tuck, asking, "What now?"

Tuck looked into Bobby's smoky brown eyes. "Does Bobby like to bottom?"

Bobby smiled at Tuck. "It's been quite a while, though. Nate wasn't much into topping. I don't know if I could handle you right off."

With a hearty laugh, Tuck tussled Bobby's hair. "Not me, stud. I ain't a twink no more. Us old farts need more time ta recharge." Tuck looked over at Odis. "I was thinkin' Odie could."

Odis scooted closer to squat on his knees behind Bobby's ass and gazed down at him, saying, "I could, if ya'd like."

Bobby grinned. "Well okay, then," he agreed, reaching down and stroking Odis's solid cock.

Tuck pulled gently on Bobby's shoulder, urging him to roll. "On your side facing me." He looked over at Odis as he opened the lube. "You watch me. It's a little more involved than bein' with a woman."

Odis nodded as Tuck slathered some lube onto his fingers. Tuck reached down and pulled Bobby's thigh upward, then stroked his fingers along the cleft of Bobby's ass. With his lubed pinky, Tuck encircled Bobby's anus, teasing and moistening it.

Odis felt his dick swell harder, and watched in anticipation as Tuck worked the tip of his little finger into the hole.

Leaning forward slightly, Bobby relaxed and opened up, pulling the pinky inside.

Tuck chuckled as his finger quickly disappeared. "Damn, stud. I guess this ain't your first rodeo." He rotated his hand and inserted his ring finger, using a gentle circling motion to loosen Bobby's sphincter.

"I said I didn't do it *often*," Bobby replied. "But I do it well," he said with a grin.

After inserting his third finger and circling wider, Tuck used his other hand to squirt some lube onto Odis's pecker. "Ya ready, stud?"

Bobby nodded and Tuck withdrew his hand. He spread the lube over Odis's pecker before guiding him down. "Super slow," Tuck told Odis. "Just line it up and let him mostly move onto you."

"Okay," Odis said with a nod. Tuck pulled on Odis's knee, urging him to spread his legs farther apart and changing the angle a little as Odis teased Bobby's hole with the glistening tip of his dick. Tuck leaned down and kissed Odis.

Bobby opened up, feeling the penetration of Odis's swollen cockhead. "Lord have mercy!"

Odis froze and Tuck broke the kiss. "You okay, stud?"

"Oh hell yeah." He nodded. "I almost forgot how good this feels." Bobby scooted back a bit more, taking about half of Odis inside.

As Odis fought the urge to lunge forward, Tuck ran his large hands over Odis's chest and teased his nipples.

Bobby bent forward and pulled off of Odis a bit. "More lube."

Tuck tapped on Odis's hip, urging him to withdraw. He liberally slathered Odis's pecker and guided him back down.

Odis held his breath as he slowly entered Bobby again. The tight sphincter pulled back his foreskin as he penetrated inside and the sensations nearly made him come. "Maybe I shoulda used a condom," he muttered as he tried to hold still.

Tuck froze. "*Why?*"

"'Cause it's so sensitive, I'm about to come right now."

Tuck pinched firmly at Odis's nipples. Bobby chuckled and said, "I wanna at least have you inside me first."

Odis resisted the pulses of the tightening sphincter from Bobby's chuckles. "Stop laughing," he said. "You're gonna make me come."

Tuck kissed Odis again, playing more roughly with his chest as a distraction. Odis moved forward a little more.

Hungry now for all of Odis, Bobby tried to keep from laughing. "Are you just gonna tease me? Give it all to me."

Odis pushed in a little more.

"Now?" Bobby nearly begged.

Tuck reached down and pushed on Odis's ass, urging him forward. Odis slid the rest of the way into Bobby and then stayed very still, trying not to blow his load from the wonderful feeling of Bobby surrounding him.

After another quick kiss, Tuck told Odis, "Stay right there and don't move." Tuck leaned down to Bobby and kissed him, enjoying his electric sparks. He moved over to Bobby's ear and whispered, "Do you have any idea how fuckin' hot this is? I'm already totally hard again."

Bobby chuckled as he opened his eyes and glanced down at the tent in Tuck's sweatpants. "I hadn't noticed. I'm too busy with his fantastic cock filling me up."

Odis lightly slapped Bobby's butt. "Stop laughing, I'm still about to blow."

Tuck grinned down at Bobby. "You just keep enjoyin' it." He leaned down right on top of Bobby's ear and whispered, "I'm gonna use your bag of tricks and make him *explode* inside you."

Bobby tried not to laugh again as Tuck moved to the edge of the bed. Just having Odis buried inside him felt glorious enough. He couldn't imagine anything better. He heard the quiet zipping noise.

Tuck positioned himself in front of Bobby's groin, admiring the fat pecker before he licked the head and drew it into his mouth. He smiled at Bobby's pleasant moans.

Bobby closed his eyes again. He'd never been serviced from both ends before and reveled in the amazing sensations.

As he worked his mouth on Bobby, Tuck quietly opened the lube. He pulled back and asked, "How ya doin', Odie?"

"Better," Odis said as he slid out a little and in again, eliciting another moan from Bobby.

Smiling, Tuck used his mouth again on Bobby and moved his hand behind Odis.

As Odis slid backward, he felt something cold near his asshole. "What—"

Tuck pushed the small plastic vibrator just inside of Odis.

Odis pushed forward. "Oh shit."

Sucking Bobby's cock completely into his mouth, Tuck flicked on the vibrator and pushed it a little farther into Odis's ass.

Bobby moaned again and opened his eyes as Tuck deftly worked his cock. "Jeezus, Tuck," he muttered.

The vibrating sensation of something foreign inside him catapulted Odis over the edge. "Fuck!" Odis yelled and clutched Bobby's hip as he saw stars. Odis exploded with an orgasm that nearly made him pass out.

Bobby nearly exclaimed as waves of Odis pulsed inside him. Tuck applied more suction and mouth-fucked Bobby's cock until he *did* scream. "Holy fuck!"

As he sucked down Bobby's essence, Tuck turned off the vibrator and removed it from Odis's collapsed body. He grinned at the sight of both men limp and panting.

Odis managed to sit up a little. As he pulled out of Bobby, he glanced over at Tuck. "What the fuck was that in my ass?"

Tuck held up the small smooth plastic torpedo vibrator. "Just a little somethin' extra Bobby had in his bag." Tuck glanced up to the top of the bed. "Was that good for ya, stud?"

Bobby just moaned without opening his eyes. "I don't think I'll ever leave this bed," he said with a gratified sigh.

Tuck gently patted Bobby's calf. "You just grab a nap, then." He turned to Odis. "I'm hittin' the head," he said as he got up and went into the bathroom.

Odis went over to the laundry basket and grabbed a towel, which he used to clean himself off. He'd have to remember to keep one closer to hand next time. He opened the nightstand drawer and fetched a clean pair of boxers and slipped them on before going into the kitchen and starting a fresh pot of coffee.

Emerging from the bathroom, Tuck smiled over at the naked sleeping figure of Bobby. He looked so contentedly peaceful, like a slumbering cherub. Tuck grabbed the afghan off the floor and draped it over the nude form before joining Odis in the kitchen. "Ah, coffee."

"It'll just be a minute," Odis said as Tuck leaned down and kissed him. Odis pulled back. "Was that good enough for ya?"

"Ya even hafta ask?" Tuck teased with a grin. "That's gotta be the hottest thing I've ever done in my life." Tuck reached down and ran his hand through Odis's hair. "Of all the times I fantasized about you, I *never* dreamed up anything like that. Almost made me come again. And that's after the way Bobby deftly drained my dick," he said with a wide smile.

"I fergot ya were a poet," Odis said as the coffee pot beeped. He turned and poured out two mugs. "Ya ever do anything with it after high school?"

"Poetry?" Tuck shook his head. "Just play around once in a while. Haven't tried to get published or anythin'." Tuck took the mug Odis handed him and followed him into the dining room. He glanced over as the sleeping Bobby shifted on the bed. The afghan slid off his shoulder, revealing the upper part of the tattoo.

Tuck turned to Odis. "What's with his tat? He got a little tense when I asked about it earlier."

"Oh, the hummingbird?"

Tuck nodded as he took a gingerly sip from the mug.

"It's sorta like a handfasting pledge he and Nathan made when they got together. Nate got one too."

"I see." He gazed over at Odis. "You never decided to get one?"

"A tattoo? Nah. Never could think of anything I wanted, really. Didn't wanna do it just for the sake of doing it, ya know." Odis took a sip. "I didn't see one on you, either."

Tuck grinned. "Maybe ya just didn't look in the right place," he teased.

"Where? Wha'd ya get?"

"You'll just hafta look for it someday," Tuck said with a teasing glint in his eye.

"Bonehead." Odis chuckled as he saw Bobby stirring again on the bed.

Bobby sat up and blinked blearily at the guys in the dining room. "Shit, I'm sorry." He untangled himself from the afghan and stood up. "Didn't mean to pass out on you guys."

Tuck smiled at him. "It's understandable. You had a long day, hangin' out in airports and all."

"Still, I hate bein' rude," Bobby said as he went into the bathroom and closed the door.

Odis got up and poured another mug of coffee, which he brought back to the table for Bobby.

A few minutes after the toilet flushed, Bobby opened the bathroom door and then dug around in the garment bag hanging on the outside hook. He removed a bathrobe and slipped it on before joining the guys at the dining table. "What time is it? Did I sleep all night?"

Odis chuckled as he glanced over at the microwave. "Just after midnight. You only slept a few minutes." He waited until Bobby sat down and had some coffee. "When ya get waked up, I'll need ya to help me with somethin'."

"As long as it's not algebra or something. My mind's not ready for that yet."

Tuck chuckled. "What's wrong with your mind?"

"All my higher functions went offline. I swear, that was the best sex I've *ever* had. Have ever dreamed of...."

Odis nodded. "I think we *all* agree on that."

The trio quietly shared their coffee.

Heimdalla twitched her ears. She jumped up and ran into the kitchen, then disappeared around the corner.

Bobby followed her with his eyes, then turned to Odis. "Why's she going into the pantry?"

"Not a pantry," Odis answered. "That's the laundry room and the—on the other side is her doggy door."

Tuck raised an eyebrow. "You can say it, Odie. That's where your grow room is, ain't it."

Odis nodded.

"I had that talk with Broyles a long time ago. As long as ya ain't sellin' or makin' a nuisance about it, the department won't hassle you." Tuck scowled. "Believe me, there's worse sharks out there in the pool."

Bobby looked over at Tuck. "Like what?"

"Meth," Tuck told him, nearly spitting out the word. "Busted three labs in the county last month, but rumor mills say there's four more out there now."

Bobby frowned. "I always thought that was more of an urban problem."

"I wish," Tuck lamented. "The way that shit rots the brain, they might as well just snort up Clorox. And the labs themselves, most of those fuckups couldn't pass high school chemistry, but they're fiddlin' with all that volatile shit right in their kitchens. Luckily, it's been a year since one blew up."

Bobby watched as Heim trotted back into the kitchen. He could swear she nodded her head, like an "all's clear" signal, before curling down on the floor again. "I'm sorry, Tuck, I never realized you had shit like that to deal with. Always pictured you'd do things like get cows off the road or rescue lost old ladies."

Tuck sighed. "Yep, there's that small-town stuff too. But it ain't *all* like a TV sitcom."

Odis glanced over at the morose looks that fell over Tuck's and Bobby's faces. He looked over at Bobby. "You wanna help me now?"

"Sure," Bobby said, putting his mug down on the table. "What are we doing?"

"Well," Odis said as he glanced over at Tuck, "Tuck's been holdin' out on us. He's got a tattoo somewhere." Odis stood up and walked around the table.

Bobby grinned. "Really, now, and you want my help to find it?" he asked as he sidled up beside Tuck.

Tuck put his hands up defensively. "Now, boys, just take a seat."

Odis grabbed his arms and pulled him up out of the chair. "Just cooperate and I won't hafta get mean," he said, studying Tuck's back for any marks.

"Yeah? And what are ya gonna do?" Tuck asked as Bobby took hold of his shoulder and leaned him forward.

"I remember where you're ticklish," Odis teased. "Don't make me use it." Odis slid down the waistband of Tuck's sweatpants and examined his toned butt.

"Over here," Bobby announced, pointing to the outside of Tuck's right flank, just below the hip.

Odis moved around and saw the tattoo, about the size of a mason jar lid. The black outline of a sheriff's star, the six-pointed kind with the rounded tips, had been filled in with a golden yellow but was otherwise empty. "Looks kinda plain," he teased.

Tuck reached down and yanked up his pants. "Well, I thought about puttin' Vic's name in it but changed my mind."

Bobby pulled down the waistband at the right side just enough to reveal the star again. "Why'd you get it there? Seems like kind of an odd place."

Tuck reached around, motioning like he was pulling a pistol from a holster. "It's right under where my gun holster sits."

Odis laughed. "Shit, and I thought ya might be sentimental or somethin'. You're just a cop down to the bones, ain't ya?" he teased.

Tuck smirked and shrugged. "Are we through lookin' at my ass? Can I sit down again?"

"Sure," Bobby said as he playfully swatted Tuck's buttcheek. "Have a seat."

Tuck and Odis sat back down as Bobby went into the kitchen and grabbed the coffee carafe, which he brought back to the table.

Bobby filled up their mugs, asking, "Isn't it a little late for coffee?"

Odis shrugged. "Don't matter. I'm too buzzed to think about sleepin' right now."

Tuck glanced over. "You're still high from the weed?"

Odis shook his head. "Nah, I… I guess it's you guys. What we did earlier, us hangin' out now, I just feel all jazzed up."

Tuck nodded. "I thought it was just me feelin' that."

"No," Bobby said as he set down the carafe. "I thought it was just that nap, but I feel all strangely energized too."

Tuck reached out to the middle of the table. Odis and Bobby also stuck out their hands, and they all clasped together. "Three musketeers," Tuck declared.

Odis chuckled. "All for one and one for all," he cheered.

"Whatever," Bobby said while smiling at the other two. They looked back, almost disappointed with his reply. "Jackpot," he said, remembering Nathan's note.

"Jackpot," the other two chimed boisterously in agreement.

CHAPTER
Fifteen

AFTER Tuck excused himself for the restroom, Odis looked over at Bobby. "So whatta we do now?"

"You mean for the night, or…?"

"Either one, I guess." Odis looked over at the suitcase on the floor. "I know I hadn't said it out loud, but you *are* welcome to stay here, or whatever."

"Sure I won't be crowding you out too much? Not exactly a lot of space here," Bobby said with a hand gesture indicating the room.

"There is that, I guess. But we can manage. At least 'til we get some more rooms added on."

"Oh." Bobby sat up. "I can help with that, with the adding-on. Had a lot of practice playing foreman with the landscaping company, and I can read my way through a blueprint. I could do the GC work—general contractor," Bobby added when he saw the confused look on Odis's face. "Since I'm at loose ends right now. It'll give me something to do and save some money."

"Ya know, ya *still* haven't told me how much the settlement was for, but I like the way yer not lettin' it go to your head. Some people just seem to lose all control when they get a huge wad of cash."

Bobby dropped his gaze to the table. "I learned that lesson a long time ago. When I got my first big fat paycheck from the majors, it was gone in less than three months."

Odis chuckled. "No shit? What all did ya buy?"

"Oh, that's the funny part. I didn't run out and buy boats and sports cars and shit. Might have been better off if I had. Instead, I thought I'd be smart and hire one of those financial advisors. He decided we should set up some 'trusts', and of course he had *his* fees, then the lawyers had *their* fees. About a third of it disappeared that way. Then he 'donated' a bunch to some offshore place—to offset the taxes, of course, he said. Which I'm pretty sure now was a backdoor embezzlement. Then he invested the rest into some speculative hedge fund that went belly-up."

Odis frowned. "That sucks. Guess there's advantages to bein' paranoid. I never let *anybody* else touch my money."

"Wise move," Bobby agreed with a nod as they heard the bathroom door open.

After stopping at the bed for his shoes, Tuck returned to the table, picking up his sweatshirt and slipping it on before leaning down against the back of the wrought iron chair. "What's up?"

"Oh," Odis said. "Talkin' about money and makin' good choices."

"Can't help with that," Tuck said with a smirk. "Never had hardly more than two dimes to rub together at the same time."

Odis chuckled and rolled his eyes. "Really, Tuck, ya make it sound like yer practically homeless."

"Well, I know what kinda money ya make at yer shows, and I can imagine the size of the checks you baseball guys get, so I'm not even in the same league." Tuck glanced at Bobby. "So what brought this up?"

"Stud *still* won't say how much they settled for," Odis said.

"Not really our business, though, is it?" Tuck told Odis with a hard look.

"I's just curious, but he's bein' so dodgy about it…."

Tuck turned his cop gaze to Bobby. "*Are* ya bein' dodgy?"

"Fine," Bobby said as he got up from the table and went to his duffel bag. He dug around in it and brought out a day planner notebook and returned to the table. "If ya just hafta know," he nearly whined as he opened up the book and yanked out the check before laying it on top of the blueprints still on the table.

"Shit," Tuck hissed under his breath.

"Oh my fuckin' Gawd," Odis declared when he saw all the zeros. "No wonder ya didn't wanna say. Is that a gazzatrillion?"

Bobby laughed. "I don't think there's such a thing as a gazzatrillion."

"Still," Tuck said with a headshake, "it's still a fuckin' lotta money."

Odis glanced up at Bobby with concern. "And ya just been carryin' that around in yer bag?"

"It hasn't left my side. I didn't even stick it in the overhead. I stowed it under the plane seat, with my feet on top of it."

Tuck laughed. "Yeah, I'd keep my feet on top of it too. And my gun in my lap."

Bobby picked the check up and put it back in the notebook. "You think there's a bank around here that can cash it?"

As Tuck laughed, Odis smirked and said, "Ya kiddin' me? Ya could prob'ly *buy* the bank in town with that kinda dough."

"Doubt that," Bobby replied while shaking his head. "And what the *hell* would I do with a bank, anyway?"

Odis chuckled. "You'd have a big vault to lock all that cash in."

Tuck just sighed and then turned to Bobby. "Ya know, I'm not any kind of financial genius or anything, but if ya wanna talk over it sometime…." His words dangled off as he suppressed a yawn. He stood up straighter and said, "I should be headin' home, guys. Not that I haven't *thoroughly* enjoyed this evenin's… entertainment." He flashed a huge grin to both men.

"You have a good night's sleep, then, Tuck," Odis told him warmly. "And don't let them talk ya into workin' tomorrow. Ya really should take a day off once in a while."

Bobby hesitantly held out his hand. Tuck stepped closer to him and pulled him into a hug. "I hope we can do better than a handshake."

Rising on his toes, Bobby brought their lips together. Tuck leaned down and squeezed him tighter as they opened their mouths and shared their electric sparks. Tuck pulled away. "Damn, stud, that's a helluva a good-night kiss."

Bobby squeezed him briefly, then let go. "So tonight's officially our ménage night?"

Odis nodded. "Yep, it's Saturday."

Tuck grinned. "Two nights in a row. You want me to call later and we can meet in town or somewhere for dinner first?"

Bobby looked over at Odis. "I thought Odie was gonna cook?" he said with a laugh.

"Fuck you," Odis barked before laughing himself. "I'd prob'ly kill us all. Just call later, Tuck. We'll figure somethin' out." Odis stood up and walked around the table. Tuck leaned down for a hug that turned into another warm kiss.

"Damn," Tuck exclaimed as he adjusted the crotch of his sweatpants. "You guys quit kissin' me like that or I'll never make it outta here."

Bobby got his ball cap and cell phone off of the table. "Don't forget your hat."

Tuck took his cap from Bobby and placed it on his head as he slipped the phone into his pocket. "Later, boys," he said with a wave before he reluctantly walked out the door and up the concrete steps.

Bobby watched his fine ass climb up the treads, then turned to Odis. "Back in a minute," he said before he turned toward the bathroom.

Odis put the note back into the brass box. Then he grabbed Tuck's mug and took it, along with the box, to the kitchen counter.

WHEN Bobby left the bathroom, he found Odis leaning over and studying the blueprints spread open on the table. Odis glanced up. "Ya really think ya can help with this? With the contractor thing?"

Bobby walked up and studied the plans a moment. "Seems straightforward enough. I'm sure I could."

Odis shook his head. Then he slumped down into a chair. "Gawd, I just—are we bein' stupid?" he asked, looking up at Bobby.

"Stupid how?" Bobby asked as he sat in the chair next to Odis.

"I mean," Odis started as he leaned toward Bobby and lowered his voice. "Are we rushin' things? After just one... and we're gonna live together now?"

Bobby nodded. "But this is what it was like with Nate. After Fourth of July, I just *knew* it was the right thing, and I didn't think twice about it when he asked me to move in the next morning."

"And you feel that now? About us three?"

"Yes." Bobby nodded again and gazed at Odis. "And you do too, don't you?"

Odis nodded.

Bobby reached out and clasped Odis's hands. "I'd already decided to fly back Monday and pack up the house and start moving. But if you have doubts about this, maybe I should hold off."

Odis wobbled his head. "No. I mean, don't hold off. I'm sure I'll get my head wrapped around all this soon enough. It's just me worryin'."

"If you're worried, we can wait. I'm sure Tuck'll understand if we slow down a little."

"No," Odis said as he squared his shoulders. "Let's go ahead. It'll all sort out. I'll try to quit worryin'." Odis stood up and went to the bathroom.

After watching Odis close the door, Bobby got up and started cleaning. He grabbed the empty beer bottles and took them to the trash can in the kitchen. He glanced down into the bin and saw that orange plastic again. Using the neck of one of the empty beers, Bobby nudged away some of the trash to reveal the cluster of prescription bottles near the bottom. Moving around the trash, he counted seven bottles in the mess, most of them rattling nearly half-full with pills. *What the hell?*

Bobby dropped the empty beer bottles on top of the mess and went back to the table.

Odis returned a few moments later, noticing the strange look on Bobby's face as he sat beside him. "What is it, stud?"

Bobby motioned toward the kitchen. "Why are all those prescriptions in the trash?"

Odis smiled proudly. "I haven't had a pill since the first day you came here. I decided I don't want 'em anymore."

Bobby's face tensed. "But don't you need them? What did the doctor say?"

"I don't need 'em as much as I need a clear mind. Really, it's nothin'."

Shaking his head, Bobby disagreed. "What were they for?"

"Anti-inflammatories and other joint shit."

Bobby studied Odis with concern. "And you just went cold turkey?"

"Wasn't hard."

"But you're supposed to taper off of stuff like that, not just quit all at once."

Odis nodded. "Well, I did anyway. I was tired of bein' fucked up all the time."

Bobby just silently studied him with a worried gaze.

"Ya know, people make *such* a big deal about how terrible weed is, but it's *never* fucked me up like those pills over there did. I mean, some days I could hardly remember my own name, much less try to get any work done in the studio." He gave Bobby a firm look. "I'm done with 'em."

Bobby threw up his hands. "Okay," he relented.

Odis smiled warmly at him. "Yer sweet, though, bein' all concerned."

"I don't think anybody's ever called me 'sweet' before."

"Well, ya are." A yawn snuck up on Odis. "I think I'm about ready to sleep now," he told Bobby as he stood up.

Bobby used the table to push himself up. "I'm starting to feel it too," he told Odis as he walked across the room and picked his suitcase up from the floor. "Is there any place I can put this?"

"Oh," Odis said, moving to the nightstand. He removed a magazine and some papers and set them on the filing cabinet. "Ya can set it there."

As Odis crawled into bed, Bobby set the case on top of the nightstand and opened it to retrieve a pair of gray boxer-briefs. He slid into the underwear and went back to the bathroom door, slipped out of the robe, and left it behind on the hook. He crawled under the covers beside Odis.

Odis rolled onto his side and scooted his back against Bobby, spooning into him. "I missed this," he nearly whispered. "It's funny, since ya were only here one night. But I missed it."

"This place already feels more like home than that huge house. You sure you don't mind me moving in?"

"No, I don't mind," Odis said as he nuzzled up to Bobby. "Where else would ya go?"

Bobby curled around Odis and spoke quietly in his ear. "Nowhere." He snuggled close, and both soon fell into a comfortable sleep.

CHAPTER
Sixteen

WHEN Bobby yawned and opened his eyes, the bright sunlight already filled the house. He found himself once again pinned between Odis and Heim. He nudged at the dog, but she merely groaned without moving. Rising slightly, Bobby managed to see the clock and read 7:18 a.m. He reclined again with another yawn.

Odis stirred next to him but didn't awaken, so Bobby settled into the bed again, thinking about Tuck. Which led to thinking about Nathan. For about the millionth time, he felt an edge of anger. Nate and his fucking secrets. He wondered once again what it was that Nate had seen to lead him to try to set all of this up. Not that Nate had been wrong, as it turned out. Bobby, Odis, and Tuck demonstrated they had this strange and almost magical chemistry as a threesome. How had Nathan even seen that? Had he picked all of it up just from meeting Odis? Or had Nate, at some point, also somehow met Tuck?

Bobby sat up again when he thought he heard something. Well, it was more of a vibration than a sound. Next to him, Heim sat up with alert ears. Whatever it was, she heard it too but didn't seem alarmed enough over it to leave the bed. Her head dropped down again, yet her ears stayed erect.

Stirring again, Odis rolled over and opened his eyes. "Mornin', stud," he greeted with a joyful smile.

"Morning. You have a good sleep?"

Odis's legs vibrated and trembled as he stretched out with a yawn. "Sure did. Ya been awake long?"

"Just a few minutes. I need to pee, but Heim has me pinned in."

"Damn dog," Odis said with a chuckle as he scooted out of the bed and freed some slack in the sheet.

Bobby got up and nearly ran into the bathroom. Odis smiled when he noticed Bobby didn't bother to shut the door. After hanging back a minute to let him take care of business, Odis heard the toilet flush and followed into the bathroom. He walked up behind Bobby and wrapped his arms around him. "Hey, I forgot to tell ya," he said with a grin as he steered Bobby to the shower. "I did some home improvement while ya's gone."

"Oh? What kind?"

"Get those shorts off," Odis said as he slipped off his boxers. "I called a plumber."

Bobby grinned at the shower as he stepped out of his underwear. "Tankless water heater?" he asked hopefully.

"Ya got it, stud."

They stepped into the lava-rock space and Odis soon had all twelve showerheads shooting perfectly warmed water around them. In comfortable silence, they enjoyed the spray while getting rained on from all directions. As they basked in the supreme wetness, they failed to hear the kitchen phone ringing over the noise of the jets.

When Odis grabbed a bottle of shampoo from the niche, Bobby leaned down and let him lather his head with the soap, smelling a kiwi-lime aroma. Then he did the same for Odis, massaging firmly with his fingers as he worked the scented shampoo into Odis's hair.

After rinsing off their heads, Odis punched some buttons on the panel. The spray of the upper jets cut off, leaving only a warm, misty fog at their feet. It soon filled the lava-rock sanctuary with rolling steam. Odis squirted a large glob of soap from the wall dispenser into his right hand before moving next to Bobby. "Now for some serious cleaning," he whispered with a grin as he gently took Bobby's semierect dick into his slippery hand.

When Bobby started to say something, Odis put his left hand up to his mouth in a silencing move. "Just enjoy," he whispered to Bobby as he stroked at his dick, quickly bringing it to life.

Bobby closed his eyes and leaned back against the polished rock wall as Odis worked his hard cock. He pulled at it and squeezed gently as he got near the head, then released it and grasped it at the base, then repeated the motion. He jacked it again with the same gentle caress. Then again.

As his knees felt weaker, Bobby pushed into the wall. He wouldn't be able to hold out much longer. This strange motion had some direct connection to his balls, which were already shrinking up close.

Odis continued to tease with the same slow rhythm, glancing between Bobby's hard dick in his hand and the concentrating look on Bobby's face. Bobby opened his mouth to speak again, but Odis put his left index finger on his lips. "I'm not stopping. Just let go," he whispered.

Odis pulled and teased more, sending a shiver into Bobby's legs. He locked his knees to keep from trembling as Odis stroked, drawing forth an electrical charge that started in his prostate and quickly zapped into his balls. His legs trembled with the next caress as his orgasm swelled. Another stroke brought the hot bloom of singing nerves as his balls clenched and his vas deferens started pumping. The semen flowed, following the bloom as it spread into his cock and up to its head.

"Oh Christ," Bobby hissed when the liquid spurted. Odis grasped his cock in the center and squeezed more firmly, feeling each pulse with his fingers. Bobby's legs spasmed, unlocking his knees as he breathed harder, trying to suck in oxygen. Odis pushed him against the wall to keep him from falling as Bobby squirted again with another spasm while collapsing toward the floor.

Odis kneeled down and kissed him, that warm fuzzy blanket feeling joining the high of the orgasm. Bobby twitched again as the final wave passed through. Odis pulled back and smiled. "You are *so* fuckin' hot."

Bobby chuckled. "*I'm* hot?" he managed to say as his breathing leveled off. "Geez, the things you and Tuck do to me… I'm surprised I don't have brain damage." Bobby gazed over at Odis, noticing he looked ethereal in the swirling steamy mist. "You really are a leprechaun," he said quietly.

"Your leprechaun," Odis replied as he leaned in for another deep kiss. Beyond the hissing of the steam jets, they didn't hear the kitchen phone ring again as they shared their tongues.

Bobby's hand wandered down to Odis's thigh, and he traced a finger higher up to stroke his balls. He pulled back far enough to say, "Your turn now." He thought he heard Heim bark but ignored it as his fingers grasped even higher.

Odis shook his head. "Not me. I'm savin' up for the main event tonight. I figured yer still young enough ta have an extra in ya," he said with a grin.

"You're only seven years older, Odie. I bet you have it in you."

Grasping Bobby's shoulder, Odis gingerly pushed himself up from the floor. His hip popped audibly as he reached down to pull Bobby up. "Not today. Ya pretty much drained me out last night, if ya recall."

"Oh, I recall," Bobby said with a grin as Odis punched the buttons to turn off the shower. "I think I'll *always* recall last night."

They opened the shower door and Odis grabbed the towels. The bathroom seemed full of the faint smoky steam as they dried themselves. Odis grabbed their underwear off the floor as Bobby opened the bathroom door. The smoky steam also hung in a faint haze in the living room.

Bobby started to ask if Odis had thought about installing a bathroom vent when he noticed the smell of something burning.

"What the hell?" Odis swore as he pushed past Bobby. Heimdalla ran over, then raced to the sliding glass door and barked sharply once.

The phone rang again. As Bobby wrapped himself up in the towel and ran to look out into the patio where Heim was pointing, Odis rushed into the kitchen and grabbed the receiver. "Hello?"

"Odis," Gertie nearly yelled, "get your butt out of there now!"

Bobby noticed the haze seemed heavier outside in the patio area. "Odie, it looks like a fire."

"Be there in a few," Odis barked before throwing the receiver back onto the hook of the wall phone.

As Bobby rushed to his suitcase, Odis ran over and yanked open his dresser. They hurriedly pulled on clothes while Heim barked sharply again, sounding insistent. Odis ran to the kitchen drawer, but his keys weren't in it. "Shit!" he cursed, looking around for his dirty jeans. He found them as Bobby grabbed his own dirty clothes and stuffed them into his duffel bag. As Odis grabbed the keys from his used jeans pocket, Bobby slid open the door, and a pungent burning odor hit them. They raced up the stairs to the garage.

The heavy haze lingered as striations of different colored layers in the nearly still air, a smelly brown fog. While Odis got the car out of the garage, Bobby ran up to the gate and punched the button. When Odis pulled up, Bobby didn't even wait for the car to come to a complete stop before he yanked open the door and nearly dropped down on top of Heimdalla.

"So much for a lazy morning in bed," Odis lamented as he sped away toward the main road. They could hardly see a few hundred yards ahead in the smoke that seemed to be growing thicker.

"Shit, what the hell's burning?" Bobby asked. Under the aroma of wood, leaves, and grass that reminded Bobby of autumn lawn care, he could also smell that pungent plastic tang and other trash.

"Smells like a grass fire. It's been so dry this winter, wouldn't take much to spark one off. Ya remembered yer phone?" Odis asked hopefully.

Bobby nodded as he unzipped the duffel and dug the cell phone out of his dirty jeans pocket.

"Call Tuck. He might know some details."

Bobby hit the Redial button and listened as the line rang a few times, then went over to voice mail. He hung up without leaving a message. "No answer," he told Odis.

"He's prob'ly on the scene, then, wherever it is," Odis replied as he drove as fast as he dared. With no wind, it was impossible to tell which direction the smoke was coming from, so they had no clue where the fire was. Odis worried they might be driving straight for it.

He relaxed a little as the foggy haze got a bit thinner when they neared the main road.

They left the smoke behind as Odis sped into town. He soon pulled into the B and B.

Gertie greeted them at the door. "Geez, Odie, ya scared me half to death. Been callin' all morning."

"Sorry, we were in the shower. Where's the fire?"

Gertie glanced down at Heim as if she didn't quite approve of the dog being in the house, but she didn't say anything. Heim just sat quietly at Bobby's feet, looking alert.

"Don't know," Gertie told them, motioning toward the dining room. "Chrystil at the sheriff's called, said she tried to call ya for evacuation but got no answer. Was checking to see if ya might be here. There was some kinda explosion out by Route 7 and Aiken's Road. The fire's burnin' south."

"Shit," Odis hissed. "It's headed straight for the house, then."

Bobby looked at Gertie as he sat in one of the dining chairs, keeping the duffel in his lap. "Was that about seven thirty this morning? Me and Heim sort of heard something."

"I guess, sounds about right."

Odis sat at the table. "Where's Tuck? We tried callin' him."

"I don't know," Gertie said. "Don't know much, really. Just glad you boys got out of there in one piece." She disappeared into the kitchen and returned with mugs of coffee.

"I'll call the sheriff's," Odis said as he stood again. "They should know more."

"Sit back down," Gertie scolded. "You'll do no such thing. I'm sure they're too busy dealin' with stuff to have pesterin' calls clogging up the phone lines."

Bobby looked at Odis, feeling the same gut-twisting concern he saw on his lover's face. "It's his job," he said aloud, not clear if he was trying to reassure Odis or himself. Heimdalla nestled up next to his leg and curled up on the floor. "Tuck's good at his job, right?"

"Right."

"Then he's fine. I'm sure they train for this kinda thing all the time. We don't even know if Tuck's out there."

Odis nodded but still looked racked with worry as he sipped at his mug.

Gertie patted Odis on the shoulder before she sat next to him. "And ya have insurance on the house, right? Ya can just rebuild, if need be."

"I ain't worried about the fuckin' house," he said quietly.

Gertie threw a glare at the language as she put down her mug and glanced quickly between the two men. "In the shower together, huh? So I guess it's... more serious now?" Her gaze landed on Bobby.

Bobby looked over at Odis, trying to read how much he should divulge.

Odis cleared his throat. "Well, yes. And—a bit more complicated too."

"I see...." Gertie sipped from her mug. "How exactly is the matter complicated?"

As Odis thought about Tuck again, his face squirreled with worry and he rose to his feet. "I'm calling—"

"Odis Tyler! No yer not. Sit your ass back in that chair 'fore I tie you down."

Odis dropped his butt back into the seat.

Bobby gazed at him with a tight smile he hoped was reassuring. "Tyler?"

Gertie looked over at Bobby. "Odis Tyler Vorleik."

"Thanks, sis. Why don'cha just go spill *all* my secrets?"

Bobby raised an eyebrow. "Oh? What secrets?" he asked teasingly.

Gertie shook her head. "He don't have any, I don't think. Just lives out there like a monk in a monastery."

Odis got a pained expression on his face. "Oh fuck," he said and then glanced furtively at Gertie, but she didn't scold him as she got up and went back into the kitchen.

"What?" Bobby asked as he reached down and petted Heim.

"That last inscription from Nathan. It's still written down at the house, and I don't remember it," Odis told him with a frown.

"Not any of it?"

"It's one of those poem puzzles that doesn't make much sense. Somethin' about a bird's nest is all I remember."

"Bird's nest?" Bobby shook his head. "Doesn't mean a damn thing to me."

"Sorry. Just hope it dudn't burn up. It's not a fireproof filing cabinet."

"Don't worry about it," Bobby told him. "Wait, isn't it on a computer printout? Maybe Gertie still has the original," he asked. He didn't really care about Nate's message, but he welcomed anything that provided even a moment of distraction from the anxiety of waiting.

Odis lit up. "Hey, Gert," he yelled out. "Ya still have my computer orders from October last year?"

Gertie stepped just inside the dining room, her hands covered with flour. "Sure. I save all that stuff. Why ya askin'?"

"Could I get a copy?"

"Right *now*?" Gertie asked as she glanced back at the bread dough on the counter. "Well, give me a sec." She disappeared back into the kitchen.

Odis leaned forward and quietly whispered, "While we're gone, try Tuck's cell again."

Bobby nodded.

Gertie returned with clean hands, and Odis followed her into the office.

When they left, Bobby retrieved his phone from the duffel bag and tried Tuck's number again. This time, it only rang once before kicking to voice mail. He hesitated but decided to end the call without a message.

Returning a few minutes later with a printout, Odis watched as Bobby gave a curt negatory shake while Gertie passed through on her way back to the kitchen.

"Come here, dog," she called from the doorway. "Let's get you outside for a bit."

Heim sat up and looked at Bobby. "Go on, you can play outside," Bobby told her. She perked her ears at the word "outside," then followed Gertie into the kitchen and out the back door.

"Dumb dog," Odis said as he put the paper in front of Bobby and pointed to the bottom. "Here it is."

Bobby looked over the note in the inscription box.

turn around the sine, fluff the feathers and freshen the nest
treasure Be un-mined, upon our Early Day of the past

Bobby just laughed as he read it. "Nathan Price. You are a bastard."

Odis frowned down. "Doesn't mean anything for ya?"

"Not a goddamn thing," Bobby nearly spit out. "You take a crack at it—you managed to figure out the last one." He pushed the page across the table at Odis.

Odis carefully read over the poem but couldn't concentrate on it. His thoughts kept getting commandeered with fears over Tuck's safety. "I'm callin' the department," he told Bobby very quietly as he took out his wallet and fished out the ratty business card.

They exchanged tense glances as Bobby slid his cell phone across the table to Odis.

In a voice loud enough to be heard in the next room, Odis declared, "Let me think about this note a minute. I'm gonna take a walk outside."

"Okay," Bobby agreed a bit loudly. He also stood when Odis did, taking the coffee mugs as Odis made his exit.

Bobby just stood at the table with the mugs in his hands. His guts churned. He hated this feeling of apprehension and waiting. And even more, he hated being forced to feel it all again.

Why in hell was he? Technically he'd only met Tucker Krickson less than twenty-four hours ago, so why the fuck should he care so much already? So deeply?

Not only did these feelings suck, they didn't make the least bit of sense. Love at first sight was mostly fairy-tale nonsense—he was lucky enough to have found it once with Nathan. Or, maybe *not* lucky. Considering that Nate was a goddamn psychic and all, it was likely Nathan "saw" Bobby ahead of time and tracked him down. It only felt like magic from *his* end.

And here he was again, waiting helplessly to hear the fate of someone else. And once again, it was Nathan's fault.

He finally turned to the doorway. Before Bobby even stepped into the kitchen, he could hear slapping and pounding noises. He walked in to find Gertie with a huge mass of bread dough, which she seemed to be beating to death. "You do homemade bread?" he asked over her shoulder.

Gertie jumped slightly at the sound of his voice. "Goodness, ya startled me." She looked over when Bobby went to the coffee pot. "Yeah, not usually so much, though. Kinda got carried away this mornin'," she said with a shrug before turning back to pushing and pounding at the bouncy mass.

Bobby filled his mug and then watched as she took out her frustration and worry on the defenseless dough. "Do you get these kinds of grass fires often?"

She shook her head. "Not often, but they can be bad when we do. 'Specially now. We've been in drought conditions for two years. Had a burn ban runnin' the last six months just to try and prevent any accidents."

"Burn ban?"

"No campfires, burning trash, outdoor welding. Things like that, ya know." Her hands stopped moving and she turned around to look at Bobby. "I know, it's not really none'a my business, but what's goin' on? I've never seen Odis so… concerned about anything before."

Bobby leaned back against the counter, not sure how much he should answer. But earlier, Odis had seemed ready to tell her, so maybe he wouldn't be talking out of turn. He could at least tell her some of it, he decided as he squared his shoulders. "It's Tuck. We're both worried about him." He studied her to try to gauge her reaction. "He was out late at the house last night. Wasn't supposed to work today, but...."

Gertie didn't show any huge reaction as she digested his words. "Were he and—have Odis and Tuck been more than *just* friends?"

Bobby nodded.

"But they had some kinda falling out a few years ago, so now they're... but I thought *you* and Odis...?"

Bobby watched the expressions on her face change as she tried to put it all together. She finally settled on looking perplexed. "What are ya tryin' ta tell me?"

Before he could think of an answer, they heard the vestibule door close. Bobby hurried back into the dining room.

With a furtive glance at the kitchen doorway, Odis handed the cell phone back to Bobby. He looked truly worried now. "Bonehead's there," he nearly whispered. "Or at least he was. Nobody knows now."

"What do you mean?" Bobby asked quietly as he leaned down.

"Might as well say it for the whole house," Gertie said from the kitchen doorway as she dried her hands on a dishrag. "Plant yer butt in that chair."

With a chagrined look, Odis sat with the others at the dining table. "The explosion this mornin'—let me back up," Odis said before taking a deep breath. "Word got to the sheriff's last night that the Thurson brothers were plannin' to do some meth cookin' today. So department decided this mornin' to make a preemptive move and bust the lab." Odis looked right at Bobby. "They *did* call Tuck in on it." He shook his head. "The sheriffs showed up with some DEA they scrounged up. Then it's all a clusterfu—I mean, nobody knows, after the explosion and the grass fire started." Odis shrugged. "Choppers say it looks like over a hundred acres is scorched, ten acres is afire, and it's still spreading. At least there's no wind to get it *really* moving."

"Then"—Gertie leaned forward—"cops got there *before* the explosion?"

Odis nodded.

"Who all's hurt?" she asked.

"Ambulances took three out to Hutchinson, but Chrystil still don't know who or how bad they's hurt. Found one of the brothers dead, the other's still missing, and there's more missing, they think, but they're all too busy dealin' with the fire to search the wreckage very hard." He looked at Gertie. "They're settin' a fire break to keep it from spreading east. Into town," he added at the end as he looked at Bobby.

Gertie sat back and quietly tried to breathe.

"How many more are missing?" Bobby asked.

Odis shook his head. "Don't know. Two of the cell towers burned out, and it's all a fu—screwed-up mess. They still got the radios, but it's limiting communications. Chrystil said she hasn't heard Tuck talkin' on it, but that don't really mean nothin', I guess."

Gertie finally found her voice. "What about *your* house?"

Odis deflated more. "Fire's already burned through there. Just hafta wait and dig around the pieces later."

"Damnation. I'm sorry, Odie. You and Bobby's a stayin' here," she announced firmly, expecting no argument.

"Appreciate it," Bobby said in thanks.

Gertie shook her head. "Not a second thought." Then she turned back to Odis. "At least it's one of the Thursons that's dead. Them boys have been nothin' but a heap'a trouble since the day they's born. They brought it on themselves," she said with a firm nod.

"Don't say a thing like that," Odis said. "They ain't exactly had an easy life. Town should'a done more when their pa ran off."

"We tried. You might be too young ta recall, but their mama'd have nothin' to do with help. Too stubborn for any charity. Right up to the day she passed."

Bobby couldn't think of anything to say. He didn't know any of these people, but he agreed with Odis that nobody *deserved* that kind of ending. He pondered the news. "Where's this hospital?"

"Hutchinson, other side of town from Walmart," Gertie said.

Odis looked over at Bobby. Bobby frowned and said, "Think we should go out there? Or call?"

"No point in goin' out there unless we knew fer sure… Chrystil said she'd call when she had more news."

Bobby sighed heavily. "I just hate waiting around."

"I know," Odis agreed.

As Gertie got up and returned to the kitchen, Odis and Bobby shared worried gazes.

CHAPTER
Seventeen

AFTER a few minutes, Gertie stormed back into the dining room. "Okay, now," she said, easing into a chair and mustering her strength. "What exactly in the hell's goin' on?" She looked right at Odis. "I can get along with the idea of ya bein' with a man, but yer stringin' along *two* men? I could smack you for that kind of disrespect."

"It ain't like *that*," Odis defended. "You've heard of a ménage à trois?"

"*What?*" Gertie leaned back in her chair, stunned. She glanced over at Bobby. "Are you guys bullshittin' me?"

Odis chuckled. "Language, Gertie," he teased.

"Oh screw you," she said with a sigh. "Can't expect me ta be composed when ya throw shit like *that* at me."

Odis squirmed, trying not to laugh. Bobby just shook his head.

"How—" Gertie struggled to compose herself. "I mean, how's such a thing even happen?"

Bobby and Odis traded questioning glances as if they were mentally drawing straws to see who had to answer. Bobby turned to Gertie. "Well, do you want the long or the short answer?"

Gertie brought her hands up to smooth her hair. "Oh good Lord." She sighed. "Suppose we start with the short answer."

Bobby nodded. "I guess the ball really got started rolling when Tuck picked me up at the airport yesterday. He was jealous of me, jealous of Odis, things got intense, and we kissed. And the funny thing is, I didn't feel like I was cheating on Odis just because I kissed Tuck. I was only cheating because Odis wasn't there too."

Odis jumped in. "Same with me the other day. We three sat down last night and talked it all out, and the three-way seemed like the best solution."

Gertie just shook her head. "I guess—there's just some things beyond what a sixty-year-old woman can comprehend. So. I'll leave you boys to do whatever it is ya feel like ya need ta do. But. Don't none of ya come cryin' to me if it all falls apart," she said, staring right at Odis. "And don't be askin' me for no advice on it either." Gertie stood and returned to the kitchen.

Turning a sharp gaze to Bobby, Odis asked, "How the hell'd that even come up?"

"While you were on the phone, we were in the kitchen. She knew something was up, and cornered me about it."

"Oh." Odis softened. "I guess I sorta started it by sayin' things were complicated earlier. At least she took it well."

"Really? Sounded to me like she decided not to take it at all."

"Nah, that's just Gertie. For her, that answer means, 'Leave me alone and let me chew on it awhile. I'll get back to ya.'"

Bobby chuckled. "Well, you prob'ly know your sister."

"She's fine. She'll come around. I'm more worried about what John's gonna say about it all."

"He seemed cool with me and didn't seem too bothered when I told them you and I made out."

"*What*?" Odis sat up straighter. "When was this?"

"That first night when I had dinner here. He even seemed upset he missed out when you shared your 'good shit' with me—his words."

"Well, I'll be damned. John Hasting, a cool dude. Who'd have guessed?"

"Why'd you say it like that?"

Odis grinned. "They didn't tell ya? John's the pastor of the Lutheran church next door."

"Well, I'll be damned," Bobby echoed. "If you'd asked me what I thought he did five minutes ago, I'd have said accountant or stockbroker. I'd *never* have guessed a man of the cloth."

"Yep, he is."

"Come to think of it, where *is* John?"

"On Saturdays he does a thing at the retirement village. I'm sure he's there. With the fire, he may stay longer, 'cause it's on the west side of town. I bet the word 'evacuate' is floatin' around over there, if it's as bad as it seems."

As they sat with anxious faces, one loud, sharp bark sounded from outside. "Damn dog."

They heard the back door open before the rapid clattering of toenails on tile heralded Heimdalla's arrival. She ran right up to Bobby and planted her rump down beside him. Bobby reached down and patted her head.

Odis chuckled. "I'll get more coffee," he said as he rose to his feet and grabbed the mugs.

Stroking Heim's head, Bobby tried not to think about her house. Odis's house. His island. He strained to overhear the conversation in the kitchen. He missed the first part of it, but Gertie's voice clearly said, "If she pees on my carpet, *yer* payin' for the steam-cleaners."

"Fine," Odis agreed as he carried the mugs back to the dining room.

Bobby glanced up when Odis set the mug in front of him. "You said the fire had burned through already?"

"Damn you. I was tryin' not to think about it." Odis fell into the chair next to him. "Yeah, it's gone," he said with a whisper. "And all yer clothes and shit was there too."

"I'm not worried about that," Bobby said. "It's all replaceable."

Odis tried to keep his face from scrunching up. "Your box too." His voice weakened and seemed to flutter. "The algiz box. That prob'ly won't be...."

"Shit." Bobby reached out and took Odis's hand. "Prob'ly not." He squeezed Odis's fingers. "But that's not something I *need*. I have all that right here," he emphasized with another squeeze of Odis's hand as he looked at the duffel bag on the table, then turned his gaze back to Odis. He looked back down at Heim, though—the pain he saw on Odis's face was causing a tight lump in his throat.

"I know," Odis said as he wobbled his head and tried to pull himself away from the depressing thoughts of loss. "I'm bein' a pansy."

"You have every right...," Bobby said, letting the thought trail off. He better shut up now, or they'd both end up bawling like fourteen-year-old girls. There'd be time for mourning later. But not right now. Not with—

The phone rang with an echoing electronic song that jangled throughout the whole house.

"Odis, grab it," Gertie yelled from the kitchen.

He jumped to his feet and rushed to the office. Bobby debated whether to follow, but Heim put her head on top of this thigh, so he reached down and patted her instead.

Good news, good news, Bobby chanted to himself. *Yes, we definitely need some good news now.*

Gertie ran into the dining room, drying her hands as she sat next to Bobby, quietly sharing his vigil. Bobby noticed she still had some kind of pasty herb-looking gunk under her nails.

After a century of the clock ticking away slow seconds, Odis returned with a tight expression. "It's not *bad* news," he told them as he grabbed his coffee.

"Well?" Gertie asked impatiently as he took a sip.

"Josh, Hampton, and one of the DEA agents are the ones at the hospital. Not in bad shape, it doesn't sound like. Mostly banged up. Fire departments from Hutchinson and Jenkins are on the way out. Jenkins crew are goin' to the scene 'cause they still have at least three missing." Odis's voice got quieter. "Tuck is one of 'em."

Bobby frowned. "Do they know if Tuck was at the house?"

"Yep. He and Hawk was gonna cover the back. Hawk's missing too."

Gertie hissed something under her breath.

"Were they actually inside the house?" Bobby wondered aloud.

"Don't know. They weren't *supposed* to be, but if things got FUBAR...." Odis let the thought trail off as he fingered at his coffee mug.

"I hope Gina's okay," Gertie said. "They just had that bad scare a few months ago when they thought Hawk had that heart attack. Lord knows she don't need another one."

"Let's hope, then," Odis said.

"Pray and hope," Gertie said as she stood up. "I'm...." She hesitated, then just nodded her head. "I'm goin' back to the kitchen," she announced as she walked away.

Odis and Bobby sat at the table, trying not to look at each other. Neither wanted to voice the morose thoughts they struggled to avoid thinking. Bobby glanced up, wanting to say something, when he saw that scrunched look on Odis's face again. Yet he couldn't think of anything reassuring. It seemed all words led to dark places best avoided. So he offered a smile he hoped was warm and then gazed back down at Heim as she curled on the floor at his feet.

Bobby drank his coffee, eyeing the printout still on the table. He read the inscription again but still made no sense of it. With a heavy sigh, he gave up trying to decipher it. Then the aroma of baking perked his nose. The scent of vanilla baking. Cookies, maybe. The thought brought a small smile to his face.

A few minutes later, Gertie emerged from the kitchen carrying a big plate of chocolate-chip cookies and a french press of fresh coffee like she did for fancy guests. She set the press on a coaster on the dining table. "I know you boys would prob'ly prefer beer or somethin', but we don't have any. Beer don't go with cookies, anyway," she said with a shrug before returning to the kitchen.

Bobby grabbed a cookie from the plate, watching it slump as he brought it to his mouth. It was still all warm and gooey. And delicious. He looked over as Odis absently nibbled at one of the cookies. He didn't smile, but he didn't look quite so stressed now, either.

The phone rang again. Odis was out of the dining room before the third note even chimed.

He returned a few moments later with a gray pallor.

"What is it?" Bobby asked as he jumped up and rushed to Odis's side.

"They found two charred bodies. One's in jeans, it looks like, so they think it's the other brother. The other's in uniform, but it's so badly burned… they aren't sure…."

Bobby grabbed Odis and wrapped him in his arms as Gertie walked briskly from the kitchen. She saw their consoling hug and froze. "No." Her face turned white as her body slumped. "Dear Lord, no."

"Two bodies," Odis repeated. "*Inside* the house." His face went blank. "They weren't supposed to be *inside*," he whispered as he buried his face into Bobby's chest.

Gertie turned and dragged herself back into the kitchen. As Bobby tried to shut himself off, to stay strong and not feel anything, the world suddenly got very noisy. He heard Heimdalla breathing. The grandfather clock in the hallway ticked in loud, slow clinks. Water gushed in the kitchen, and the momentary squish of the soap dispenser echoed. A motorcycle growled as it passed by outside.

Odis clutched tightly at his back, as if he was trying to hold himself up. Bobby pulled him over to a chair and sat him down as Gertie slowly walked through to the office with wet hands. "I'm making some calls," she said to no one in particular as she passed by.

Odis wouldn't release his grip, so Bobby half squatted and half kneeled on the floor. As Bobby hugged Odis tighter, he sniffled. Bobby moved his mouth by Odis's ear. "You said they weren't sure."

"If it ain't Tuck, then it's Hawk. And if *one* of 'em was in the house...." Odis loosened his arms and pulled back to stare into Bobby's face. "Aren't they supposed to go in pairs?"

Before Bobby could answer, Gertie inched back into the dining room. She stopped partway in, just staring down at Heim sleeping. "Alice is bringin' Gina over. Couldn't reach John. What about the fire?"

"Fire break's holdin' up. It's moving more or less south now." Odis sniffled again. "Choppers are dumpin' water and seem to be slowin' it down. If the wind don't pick up, they think it might die out soon."

"Well." Gertie took her gaze off the floor. "Lunch'll be ready in a minute." She went back into the kitchen.

Bobby stroked the back of Odis's hand. "He's cautious, right? Follows protocols? I bet he *didn't* go in the house," Bobby said firmly, trying to believe it himself.

"If... Hawk'd almost be worse. He's kinda the town hero. Has been since high school. The golden boy quarterback. Firm but compassionate cop. Always there with a smile to pitch in when somethin' needs done." Odis brought his hands up to his face and clutched his cheeks. "Shit." A sudden glaze of guilt enveloped his eyes as Odis dropped his hands and pulled back from Bobby. "While it... we were in the *shower*," he said with a cringe.

"That doesn't have anything to do with—"

"Yes," Odis hissed as he pushed Bobby away. "While we... somebody *died*."

Bobby fell back onto his butt on the floor. "Odis," he said without trying to get up. He just gazed up. "Odis."

"It was so *wrong*."

"How can it be wrong? We didn't know."

Neither man turned when Gertie rushed from the kitchen, carrying a giant glass baking dish with some kind of steamy cheese casserole bubbling inside. She set the dish on more coasters on the dining table. "Lunch is ready," she announced, suddenly noticing Bobby sitting on the floor. "Macaroni-chicken casserole," she told the despondent-looking Odis. "Get yerselves up here and eat."

Bobby pushed himself from the floor and sat in a dining chair while Gertie brought back a serving spoon with plates and silverware. "Eat," she commanded again before turning toward the kitchen. The phone rang. Gertie nearly ran into the office to answer it.

CHAPTER
Eighteen

BLACKNESS.

Throbbing.

Tuck woke up from the horrible blinding dream again. His right hand felt strangely numb, yet sent shooting pulses of pain up his arm every once in a while. The last few times he had tried to move his hand, he blacked out. He decided to be smart this time and *not* move his hand. *Be smart*, he yelled at himself.

The air felt so stale and stuffy as Tuck tried to take a deep breath. He felt totally restricted and tried to ignore the impression of being trapped in a coffin. He thought back to his situational training. Wasn't that step one? No negative thoughts? *No*, he recalled. *Step one is breathe.*

Just breathe.

One slow breath as deep as you can.

Let the oxygen clear your mind and chase away the panic.

Exhale.

Check.

Second slow breath. *Step two: physical evaluation. Catalogue all pain and numb sources.*

His right hand pulsed with obvious injury. He forced himself to ignore it and focus on everything else.

A cold numbness seeped into his right leg near his ankle.

With each breath, he felt a slight jag in the area of his left-front ribs. Not internal. Felt more on the surface, like skin or muscle damage.

Something on his forehead by his left eye felt sticky and wet, but there was no pain or numbness associated.

He focused, but nothing else surfaced.

Check.

Third slow breath. *Step three: evaluate environment.*

He blinked just to make sure his eyes were open but still saw only darkness. He was lying mostly on his back, angled a bit to the right side. He felt the closed-in pressure all around but sensed the space was more triangular. *Not a coffin*, he reassured himself.

Just breathe.

He tried to move his right foot but got no play. It seemed trapped by something.

He tried to move his left foot. He could raise it about an inch and a half and move it backward about two inches, but it was pretty much trapped as well.

He tried to move his left hand. It was resting on the right side of his stomach. He couldn't move the elbow back or really move the hand away from him, but he could slide his hand up his body all the way to his chest. He slid his left hand back down, and near his thigh, he felt something beside him brush his fingertips. He pushed with his fingers slightly, rubbing moist, bare flesh that felt impossibly cold.

Just breathe.

It's not my right hand. No, he insisted, fighting the image of a cold amputated hand curled up next to his leg.

Breathe. Breathe. Deep breath.

He slid his left hand back up to his stomach.

One slow breath as deep as you can.

Let the oxygen clear your mind and chase away the panic.

Exhale.

Step Three: evaluate environment.

He swiveled his head to the left and right and felt no resistance. He slowly raised his head up, barely gaining half an inch before his forehead pushed into something very hard and solid. Something metallic.

Tuck inhaled deeply through his nose, smelling for any traces of gasoline or other chemicals. The air just smelled cold, wet, and stale with no dangerous odors.

He tried shifting his hips, but they wouldn't move. He couldn't think of anything else to try.

Check.

Next slow breath. *Step four: listen.*

Tuck closed his eyes and tried to ignore everything but his ears. He could hear the slow drip-drip sounds of something. He listened closer. Actually, it seemed like three or four different drip sources.

He listened closer. He thought he heard some kind of shifting or shuffling noise. "Hey," he tried to yell, but his voice barely escaped his parched throat in a whisper. "Hey!" he tried again with the same result.

He tried banging his left hand in front of him but couldn't get enough leverage to make much more than a faint noise.

He listened. Only the plinking sounds of drips surrounded him.

Check.

Next slow breath. *Step five: search for tools to free yourself.*

Tools. Radio, Tuck instantly thought. The microphone piece of his personal radio rested on his right shoulder. He moved his left hand along his body again, but easy movement stopped at his chest. Digging into his uniform shirt with his fingers, he slowly managed to claw and inch-worm his hand up to his shoulder. He reached out for the mic but felt only the Velcro strap. *Shit.* The microphone must have been knocked loose. Now it lay somewhere under him or at his side.

"Fuckin' shit," he hissed aloud as he groped around his empty shoulder, hoping to maybe find a section of the coiled cord he could use to pull the mic out from under him. His fingers found nothing but Velcro and more shirt fabric.

Breathe. Just Breathe.

Tools. Cell phone. Tuck felt his heart sink when he remembered. *Oh shit.* It was still at his apartment. He'd set it on the hall table when he grabbed his keys and did the quick mirror check as he rushed out this morning. *Fuck.* He'd forgotten to grab it again. *Fuckin' fuck.*

Breathe. Breathe. Deep breath.

Tools. Maybe the handset is on the floor within reach.

He tried sliding his left hand down across his body toward the floor. At first he felt fabric; then he felt his right forearm. When he pushed on it somewhere near his right wrist, his arm responded with a squeal of pain.

He tried shifting his left hand and nudging it around the arm as far as he could but only felt more of his arm.

Even if he could find any tools, it seemed unlikely he could use them.

Free yourself.

His only point of real mobility was his left foot. Tuck tried scooting his left knee up, then kicking downward forcefully. His foot encountered nothing, so the force rotated his body slightly, sending another squeal of pain from his right hand.

He moved his left foot back as far as possible, then kicked forward as hard as he could. With a grinding noise, the walls of his prison shifted, squeezing down more tightly around him. He tried to ignore the disgusting squishing sound he'd also heard.

Shit.

Tuck tried rotating his shoulders to free his left hand again. *Fuckin' shit.* As his right arm moved, a screaming agony from his right hand blinded his vision with hot stars of light before blackness engulfed everything and he passed out again.

ODIS wouldn't even look at Bobby as he forked at the casserole noodles, occasionally shoveling some of the food into his mouth to avoid Gertie yelling at him again. Gertie was too focused on Gina to really notice, though.

Bobby looked over at Gina. Beneath the roughly pulled-back hair and streaked makeup, she had the appearance of a nicely fading beauty queen. Under normal circumstances, the woman probably looked stunning.

"Gina," Gertie reassured her, "we still don't know anything. Tuck and Hawk are just missing, that's all."

Hawk's wife just nodded as she picked at the food on her own plate. Looking up, Gina glanced over at Bobby, only truly noticing him for the first time. "Yer that athlete guy," she said, motioning toward him with her fork. "I heard somebody famous was in town."

"I guess that's me," Bobby replied with his public smile.

"The baseball guy," she continued as if not hearing Bobby's acknowledgement. "The fa—gay one." Gina's face quickly collapsed as her shoulders slumped. "Hawk. He had wanted to meet you," she groaned as her eyes watered.

Gertie jumped up and patted her shoulder. "No. No tears. Hawk *will*. We'll make sure he meets Bobby. Won't we?" she said, looking over for confirmation.

"Of course. I'd be happy to meet Hawk," Bobby agreed.

As Gina pulled herself together, the phone rang. Gertie glanced over at Odis, who seemed oblivious. "I'll get it," she said before hurrying away.

At this point, Bobby didn't care if it was good news or not. He just wanted this sickening waiting to be over one way or another. He felt Heim stir at his feet. He slipped her a piece of his buttermilk biscuit since Gertie wasn't there to see. Heim sat up and put her head on his thigh, quietly agreeing to accept more.

Gertie returned all animated. "Gina," she nearly sang, "they found Hawk."

"Is he…?"

"Sounds like he's fine." Gertie rushed over and patted Gina's shoulders. "They're just takin' him over to Doc Murphy's office, not even goin' to the hospital. Part of the floor collapsed and he fell into the crawl space under some junk."

Odis deflated completely. "Then it's…."

Gertie glared at him across the table. "We don't know that. Don't even say it." She turned back to Gina. "Now, finish yer plate and we'll get over to the doc's office in a bit."

Wiping at her eyes, Gina sat up straighter and actually tasted the casserole. "This is good," she told Gertie a minute later.

Bobby glanced over at Odis. The little man looked like he was ready to curl up into a ball in the corner. Part of Bobby thought that might be a good idea and wanted to do the same.

TUCK'S mind lingered in a foggy daze. He wondered how long he'd been here, but he'd lost all sense of time. It could be less than an hour or several days; he had no way to tell. He didn't feel hungry, though, so it probably hadn't been too long. Unless his injuries were dulling his appetite. *No, quit thinkin' about shit like that. Just breathe.*

His mind turned to worry about Odis and Bobby. It felt kind of strange to think of them. In all his years on the force, he never had anyone else to be concerned over. Well, Vic had been around, but Tuck had never been apprehensive about Vic's feelings when dealing with bad situations. This reaction with Bobby and Odis was new and different.

Tuck wasn't sure which man concerned him more. Bobby, he thought, would be the stronger of the two, but that poor guy had been through so much shit recently, this would just be like more aggravation on top of it. Tuck hated that he was putting Bobby through this again.

On the other hand, Odis was so sensitive. Chances were he'd completely fall apart, but he also had that streak of optimism. He would bounce back much quicker in the long run. Bobby would have to be strong enough to carry them both through initially.

Stop it! Tuck yelled at himself. *It's prob'ly only been an hour. The guys prob'ly haven't even heard there's a situation yet. They're fine*, he told himself. He closed his eyes and breathed.

Some kind of sound pulled Tuck to alertness. He listened and heard more shuffling scrapes. "Hey," he yelled, his voice echoing in desperation around him. He tried moving his left hand again to knock or make some kind of noise, but it was wedged tightly against his chest now.

The sounds stopped.

"Hey," he yelled out again, forcing his voice to be as loud as he could.

"Over here!" a muffled voice called from above somewhere. Thrashes of movement crashed terribly loud in his ears. Tuck squinted when an intense light hit his face. Something shifted on his right hand, and a torturous throb blinded him with hot stars again before he passed out.

JOHN was just walking into the B and B when the phone rang again. "I got it," he yelled out as he turned in the hallway and went into the office.

Bobby glanced over at the despondent figure of Odis, who wasn't even pretending to eat anymore. Odis just stared out at the opposite wall like a catatonic patient. Bobby hoped it wasn't bad news—he didn't know if Odis could handle any more.

Moments later, John came into the dining room with a hard-edged serenity plastered on his face. "They identified the bodies. It's Willy

Thurson and Carl Travie." John looked around the table. "Hey, Gina, guys," he greeted each with a nod.

Gertie got up. "I'll grab ya a plate," she told John as she went to the kitchen.

"Thanks, hon." John took the chair next to Odis, looking him over. "How you boys holdin' up?"

Bobby just shrugged. Odis didn't seem capable of even that much effort.

Gertie returned and handed John a plate before sitting next to Gina again. She wrapped her arm around Gina's shoulder in a comforting hug. "We're heading out to Doc's in a minute. That's where they took Hawk," she added, not sure how informed John was.

"What about Tuck?" John asked while loading up his plate. He noticed Odis flinch slightly at the mention of the name.

Gertie shook her head with a furtive glance at Odis. "No word."

The phone rang again.

Gertie gave Gina a pat on the shoulder and glanced over at Bobby as she stood. "Why don't you boys head upstairs for a bit. Grab the yellow room again," she said over her shoulder as she went to the office.

Bobby gazed over at Odis, pretending an ease he didn't feel. "How about it, Odie? Let's go upstairs."

Odis blinked but showed no other response.

John looked over, trying not to show worry. "Go ahead, Odis. You can stretch out a minute."

Gertie rushed back into the dining room. "They found Tuck," she nearly yelled. "They're rushing him to Hutchinson now. He's mostly okay," she said, looking down at Odis.

Odis snapped back into himself. "He's not...?"

"No, he's okay, mostly," she tried to say cheerfully, but she threw a concerned glance at Bobby before plastering on a smile.

That look left Bobby very anxious about her definition of "mostly." He put some spirit in his voice as he smiled over at Odis. "We can go to the hospital in a bit, if you wanna eat something first," he gently suggested.

Odis shook his head. "Not hungry."

"That's okay." Bobby nodded. "Maybe we should go upstairs first. Freshen up a bit?"

Odis thought on it a moment. "Okay. We should do that. I guess."

Heimdalla stood up when Bobby did. He patted Odis on the shoulder. "Let's go, then."

After pushing to his feet, Odis led the way to the stairs. When he was on the second tread, Bobby told him, "Oops, I forgot my duffel. I'll see you up there in a sec."

Odis nodded as he continued climbing the steps.

Heim followed Bobby back to the dining room. Gina looked over when he bent down to grab the duffel from under the table. "Where'd the dog come from?"

John looked over and quietly chuckled. Bobby stepped up close to Gertie. "How bad?" he asked quietly.

"His hand was crushed under a freezer," she said in a low whisper. "He's goin' straight to surgery, so stall awhile or ya'll just be sittin' around the waiting room."

Bobby nodded curtly and then went up the stairs to find Odis. Heim stuck right beside him as they climbed the treads.

John turned to Gertie. "Any word on his house?"

"In the burn zone," she said as she gathered up the dirty dishes.

"Lord, give us strength," John prayed under his breath as he turned back to his plate.

UPSTAIRS, Bobby found Odis in the little side bathroom, leaning against the sink. "You washing up?" he tried to ask cheerfully.

"Oh," Odis replied before he remembered to turn on the faucet. He splashed some water on his face and then gazed at the reflection of Bobby's eyes in the mirror. "How bad is it, really?"

Bobby dropped the smile. "His hand's hurt. They might take him to surgery when he gets to the hospital," he fudged. "So we should prob'ly hang out here a few minutes before heading over. They'll have to get him all checked in and everything first, anyway."

Odis smiled tightly. "Don't ever go play poker at the casino," he said while turning around. "Yer not a very good liar."

Bobby tried to look innocent.

"Just tell me," Odis insisted.

"It's his hand. It was stuck under a freezer. He's going to surgery for it."

"Humph." Odis walked into the bedroom. "And I don't suppose that freezer just lightly floated down to gently rest upon his hand before it got stuck."

Bobby shook his head.

"*Which* hand? How badly crushed? Just *some* of the fingers?"

"I don't know. They'll know more when he gets to the hospital, I'm sure."

Odis opened his mouth to speak again, but Bobby reached out, grabbed him, and pulled him into a close hug, smashing Odis's face into his chest. "Don't ask. I don't have any answers. Just hug me, Odie. He's alive, that's the important part. Right?"

Odis nodded against Bobby's chest before wrapping his arms around Bobby's back. His relief couldn't overshadow the cold sense of dread he felt throbbing in his guts. He let Bobby's warm scent comfort him.

Bobby dragged him toward the bed, and they reclined back against it. He scooted them all the way onto it and then spooned up behind Odis, hugging the little man tightly in surrounding arms. "Let's try and sleep a little," Bobby said. "I know how hard it is to try and sleep at a hospital, if we're there late, so try and nap now."

"All right," Odis agreed, closing his eyes. "You think he's gonna be okay?"

Bobby wanted to say, *Sure thing, Tuck'll be fine*, but felt it would be a lie. "I don't know," he soon admitted.

Odis nestled up against him, trying to absorb Bobby's strength and warmth. He needed all of it that he could get. As he worked on breathing slowly, he felt Heim jump onto the bed.

CHAPTER
Nineteen

A KNOCK at the door roused them. Bobby hadn't actually slept, but he thought at one point Odis had dozed, at least a little. Brushing at his now wrinkled shirt with his hand, Bobby got up and went to the door.

He blinked as he opened it to find John in the hallway. "Gertie's back. We're gonna head over to Hutchinson. You guys wanna come along?" John asked, peeking into the room to see Odis curled up almost fetally on the bed. "Or ya could just follow us later," he suggested.

"Any news?" Bobby asked, looking around for a clock. He felt Heimdalla push up against his leg.

John shook his head. "Didn't expect to hear any yet. It's only one thirty," he added.

"Then we'll head out a little later," Bobby said with a nod.

"Good, then." John returned the nod and went back to the stairs as Bobby closed the door.

He turned around to find Odis still curled up, but his eyes were open.

"I almost don't want to," Odis whispered.

"Want to what?" Bobby asked as he crawled back onto the bed.

"Go to the hospital. It's never been my favorite place."

Bobby curled up behind Odis again. "Mine either," Bobby agreed.

Odis sighed and pulled him closer. "It looks like ya've been adopted."

"Huh?" Bobby asked.

"Heimdalla. Never saw her act that way with *anybody* before. Looks like she adopted you. Yer her human now."

"Oh, guess so," he said as the dog jumped onto the bed and squatted beside him again.

They rested quietly a moment before Odis asked, "You have a flight Monday?"

"I'll change it," Bobby reassured him. "I won't leave while things are…." He trailed off, not wanting to even consider finishing the thought.

"I don't want you to go at all," Odis said. "Not ever."

"I have to, though, eventually. Still some loose ends."

"I know." Odis tried to push back the empty loss of his house. He shivered as he tried to fight a sob. "Ya like this room?"

"Sure, seems like a nice room. It's where I stayed the other night."

"It's my old room," Odis said, shivering again. "I guess it's home again, now."

Bobby tightened his arms in a reassuring hug and nuzzled up next to his ear. "Then it's a great room," he whispered. "The best one we could have."

Odis looked at the rug on the floor. "I wonder if it's still there?"

"What is?"

"My desk used to be over there. When I's, oh, I guess about twelve, I spilled some red Testors paint over there on the floor." Odis almost chuckled. "I was such a goofball, though, I didn't really try to clean it up, I just moved the rug over to hide it. The paint sat there so long before Mamma found it that red splatter had stained deep into the wood." Odis shivered again. "I was such a mischievous kid."

"You still are," Bobby whispered in his ear. "A mischievous leprechaun."

"I still miss her sometimes," Odis said with a heavy breath. "You'd have liked Mamma. Gertie's just like her. Sometimes I can close my eyes and pretend she's Mamma."

"I like Gertie," Bobby agreed.

"What's *your* mamma like?"

Bobby pulled back just a little to slide his arm out from under Odis before it fell asleep. He raised his hand and ran his fingers through Odis's sloppy-looking hair. "Not today. Okay?"

Odis rolled over onto his back to look up at Bobby.

"I promise I'll tell you someday. Just… not today?"

"Okay," Odis agreed with a nod. He rose and met Bobby's lips with a quiet kiss. "I don't think I'm gonna sleep anymore."

"You wanna go over now?"

Odis looked over at Heim. "Better take yer dog outside first."

"Fine." Bobby scooted off the bed, and Heimdalla jumped down to the floor. "Come on, then, dog, let's go outside."

She perked up and wagged her tail, following Bobby out the door. Odis crawled from the bed and went into the bath to get himself at least somewhat presentable.

THE guys didn't talk much in the car as Odis drove. Neither man wanted to discuss what they might face once they got to the hospital. Soft silence seemed like the safest option.

They entered the tiny building and were assaulted with that unique hospital odor as they walked through the doors. Odis spoke with a nurse at the counter, then led Bobby down the left hallway. At the end of the hall, they found a waiting room area lined with plastic chairs. Gertie jumped to her feet when they approached.

"News?" Odis asked hopefully.

Gertie shook her head. "Still in surgery. Everybody else is doing well. Hawk's here now too." She motioned to the chairs. "He had a bad bruise on his back right behind his kidney. They wanted to run scans and make sure there's nothing internal."

Odis glanced over as he sat. "Is that why we're in the ER?"

Gertie nodded. "Josh is just over there," she said, pointing to another curtained area. "He's okay. They'll prob'ly turn him out soon. I don't know if they got Ham a room or not."

Bobby just smiled and tried to look supportive. None of these names meant anything to him. He wondered how long Tuck had been in surgery.

"Darlin'," a female voice called out. Bobby glanced up to see Gina emerging from behind a curtain, looking right at him. She almost glowed, not looking at all like the crumpled woman he had shared lunch with earlier. "There ya are." She called him over with her hand as she turned back. "He's here now, hon."

Gertie patted Bobby on the back. "Go meet Hawk," she urged with a slight hand push.

Bobby stood up, put on his public smile, and then walked over to Gina. "Hi again," he told her.

She grabbed his arm and dragged him to the bed. "Hawk, here's Bobby. I'm gettin' some coffee," she said as she disappeared around the curtain.

Bobby looked down at the bed. The man looked to be nearly the same build as Tuck, only a few years younger. He also had the same bold Nordic features, but with more blue in his eyes, making them look more turquoise. It was easy to see that golden boy image Odis had mentioned. "Hello, Hawk," he greeted. "Gina said you wanted to meet me?"

With a smile, Hawk reached out and grabbed his hand. "Sure did." He gave Bobby's hand a vague shake. "*The* Bobby Lane," he said, trying to sit up a little. "Have ya met my brother yet?"

"Your brother?"

"Tuck," he said. "Have ya met Tuck yet?"

Bobby nearly laughed. When he looked at the man, it was so obvious now why he resembled Tuck so much. "Yes, we've met," he said cautiously.

"Good, good." Hawk nodded. "I think he really needs to meet you."

"He did. We had beers at Odie's house last night."

"Shit," Hawk cussed under his breath. "I heard about the fire. I hope maybe Odis can salvage some of it. At least some."

"Let's hope," Bobby agreed.

Hawk looked over at him with a suddenly serious face and lowered his voice. "Do you know who else is here? They won't tell me a damn thing."

Bobby looked over at Hawk, deciding what to say. If they hadn't told him Tuck was here, there must be a reason. Bobby didn't know Hawk like they did. Maybe he was the hotheaded type who would plow through the hospital until he found his brother if he knew Tuck was hurt. "Well, Josh, some DEA guy, and... I wanna say Humpty, but I know that's not right."

"Hampton?" Hawk offered.

"Yes, Hampton. Those guys were brought in a while ago. They'll prob'ly release Josh in a bit, they said. Don't know about the other two."

Hawk shook at his hand again. "You should go say hello to Josh. He's a huge baseball nut, and he'd be thrilled to death to meet a player."

"Okay," Bobby agreed as Gina returned.

She smiled at Bobby and then looked over at Hawk apologetically as she sipped from her cup. "They said ya can't have any in case they hafta make ya pee blue again."

"Tell that dang nurse I'll pee when I wanna," Hawk grumbled. He looked over at Bobby. "Go find Josh. Let me smooch on my wife a minute," he said, gazing over at Gina.

"Okay, see ya later, Hawk," Bobby said. He walked around the curtain and returned to the waiting room. He decided not to notice that Gina had handed the coffee cup to Hawk as he'd left.

Odis smirked at him. "Cantankerous?" he asked. When Bobby nodded, he sort of grinned. "Then he's fine."

"I'd say so. But nobody said he was Tuck's *brother*." He glared over at Odis.

"Sorry." Gertie patted his arm. "Just got caught up in things and fergot ta mention it."

Odis shrugged. "Sorry."

Bobby glanced over at the other curtains and then turned to Gertie. "You said Josh was over there?"

Gertie nodded.

"Hawk said I should meet him."

"Oh, sure." Gertie got to her feet. "I'll introduce ya," she said as she led Bobby across the room. They stepped behind the curtain. A young darker-haired guy who didn't hardly look to be thirty yet struggled to rise. "Hey, Josh," Gertie called out. "Ya got a visitor."

Josh sort of sat up. He tried to smile, but the movement must have pulled on the short, neat row of stitches across his left cheek, and he winced. "I do?" He turned to look at Bobby. In just a few seconds, recognition dawned on his face. "Bobby Lane!" he nearly shouted.

"I'll leave ya boys to it." Gertie quietly slipped out.

Josh nearly lunged out of the bed trying to grab Bobby's hand.

"Hi," Bobby said as he rushed forward to keep Josh from tumbling out. "Hawk said I should meet you."

Josh grabbed his hand and pumped vigorously at it. "Hi, hi," he repeated in a starstruck daze.

"Maybe you should lie back down?"

"Oh, sure," Josh agreed and released Bobby's hand before reclining. "I can't believe it. Bobby Lane. That was one hell-uv-a game with the Orioles two years ago. Ya caught three flies in one inning, had all the outs ta yerself. Hell-uv-a game. I nearly pissed my pants that day. Didn't wanna get up from the TV."

"Well, nice to hear from a dedicated fan." Bobby smiled, not sure what else to say.

Josh seemed to merrily reminisce a moment. Then his face turned more serious. He grabbed Bobby's hand again. "I'm sorry. Ya don't know how *pissed off* all that bullshit got me. I was ready to go up there and start kickin' some commissioner asses. I still will if ya need me to."

"No." Bobby patted his hand, feeling a slight lump in his throat from Josh's protective sincerity. He was still surprised by how supportive most of the straight guys could be. "We got it settled."

"Good." Josh lay back again. "Have ya met Tuck yet?" he asked.

"Yes," Bobby said with a nod, feeling puzzled and a bit curious. This was the second time someone had steered him toward Tuck.

"Good," he replied. "I think he should hang out with ya."

"Is there a particular reason?" Bobby quizzed.

Josh hesitated with his words, as if he had a destination in mind but didn't know quite how to navigate the terrain. "Well, yeah," he said slowly, struggling. "Maybe... maybe you can inspire him," Josh finally said.

"He needs inspiring?" Bobby wondered aloud. Tuck was such a go-getter. He didn't seem to need any inspiration.

Josh hesitated again while nodding his head. "Let him know—let him see—he doesn't hafta keep secrets."

"Secrets?" Bobby asked, but before the word had fully escaped his mouth, the crux of Josh's conversation smacked Bobby in the face. Josh was voicing his suspicions about Tuck and saying it didn't matter. He was opening the door for Tuck to come out.

Josh just nodded when he saw the realization on Bobby's face. Josh shook his hand again. "*Now* ya understand me."

Bobby nodded back. "I do." He didn't feel it was his place to discuss it further—this would have to be Tuck's conversation to resume. He had to bite his tongue, though, remembering in the SUV ride when Tuck talked about coming out to the department. Josh might be relieved to hear about it, but Bobby felt mentioning it would border more on gossip. He just nodded again.

"Where *is* Tuck?" Josh suddenly thought to ask. "He shoulda been here by now."

"He's here in the hospital somewhere," Bobby answered vaguely, hoping Odis was wrong about his lying skills.

"Oh," Josh replied, letting go of Bobby's hand. "You should get along, then. I'm sure you're actually here for somebody else."

"Yeah," Bobby agreed noncommittally. "I heard they're gonna kick you out soon anyway."

"So they keep sayin'."

"You take care," Bobby said with a smile. "And I'll remember our talk too, next time I see Tuck."

"You do that," Josh said with a wave as Bobby left his cordoned-off area.

He found Gertie and Odis were still sitting in the same spot. Gertie shook her head when Bobby glanced at her as he approached. She stood up. "Keep my seat warm," she told him. "I'm gonna... scratch up some drinks."

Bobby sat in her chair next to Odis as she moved away down the hall.

"How's Josh?"

"Seems good. He's a big fan."

"Is he...?" Odis asked, sounding almost jealous.

"No." Bobby shook his head. "I don't think. Just a baseball fan."

"Oh. Ya never know."

They sat quietly for a time. One of the nurses went into Hawk's area; then they heard Hawk grumbling at her about something. She emerged with an exasperated look on her face.

Gertie returned, carrying a plastic tray with some drink cups and packets of peanuts. She handed the tray to Bobby before sitting next to him. "Have some peanuts, Odie. Ya didn't eat any lunch."

Bobby leaned back and set the tray in his lap. The drinks looked too pale to be coffee.

"It's tea, some kind of weird jar-deer-ling stuff. Supposed to be good, though," Gertie said, answering the question on his face.

Odis looked over at the tray. He picked up a packet of peanuts and opened it with his teeth before grabbing one of the drink cups.

Bobby tried not to sigh. He hated all this waiting. He just felt so useless. His only value was letting his lap serve as a table.

He suddenly realized he hadn't seen John. He turned to Gertie. "Where's John? I thought he came with you."

"He did. He wandered up to the second floor. Children's ward, I think he said."

Odis nodded as he chewed some peanuts. "Not a surprise. He hates sittin' around too."

Gina stepped from behind Hawk's curtain, sighing and shaking her head. She walked up to the group and glanced over at Odis. "Are all the Kricksons so damn stubborn?"

"Yep," Odis said with a nod.

Gina turned to Bobby. "He wants to talk to ya again, darlin'."

"Oh?" Bobby said, surprised. "Okay." He picked up the tray and stood before Gina grabbed the tray from him and stole his seat. "Be back in a minute, I guess," Bobby told them as he headed for Hawk's area.

"Hey, Bobby," Hawk greeted with a dopey grin. "Did ya find my brother yet?"

"I didn't know I was supposed to be looking for him."

"Well a'course ya are. You're supposed to be meetin' him." Hawk scrunched up his brow. "No, wait, ya already *did* meet him. Shit. These damn pills are messin' with my head."

Bobby thought he should keep the conversation going before Hawk got around to asking where Tuck was. "*Why* was I supposed to meet him?"

"Well, 'cause he's needin' to." Hawk nodded, satisfied with his grasp of English.

Bobby thought he seemed to be dodging the answer. Hawk probably shared the same reason that motivated Josh into making the same suggestion, but Bobby wanted to keep the man talking. "Why does he *need* to meet me?"

"Dammit, man." He sucked in a breath. "Just talk ta him. Okay?"

"Okay," Bobby agreed warmly. "But I have the feeling there's something specific you think I should say."

Hawk grabbed his hand. "He's my brother. I don't want him ta keep livin' like a hermit 'cause he thinks he hasta keep things quiet. Talk to him."

"Keep *what* quiet?"

"I didn't just fall off the turnip truck yesterday," Hawk threw out with a slight slur.

Bobby decided it was time to throw him a rope. "You think he's gay."

"I'm pretty damn sure," Hawk said firmly. "Last time he took out a girl was for his senior prom, and I'm guessing that was just for appearances' sake. A gazillion years ago."

"And how is my talking gonna help him?"

Hawk stared at Bobby, wondering why he was being so stupid. "At least *don't* let him get back with Vic. Tuck's banged his head on that brick wall long enough. I don't think he'd take that advice from me, though. You, he just might listen to."

"Okay, no more Vic. Anything else?"

"Can't ask for anythin' else since ya already done hooked up with Odis."

"What makes you say that?"

"News travels," Hawk said with a shrug and a yawn. "Where *is* my damn brother, anyway? Tuck shoulda been here by now."

"Don't know," Bobby said with a tight smile. "Let me go see if I can find out."

"You do that, and talk ta him," Hawk repeated while closing his eyes as Bobby slipped out.

He emerged from the curtain to see Gertie partway down the hall, conversing with a nurse. Gina and Odis sat in the chairs, chatting about somebody they knew. Bobby moved toward Gertie. The nurse nodded and scurried away as Bobby stepped up. "Gertie?"

"Outta surgery, finally," Gertie said quietly. "They're moving him into ICU now. We can go up in a little bit."

"How'd it go?"

"Did the best they could. Won't say much more than damage to his right hand."

Bobby frowned. "Hawk was asking about Tuck. Should we tell him?"

Gertie shook her head. "Doc's still worried about his kidney. He needs to stay put for a while. Gina said they gave him something to knock him out for now."

CHAPTER
Twenty

TWENTY minutes later, when Odis and Bobby followed Gertie away from the elevator, they found John pacing the hall in front of the ICU. He plastered on a smile and rushed over to the gang, pointing toward the lounge couches against the wall. The worn maroon cushions looked much more inviting than the hard plastic chairs in the ER.

Gertie hugged him briefly before sitting down. "Any details?"

John nodded. "His right hand," John started but threw a puzzled look over at Odis when he saw relief wash over the small man's face.

"Tuck's left-handed," Odis announced, looking over at Bobby. "Ya didn't notice?"

Bobby thought back and recalled Tuck pantomiming the drawing of his gun, remembering how Tuck had reached around himself with his left hand to the location of the imaginary holster on his right hip.

"Oh." John relaxed. "That kinda makes a bit of difference, then." He continued as the other faces watched him expectantly. "They cleaned up the crushed bones, put in a few pins and rods to stabilize things so the bones can heal. But the big concern is the long period of time with reduced blood flow. After four hours, the tissues may not—may be too far gone to recover."

"How much of his hand?" Bobby asked. "Are we talking one or two fingers, or—?"

John took a deep breath. "From what I gather, the freezer mostly rolled on top of him, but the door handle landed longways across the top of his palm."

Odis winced. "*All* his fingers?" he asked aloud.

"He'll hafta have at least one more surgery to yank out the rods, if nothing else. They got him here in ICU to keep a close eye on the fingers. Any signs of necrosis and they'll have to amputate. They told me they haven't put on a more permanent cast yet but prob'ly will in a few days."

Bobby glanced around, noticing they were the only ones in the waiting area. "Where's his family?"

Gertie patted him on the arm. "It's just Hawk, Gina, and their little ones. And us, I guess. His mother passed on years ago," she added.

They sat in silence a few moments before Klyve, the weary nurse, stretched his back and wandered over to the couch. "Y'all here for Mr. Krickson?" he asked.

All heads nodded.

"He's wakin' up now. We can let somebody back, but only one at a time." He looked around for a volunteer.

They glanced from one to the other. Odis spoke up. "You go first, Gertie. Let him know we're here."

"All right," she said while standing. "Guess I'm first."

"No cell phones," the nurse told her.

Gertie handed her purse to John, then straightened her shoulders to steel herself before following Klyve into the ICU.

TUCK could hardly open his eyes when he heard someone come in. He managed to focus on a nurse, then saw Gertie standing behind him.

"Hey, Tuck." Gertie stepped forward. "They said you were awake now."

Tuck tried to speak, but his throat seemed to be stuffed with dry sponges. Klyve rushed over, picked up a plastic cup, and stuck the straw into his mouth. He sipped at the water, the liquid so cold it chilled his teeth with zings of awareness. He cleared his throat and tried his voice again. "Hey, Gertie."

"Odis and Bobby are here," she said as she stepped a little closer, trying not to look at the huge wad of mummy wrappings covering Tuck's right hand. "They're only lettin' us in one at a time, though. I think the boys are havin' a wrestlin' match in the hall to see who's next."

"They holdin' up okay?" Tuck managed to choke out.

Klyve put the water cup into Tuck's left hand. "I'll check back in a minute," Klyve said before leaving the cubicle.

Gertie nodded as Tuck got another drink. "It was scary for a minute. But mostly okay now."

"I overheard talk of a grass fire as they threw me into the ambulance. Nobody's sayin' more...."

Gertie nodded again, watching Tuck closely. "It burned south."

"How *far* south?"

"Almost eight miles, last I heard."

Tuck knew the local geography intimately enough to realize those details put the fire right through the Vorleik property—Odis's house. "But they made it out," he said before another sip.

"Fine and dandy. That damn dog too," she added with a chuckle.

"Good." Tuck paused a minute. "Who else is here? I mean, hurt?"

He saw Gertie hesitate. "You got the worst of it, I think. Josh and Hampton just had bumps and bruises. Hawk is still under observation. He took a bad bang to the kidney."

"Shit," Tuck hissed. He was kinda surprised Hawk hadn't stormed his way in by now. His baby brother could be a downright obsessive nuisance at times. "You have him chained down somewhere?"

Gertie chuckled. "Just passed out downstairs. I don't think they told Hawk yer here yet." She smiled at him. "Glad to see ya awake again. I better get out afore the boys start clawin' the walls. Who should I send back next?"

"I can't have two?" Tuck asked. He didn't want to decide. He wanted to see both men.

Gertie gave him a look. "Nurse was pretty insistent it only be one at a time. And we're gonna hafta have a talk about this... unusual situation one of these days soon."

Tuck's mouth dropped open. "They told you?"

"You *know* Odis can't keep nothin' from me."

"Oh. Right." Tuck stopped to think. He could really use the warm glow of Bobby's smile right now, but Odis was probably growing ulcers as they spoke. "Better send worrywart in first, I guess."

Gertie nodded and left the cubicle. A short walk later, she exited the ICU area and approached the couches while glancing down at her watch. "Your turn, Odis," she told the waiting men. "He's in room two."

Nodding, Odis pushed to his feet and walked in. He took a deep breath before entering Tuck's room, just to prepare himself for the horrible battering he expected to see. Yet other than the large bundles of gauze on Tuck's right hand, Odis couldn't tell he had even been hurt. No marks, bruises, or gashes marred his face or visible arms. "Hey, Tuck," he said with a smile as he hurried to the bedside. Before even thinking about it, Odis planted a big kiss right on his lips, leaving Tuck breathless.

Returning for another examination, Klyve saw through the glass of room two what looked like a little man trying to suck the life out of Tuck. He smiled and swerved to check on room three instead.

Odis pulled back and then punched Tuck in the left arm. "You bonehead. I told ya not to go to work today, didn't I?" He grabbed Tuck's left hand in a clutching embrace.

With an exaggerated grimace, Tuck said, "I know, I know. So much for our date tonight."

All of the bravado seeped out of Odis as he looked over at the bandaged hand. "So, does it hurt?"

"Nah, I'm just not supposed to move it. They said it's not in a cast yet."

A weak edge crept into Odis's voice. "You really had us worried, stupid bonehead."

"I'm fine, Odie," Tuck said while shaking his hand. "Takes more than a damned appliance to best me."

"How long ya gonna be stuck here?"

"Haven't heard nobody say. Prob'ly just a day or two, I bet."

With a loud noise at the door, Klyve stepped in. Odis moved from the bedside and dropped Tuck's hand self-consciously. Klyve glanced over the monitors, made a few scratches on the chart, and then pulled back the sheet to poke at Tuck's right toes before scratching more notes. "Behave yourselves," he said warmly as he left the room again.

Tuck reached out and took hold of Odis's hand again. Tuck said, "He seemed a little snippy."

"Well, he hasta put up with the likes of you all day, I'm sure."

"The likes of me? We could always send him down to Hawk's room."

Odis gave a strained laugh. "Oh yeah, he's still downstairs. It won't be pretty when he wakes up." He reached out and stroked Tuck's forehead, then trailed his fingers down his cheek. "It's not as bad as I thought. I was expectin' to see ya covered in bruises and shit."

"I'm a tough old guy."

"Well, at least ya got *that* going for ya."

Tuck gave him a studying look. "I bet ya haven't eaten a damn thing today."

"I had some peanuts a while ago."

Tuck scowled playfully. "*Peanuts*? Seriously?"

Klyve poked his head in the door. "There's other people still waiting."

Odis flipped off the door, then quickly kissed Tuck again. "Guess I hafta go."

"Go get some food. Some *real* food."

Reluctantly, Odis released Tuck's hand and went to the door. "I'll be back later," he said before leaving.

Tuck clenched his eyes shut and let out the strangled sigh he'd been holding.

Bobby came in moments later. He walked right up to the bed, grasped Tuck's face in his hands, and kissed his forehead. Tuck wrapped his good arm around Bobby and pulled him close. Bobby leaned down and shared a warm and comforting kiss.

As he passed by room two, Klyve glanced through the glass and froze. It wasn't so much that Tuck was kissing *another* guy, it was the way their kiss brought to mind all those silly "springtime in Paris" kind of romance movies. Tuck's hand moved up behind the other guy's head as the visitor's hands drifted down to his chest, then started wandering down farther. This was starting to look more like porno than Paris. Klyve headed for the door, banging against it loudly before opening it. They had parted lips, but the other man hadn't moved away.

Klyve made a show of grabbing the chart and peering over the monitors. He glanced over at Tuck, expecting him to look chagrined at being caught with another man, but only saw a blissful smile on his face. "Don't stay long, I'm coming right back," he announced as he exited.

Bobby watched the nurse leave. "Prickly ass," he said as he squeezed Tuck's good hand.

Tuck nodded as he slumped back into the bed. "How's Hawk?"

"Seems fine. He's just in observation. Which brings up an interesting topic."

"Oh?"

"You remember that talk we had on the way from the airport, about you and the department?"

Tuck nodded.

"You should seriously consider it. Both Hawk and Josh practically demanded that I meet you and talk to you."

"Really?"

"They've both got you figured out. And I bet they aren't the only ones."

"What did Hawk say?"

"He's afraid you'll turn yourself into a hermit trying to keep everything quiet. And he didn't seem to be a big fan of Vic's."

Tuck winced. "How'd he even *know* about Vic? I kept that under wraps."

Bobby gazed at him. "He's a cop and a worried brother. Easy math, I'd say."

"Right. I guess I'll hafta have a chat with him, then."

Trying not to look at the bandages, Bobby sat on the left edge of the bed. "Does it hurt?"

"Not too bad," Tuck admitted. "Throbs, mostly. Have ya been to check the house?"

Bobby shook his head. "We came straight here from the B and B. Gertie put us up in Odie's old room for now."

Tuck looked over and saw the nurse hovering outside the door. "I think yer about ta get thrown out." He rose and kissed Bobby again. "Make sure he eats."

"I'll try, but he can be as stubborn as you, I'll bet." He glanced at Tuck with concern. "I hope you passed out through it."

"Mostly, I did. It already seems like some kind of weird dream. Or maybe a drug trip. But I…." He gazed at Bobby with a touch of remembered fear in his eyes.

"What?" Bobby asked gently. "Was it frightening?"

"I kinda—I did get scared once, when I thought my hand got amputated."

Bobby winced at the thought and tried not to show it on his face. "Well." Bobby looked over at the bandages. "I'm not gonna blow smoke up your ass and say it's all fine. The hospital people still seem pretty worried."

With a clatter, Klyve pushed his way into the cubicle. "Time's up," he announced with a hard look at Bobby.

Tuck gave his hand a so-long squeeze before Bobby got up to leave.

Klyve watched until Bobby made it out of the ICU area. Then he turned a hard glare on Tuck. "What the fuck, dude?"

"Not that it's any of your business, but Bobby is my boyfriend."

Klyve stepped closer. "That's pretty damn obvious. But what about the short guy who was here before him?"

Tuck bristled. "I don't hafta explain myself to you."

"No, you certainly don't," Klyve said as he walked around to the right side of the bed and gingerly peeked inside the bandages. "But I've got enough to deal with here just doing my job. I'm not runnin' interference for ya too, tryin' to keep your boyfriends separated."

"Didn't ask you to." Tuck watched him carefully examine his hand. "How bad?"

"Looking *much* better. Barring necrosis, you've got at least two more surgeries to look forward to." He carefully rewrapped the hand. "You've got a long road ahead, dude."

"Tuck. Call me Tuck."

"Okay, Tuck. I'm Klyve," he said as he got the chart and made more notes. "Any *more* boyfriends I need to know about?"

Tuck sighed as he sank back into the bed. "No, but ya might wanna be on the lookout for my brother. I expect he'll show up soon."

"You don't want him in here?"

"Oh, I do. But he can get a bit… worked up."

"I'll keep that in mind." Klyve put away the chart and left.

Closing his eyes, Tuck nestled back into the bed.

GERTIE glanced at her watch as Bobby emerged from the ICU area. Then she stood up. "I need to get back." She looked over at Odis. "You boys should come along too. Eat some supper and come back in the mornin'."

Odis shook his head. Bobby stepped up to him and put his hand on his shoulder. "Odie, we should at least go eat. We can come back a little later."

"Yer gonna insist, ain't ya," Odis said with resignation.

"We'll meet ya there," Gertie told them as she and John went to the elevator.

"It wouldn't do any good for Tuck to see you all run-down, now would it?"

"Oh. Okay." Odis stood up. "Can we make a quick detour first?"

"I guess. Where to?" Bobby asked as they headed for the elevator, but Odis pulled on his arm and led him to the stairwell.

"It's only one floor. Who knows how long we'll hafta wait," he explained as they started down the concrete steps of the emergency stairwell. "I gotta see. Gotta see how bad the house is. It's all I've been thinkin' about."

"Yeah, okay," Bobby agreed as they exited the stairwell and headed to the front doors.

They didn't talk much on the drive out to Odis's property, a quiet exhaustion draining away their words. The fire damage became obvious as they reached the country roads on the west side of town. Black-and-gray swirly smears marred the barren rocky moon surface of a landscape.

When Odis pulled up to the gate, Bobby could see—or rather not see—the garage ahead. The building's stump of charred remains etched across the ground with dark blueprint marker lines, as if declaring "build here."

Bobby opened the gate, and Odis waited for him to get back in the El Camino before he pulled ahead. He looked over to the left as they rolled slowly down the driveway. With the camouflage of grass and bushes burned away, the outlines of the concrete roof stood out in a discolored gray.

Odis parked and they quietly walked down the steps. Odis brushed aside the scattered glass shards from the sconce lights with his sole of his shoe as they descended deeper. At the bottom step, Odis paused, closing his eyes and taking a deep breath. "It's only stuff," he whispered before opening his eyes, reaching beside him and grabbing Bobby's hand, then moving forward again.

The singed patio area looked like a dusty black chalkboard. They glanced over it. The large pane of picture-window glass nearest the stairs had a huge spiderweb crack close to the top, the safety glass drooping into a strange and beautifully warped and fused blob, like a tired eye trying to blink. The second windowpane had one long gash of a crack diagonally near the middle, but it held together. The rest of the windows just looked dirty. The inside appeared untouched.

Odis smiled. "I'll be damned."

"Yeah," Bobby agreed. They quickly stepped up, opened the sliding door, then walked inside.

Bobby coughed at the stale lingering smoke in the air. A startled bird flew up from its new roost on one of the wrought iron chairs and banged into the glass. They managed to herd it out through the open sliding door.

"Well, it needs a good cleaning," Odis said, glancing toward the black face of the microwave. "And the power's out."

Bobby nodded in agreement. The only real damage he spotted was the red rubbery blob that once had been a toy ball puddled near the glass wall. The heat didn't seem to have penetrated very far past the glass.

Odis pulled him toward the sleeping area. "Grab yer shit while I get some clothes." As Odis dragged out a large duffel and stuffed it with the contents of his dresser, Bobby zipped up his suitcase, then sealed up the garment bag hanging on the bathroom door.

Odis picked up his duffel and dragged it to the kitchen area. He disappeared into the laundry room and returned a moment later with a sheet of poster board and some duct tape. Bobby watched him drag a wrought iron chair from the table set to the window and tape the poster board over the opening in the first pane of glass. "Not watertight, but it'll keep the damn birds out," Odis commented as he worked.

After covering the window, Odis grabbed Bobby by the arm and led him out. "I got yer box," Odis said as Bobby followed him up the stairs and back to the car.

Odis turned the car around and pulled out of the driveway, not bothering to close the gate as they left. He smiled at Bobby as they cruised down the road, the dimming light of dusk lending even more of a feeling of moonscape to the blackened earth around them. Odis glanced over. "I'm so relieved. We can get it all fixed up and be back in before middle of next week, I bet."

Bobby nodded. "I'm kinda surprised, but I guess I shouldn't be, since it's concrete and all."

Odis nodded. "I designed it with tornadoes in mind. Wanted to make sure it would hold up if one blew through. Never even thought about a grass fire, though. I'll hafta check the roof carefully, make sure the concrete didn't crack anywhere from the heat. It'll hafta be patched and sealed up right away if there are any cracks," he thought aloud as they neared the main road.

A few minutes later, they stepped into the B and B, welcomed by the wonderful aromas of baking bread and spicy roasted meat. They found John already sitting at the dining table and Gertie setting out a full spread. A huge rack of lamb filled up the center of the table, surrounded by a loaf of fresh bread and numerous vegetables.

Odis dropped his duffel in the hallway. "Geez, Gertie, how many people we feedin'?" he asked with a chuckle.

Bobby set down his suitcase in the hall and draped the garment bag over one of the chairs before joining them in the dining room.

Gertie smiled at the joviality in Odis's voice and pointed at the chairs. "Don't know fer sure. Told Alice and Gina to drop by. Don't know if they will or not. Wanda Travie, Carl's widow, is supposed to be comin' by later." Gertie glanced at the suitcases in the hall. "I take it ya went by the house?"

The scent of the perfectly seared lamb made Bobby's mouth water as he sat down.

Nodding, Odis approached the dining table. "Yep, and it's still there. Just some broken windows is all. Easy to fix. Garage burnt up, though." He chuckled as he looked over the spread of food. "Just like Mamma— always cook when ya get worried."

"Shut up and eat," Gertie said as she served out sliced rib sections onto the waiting men's plates.

Bobby grabbed some of the mashed potatoes and green beans as the door buzzed. Gertie waved at Alice to come in.

She looked like an older and slightly mousier version of Gina. "Smells heavenly," she complimented while taking a seat next to Gertie.

"Gina not comin'?" Gertie asked, picking up a clean plate from the stack and handing it to Alice.

"Nah, she wanted ta peek in on Tuck and hang around for Hawk ta wake up. Doc said Hawk's fine, just ornery, as normal. So they're sendin' him home."

Gertie looked over at Odis, glad to see how he dug into the meat and corn on the cob with gusto. "Then ya boys might wanna eat fast and run back. Odie can help handle Hawk, if he's in a mood."

Odis and Bobby nodded in agreement as they devoured their dinners.

CHAPTER
Twenty-One

ONCE back at the hospital, they found Gina in the ER, still waiting for Hawk to wake up. He was expected to be out another thirty minutes, so Bobby and Odis ran back upstairs to squeeze in a visit with Tuck. Bobby motioned for Odis to take the lead. "You go in first. That way, you can be waiting here in the hall if Hawk shows up early."

"Okay," Odis agreed, and he went in. He didn't see a nurse anywhere, so he rushed right into Tuck's room. "You awake, bonehead?" he called out while pushing open the door.

Tuck grinned and blinked over at the doorway. "Am now, asshole."

"Good. I heard somewhere ya can't heal when ya sleep 'cause yer not awake to think about it," Odis teased as he approached the left side of the bed and kissed Tuck.

After a nice moment of sharing lips, Tuck pulled away. "And where'd ya hear nonsense like that?"

Odis shrugged. "One of those fundamentalist channels. Twenty Thousand Club, I think. The ones that don't believe in hospitals or shit."

Tuck chuckled. "Oh, I'm sure they have sound medical advice, then. Maybe you should ask Klyve about that next time he's by."

"Klyve? Oh, is that the snippy nurse?"

Tuck nodded. "He's actually a good guy, just seems really tired."

Odis took time to glance around the space. He looked curiously at Tuck. "I don't see any kind of bathroom nearby," he said with a questioning tone.

"Catheter," Tuck replied. "They don't want me movin' around 'til they get a cast on my hand."

Odis scowled and reflexively covered his groin with his hand. "Doesn't that hurt?"

"I don't know. Wasn't awake when they put it in. Can't be too bad, though, since sounding is such a hot activity."

"*Sounding?*"

Tuck chuckled. "I ferget yer a slow straight man sometimes. It's puttin' things down the urethra for pleasure."

"Hey," Odis said as he punched at Tuck's arm. "Who says I'm slow? I'm just not up on all this jargon." Odis turned curious. "What kinds of things?"

"Thin metal or plastic rods. Look it up on the Internet if ya really wanna know more."

"I will," Odis said firmly. "Have *you* ever done that?"

"No sex talk right now, okay? Seein' how's I'm stuck here like this, with no privacy, even."

"Sure, sorry," Odis agreed. "But you brought it up. I should go," he said with a hand squeeze. "Bobby's waitin' his turn, and just so ya know, Hawk's due awake any time now."

Tuck tried to smile peacefully. "Good to know."

Odis gave him a quick kiss and left. "All yours, stud," he said a minute later as he passed Bobby and sat down on the maroon couch.

Bobby handed him his cell phone and went into the ICU. He grinned back at Tuck as he slipped in the door. "Hey," he said warmly.

"Hey, stud," Tuck answered as Bobby sidled up to the bed. They kissed. "He looks better."

"We had some dinner at Gertie's."

"Damn, makin' me jealous. Don't even tell me what she made."

"Okay, I won't, then." Bobby glanced around at all the pinging and beeping machinery. "Why do they have you hooked up to all this junk?"

"Who knows?" Tuck said with a shrug. "I can't even tell what half the shit's for."

"You doing okay?"

"Sure. Mostly just bored. They won't let me even stand up out of bed."

"Sorry," Bobby said with a comforting hand pat. "Prob'ly won't get better anytime soon." Bobby heard a familiar grumbling voice out in the hallway and felt Tuck tense up under his caress.

"Loki's nuts, here we go," Tuck quietly mumbled.

"Should I—"

Tuck grabbed his hand. "You stay right here."

ODIS blocked the door to the ICU wing with one hand planted on each side of the doorframe, trying his best to look formidable as he stood up to the six-foot-three Viking warrior. "No. Bobby's already back there. Only one at a time."

Hawk scowled. "Don't feed me bullshit, Odie. I'll rip you in two if you don't get outta my way."

Klyve stepped up behind Odis holding a squared-off plastic gun. "You heard the little guy. Back up to the couch."

"And who the fuck are you?" Hawk glowered down, keeping his eyes on the gun in the nurse's hand as he shifted slowly to the right.

"I could ask you the same fuckin' question," Klyve replied. "But all *you* need to know is I'm the one in charge of keeping the peace here."

Hawk took another slow step to the right, watching Klyve wielding what looked like a Taser as he stepped forward. Hawk studied his movements, learning his tells.

"Couch," Klyve repeated as he motioned with the gun. "Not only am I the senior nurse on this floor, I'm also a Vartlett. Do I need to call my cousin Charlie?"

"No." Hawk took another step back and relaxed his shoulders. "No need to bring Mayor Vartlett in on this."

"Didn't think so. Now, have a seat and wait your turn." Klyve looked at Hawk's bare feet and the haphazardly tucked hospital gown he wore as a shirt with his jeans. "Before I change my mind and start calling all the stations to find out where you escaped from."

As Hawk took two steps back toward the couch, the elevator door opened with a ding and Gina rushed up. "Hawk!" she yelled. "They didn't say you could leave yet."

Hawk perched on the edge of the couch. "I'm not leavin' 'til I see my brother."

"And you're not gettin' anywhere near him until you calm down," Klyve said firmly. "Tuck and the other patients need a quiet environment."

Gina glared at her husband as she sat down beside him.

"Okay," Hawk said.

Klyve glanced over at Odis. "If you can behave, I'll let the little guy take you back, but only for five minutes. I have to check him for rounds soon."

Hawk stood up and nodded.

"I didn't hear you."

"Okay," Hawk agreed aloud. "Five minutes. Got it."

Klyve stepped back into the ICU and let Odis and Hawk pass. "Behave," he said, waving the gun at Hawk as he stepped by.

Odis led him into room two. "Ya got a visitor," he announced as Hawk walked in.

Hawk froze in the doorway, taking in the sight of all the busy machinery. He saw the mummy-wrapped hand, then saw Tuck's left hand in Bobby's. His brow furrowed, etched with heavy concern. "You okay, midget?" he asked, trying to keep his voice normal.

Odis glared at the slur, but Hawk was looking right at Tuck and didn't notice.

"Yeah, I'm fine," Tuck told him. "Was that *you* makin' all that ruckus in the hallway?"

Hawk dropped his gaze. "Sorry. I was kinda pissed nobody told me ya was here."

"You upset people when ya carry on like that," Tuck chastised as he pulled his hand away from Bobby and held it out. "Ya gonna hug me? Or just stand there lookin' stupid?"

Bobby stepped over to make room for the big man to get close. Hawk very gingerly put his arms around Tuck and lightly squeezed before pulling back. "What happened to your hand?"

Tuck frowned as if he wasn't sure how to answer. "Freezer landed on it," he finally said.

"Fuck," Hawk muttered. "Which one was it? I'll go shoot it for you."

"Ya idiot." Tuck chuckled. "No need for that." He patted Hawk's arm. "You better get back downstairs before they start lookin' for ya."

"Okay," Hawk said, his eyes glued to the bundled wrappings on Tuck's hand.

Odis stepped up and grabbed the billowy side of Hawk's gown-shirt. "Let's hurry, before Klyve throws ya out." He pulled Hawk back toward the door and started dragging him out.

"I'll come back later," Hawk promised.

"In the morning."

"Okay, mornin'," Hawk agreed as he stepped out the door.

Tuck visibly exhaled when he saw his brother step out of the ICU into Gina's arms. "Sorry," he said to Bobby.

"Why are you apologizing?" Bobby asked as he held Tuck's hand again. "Hawk obviously loves you."

"He doesn't handle emotion well. Never has. He just growls and stomps around like a wild bear. It can be embarrassing."

"Better that than a brother who won't even look at you," Bobby replied.

Something in the tone of Bobby's voice grabbed Tuck's attention. It was just the slightest tremble—a quiet thing, easily unnoticed, that hinted Bobby was speaking from a place of painful experience.

Klyve came in before Tuck had a chance to ask about it. Walking to the charts, he threw a glance at Bobby. "Time's up."

"Okay." Bobby smiled at Tuck. "We'll be out in the waiting room. I'm trying, but I doubt I'll be able to drag Odis out again."

"See ya, stud."

After Bobby left, Klyve smirked over at Tuck. "That little guy of yours sure has some big-assed balls. Had to rescue him with a stapler." He went around to Tuck's right hand and slowly opened up the bandages.

"A *stapler*?" Tuck asked.

"Square plastic, gun shaped, looks like a Taser. I thought yer brother was gonna chew him up."

Tuck chuckled. "Odis is like one of those Jack Russell dogs. He fergets he's a half-pint."

Klyve carefully examined Tuck's fingers. "He'd have got his own blows in, I'm sure. But you tell that brother—"

"Hawk," Tuck told him.

"You tell Hawk if he ever acts like that again, he's not comin' back. I'll lock the door on his ass."

"He should be all right now that he knows I'm not dyin'."

Klyve nodded as he began rewrapping the hand.

"How is it?" Tuck asked.

"Doing well, I'd say. Good color. We can prob'ly throw a cast on it tomorrow, sad to say."

"Why sad?"

Klyve walked over the chart and made his notes. "Because you won't hafta be in ICU anymore. They'll put you in a regular room or maybe even throw ya out the door altogether."

"Oh."

After putting away the chart, Klyve looked at him. "It's not often I get guys I actually like hangin' out with around here."

Tuck just kind of half smiled, not sure how to take the compliment. He thought it might be nice to have Klyve over for a beer someday—it seemed like they could be good friends. Then he remembered about the house. "Shit."

"What?"

"Could ya send one back for a sec? I fergot to ask if they checked Odie's house. It's in the burn zone."

Klyve hesitated, then smiled slightly. "Let me finish my rounds first, and I will."

"Thanks," Tuck told him as he left.

AFTER finishing his rounds, Klyve returned to the central station to give the various room monitors a once-over. He glanced up toward the waiting room and saw Bobby and Odis on the couch. The two guys were cuddled up next to each other in the empty room in a strong embrace.

As Klyve stood up, something in his heart melted a little bit. He forgot all about being the tough nurse as he crossed the threshold of the ICU area and walked up to the men. Odis pulled away quickly when he realized someone was approaching. Klyve smiled. "Why don't you come back a minute. Tuck said there was somethin' he needed to ask about."

Bobby looked over at Odis. "You go."

"No," Klyve cut in. "Both of you. Hurry before I change my mind."

Both men jumped to their feet and followed Klyve back to room two. Klyve motioned at the door. "Hasta be quick, though. My relief comes in at nine, so ya gotta be out by then."

"Okay," Odis said as he walked in.

"Thanks," Bobby said and turned before the door closed.

Tuck grinned up at the sight of both of them coming in. They rushed to the left side of the bed and pushed up close as Tuck wrapped his long arm around both of them. "Hi, guys." They held the strangely awkward hug a minute before pulling back.

"Hey," Bobby said. "The nurse said you had a question?"

Tuck glanced at Odis, then looked back to Bobby. "The house. Did ya check the house yet?"

Odis nodded. "It held up. Just some cracked windows. The garage is a goner, though."

"Probably only take a couple of days to repair the windows," Bobby added. "The house can be fixed before you get out of here."

"Don't know about that," Tuck said with a smile. "Klyve said I'll prob'ly get a cast tomorrow, then I'm outta the ICU."

"Really?" Odis asked with enthusiasm.

"Really."

Bobby reached out and ran his hand through Tuck's hair. "And what about after that?"

"Not sure," Tuck admitted. "They're still bein' dodgy about answers."

Bobby nodded. "Still great news, though." He glanced over at the time stamp on the EKG monitor, which showed 2056. "We better go, Odie. Don't want the new nurse throwing us out."

Odis hugged Tuck's neck. "Get some sleep," he told Tuck as they left. "We're goin' back to the B and B."

Bobby threw him a kiss before the door closed.

"Good night, boys," Tuck called out after them. He settled back into the bed, relieved to see Odis in such good spirits. Maybe Tuck could fall asleep now, for just a few minutes.

HOURS later, the night nurse let herself into room two to do her rounds. Tuck didn't stir. He continued snoring softly in his bed. The nurse glanced over the monitors, checking for any abnormalities. Not finding any, she went to the right side of the bed and unwrapped some of the bandaging on the hand. The color looked good both on the skin and in the nail beds of each finger.

Glancing up to make sure Tuck was still asleep, the nurse retrieved the sensitivity reflex tool from her pocket. The small spiky wheel was affixed loosely inside the long handle, similar to a pizza cutter. The wheel spun like a miniature boot spur as the nurse ran the pointed spikes over the tip of Tuck's index finger. The finger jerked back slightly. Same for the second finger. When she ran the wheel over his ring finger, though, it didn't move. Also no response from the pinky finger.

She put the reflex tool back in her pocket and bandaged Tuck's hand again before making detailed notes in his chart. He still snored, unaware, as she let herself out.

TUCK fidgeted his legs in the bed when Klyve came in the next morning after shift change. "Please, can't I get up or somethin'?"

Klyve smirked as he set down the fresh pitcher of water on Tuck's nightstand. "Good mornin' to you too, sunshine." He checked over the monitors and reviewed the charts.

"Oh, mornin', Klyve," Tuck said once he remembered his manners. "I'm 'bout to go outta my mind with boredom. Can I at least get a TV or somethin'?"

"Maybe." Klyve tried not to show any concern as he read over the night nurse's notes. "Most of the people who visit me here aren't hardly conscious," Klyve said as he went around to the bandaged hand. "But we do have a roll-around set. I'll see about gettin' that TV in here for ya."

"Thank you."

After unwrapping Tuck's hand, Klyve examined it. "What's that time stamp on the EKG say?" he asked, getting Tuck to turn his head away.

"It says 9:11."

After pinching Tuck's pinky slightly with his fingernails, Klyve was disappointed to see no reaction. He had been hoping the night nurse might be wrong. He wrapped the hand up again. "Behave yourself and I'll be back soon."

"I'll try," Tuck grumbled.

Klyve nodded with a smile as he left room two, but it quickly fell off his face as he rushed over to the monitoring station. With it being Sunday morning and all, he might have a tough time getting hold of Tuck's doctor. That thought didn't slow him any as he grabbed for the phone.

ODIS slipped in not long after Klyve left. "Mornin', bonehead."

"Hey." Tuck's face lit up with a grin. "Great to see ya, Odie. Did ya happen to see a TV in that hallway?" he asked as Odis approached the bed and kissed him.

"No. Was I supposed ta?"

"Hopin', maybe," Tuck replied. "Klyve said he'd see about gettin' one."

"Oh. I didn't see Klyve out there. Maybe that's what he's doin'."

Tuck looked over Odis. "At least ya got some sleep, looks like."

"Yep, and I even ate some breakfast."

"Asshole," Tuck grumbled. "They still haven't fed me yet."

"Yer kidding, right?"

"Well, they have these protein bar things that are as bad as army rations, but no *real* food."

Odis kissed his forehead. "I'll send Bobby in and see if I can't find Klyve and have a little talk with him about that."

"And the TV," Tuck added as Odis left.

He bounced his leg in the bed until Bobby arrived. "Hey, stud."

"Hey, Tuck," he said. He rushed up and smothered him with a kiss.

Tuck pulled him close and smelled the sandalwood shampoo in his hair. "Is the house really okay?" he asked when he pulled away and looked at Bobby for the truth.

"Oh yeah, just some broken windows. With the house being built like a concrete bunker, the fire couldn't really get at it."

"Good, good." Tuck tried to rise and peek out through the glass. "Where'd they go now?"

Bobby squeezed his hand. "Calm down. You're starting to sound like your brother."

"Oh fuck you, I am not," he said a little harshly. Hearing his own tone, he took a deep breath. "I'm just bored and want outta here."

"I know, but you have to get your cast first. So be nice to the hospital people."

"Yeah, yeah," Tuck agreed, pulling Bobby in for another kiss. The twitch in his groin caused a strange painful sensation that made him stop short.

Bobby nearly jumped back. "What's wrong?"

"Damn catheter," Tuck grumbled. "Guess I can't do any *real* kissing either."

"My, aren't we a grumpy Gus this morning."

Tuck scowled at him. "You would be too, endurin' all the shit I gotta deal with."

"Dial it down a little," Bobby said with calm sincerity. "I know all this must suck big-time, but don't take it out on everybody else."

Tuck dropped his gaze. "Right."

Bobby nodded. "I'm sure I can find Hawk's number. I'll call him in here and have him sit on you or something if you can't behave."

"Don't do that. I could do without all his drama again today."

"Okay. But I'm keeping it an option," Bobby threatened as he moved in close and hugged Tuck around the neck.

Tuck flinched again. "Maybe we shouldn't do that."

Bobby pulled back. "Sorry. We missed our threesome last night."

"Don't remind me. Did you and Odie?"

"No, we both pretty much passed out right after crawling into bed."

"Busy day?" Tuck asked sarcastically.

"Just a little. Odie's house almost burned down, and some bonehead went missing and scared us half to death."

"How long was I…?"

"Over four hours. They didn't tell you?"

"Nobody tells me shit here," Tuck grumbled, then paused for a deep breath. "Other than me and Hawk, I don't even know who else was even hurt."

"Josh and Humpty came in, but they didn't even stay overnight."

"Humpty? You mean Hampton?"

"Yes. Why can't I ever remember that guy's name?"

Tuck nodded. "Oh, I do remember Gertie mentioning them yesterday. Who else?"

Bobby shook his head. "Didn't hear of anybody else."

Pulling him closer, Tuck lowered his voice. "What exactly happened?"

"The only answer I've heard is 'we're still piecing it together'. So you'll hafta ask somebody else. I'm sure with the casualties, they'll do a thorough investigation."

"*Casualties?*" Tuck sat up and scowled. "Nobody ever fuckin' said *shit* about—who died?"

"Both the Thornson Brothers and Travis."

"Thursons," Tuck corrected. "And Travie, Carl Travie?"

Bobby nodded.

Tuck collapsed into the bed. "Oh Loki's nuts. That poor kid. He was only twenty-two. Just came on board less than a month ago, right out of the academy. Fuckin' shit."

Bobby gave his hand a comforting squeeze. "Sucks."

Tuck bowed his head. "How…?" he finally asked.

"He and the brothers were inside the kitchen, near where they think the explosion happened."

Tuck bolted upright. "*What?*" He gave Bobby a hard stare. "Did you say inside the house?"

"Yeah." Bobby nodded.

"Fuck no," Tuck barked. "This." His brow crinkled. "It isn't adding up." He looked over and saw the confusion on Bobby's face. He leaned forward and used the sheet and his finger as an imaginary whiteboard. "The house was basically a square." He traced one out as he explained the game plan. "Hawk and I were covering the back porch, on the east side." He indicated it with his finger. "Josh and Hampton were covering the south windows. Carl and one of the DEA guys were on the north bedroom windows. The rest were going to burst in the front door at the west with a surprise ambush."

Bobby nodded that he understood so far.

"So how did Carl end up *inside* the house? And how'd he even *get* there? He didn't slip by Hawk and me, I can guarantee that. And it seems unlikely he could have gotten past the gang of officers at the front door."

"What about the DEA guy on the north side with him? Maybe he knows something."

"Shit, I don't even remember a name. I was still kinda ticked off about getting dragged out and wasn't really paying attention."

"I'm sure somebody knows who it was," Bobby offered. "Who drew up the game plan?"

Tuck nodded. "Fenton. I *need* to talk ta Fenton." He glanced over at Bobby. "Did ya bring yer cell phone in?"

Bobby shook his head. "Left it in the car. They have a real bug about letting them back here."

Tuck glanced around but didn't see any pens or paper. "Shit. Check the nurse's station?"

Bobby slipped out and came back a minute later with a Post-it pad and a pen.

Tuck took them and scratched out a number. "Please, go call him now. I need to know what in Valhalla's goin' on."

"I'm sure they also realize something's fishy." Bobby hated seeing that look of frustration on Tuck's face. "I'll go call right now." Bobby gave him a quick kiss before leaving.

"Thanks." Tuck leaned back and tried to ignore all the beeping noises and relax.

CHAPTER
Twenty-Two

ON HIS way out of the ICU, Bobby couldn't help but notice the tall, thin guy pacing around the waiting room. The rough-looking tattoo-covered man appeared to be about his age. He paced quickly back and forth like he was trying to work up the energy to go inside. Bobby gave him a nod. "You here to visit somebody?"

The biker guy smirked. "Tryin' to," he admitted. "I just don't know if I wanna see how bad it is."

Bobby gave him a warm smile. "Trust me, not knowing can lead to imagining things much worse than they really are. Just take a deep breath and go in."

"Okay," the biker guy said. "I will."

Bobby headed for the stairwell as the guy took a breath and walked into the ICU.

"That was fast," Tuck said as the door opened. He looked over, but it wasn't Bobby squirming in the doorway. "What the fuck?"

"Hey, Tuck," Vic said, stepping the rest of the way into the cubicle. "I heard ya had an accident."

Tuck scowled. "Ya make it sound like I peed on the carpet." He threw Vic a hard look. "What are ya doin' here, Vic?"

"Dude," Vic said as he put his hands up defensively, "I came to visit a friend in the hospital. We *are* still friends, right?"

Tuck was skeptical but said, "Sure."

Vic stepped closer, looking over Tuck. "What all happened?"

"What did ya hear?"

"Don't be that way, Tuck," Vic scolded as he moved closer. "Never could give a straight answer."

"Meth lab explosion."

"Well, ya don't look *too* bad off," Vic said as he sat on the left edge of the bed. "It didn't hurt yer pretty face," he said as he reached out for Tuck's cheek.

Tuck pulled back. "I'm not fuckin' pretty. And don't touch me."

"Sorry," Vic whined, dragging out the word and sounding less than sincere. "Thought ya'd be happy to see a friend."

Tuck bit his tongue when the door opened again. He looked up to see Odis, who froze when he saw the guy sitting on the bed. "Hey, Odie," Tuck said cheerfully. "This is Vic."

Vic turned around and studied him. "So yer the little Odie I've heard so damn much about."

"And you must be the asshole Tuck dumped," Odis said as he stepped around the man. He pushed him back to lean in and kiss Tuck.

Vic blinked at them. "Really, now, little straight man. Who do you think yer foolin'?"

Before he could answer, the door opened again. Bobby stepped in about halfway. "How rude. I turn my back for one minute, and you guys start without me," he joked, looking over at the biker guy on the bed.

"And who the fuck are you?" Vic bristled as he stood to his feet.

"I'm Bobby Lane." Glancing over at Tuck, he questioned with his eyes.

"We're past room capacity," Tuck announced with an edge in his voice. "Time to leave, Vic."

Bobby glared over at Vic. "Sounds like a great idea. I'll see you out," he said in a hard tone.

"So much for bein' nice. Fuck you, Tuck," Vic barked out as he headed for the door.

"Those days are over," Tuck yelled back. "I've got new boyfriends now."

Bobby nudged Vic on the shoulder when he paused in the doorway. Vic turned back and said, "Yeah, right. Yer just tryin' to fuck with my head."

Odis glared at the door as they left. "I'll kick his ass if he comes back," he promised Tuck as he hugged his neck.

Tuck chuckled. "I can handle Vic," he said before kissing Odis.

As Vic walked out the ICU area, Bobby stomped right behind him.

Vic turned when they got to the hallway. "I don't know what kinda game y'all's playin', but if ya really *are* his boyfriend now, better enjoy it while ya can."

"Keep moving. Elevator's over there." Bobby gave his shoulder another hard nudge.

Vic started down the hall. "You wait. You'll find out how selfish he is soon enough."

Bobby nearly laughed. Maybe Vic knew a few more things about Tuck than he did, but Bobby had never seen or heard *anything* to make him think of Tuck as selfish. If anything, he had shown himself to be more of a self-sacrificing kind of man. "If you really think that, you don't know a damn thing about Tuck."

"Oh, I do. Especially in bed." Vic stepped into the elevator. "Just wait, you'll find out," he called out as the doors closed in his face.

Bobby just shook his head and went back to room two. He walked in and sat on the bed next to Odis. "You won't believe what that asshole said."

Odis glanced over curiously. "What?"

"He called Tuck selfish," he said and chuckled along with Odis. They both stopped when they looked over and saw the hurt expression on Tuck's face. "Sorry to laugh, Tuck. I know it's not true."

Tuck peered from Odis to Bobby, trying to decide how much to divulge. He quickly decided to be honest. "Well, from *his* side, I guess it's true."

Odis frowned in disbelief. "What do you mean?"

"Vic—he wanted to do things I wanted no part of. I refused to help him."

"What things?" Bobby asked pointedly.

"He liked—he wanted me to choke him while we did it." Tuck dropped his gaze as he spoke. The words seemed distasteful for him to even say.

Odis gaped like a fish. "What the fuck?"

"Erotic asphyxiation," Bobby explained. "Lack of oxygen until you pass out, hopefully right at the point of orgasm."

"Seriously?" Odis gasped. "People actually *do* that?" He glanced over at Tuck. "How do they keep from killing themselves?"

Tuck shrugged. "Sometimes they don't."

"Shit," Odis spit out. "Just when I thought I'd heard of every kind of thing there is out there, out pops another one." He got to his feet. "And yer not selfish for sayin' no to something that made you uncomfortable."

Tuck looked over at Bobby, questioning with his eyes.

Ignoring Odis as he paced around, Bobby wobbled his head. "Fenton wouldn't say anything to me. Promised to come by later."

Tuck nodded he understood. They all turned when the door opened. Odis bristled, getting ready to kick ass, but it was only Klyve. "Out," he said when he saw both guys inside. He turned to Tuck. "Doc's coming by in a minute."

"What about my TV?" Tuck whined like a three-year-old.

Klyve sighed exasperatedly. "Sorry, forgot," he said as he closed the door behind Bobby and followed them. "And the one-at-a-time rule applies unless ya ask me first," he scolded the men as he herded them to the waiting room.

"Sorry," Odis apologized.

Klyve smiled. "Doctor's coming by to look at his hand. Go downstairs and grab some lunch or somethin', it might be a while."

"Okay." Bobby nodded. With a gentle nudge on the shoulder, he steered Odis toward the stairs.

Klyve turned and went back to the ICU as the other men went down the hall.

Odis seemed to breathe heavily as they entered the stairwell. He moved quickly ahead of Bobby down the first half, rounded the central landing, and made it halfway down the second half of stairs before he seemed to wobble. "Shit," he groaned as he froze and clutched at the railing.

"You okay?" Bobby stopped beside him, noticing the way Odis clung tightly at the metal bar with both hands.

Odis wobbled again and his eyes glazed over. "I'm not fee—" Odis said as he lost his grip on the railing and slid back. Bobby jumped forward and caught him as he fell.

"Odis!" Bobby yelled as he tried to stand him on rubbery legs. "Shit," Bobby hissed. He got his arms under Odis's armpits and dragged him down the rest of the stairs. He somehow managed to open the stairwell door without dropping Odis and mostly carried him out into the hall. "Help!" he yelled out, but with a quick glance, Bobby saw only a vacant hallway. But he did see an empty wheelchair near a doorway a bit farther down the hall.

"Loud voice," Odis whispered as Bobby carried the rag-doll-limp Odis to the chair and set him in it. He pushed the chair as fast as he dared toward the ER area.

"Help!" Bobby yelled out again as he approached the ER.

A nurse came up when she saw the wheelchair. "What happened?" she asked as she kneeled down and looked at Odis while grabbing his wrist.

"We were coming down the stairs, and it looked like he got dizzy," Bobby explained as another nurse rushed up and started waving a flashlight around in Odis's face. "He collapsed and hasn't been coherent since."

The first nurse stood. "Weak pulse," she said, grabbing the chair handles from Bobby.

Nurse number two announced, "Unresponsive pupils," before looking at Bobby. "Is he on any medications?" She grabbed Bobby's arm and led him to the ER station as nurse number one whisked Odis toward the curtained cubicles.

Bobby shook his head. "He *was* on some things, but he stopped taking them last week."

"Any idea what they were?"

Bobby shook his head again. "Arthritis stuff. I don't know exactly."

"Name," the nurse asked when she got to the computer.

"Odis Tyler Vorleik," he told her.

"O-T?"

"No. O, D as in dog, I, S." While she typed, he spelled the last name also. Bobby read her name, Evie, off of the Velcro-adhered patch on her chest as she peered over the computer screen and hit a few keys.

"Find it?" Bobby asked.

"Yeah," Evie said as she reached for the phone and dialed a number she read off the screen. "Why don't you have a seat?"

Bobby ignored her suggestion and ran to the curtains. He found two nurses with Odis, who was now stretched out on the bed with a clothespin clip thing attached to his thumb and one of the nurses using a blood pressure cuff on his arm. "Out," nurse number one said as she body-blocked Bobby from stepping near the bed.

"How is he?"

"Out," she repeated. "Call his family."

Shit. It must *be bad if they want me to call.* Bobby reached down to his pocket. He'd absently slipped the phone in after making that call for Tuck earlier. At least he wouldn't have to run back to the car first. He pulled out the phone as he walked to the row of plastic chairs and dialed the B and B.

UPSTAIRS, the doctor arrived at Tuck's room. "Hello," he said, reading the chart from the bed, "Mr. Krickson. You feeling better today?"

Tuck nodded apprehensively. "Do I know you?"

"Sort of." The young doctor moved around the bed to Tuck's right side. "I'm the ortho who patched up your hand yesterday. Dr. Grinboe."

"Hello." Tuck nodded with more feeling. "You gonna put my cast on?"

The doctor slowly unwrapped the bandages until all of Tuck's hand was revealed. Klyve stepped into the room and nodded to the doctor as he handed him some kind of X-ray printouts. After looking at the pictures briefly, Dr. Grinboe tapped slightly at the knuckle joining Tuck's index finger to his palm. "Does this hurt?"

"Not pain, exactly," Tuck replied. "More like, it's not totally happy about getting poked at."

"Scale of one to ten?"

"One. One and a half, maybe."

The doctor moved his finger over to the pinky knuckle. "And this?" He pushed, then applied more pressure.

"Nothing?" Tuck tried to sit up, but the slight rotation to his wrist when he moved changed the angle of his palm and made him wince. "That's not right, is it?" he asked, realizing how stupid the question was as the words left his mouth.

The doctor studied the printouts more closely. "No," he finally admitted. He turned back to the hand, very delicately running his finger across the metacarpal bones near the wrist, feeling for the pins. Then he turned back to the scans. "It's one of two things," he explained as he set down the pictures before looking straight into Tuck's face. "Either you suffered some nerve damage from the initial injury, or some of the hardware we put in yesterday is pinching or blocking nerves."

"You gonna be able to do an MRI or somethin' and figure out which?"

The doctor paled visibly when Tuck mentioned an MRI. "No. With the metal in your hand, we can't let you anywhere near a magnetic machine. And that wouldn't be able to tell us much anyway." He looked back at the hand. "I could just throw a cast on it and reexamine it in six weeks, but frankly, I'm concerned it *is* the hardware. Leaving this unattended that long could cause further serious damage."

"Shit," Tuck muttered.

The doctor sat up and looked right at Tuck again. "I think our only viable option is to go back in." He studied Tuck as he continued. "If we go in local, I can remove the pins and see how much nerve traffic is restored."

"What do you mean?"

"You stay awake so you can talk to us. We just numb up the hand with some shots."

The doctor looked a little miffed when Tuck turned to Klyve. "That sound right to you?"

"Oh yes." Klyve nodded. "Best all around, I think." He turned to Dr. Grinboe. "When are we talkin'?"

"ASAP," he replied. "As soon as I can book an OR."

Tuck tried to peek out of the glass at the waiting room, then looked to Klyve.

Klyve looked out the doorway before shaking his head. "I'll let them know when they get back."

Tuck turned back to Dr. Grinboe. "Okay, then, let's do it."

BOBBY paced the short area in front of the plastic chairs. Gertie was on the way, but he couldn't tell her much over the phone because they still wouldn't let him back to Odis's curtain or tell him anything about his condition. He paced another length before frustration drove him back to the ER station.

Evie didn't even look up. "Nothing's changed in the last ten minutes. Dr. Murphy should be here any time now."

"Is he conscious? When can I see him?"

She looked up, trying to hold a mask of patience on her face. "Go. Have a seat. I'll let ya know the second anything happens." Evie pointed to the chairs. "Now."

Drooping with resignation, Bobby walked back to the row of plastic chairs, but he didn't sit down. He glanced over to the hallway. Gertie hadn't arrived yet, but a guy, about Bobby's size and in his midthirties, wandered around near the cafeteria. The guy glanced over and saw Bobby looking at him. As recognition showed in his eyes, he hurried down the hall.

Oh great, another fan to deal with.

When the guy approached, Bobby thought his horseshoe mustache looked out of place without a complementary cowboy hat on his head. "Are you Bobby Lane?"

"Yes," Bobby said with his hands clasped in front of his chest.

"I'm Billy," the guy told him as he offered his hand for a shake. "You called me earlier?"

"Fenton?"

"Yep, Billy Fenton."

Bobby shook his hand. "Tuck's upstairs in ICU, if you came to see him."

Billy shook his head. "Was just up there. They said he was goin' back into surgery, so I was tryin' to find ya. Why you waitin' in the ER?"

"*Surgery?*" Bobby squawked. "When?"

"Don't know, man. Thought maybe you might know."

"Shit!" Bobby spat as he looked toward the curtains. "Fucking shit." He ran back over to the ER station. "Can you look up Tucker Krickson and find out why he's in surgery again?"

Evie started to say something as she looked up, but seeing his desperation, she went to the computer without further protest. "Spell it?"

Bobby spelled out the name for Evie as he fidgeted against the counter. Billy stepped up beside him.

"He's an ICU patient?" She looked up to see Bobby nod. "Just says 'follow-up'. No details or ETA posted."

"Shit," Bobby nearly howled. This had started out such a good day, but now it felt as if a demon of disasters was running around destroying everything. He refrained from kicking the counter and tromped back to the chairs. He paced the length in front of the seats, then sat down, trying to force himself to calm before he exploded and punched something. Part of his frustration even turned to Nathan. If he was such a fucking great psychic, why hadn't he seen any of this shit coming?

"Hey, Billy," he heard Gertie's voice say. "What'cha doin' here?"

"Came in to see Tuck, but he's in surgery, so I came to find Bobby."

"*What*? Surgery? Since *when*?" Gertie squealed, glaring over at Bobby.

"Don't ask me," Bobby said as he help up his hands in defense. "I just found out about it."

"Well, butter my cracker," Gertie said. "What about Odis?"

"No news. At least, they won't tell *me* anything. You could try," Bobby told her as he jerked his head toward the ER station. Then he jumped to his feet. "While you do that, I'll run upstairs and see if I can get any info on Tuck."

Gertie nodded as she headed toward the counter.

Bobby went down the hall to the stairs. When he entered the stairwell, he waited until the door closed behind him. Then he turned and kicked at the metal doorframe as he let out a frustrated howl. "Fuck," he yelled. *This just isn't fair*, he felt like screaming. *We made it through all that shit yesterday, and everything seemed to be okay this morning. Wasn't that enough? Why more of this shit?* He took a deep breath and then charged up the stairs.

As he headed toward the ICU, Klyve ran up as soon as he saw him. "Where you been? I had them page you in the cafeter—"

"Tuck's in surgery?" Bobby asked, cutting him off.

"Yeah. Doc thinks the pins are pinching nerves, and he wants to reposition them. Tuck agreed."

"We never made it to the cafeteria. Odis is in the ER and they won't tell me shit."

"*ER?*" Klyve nearly gasped. "How'd that happen?" He lightly grasped Bobby by the shoulder and led him to the ICU station.

"We took the stairs and he got dizzy and collapsed on the way down. I dragged him to the ER."

Klyve pointed to a chair for Bobby to sit in and went to the computer. "Last name?"

Bobby spelled the name, and Klyve soon had his details pulled up. Klyve read over the screen and then looked over, asking, "Did he eat breakfast?"

"Yeah, but just some toast, I think."

"Well, that's not really a breakfast. Looking at the physical stats, I'd guess his blood sugar and blood pressure just bottomed out at the same time, which they're treating him for. It shows his doctor's there, so we should know more soon."

As Bobby listened, he began to relax a little. "Okay. Now what about Tuck?"

Klyve looked over at him. "He's having some nerve problems in the hand. The two outside fingers have no tactile feeling. Let's hope it's the pins." He turned back to the monitors. "I need to make rounds, but stay here a minute."

"Okay," Bobby agreed as Klyve gathered up a clipboard and went to room three.

Bobby looked over at the banks of monitors but couldn't make heads or tails of all the busy stats scrolling and flashing across. It might as well have been the control station of some alien space vehicle. He hated sitting here waiting, doing nothing. The thought of going back downstairs to the ER crossed his mind, but he'd told Klyve he would stay put, and he'd probably just do more waiting down there anyway. He spit out an exasperated sigh.

Klyve returned and motioned for Bobby to follow. He led them to a storage closet. "Help me with this," he asked as he went in and wheeled around a metal cart with a large TV mounted on it. Bobby helped him steer it out of the closet, and they wheeled it to the front of room two. "Tuck's been asking about a TV. This will make him happy. Let's just leave it here 'til he gets settled back in the room." He led Bobby back to the ICU station.

Bobby sat down again. "How long is Tuck gonna be in surgery?"

"Don't know. Prob'ly two hours, at least," Klyve said as he took the larger seat. He rolled it over closer to Bobby and asked in a quieter voice, "I know it's none of my business, but I'm just gettin' really curious. What's the deal with you three?"

"I wish I had a good answer for that," Bobby replied. "This three-way thing just kinda happened Friday night."

"So they were a couple, then you got involved?"

"No, not really. They knew each other, kinda pals since forever, but I met Odis first and we kinda had a thing. Then I met Tuck and it got more complicated."

Klyve looked over the monitors. "And you just met Tuck Friday?"

"Yeah. He picked me up at the airport."

"Well, shit," Klyve said. "If that doesn't just make me all kinds of jealous. I can't even find *one* boyfriend, and you've gone and got two."

"Sorry." Bobby couldn't really think of anything else to say.

"At least it gives me hope to keep tryin'," Klyve said with a shrug. "And you really only met him two days ago?"

"Yeah. Is that so hard to believe?"

"I've seen a lot of patients and their visitors in and out of here. The comradery between ya guys when ya were goin' at it yesterday seemed more like people who've known each other a while. A *long* while. It's just a little unusual."

"Oh," Bobby replied. "I did have a psychic say we were supposed to be together, if that makes any difference."

"Psychic?" Klyve asked as something on the monitors caught his attention. "Hold that thought." He jumped up and rushed to room four.

He returned a moment later, shaking his head. "Just shifted over and pulled off one of the leads," he explained to Bobby as he sat down again. "Now what's this about a psychic?"

Bobby took a deep breath. He spent the next thirty minutes explaining to Klyve all about Nathan and the weirdness since October.

"Damn," was all Klyve could reply. "That Nathan must have really loved you if he spent his last days playing cupid for your future."

Bobby shook his head. "I don't know about that. I'm still kinda pissed about all the damn secrets he kept."

"Hm." Klyve pondered. "Haven't ya ever told a little white lie?"

"Of course," Bobby admitted.

"Well, this is just a bigger version of that, isn't it? He wasn't tryin' to be deceitful or hurtful by not mentioning things, or tryin' to cover up any transgressions." Klyve nodded at his own words. "Just a little white lie to keep the peace. Maybe you should try lookin' at it *that* way."

Bobby started to reply, but his cell phone rang. He fished it out of his pocket and saw an unknown number. "Hello?" he answered tentatively.

"Bobby, you still in ICU?" Gertie asked. "Odis is awake now. Come on down if ya want."

"Okay, be there in a minute," Bobby answered before hanging up. "Odis," he explained to Klyve.

"What's your number? I can call when Tuck gets back."

Bobby gave him the number, then got up and headed for the stairs.

CHAPTER
Twenty-Three

BOBBY didn't see Gertie or anyone when he returned to the ER, so he went to the curtained area where they had taken Odis. He found Gertie next to his bedside.

"Hey, stud," Odis said with a smile.

"What the hell, Odie?" Bobby asked.

"You were right," Odis admitted. "Doc chewed me up one side and down the other for goin' cold turkey on the pills."

Gertie just shook her head. "Always been a stubborn fool."

Bobby stepped up and took the hand that didn't have the IV in it. "And you're okay now?"

"It was just low blood sugar. Right as rain now."

"And he's putting you back on the pills?"

Odis wobbled his head. "Different ones. He said, with the kind of arthritis I got, I need to be on somethin' or my body's just gonna destroy itself and eat up my joints. So we'll try some different ones until we find somethin' that doesn't make me all foggy."

Gertie spoke up. "What about Tuck?"

"Something with the pins," Bobby explained. "Pinching his nerves or whatever. They took him back to surgery to fix it."

Gertie nodded. "Can I leave you boys to yerselves now? Or will another disaster strike?"

"Go on," Odis told her. "We should be fine now."

"Let's hope so," Gertie replied before turning to Bobby. "Oh, by the way, that dumb dog of yours is waitin' for ya. Been parked in front of the vestibule door ever since you left."

"Shit," Odis hissed out. "Forgot to feed her. We shoulda grabbed some food when we's at the house yesterday."

"I suppose I can scratch up some kind of food for her," Gertie replied with a sigh. "Keep me posted, but let's try for *good* news from now on."

Bobby sighed. "I'll certainly try."

"Later, sis."

Gertie nodded and then stepped beyond the curtain.

"I'm sorry," Odis said. "Last thing I remember, I was on the stairs. Nurses said you carried me in here."

"I used a wheelchair, but yeah."

"I wasn't feelin' good yesterday, either. But I thought it was just from all the shit goin' on."

"Well, before all this, I was gonna suggest you go visit the doctor Monday, just to make sure about quitting the pills. Don't suppose you need to now."

Odis shrugged. "Oh, he wants me in his office tomorrow. Prob'ly to chew me out again when I'm more alert."

Glancing around, Bobby asked, "What happened to Fenton?"

"Went to get some lunch, I think he said. He's comin' back. So, Tuck's back in surgery?"

"Klyve said something about the nerves in his pinky not responding, so the doctor went in to fix it."

Odis scowled. "Damn shit. I thought we caught enough of it yesterday."

"That's my opinion too," Bobby agreed with a nod. "Let's hope nothing else goes wrong."

With Bobby sitting on the edge of the bed and holding Odis's hand, they shared some quiet moments before a male voice could be heard outside. Fenton stepped around the curtain.

Odis sat up a bit to greet him. "Hey, Billy."

"Hey," he threw back before turning to Bobby. "What's up with Tuck?"

"Just a quick surgery to fix the pins in his hand. Should be out soon."

Fenton shifted his weight from one foot to the other, trying to ignore the clasped hands of the two men. He nervously ran his index finger and thumb down along the curves of his horseshoe mustache. "I'll wait upstairs, then," he finally said before exiting quickly.

Bobby looked over at Odis. "What's up with that?"

"Who knows."

They shared more silence until Bobby's phone rang. "Hello?" Bobby nodded. "Okay, call me when he's done?" he asked before hanging up. "Tuck's out of surgery. Fenton's in with him now."

"Why's Billy here, anyway?"

"Oh, Tuck found out about Travis—"

"Travie," Odis corrected. "Carl Travie."

"Right. Anyway, he wasn't supposed to be inside the house, and the whole scene just wasn't adding up. Tuck asked me to call Fenton so they could compare notes."

"Humph," Odis grunted.

Before he had time to reply further, Evie came in. "We're takin' the IV out." She turned to Bobby. "Waiting room," she told him firmly.

Bobby patted Odis's hand, then got up and went to the plastic chairs. He was more than ready for all this hospital shit to be over. After sitting down, he found his mind turning to Nathan again, pondering over his abilities. Bobby had no idea how those powers had worked. *Had* Nate even been able to see this? Or did he see it and *choose* not to give a warning? The rambling thoughts left Bobby feeling more pissed at Nathan for abandoning him in the dark without any answers. Tuck's words from the airport ride soon trickled up. *There must be a reason Nathan didn't say anything.*

Evie stepped up and interrupted his musings. "We're keeping Odis a little while longer," she told Bobby. "Go get some food or something."

"I'm fine. Can I go back in?"

"Suit yourself," she said with a shrug before going back to the ER station.

Bobby's phone rang as he stood. "Hello?"

"Hey," Klyve's voice said. "He just left."

"I'll be up in a minute. See ya," Bobby replied before hanging up. He walked across to the patient area and peeked his head behind Odis's curtain. "I'm going upstairs. I'll come back if you don't show up soon."

Odis nodded. "Okay. Later, then."

Odis settled back into the covers, marveling over Bobby. It was hard to believe he'd only been around eight days. The guy had turned his world upside-down and inside out in such a short amount of time. He'd never had a girlfriend or wife be so loyal and caring, even after years of being together. Odis smiled to himself. Bobby was such a pleasant surprise.

BOBBY entered ICU room two and noticed right away the fancy-looking air-inflated plastic cast covering Tuck's lower right arm. "Hey, Tuck," he tried to say cheerfully.

Tuck gazed back with a silly grin. "Hey, stud. I hadda new surgery," he declared a bit loudly, holding up his right arm as if it were a trophy.

"I heard," Bobby said as he approached. "Did they give you drugs?"

Tuck grinned and grabbed Bobby's hip with his left hand and pulled him close. "I think maybe one or two, and a whole lotta buncha shots."

Bobby leaned down for a kiss, but Tuck's mouth tasted like some kind of sour chemical factory, so he pulled back quickly.

"Ya not happy to see me?" Tuck asked with an exaggerated frown.

Bobby kissed his forehead. "Very happy, but your breath is kinda rank."

"Ya taste that too? Thought it was just me." Tuck looked around. "Aww, and I didn't bring a toothbrush. Not that I have me a bathroom anyway."

Backing up, Bobby retrieved the water cup from the tray table and handed it to Tuck. "Drink some of this. Swish it around inside your mouth and it should help. I'm going to run out for a second," Bobby said as he went to the door.

"Okeee." Tuck grinned before he slurped up some water through the straw and swished it loudly between his teeth, his cheeks inflating and deflating like a puffer fish.

Bobby stepped out and looked around for Klyve. He spotted the nurse leaving room four and met him at the ICU station. "So how was his surgery? He doesn't seem coherent enough to give a good answer yet."

Klyve nodded. "They gave him nitrous. It should wear off pretty quick."

"What about the surgery?"

"Oh." Klyve pulled up some info on his computer screens and read over it. "Went well. They removed one of the pins and sensations returned. So doesn't seem like there was any nerve damage from the injury. Can't really tell for sure 'til his bones heal enough we can have him try moving the fingers around. But it all seems in order so far."

"Good." Bobby nodded. "Oh, he was complaining about a bad taste in his mouth. Do you have a toothbrush or mouthwash or something?"

"Sure, let me get a kit," Klyve said as he bent down to one of the cabinets and got out a plastic zippered bag with basic toiletries in it. "Should have what ya need in there." He handed the kit to Bobby.

"Thanks."

After returning with the bag, Bobby opened it to find some kind of minty cotton swabs. "Smile wide," he told Tuck, and then he ran the swabs over Tuck's teeth, which seemed to clean his mouth without the foaming of normal toothpaste.

Bobby had Tuck sparkly fresh in no time. Afterward, they enjoyed a much more pleasant kiss.

"Thank ya, stud," Tuck said when he pulled back, his voice sounding more like his normal tone. "Where's Odie?"

"He's still downstairs," Bobby told him. "He kinda fainted when we went down earlier, and they wanted to check him out." He didn't want to worry Tuck unnecessarily at the moment.

"Fainted?" Tuck shook his head. "Odie doesn't just run around faintin'. What happened? The truth this time."

Bobby took a breath. "He went cold turkey off his meds Monday, and his blood sugar is just a little screwy now. They'll get it straightened out."

Tuck studied him closely. "Ya better not be blowin' smoke."

"I'm not." Bobby shook his head. "I wouldn't do that to you, Tuck. He'll be up here in no time, I'm sure. It's really nothing to worry about."

"Okay, I'm trustin' ya on that."

Bobby sat on the edge of the bed. "What did Fenton say?"

"Not much." Tuck frowned. "Just wanted to hear my side of things. Making sure Travie didn't slip in past us. He was pretty close-lipped on everything else."

"Did you know that Travie guy very well?"

"Not really. He'd just started. I'd never worked with him or hung out with him. He was so young, I kinda didn't know how to relate to him."

Bobby nodded. "I know what you mean. It's like these younger kids grew up on a different planet or something."

"Well, they kinda did. Computers and microwaves in the house from the day they were babies, thousands of channels on the TV, cell phones and texting practically from the minute they could read. Grew up with whole different ideas of how the world works."

"Never thought of it that way," Bobby admitted.

"Instant grat is the worst of it, though. Had ya gotten around to dating again?"

"No, I *barely* got around to leaving the house before I came to Texas. And what do you mean by instant grat?"

"The whole instant gratification thing. Hafta have whatever I want, right now. It's completely changed dating. Or should I say, it's killed dating."

"*What?*"

"Well, the whole idea of getting to know someone has gotten passé, I guess. Ya meet online or through friends or whatever. First they google ya to decide if they wanna meet up for coffee. Once ya *do* meet, if there's not an instant click in, like, the first five minutes, it's 'so long to ya'. No time allotted for actually talking, getting to know each other."

"That sounds harsh," Bobby said with a frown.

"Sure is, but the *worst* part is, if there *is* a click, it's expected ya'll have sex within the next five minutes, or at least within thirty minutes. Then, *if* the sex is satisfying enough, you might go out to dinner after."

"How long has it been like that?"

Tuck shrugged. "The new rules have been slowly creepin' in over the last ten years or so, but it's really noticeable now." Tuck clasped his hand. "Yer lucky ya don't hafta go through it."

"Who says I won't?" Bobby said flippantly, but he regretted the tease when he saw the hurt look flash on Tuck's face.

"I hope ya don't mean that."

"It was a joke, Tuck," Bobby tried to reassure him with a hand squeeze.

"I still mean what I said in the car. If this three-way thing don't work out, ya better at least stick with Odie, or I'll kick your ass."

Bobby leaned in and kissed him, sharing their sparks until Tuck nudged him away. With a smile, Bobby said, "I don't think we have to worry about that."

Tuck smirked at him. "And no more kisses like that. I've still got the damn catheter."

The door opened and Klyve poked his head in. "Can ya help me real quick?"

"Sure," Bobby said, guessing he wanted to move the TV inside. Bobby held the door open and helped Klyve navigate the cart into the room. After lining it up against the wall, Klyve set to work connecting all the cords.

"Cool, my TV," Tuck cheered.

Klyve finished the connections and turned it on. "Yep. They wanna keep you one more night because of the anesthesia." Klyve smiled over at Tuck. "They wanted to move ya to another room downstairs, but I told 'em no point in shufflin' ya around. So ya get to stay."

Tuck shrugged. "Might be nice to have a bathroom."

Walking over and handing the remote control to Tuck, Klyve said, "But I know who's on duty tonight. Trust me, yer better off here. Besides, they'll prob'ly kick ya out tomorrow anyway."

"Okay, then," Tuck said with a grin.

"Not too loud," Klyve warned on his way out the door.

Bobby grinned back at Tuck. "Kicked out tomorrow."

"*Maybe*, the man said," Tuck emphasized.

The door opened again and Odis strolled in. He rushed up and ruffled Tuck's hair.

Tuck smirked at him. "Have a nice nap, bonehead?"

"I dunno if I like having all these boyfriends. Ya guys gossip as bad as the church ladies. I'll never be able ta keep anything secret."

"*Us?*" Bobby asked, trying to sound wounded. He turned to Tuck. "He called us old church ladies."

"I am *so* offended," Tuck whined.

"I never said 'old', ya drama queens."

Bobby stepped behind Odis and put his arm around his neck. "Straight boy's just *full* of insults today. I don't think we should even tell him, since we're such bad gossips and all."

"Tell me what?"

"Nah, don't wanna be accused of gossip," Tuck agreed with a headshake.

"Tell me *what*?" Odis repeated.

Lowering his arm, Bobby gave an affectionate squeeze to Odis's chest. "Klyve said Tuck will prob'ly go home tomorrow."

"Woo-hoo!" Odis called out, then dropped his head for being too loud. "Guess we'll hafta celebrate tomorrow night," he said with a mischievous grin.

Tuck smiled at Odis's enthusiasm. "So what about the house? What all needs done?"

"Just two windows need replaced, but those are a bitch of a special order so may take a few days. Still need to check the roof for cracks, but didn't see anything obvious."

Nodding, Tuck asked, "And what about the studio?"

"Oh shit." Odis's eyes flew wide. "I fuckin' forgot to check. Shit," he spit out,

"It's probably okay," Bobby said as he hugged Odis. "I didn't see any damage on the east side of the house."

"I'm sure he's right," Tuck agreed. "So I guess we'll all hafta hang out at my apartment tomorrow. If I do get out."

Odis glanced between the two men. "Whose turn is it tomorrow night?"

"I don't remember," Bobby admitted. "And I don't think we should worry about it. We'll drive ourselves crazy trying to hold up to some kind of schedule. Let's just play it out by ear for now and worry about a schedule if it seems like we need one." Bobby held out his right hand, and Odis and Tuck reached out and made a three-way clasp.

"Agreed," Odis and Tuck chimed in.

"Jackpot," Tuck said, and they all shook on it. "Now, get back over to Gertie's and let a man watch his TV in peace." He flipped the TV channels around until he found the NASCAR race.

"You heard him, Odie. Think we can talk Gertie into making some lunch?"

Odis laughed. "I'm sure she's done finished lunch and started on dinner by now. We'll see you later, Tuck," he said as he leaned in for a kiss.

Tuck smiled. "Morning. See me in the morning," he said with a look to Bobby.

"He's right," Bobby agreed as he pulled Odis away. "Let's let the bonehead rest for one night, or he won't be worth a damn tomorrow."

Tuck smiled at Bobby as they left. With a quick nod, Bobby silently promised to look after Odis.

"Oh wait," Tuck called out. Bobby froze in the doorway. "Check with Klyve and see if ya can track down my keys and hit my apartment. Odie knows where it is. Bring me some clothes ta wear outta here tomorrow."

"Can do," Bobby said with a smile before he turned and left.

Once the guys were gone, Tuck nudged down the volume then flipped through the channels until he found Paula Deen. Not only did that lady crack him up, she also made some great recipes. Tuck hadn't tried any *real* cooking in a while—it always seemed depressing to make a bunch of great food and be the only one sitting at the table to eat. But maybe now…. Yes, he decided. It wouldn't hurt to spend some time in the kitchen again.

Bumping the volume up one notch, Tuck settled back into the bed to watch Paula at work.

IT DIDN'T take Klyve but a minute to retrieve Tuck's keys from the personal items that had already been bagged up. When the guys got into the hallway, Bobby steered Odis to the elevator, saying, "Let's ride this time."

"Okay," Odis reluctantly agreed.

After the short drive back to Brungess, Odis pulled into a rear parking lot behind one of the storefront brownstones on Main Street. He let Bobby in through a back door and led him up a flight of narrow stairs.

"Here we are," Odis said while unlocking the door and pushing it open.

Bobby wasn't sure what he had expected, but the small space they stepped into appeared very clean—nearly spotless and well organized. A huge flat screen, at least fifty inches or more, hung on the back wall facing a new-looking cream couch. Along the side wall, a long row of bookshelves, packed tightly with various volumes, warmly filled the space.

Odis ducked into the first doorway. "You get the clothes while I pee," he told Bobby.

Bobby stepped around the cozy kitchenette to the other door. The bedroom held more of the smartly styled furnishings. He went to the closet and looked at shirts. He scanned them until one caught his eye: a short-sleeved western shirt of grassy green adorned with some kind of Navajo rug pattern in yellow and brown. He smiled, thinking how well it would go with Tuck's eyes. When Bobby noticed it had snaps, he pulled it out and set it on the bed. With the cast on Tuck's hand reaching all the way up to his fingertips, it was unlikely he would be able to successfully fiddle with any buttons.

Bobby saw some denim behind the pairs of brown uniform pants. He slid back the uniforms and found various pairs of jeans on hangers. He looked through, trying to find a pair with zipper and snap, but all Tuck's jeans were of the button-fly style. He was about to give up before, toward the back of the closet, he found a pair of slate-gray jeans, which had the fasteners he was looking for. He pulled them from the closet and set them on the bed with the shirt.

At the dresser, Bobby pulled out the top drawer and burst out laughing. Inside, he found five very neat vertical columns of stacked underwear, each composed of a different style. On the far right were long boxer-briefs, next to them a column of full briefs, then bikini briefs. Flanking those was a column of sexy mesh briefs, and lastly jockstraps.

Stepping into the bedroom, Odis asked, "What's so funny?"

"Tuck," Bobby replied. "He's got everything so neat and organized, it's like shopping at Lord & Taylor or something."

Odis chuckled when he peeked over and saw the underwear drawer. "Prob'ly 'cause his pa was such a slobby pig. When we were younger, he made me promise to threaten bodily harm if I ever caught him living like that. Used to cuss up a storm when he had to spend hours cleaning up after his old man. I don't know if he'd have gone to the trouble if it weren't for Hawk's sake."

"How much younger is Hawk?"

"Six years, or is it seven? Don't recall exactly." Odis picked up a pair of the sexy silk mesh underwear. "Think he actually wears these anywhere?"

Bobby chuckled. "I bet he wears them under his uniform to feel secretly sexy."

Odis laughed. "Oh my God, I can't get that out of my head now." He slugged Bobby in the arm. "Thank ya so much," he said sarcastically before chuckling again. "I really bet he does, though." Odis let out another chuckle as he put the underwear back on its stack.

"What should we take?" Bobby asked.

"Yer askin' me? I don't know."

Bobby looked over the selection. "The boxer briefs have a large fly. Should be okay for one-handed operation," he said as he chose a seafoam pair and closed the drawer.

"One-handed?" Odis puzzled aloud briefly. "Oh right, stupid cast. I guess he kinda is one-handed now."

Bobby opened the next drawer and found neatly arrayed balls of socks. "What about shoes?" he asked Odis.

Odis looked over at the clothes laid out on the bed. "I know just the thing to go with that." Odis went to the closet. "Pick out some long socks," he told Bobby as he dug around in the shoe rack on the floor.

Bobby found some socks and took them to the bed, and Odis stepped out of the walk-in closet, carrying a very fancy-looking pair of cowboy boots, their bumpy-looking leather dyed a grassy green. "His ostrich boots," Odis declared. "He won't hafta mess with laces this way."

"Brilliant," Bobby agreed with a grin. Looking over the ensemble, Bobby said, "Only one thing missing."

"Oh no," Odis warned. "He'll shoot us if ya bring a cowboy hat. He hates bein' stereotyped."

Bobby laughed. "Hey, we found all this shit right in his closet. What about a belt?"

"Hates belts," Odis told him. "He told me once a belt means yer too poor to afford pants that fit."

"Humph. Not snobby at all, is he."

Odis laughed. "He has his moments."

"I guess this is all we need, then." Bobby picked up the shirt and jeans by the hangers, and they gathered up the rest of the clothes before locking up. Neither man spoke on the short drive to the B and B. They left Tuck's clothes in the car and went inside.

Heimdalla nearly tackled Bobby when they walked in the door. "Hey, girl, we're back," he said as she bounced around in unbounded excitement.

Gertie greeted them from the living room. "Hey, boys. Didn't expect ya back so soon."

Odis said, "Tuck wanted some rest, so we bugged out."

"Yeah," Bobby agreed with a nod. "And we need some rest too, I think."

"Made up some rice with chicken livers for the dog," Gertie said as she stood up. "She seemed to like it."

"I'll bet," Odis chuckled. "Prob'ly won't get her to eat dried food now, after ya spoil her."

"I'm not the one who forgot her food," Gertie scolded. "I've got some leftover lunch I could heat up, and some corn on the cob from last night."

"Okay," Bobby said, following her into the dining room with Heim tagging along at his side. "I guess we could eat a bite first."

"Odie, there's lemonade in the fridge. Grab some glasses while I get this going."

"On it," Odis said as he went into the kitchen.

Bobby took a seat at the table, and Heim tried to crawl in his lap. "Ooomph, get down. You're too damn big," he told her as he pushed her down. She parked on her butt at his side.

They ate one plate of food each and then went upstairs. Bobby closed the door after Heim came in. Odis paused just long enough to kick off his shoes before crawling onto the bed. Bobby took off his shoes, crawled onto the bed, then spooned in behind Odis. Heim jumped on the bed and sat behind Bobby's knees.

All three let out a quiet sigh.

CHAPTER
Twenty-Four

MINUTES later, Odis rolled onto his back. "I'm sorry. I feel like I'm lettin' ya down, since I don't wanna do anything."

"What?" Bobby asked with confusion.

"I know how young men are. I'm sure you prob'ly wanna fool around."

"Oh hush, I'm not *that* fuckin' young. And I'm quite satisfied with this." He squeezed Odis close for emphasis. "This is all I want right now. I may be more worn out than you are, since I didn't get a nap today."

"It wasn't really a nap," Odis said as he looked up into Bobby's eyes. "It's kinda weird how you make me feel something I never even thought I wanted."

Bobby looked down into his blue eyes, as richly deep as the sky, and felt himself nearly falling into that depth. "What do I make you feel?"

"Safe. Secure." Odis reached up and rubbed his hand along Bobby's forearm before letting it rest in the middle. "I've never felt this before. I didn't know I wanted to."

"Maybe that's part of why you've had attractions to men, as a way to fill that need."

"Could be."

Bobby squeezed him again. "I kinda like keeping you safe. I never got to be a big brother or anything."

"You didn't for Nathan?"

Bobby shook his head. "He was so confident and independent, he didn't need it. Which was good at the time, with my career. I could go on the road and not worry about him."

Odis put together the family dynamic of what he'd said. "So you were the youngest?" Odis asked, not sure if Bobby would answer, since he was so reluctant to talk about his family.

"Yeah," Bobby said with a nod. He paused before abruptly adding, "I just had one older brother."

"Oh." Odis rubbed his arm again when he noticed the use of the past tense. "When did he pass?"

Bobby gazed down into Odis's eyes for so long, Odis thought he wasn't going to answer. Then Bobby's eyes started to moisten up and he rolled away onto his back. "He—"

Odis turned onto his side to face Bobby, showing a supportive face without saying anything.

Bobby finally spoke again. "It wasn't pretty when I came out," Bobby said as he sat up. "And I know you deserve to hear about it, but so does Tuck." He turned to Odis. "It'll be hard enough getting through it once. I don't wanna have to keep repeating it." He reached out to Odis's neck and pulled him close enough to kiss his forehead. "Okay?"

"Sure," Odis agreed. "It can wait 'til we're all together."

"Okay," Bobby said as he got up and went into the bathroom. Heim jumped down and followed him in before he closed the door.

Odis lay on the bed, trying to ignore what sounded like a sob. At that moment, he felt so grateful for the relationship he had with his sister. He felt a little stab of guilt when he couldn't remember the last time he'd told Gertie how much she meant to him.

TUCK was flipping through the channels, searching for something else to watch, when his door opened. He looked up to see Josh standing in the doorway. He bumped down the volume.

"Hey, dude," Josh said as he slowly walked in.

"Hey, Josh. Ya didn't get enough of the hospital yesterday?"

"I heard ya got attacked by a freezer," he teased back as he got closer.

"Looks like ya had yer own fight," Tuck said when he noticed the bandage on his cheek surrounded by various blooming bruises.

"Somethin' like that. So, how are ya?"

"Doin' okay, I guess," he said, raising his right arm to show off the cast. "Looks like I took a little more damage than you."

"Nothin' an old, tough dawg like you can't handle," Josh said with a nod. He sat in the chair near the bed. "Did ya hear that Bobby Lane's in town?"

Tuck nodded. "I heard."

"Well…." Josh hesitated. "I think ya should talk to him. Have a beer with him."

Resisting a smile, Tuck sat quietly. He felt a strange pleasure from watching Josh squirm and was curious about how far the younger man would take the conversation.

Josh looked at his eyes briefly. "I heard he's been hangin' out with Gertie's brother. Shouldn't be too hard to track him down."

"Okay," Tuck said flatly. "And why should I do that?"

After glancing at him quickly, Josh shifted in the chair and looked up at one of the monitors. "I… just think you should."

"Why?"

"Because." Josh clasped his hands in his lap and finally met Tuck's gaze. "He might be a good role model."

"But I'm not a baseball player."

Josh sighed in exasperation. "Jeez, yer just as hardheaded as yer brother sometimes."

"So Hawk should meet him too?"

"He already did, but that's not the point."

"Then what *is* the point?"

Josh shifted in his chair again. "The point is, *you* should meet with Bobby."

"And ya still haven't said why," Tuck replied, biting the inside of his cheek to keep his face stoic.

"Dammit, Tuck," Josh said as he hunched forward. "Ya don't need to be such a hardass. Doesn't make any difference to me, or nearly anybody else… who you are. Ya don't hafta keep everything private."

"Ah," Tuck said, finally allowing a smile. "But there's the rub, ain't it? You said 'nearly anybody'. That's *my* point of concern."

Josh shrugged. "I can't account for everybody."

"No. And I'd already guessed that you, and quite a few others, wouldn't give a howlin' hoot about such things. Some, though, I'm not so sure about."

"Like who?"

"Well," Tuck said before pausing. He looked over Josh, trying to judge just how far he wanted this conversation to go. Of everybody at the department, he trusted Josh as much as he trusted Hawk, so maybe.... "Broyles, for one. I think he'd come around in the long run, but it will probably freak his shit at first."

"Right," Josh said with a nod. "And the fact he's the boss doesn't make that easy."

"No, it doesn't. And I don't know about Fenton, either. I can't ever seem to get a bead on that guy."

"Know what ya mean. That dude's kinda weird sometimes."

"As for Bobby, we've already had beers."

Josh looked up hopefully. "When?"

"Friday. I was the one that picked him up at the airport."

"No shit?" Something seemed to click, and Josh suddenly grinned. "Was he the 'something that came up' Friday night ya called me about?"

Tuck nodded.

"Well, holy shit. Then you...?"

"You sure you wanna ask that?" Tuck questioned aloud.

"It's *Bobby Lane*. How could I *not* ask?"

Tuck smiled. "Yes, we did."

"Holy shit. And did he... is he... was it good?"

Tuck shook his head. "I can't believe you just asked me that. I thought ya were a straight boy."

Josh smirked. "If some hunky baseball star wanted to share my bed, I wouldn't say no. Shit, I'd prob'ly even catch."

Tuck tried not to chuckle at his euphemism. "A little bit heteroflexible, are ya?"

"Could be," Josh said with a blush. "So when Bobby was here yesterday, he was comin' to visit you?"

"Yep. Thurson brothers kinda screwed up our weekend plans."

"That sucks." Josh glanced around, trying to look casual. "Well, ya gonna see Bobby again?"

"Why? You wanna date him?"

Josh smirked at Tuck but didn't say no.

"We have plans for tomorrow night, if I get released."

"Oh, that's chill," Josh said as he stood up. "Well, you'll hafta make yer own decisions, but I wanted to let ya know ya got allies. Lots of them."

"I appreciate it." Tuck shook his hand.

"And talk to Hawk. Like *now*. You know how he is—he's either at zero or a hundred. He knows somethin's up, but he's keepin' at zero. Don't wait 'til he hits a hundred and explodes."

"Okay, I will," Tuck said with a nod. "Ya wanna do me a favor, then?"

"Sure."

"Step out in the hall and call him. Not supposed to use yer cell phone in here."

"No problem," Josh said as he went to the door. After pushing it open, he let it close without stepping out. "Don't look like I need to," he said as he turned back to Tuck. "I think that's his giant mug out there now."

"Good. Ya better clear out, then. He ain't gonna listen to no one-at-a-time rule." He smiled at Josh. "Thank ya for the visit. I really do appreciate it."

He smiled back. "It was a nice chat," Josh agreed. "I'll see ya later, Tuck."

Tuck took a deep breath and settled back into the bed, preparing himself. It didn't take long for Hawk to burst in.

Hawk stepped into the room gingerly. "Hey, midget. Still here, I see."

Tuck held up the cast. "But prettier since the last time ya's here."

Walking slowly to the bed, Hawk looked over the cast. "So that's really all that got hurt?"

"Nah, also got some bruises starting to hurt too."

Hawk glanced over him with a critical eye. "I don't see no bruises," he said after a minute.

Tuck lifted up the hospital gown on his left side, showing a huge purpling, dark-red bruise that started near his left hip and reached all the way to his ribs in a vaguely round pattern.

"Shit," Hawk spit out. "That looks like it hurts." Hawk untucked his shirt and pulled it up on the right side, turning so Tuck could see the curved crescent bruise on his lower back. "I got one too," he said with a touch of bragging in his tone.

"Sure did. You sure that was the explosion? Looks more a horse kicked ya."

"Who knows? Yers looks like a fucked-up Easter egg," Hawk said with a laugh as he tucked his shirt back in. "I don't remember a fuckin' thing after Fenton squawked roll call. It *might* have been a damn horse."

"I remember us crouching in position, then a white light, but nothing after that." He motioned for Hawk to sit in the chair. "Come here a minute. I think it's time we had a talk."

After a brief "oh shit" expression flashed on his face, Hawk pulled the chair right up next to the bed and sat. He tried to casually ask, "What's up?"

Tuck looked at his brother. "First," he said after a deep breath, "I need ya to promise me not to get all riled up."

Hawk's face fell into concern. "What? Is it…?" he asked while staring at the cast.

"No, no. Nothin' about that." Tuck reached out and bumped his arm to get him to look back at him. "It's more personal."

"Okay," Hawk said with a wavering nod.

"How much do ya know about Vic? And how'd ya even find out about him?" Tuck asked very quietly.

"Chrystil." Hawk looked up at the monitors. "She saw ya hangin' around the auto shop when she took her truck in ta Walmart for some new tires last year. She said you's kinda chummy with one of the mechanics." Hawk looked over at the cast on Tuck's hand. "So I followed ya that weekend ta find out what was up." He glanced very briefly at Tuck. "And I saw ya with that biker guy."

"What did ya see?"

"Does it matter? I ain't stupid, ya know. I kinda figured, for a long time now, that you was *that* way. And I don't give a flyin' fuck about it. I just want ya ta be happy. Which I don't think ya are."

"Okay," Tuck said. "How'd ya find out his name?"

Hawk looked at him as if he'd suddenly gone stupid. "Standard investigatin' techniques, ya dumb midget. Went back to Walmart and asked around," he said as he rolled his eyes.

"Right." Tuck bumped him in the arm again to get Hawk to look back at him. "And what did ya find out?"

"He's got a criminal past." Hawk looked him in the eye.

"We were *all* dumb kids. Public drunk and joyriding at fifteen doesn't make someone a hardened criminal," Tuck defended.

Hawk smiled. "I know, but I wanted ta see if ya did yer homework. That was the only thing *I* found on him. But he still seems kinda shady."

"Well, ya don't hafta worry about him anymore. We broke up. For *good*," Tuck said strongly.

Hawk raised his eyebrows and stiffened his shoulders. "What'd he do?"

"Calm down, he didn't do nothin'. Let's just call it irreconcilable differences."

"Okay." Hawk relaxed a little bit. "So what next for ya?"

Tuck hesitated as he looked at his brother. "I—I met Bobby," Tuck finally threw out.

"Really?" Hawk asked as he perked up visibly. "Oh yeah, he was here in the room with ya yesterday."

"Yep. I picked him up at the airport Friday."

Hawk's brow furrowed with confusion. "So ya knew him before the hospital?"

Tuck shook his head. "No, Odie knows him." Tuck looked sternly at Hawk. "And this is where it gets complicated. Promise me ya'll keep a lid on yerself."

"Okay," Hawk agreed with a tentative nod.

Tuck took a deep breath, trying to think of how best to explain this. He knew it wouldn't take long for the gossip mill to start churning, and he had to tell Hawk before he heard some twisted thirdhand version of the truth. He struggled for what to say.

"Okay," Hawk said again. "Spit it out."

Tuck decided to try from a more analytical angle, even though he doubted Hawk could follow that line. Bless his heart, his brother wasn't exactly the sharpest pencil in the box. "Have you ever heard of a ménage à trois?"

Hawk's brow crinkled. "Is that like a zoo?"

"No, not a *menagerie*." Tuck resisted a sigh. "A committed three-way."

Hawk seemed to concentrate on the words a moment. With a lowered voice, he asked, "Ya mean like those Mormons?"

"No, not *polygamy*. A three-way." Tuck sighed.

Hawk looked into his eyes. "What's the difference?"

"With polygamy, the wives may not like each other or even necessarily know each other. They each have an individual commitment to the husband. It's sometimes more like they're property of the husband." Tuck scanned Hawk's face to see if he was following. "With a ménage, all three are committed to each other."

Hawk still looked confused. "I still don't...."

"Okay." Tuck sat forward a bit, deciding to change tactics. "Let's say you fell in love with Chrystil and married her."

Hawk nearly scowled. "Gina hates her. She'd kick my ass fer doin' somethin' like that."

"Let's say, for whatever reason, Gina didn't have a say. Even though they hate each other, they both love you and are both your wife." Tuck reached out and bumped his arm. "Can ya picture that?"

"Sure, I guess."

"Okay, that would be like polygamy. Now try to picture somethin' different. Let's say Gina was into girls as much as guys. And she met some girl, like Holly for instance, and they started falling in love. Then *you* meet Holly, and you fall in love with her too. So all three of you decide to share the relationship equally, together. That's a ménage."

Hawk sat back and thought about all that a minute. "So yer sayin' this Holly, Gina, and me would all love each other together? And all have sex together?"

Tuck nodded. He could see from his brother's face when all the gears started pulling together and the machinery turned. "So Odie. He's into guys too?"

Tuck nodded.

"And... so ya got *two* boyfriends now?"

Tuck nodded again. "I guess you could put it that way."

Hawk frowned slightly. "And that makes ya happy?"

Tuck grinned. "*Happy* isn't even the word for it."

Hawk's lips lifted a little at the corners, but he still looked concerned. "I'm glad for that. I really am. But you know the town's gonna talk, and some of it... won't be nice."

Tuck studied him to make sure he was being truthful. "It wouldn't bother you, having Bobby as a brother-in-law?"

"Hell no," Hawk said with a smile. "He's a famous athlete. And kinda good-looking too, I guess. Who would mind that?"

"And what about Odis?"

"That little shrimp?" Hawk asked with a smirk. "I always thought he was smarter than you, and he's got some balls too. Yesterday I thought he was gonna bite my nads off. He wasn't gonna let me back here, not as long as he was conscious." Hawk let out a short chuckle.

Tuck also chuckled. "I thought ya learned not ta mess with pit bulls."

"I know. I still got a scar on my calf from that mean bitch." Hawk sat up with a serious expression. Then he reached out and took Tuck's left hand and looked him in the eyes. "I'm glad. I'm really glad ya finally told me. Ya didn't hafta wait so long, midget."

"And it really doesn't bother you? I mean, everything?"

Hawk chuckled. "With two boyfriends, ya'll prob'ly be gettin' more than me now. Don't bother me at all, other than maybe a little jealous," he said with a smirk.

"That's good. I was almost afraid to tell ya, but I knew I had ta say somethin' before any rumors start."

"You didn't hafta wait for rumors. I mean it, I want ya to tell me *everything* from now on. Even the bad stuff. I can't be a good brother if ya don't let me," Hawk said with a stern look.

"Okay, I promise. I'll tell ya everything."

"You better." Hawk released his hand and patted it before sitting back in the chair. "How ya think Broyles is gonna handle all this?"

"I don't know. He is a concern."

Hawk nodded. "It took a while for him to come around to ya bein' gay. This is gonna really freak him."

Tuck nearly jumped out of the bed. "He *knows*? Broyles knows? Since *when*?"

"Calm down." Hawk stood and hovered over him. "About a year, but he had his suspicions way before then."

Tuck lay back down. Then the timing hit him and he glared at Hawk. "*You* told him?"

"He already had suspicions," Hawk said in defense. "And I had to tell him *some* reason why I was investigatin' Vic. Seemed easier not ta lie."

Tuck glared at him as he breathed through his nose. He couldn't believe his brother would go behind his back like that. It felt like a cruel betrayal.

Hawk hovered over him, trying to look like an innocent baby brother. "Come on, Tuck," he nearly pleaded. "Ain't none of us stupid. I don't know of anybody who hasn't figured it out by now."

"Still." Tuck turned his eyes away and focused on keeping his words steady. "That doesn't give ya the right to go blabbing it everywhere."

"I didn't," Hawk said in a wounded tone. "Broyles was the only one I talked to, and he even kinda started it, anyway."

Tuck softened a little as he stared at his cast. "Yer still an ass."

Hawk sat on the edge of the bed and got in front of Tuck's gaze. "I'm sorry. I wasn't tryin' ta be."

"Maybe not," Tuck said with a sigh. "I should have been the one to talk to him. What if he'd kicked me out of the department?"

"Shit." Hawk scowled. "I didn't think of that."

"Right. So if I'd talked to Broyles, and that happened, it would have been *my* doing. You'd have hated yerself if I'd been fired because of somethin' *you* said."

"Okay, I'm sorry. I won't say another word to anybody else."

"Ya don't hafta go that far, just be more careful," Tuck said, realizing he was making a silly request of his brother. The guy probably couldn't even find the word "caution" in the dictionary, much less apply it.

"Okay," Hawk said with a nod. "Then I can kick somebody's ass if they say shit about you and Bobby and Odis."

"Is that being careful?" Tuck asked sharply.

"Maybe I could put on a mask first?" Hawk asked with a twinkly smile.

Tuck chuckled at the mental image of his brother in a superhero costume running down the street and then slugging people. "No, don't think that'd work. Yer one of the few six-foot-three guys around here, as far as I know."

"Right. So much for being anomalous."

Tuck laughed, wondering if his brother understood the joke he just made. "I think you mean anonymous."

"I *really* am sorry," Hawk said as he leaned forward. "I just wagged my jaw without even thinkin' how it could go bad."

"It's okay. I know you were just tryin' to look out for me."

Hawk leaned in and hugged Tuck. "I should go." Hawk stood up. "Time ta get my six-foot-three anomaly ass home," he said with a wink.

Tuck laughed as Hawk left. Damn bastard *did* know the joke he made. Tuck laughed again when he realized how deftly Hawk had played him past his anger after he'd learned about getting outed to Broyles. That damn little shit. Hawk was sure slick when he wanted to be.

With another chuckle, Tuck turned up the TV and flipped the channels, looking for something interesting.

CHAPTER
Twenty-Five

THE next day, it took until almost two in the afternoon to get Tuck out of the hospital and settled into the El Camino. After absently banging his cast against the door, Tuck crammed in next to Bobby, who sat in the middle for the drive back to Brungess. Odis started the car. Once he pulled out of the parking lot, Tuck let out a huge sigh.

Bobby looked over at his scruffy face of gray-and-blond stubbly growth. "You okay, big guy?"

"Oh sure." Tuck nodded. "Just such a relief ta be outta there," he said as he rubbed his left hand across his chin. "Can't wait ta get home and shave. Gettin' all itchy."

Odis chuckled. "Never did like a beard, did ya."

"Nope." Tuck's eyes suddenly lit up. "Oh. I haven't told ya guys. I had some visitors yesterday."

"Who?" Odis and Bobby asked at nearly the same time.

Tuck chuckled, thinking it was like being in a car full of barn owls. "Hawk, of course. He came by, which is a tale in itself. But before him, Josh dropped in."

"Josh?" Odis asked as he reached over and turned the radio off so they wouldn't have to talk over it.

"Oh, this should be interesting," Bobby said with a grin.

Tuck nodded. "He started with sayin' that Bobby was in town, hangin' out with Gertie's brother, he said, and I should track you down and have a beer with you," he told them as he smiled over at Bobby.

Odis guffawed. "Really?"

Bobby nodded. "Josh told me Saturday, when I saw him in the ER, that I should meet with Tuck."

"And what did ya say ta that?" Odis asked Tuck.

"Oh, I didn't say anything right away. It was too much fun watchin' him squirm around. He finally said nearly everybody in the department had my number, so to speak, and I have allies if I wanna come out for real."

"Wow," Odis replied. "Are ya gonna do that?"

"Let me tell ya about Hawk's visit before I get into that one. There's one more thing about Josh I wanna mention first."

"What's that?" Bobby asked.

"When I told him I'd picked ya up at the airport Friday, he put two and two together about me callin' to cover my shift. Then he asked me if ya were any good."

Bobby chuckled. "I see."

Odis shook his head. "Josh? He actually asked that? I thought he was straight."

Tuck laughed. "And so are you, Odie. Or are ya changin' your mind about that?"

Odis shook his head. "I'm not sure about anything anymore," he admitted. "All I know is I've got these two guys that keep punchin' my buttons. I don't even notice anybody else."

"Better not," Tuck said in his authoritative voice. "This is a complicated enough mess without draggin' anybody else into it."

Bobby reached down and rubbed the nearest thigh of each man. "I've already got my hands too full to think of anybody else."

"No worries." Odis glanced over. "So what happened after that, with Hawk?"

Tuck paused as they pulled onto Main Street. "Let's get inside before I start *that* story," he said as Odis neared his building.

On Bobby's last visit, they had come in through the back, so he hadn't noticed Tuck lived above a closed-down storefront. It appeared the place was still fairly well maintained despite being vacant—for several years, from the looks of it.

Odis pulled through the alley to the back and parked near the door. Bobby studied Tuck moving a bit carefully up the stairs to his apartment.

Once inside, Tuck went right to the kitchenette and started making coffee. Bobby watched as Odis plopped onto the couch and turned on the TV.

Bobby stepped into the kitchenette. "You doing okay?"

"Oh, sure, I'll have this brewin' in no time. Then I'm hoppin' in the shower."

"I mean, you don't seem as spry as you normally do."

"Oh." Tuck finished adding the water to the coffeemaker and turned it on. "I got a couple a sore spots, but I think it's mostly just from layin' around in bed fer two days."

"Sore spots?"

Tuck nodded and then headed to the bedroom door. "Help me and I'll show ya," he said with a smirky crooked grin. Bobby followed him into the bedroom.

Tuck managed to open the shirt snaps mostly one-handed, then pulled open the left side to show the large Easter-egg-shaped bruise just below his ribs.

"Geez," Bobby said as he sucked in a breath. "No wonder you're sore."

"A few inches higher and it woulda surely broken ribs."

"What *did* that? Looks like somebody punched you," Bobby said as he stepped closer.

"Doorknob, I think. Who knows?" Tuck said as he wrangled out of his shirt, then sat on the edge of the bed. "Help me with the boots?"

"Sure," Bobby agreed as he went and kneeled down in front of the bed and took Tuck's right cowboy boot by the heel. Tuck winced and sucked in a breath as he pulled on it. "Sorry," Bobby said when he stopped. Being more careful and watching Tuck's facial expressions, he managed to wriggle the boot off Tuck's foot. He took hold of the other boot and pulled it off without Tuck flinching.

Tuck stood up again, unsnapping and unzipping the pants without assistance. He pushed the gray denim down to his thighs, then bent to grasp the leg cuff, but couldn't seem to manage the maneuver with only one hand.

Bobby nudged him to sit on the bed. "Let me help." Once Tuck sat, Bobby grabbed the cuff of each denim leg and pulled the jeans off.

"Ouch," he muttered when he saw the wide gash of a bruise across Tuck's right leg, a deep purple line just above the ankle.

"Yeah," Tuck said with a nod as he also looked down at the nasty purple wound. "Klyve said I's damn lucky it didn't break my leg."

"Looks like it," Bobby agreed as he glanced over Tuck in nothing but the seafoam boxer briefs. He saw several other minor scuffs and bruises on Tuck's legs and stomach, but none looked nearly as dramatic.

Tuck smiled at Bobby's admiring gaze. "I'm guessin' it was *you* that picked out these clothes? Doubt Odis is that fashion conscious."

Bobby nodded. "He actually got the boots, though, when he saw what all else I had laid out. Don't forget that he's an artist. He might not know the difference between Armani and Valentino, but he can tell what looks good."

"Sure." Tuck nodded. "I couldn't tell ya the difference, either," he admitted. "Thanks for findin' the snap-and-zipper jeans. I fergot I even had 'em, and buttons are gonna be a bitch." He held up the plastic finger-encasing cast as proof.

Tuck stood up. "I'm gonna shave and shower, as best I can, anyway."

Bobby noticed the slight swelling in the groin of Tuck's boxer briefs and gazed up with an innocent smile. "Need help with that?"

Tuck grinned back. "I need ta get cleaned up first, with no distractions." He led Bobby back out into the living room. "Go keep Odie company. I'll be done in a jiffy." Tuck continued around the kitchenette to the bathroom and closed the door.

"Is he parading around nekkid?" Odis asked as he turned and looked over the back of the couch.

"Nah, still had undies on." Bobby stepped around to the front of the couch and sat near Odis, watching the laser shoot-'em-up sci-fi scene on the TV. "I didn't know you liked sci-fi," he commented.

Odis chuckled. "Give 'em six-shooters and cowboy hats and most of 'em's just like a western in disguise."

Bobby chuckled along. "Never thought of it that way."

They watched a few more minutes of the guys in shiny armor trying to rescue some long-haired blonde girl dressed in a racy robe and high heels.

"See," Odis said like a voice-over. "She's the Indian squaw that's done got kidnapped by the cavalry, and them's her brothers come ta rescue her from the fort."

Bobby chuckled. "And where are the horses?"

Odis smiled. "You watch. In a minute they'll run back to their tired-lookin' ponies and skedaddle."

They watched the TV as the shiny armor guys led the robed woman away, shooting lasers behind them as they fled down the spaceship corridors until reaching some sort of docking hanger. Bobby laughed when he saw the tiny scarred-up scout ship they all crammed into before scurrying away into space.

With a nod, Odis said, "What'd I tell ya? Tired-lookin' pony."

Bobby laughed and gazed over at Odis with a wide grin, admiring how clever and intuitive the little man could be. And the best part was that Odis didn't do it in a haughty or bragging kind of way. He didn't even seem to realize how smart and talented he was. Bobby leaned forward and kissed his mouth.

Like a thirsty man finally finding water, Odis immediately leaned forward and kissed back. With heated force, he put his hands behind Bobby's head and pulled him close, enjoying the fuzzy warmth they shared a few moments before pulling back.

"Wow," Bobby said when he could breathe again. "What brought that on?"

Odis shrugged. "I guess 'cause we hadn't kissed in two days, I just realized."

"Right," Bobby agreed. "I guess we haven't."

When they heard the bathroom door open, both guys looked over the back of the couch. Tuck emerged, draped with a smaller pale-blue towel wrapped around his waist like a terry cloth kilt. He went to the kitchenette and poured himself a mug of coffee before looking over at the other men watching him. "Do I hafta play hostess, or can ya guys get yer own coffee?"

Odis huffed. "Who says I want coffee? Don'cha have any beer?"

Tuck nodded. "*I'm* plannin' on stayin' up late, since I got guests to entertain," he said with a lecherous grin. "But suit yerself. You know where the fridge is."

Bobby grinned back. "Coffee sounds good to me."

"Well." Odis also broke into a grin. "Coffee it is, then," he said as he stood up from the couch.

When Tuck stepped away from the kitchenette counter to give him room to go in, Odis saw the Easter-egg bruise. "Fuck," he muttered. "Ya been hidin' that the whole time?"

Tuck stuck out his right foot and turned it slightly to show off the ankle bruise. "Here too."

"Shit," Odis hissed. "I thought you's okay," he said as he poured two mugs.

Sticking out his right arm, Tuck waved the cast. "And ya didn't notice this?"

"Bonehead," Odis scolded as he stepped back out and carried the two mugs to the coffee table. "I mean, other than *that*, I thought you's okay."

"I am," Tuck said as he followed Odis to the couch. "Just kinda sore is all."

"Thanks, Odie," Bobby said with a nod toward the mug. He turned to Tuck as he started to sit on the couch beside him. "Maybe you should sit in that chair." Bobby motioned to the recliner against the flanking wall.

"Oh?" Tuck asked as he froze in place.

Bobby waggled his eyebrows as he flicked the hem of the short towel. "Better view."

Tuck chuckled warmly and sat down. "Is that all ya want? Just a peep show?" he teased as he unclasped the towel and slid it partway off his lap, just enough to show pubic hair.

Odis turned off the TV and set the remote on the table before looking over. "Sure ya should be doin' somethin' strenuous?"

"There may be certain things I can't do, but I'm sure we can work around it."

"What things?" Bobby asked.

"Standing up too long or havin' somebody sit on my chest. I think those are out."

Bobby reached out and rubbed Tuck's bare thigh. "I hadn't planned on sitting on your *chest*," he said with a grin. "I can think of more interesting places to sit."

Odis leaned over as he watched the towel in Tuck's lap tenting upward. "Oh, I was kinda thinkin' somethin' else."

Tuck gazed over. "What were ya thinkin'?"

Odis swallowed and then seemed to lose some resolve. "Oh!" he suddenly blurted out. "Ya never did tell us about Hawk's visit."

Bobby and Tuck glanced over questioningly at Odis's sudden change in tone. Tuck nodded. "Right, I never did. Learned a few interesting things," he said before sipping at his mug. "Found out Hawk'd known about Vic since last year, had him tailed and investigated, and also managed to out me to Broyles in the process."

"Holy fuck!" Odis exclaimed. "That stupid-assed shithead. I'm gonna kick his ass!"

"Calm down," Tuck said with his authoritative voice. "He wasn't doin' anything to intentionally hurt me, and he apologized for bein' a stupid ass. And now it turns out I don't hafta worry about Broyles if I 'come out' officially. So he kinda did me a favor with that."

Bobby nodded. "Sounds like good news."

"It is," Tuck agreed. "So now there's only one guy I have any concerns over. Fenton."

"Right," Odis said as he got himself under control. "I've always wondered if he weren't a closet-case."

"He *was* kind of weird in the ER when he saw me and Odie holding hands," Bobby agreed. "But that's just *one* guy, and he's not your boss or anything, right?"

"True." Tuck took another sip. "Josh was pretty much tellin' me Fenton would be a loner if he *did* kick up some shit."

"So," Bobby said as he patted Tuck's leg. "How 'official' were you planning to be? Like, do an interview in the town paper, or something?"

Tuck scowled at the thought. "Just gonna let it unfold naturally, I guess."

"Trust me," Bobby said, "if you're gonna do this, you need to get in front of it and own it. Or the shit'll get all twisted up on you."

Scowling again, Tuck looked over at Odis.

"Don't ask me," Odis told him. "I ain't got no advice."

Tuck decided to change the subject. "You guys gonna stay over for a few days? It's just a queen-sized bed, but I think we can manage."

"Not after tonight," Bobby said. "Gertie only managed to get my flight bumped up one day without any charge, so I'm flying out tomorrow."

"Oh," Tuck answered weakly. He stared down at the cast. He hated feeling so helpless, but he was a little concerned about being stuck alone if he *did* end up needing help.

Bobby noticed where Tuck was looking. "Maybe Odis could stay here with you?"

"I wouldn't be around much, though," Odis admitted. "Got the window people and other stuff with the house I gotta take care of."

"Oh," Tuck said again.

Bobby brightened when he had a sudden thought. "Why don't you come *with* me, Tuck? I could use the help getting packed up and all."

"Really? I don't know if I'd be much help, though," he said as he waved the cast around.

"I need to drive my car down too—you could help with that. We could get farther in a day if we take shifts."

"*That* I could help with," Tuck agreed. "But won't that be expensive? Gettin' a last-minute plane ticket?"

"I got money," Bobby said. "Might as well spend some."

"Speaking of which," Tuck suddenly realized, "where's yer duffel? Haven't seen ya draggin' it around."

"Opened an account this morning while Odie was at the doctor's. The bank has it now. Well, the check, anyway. I kept the duffel."

Odis and Tuck chuckled at the joke.

"So how about it? Come with me?"

"Okay," Tuck slowly agreed. "I suppose. I'll go with ya." He smiled.

"Good." Odis nodded. "Then I won't hafta worry about your bonehead butt wastin' away over here," he said as he got up from the couch and went into the bathroom.

"This'll be fun," Bobby said with a grin. "I can show you around. Have ya ever been to the East Coast?"

"No, sure haven't."

"Then there'll be lots for ya to see."

Tuck chuckled. "I think ya've been here too long already."

"Why ya say that?"

"Yer startin' ta sound like a Texan," Tuck teased as he lightly punched Bobby's arm. "It's cute."

"Oh, hush. I'm not 'cute'. I agree with Odie on that one."

Tuck looked at him questioningly.

"He told me 'cute' is for puppies and kittens—shouldn't apply to a grown man."

Tuck laughed and hit his arm again. "Ya *have* been hangin' around us too long."

Bobby scooted closer and swatted Tuck's arm. "I said hush." He gazed up at Tuck, their eyes locking together. Tuck grabbed a handful of Bobby's shirt and pulled him to his face. Their lips touched, and sparks nearly made Bobby's hair stand on end as jolts coursed through him. He leaned forward and wrapped his hands around Tuck's shoulders before nearly collapsing against him.

Tuck pulled back and grinned. "Fuck a duck."

Bobby gazed. "Where'd you learn to kiss like that?"

Chuckling, Tuck wrapped his casted arm around Bobby's neck. "Don't think that's the kinda thing ya learn. It's chemistry, as they say."

"I'll say. It's *somethin'*," Bobby said with a grin as he looked down at Tuck's erection peeking its way out from under the towel in Tuck's lap.

The sound of a clearing throat came from above them. They both looked up to see Odis standing behind the couch, smirking at them. "I leave for two minutes…," he teased as he shook his head and came around the couch.

"Then get over here," Tuck said as he scooted closer to Bobby and made room on the other side. Odis sat next to him. "Ya won't miss us while we're gone?"

"Prob'ly get a whole lotta work done with you guys outta the way. Get the house totally back in shape." Odis looked over at Bobby. "Ya takin' yer dog with ya?"

"*My* dog?" Bobby blanched.

Tuck laughed. "What's this? Bobby got a dog?"

"Heimdalla adopted him," Odis told Tuck. "She's gonna be a miserable bitch while yer gone."

"Adopted?" Tuck asked.

"Since Saturday, she's been Bobby's shadow when we're at the B and B."

Bobby shook his head. "I'm sure she'll be okay once you get moved back into the house. It might just be trauma from the fire and all."

"No," Odis said. "Don't think so. She was gettin' chummy with ya Friday night, before the fire even happened."

"I don't think I can take her on a plane last-minute. That's the sort of thing they need advance warning on." Bobby stood up and fished his cell phone out of his pocket. "Speaking of which," he said while scrolling the screen and punching buttons before bringing the phone to his ear. "Hey, Gertie," Bobby said. He paused and nodded. "Oh, settled in now. He's fine. You busy right now?"

Odis looked over at Tuck and lowered his voice. "You sure about this? Did you tell him?"

Tuck shook his head. "That was a long time ago. I'm not a kid anymore. Nothin' to tell," he said flatly.

"Okay, then," Odis drawled, not sounding the least convinced. "Better call Hawk, though. He'll get mad if ya leave town and he don't have time to dote over you first."

Tuck smirked. "My brother doesn't dote."

"Bullshit." Odis chuckled. "He's as bad as Gertie."

"Dammit." Tuck fastened the towel and stood up. "I was hopin' for some playtime," he said as he headed to the hall table and his cell phone.

"We got all night, don't we?" Odis said while waggling his eyebrows.

Bobby hung up his phone. "All night for what?"

"Playtime," Odis said with a grin.

Tuck grabbed his phone and made his way with a slight limp to the bedroom.

"You need help?" Bobby asked.

"Nah," Tuck replied as he paused in the doorway. "I'm just gonna throw on some sweats."

Bobby looked over at Odis. "Why's he gettin' dressed?"

"Gonna call Hawk and tell him about the trip. He'll surely run over here."

"Oh. Gertie's gonna check on gettin' a ticket for Tuck."

Odis laughed at Bobby's language. "We'll have ya turned into a Texan in no time."

"Shut up," Bobby said with a smirk. "Tuck's already made fun of me. Don't need *you* in on it too."

"I'm not teasin'," Odis said with a grin. "I think it's sexy, you gettin' all Texa-fied."

"Hush." Bobby smirked again. "I'm gonna go check on Tuck," he said as he went to the bedroom. He walked in to see Tuck already dressed in sweatpants and a T-shirt, getting a pair of socks from his dresser drawer. "Odie said ya called Hawk."

Tuck nodded. "The Hurricane will be here shortly."

"Hurricane?"

"That was his nickname in high school. Hurricane Hawk," Tuck said as he sat on the bed and struggled with trying to pull on a sock with just one hand.

Bobby laughed. "I can definitely see that," he said as he moved to the bed to help.

Tuck smiled down as Bobby took over the socking operation. "Nathan musta really loved you."

Bobby scowled. "Yer bringing him up? Shit, I can't even go a day without hearing his name."

"Sorry," Tuck said with quiet sincerity. "I didn't mean anythin' bad."

Bobby softened. "I know. It's just kinda frustrating, being reminded all the time."

Tuck just nodded quietly.

"There," Bobby said as he stood up. "All dressed now."

"Unfortunately." He stood up and followed Bobby to the living room.

CHAPTER
Twenty-Six

IT WASN'T long before a hard knock sounded at the front, right before the door burst open. "Ya just got out of the hospital," Hawk yelled as he came down the hallway. "Ya can't leave town."

"Yes, I can," Tuck said as he stood up from the couch. "Take it down a notch."

Hawk stepped closer and appraised him. "You *sure*? What if ya have a relapse?"

Tuck nearly laughed. "A relapse from what? It's a broken hand, not fuckin' pneumonia or somethin'."

"Still," Hawk tried to argue.

"I won't be doin' anything but sittin' around here for six weeks anyway. I might as well be productive and help Bobby move."

Hawk looked over at Odis and Bobby sitting on the couch, as if he just realized they were there. "Oh. Bobby's movin'?"

"Yeah. I told ya about things yesterday."

"I know, just didn't think... I guess he would hafta move, huh?" Hawk walked around and sat in the reclining chair, looking a bit calmer. "So this? All *three* of ya guys are really...? It's for real?" He glanced over at Odis.

"Yes," Odis said with a nod. "It really is real."

Hawk turned his gaze to Bobby. "And yer gonna take care of him? Out there?"

Bobby chuckled. "I don't think Tuck needs taken care of. He's a big strong man. But I'll keep an eye on him."

Hawk studied Bobby a moment and then nodded. "Ya better." He glanced over at Tuck. "I still don't understand all this, but I ain't gonna get in front of yer happiness." Hawk turned a harder gaze to Odis and Bobby. "But I'm watchin'. I won't hesitate ta stomp either one of yer asses if ya do him wrong."

"Fuck you, Hawk," Tuck barked. "I ain't yer fuckin' *sister*. I can take care of myself. Don't you go meddlin' with this like ya did Vic."

Hawk bristled and stood up. "I only had ta get after Vic 'cause *you* didn't tell me about it. I had ta get some answers some way."

"Right," Tuck said strongly. "I didn't tell ya. *But* ya could have fuckin' *asked* me instead of goin' all Wild West over it."

The two glared over the coffee table, staring each other down. After a minute, Hawk finally dropped his shoulders and let out his breath. "I just worry about ya," he said softly.

"Don't need ya to, but I'm glad you do. I know it's because you love me."

Hawk smirked. "Don't start throwin' *that* word around, or I'm outta here."

"Why not?" Tuck stepped forward and grabbed Hawk in a tight hug. "I'm not afraid to say I love my brother."

Hawk rolled his eyes and patted Tuck on the back as if he was placating a toddler. "All right, enough."

Tuck winced from the pressure on his bruise when he tightened his grip. "Say it."

Hawk squirmed and tried to break Tuck's hold.

"Say it," Tuck demanded.

"Okay, I love my brother. Now let me go."

Odis glanced over at Bobby, ready to make a joke, until he saw the tear forming in the corner of Bobby's eye. Odis turned and threw Tuck a look.

Tuck caught the look and glanced back at Bobby. Remembering that comment Bobby made about brothers in the hospital, Tuck released Hawk. "Now get on outta here. I got some packing and shit. And I promise to call every day."

Hawk smirked as he headed for the door. "Ya don't hafta go *that* far. Just one or two calls will do. Have a nice trip, then."

"I will," Tuck yelled as Hawk closed the door behind him. He quickly turned his attention to Bobby, who was trying his best to look normal, but his moist eyes betrayed him. "You okay, stud?" Tuck asked gently.

Bobby nodded. "Mostly," he tried to say without a sniffle.

Odis patted his shoulder. "This has to do with *your* brother, don't it."

Bobby nodded as Tuck sat on the couch next to him. "The one who won't look at you," Tuck said.

Bobby grabbed his mug from the coffee table and drank.

Odis frowned. "That must be cold by now. Let me get ya a refill."

"I don't care," Bobby said.

"We're all here now," Odis told him with another shoulder pat. "Just go ahead and tell us. Then ya won't ever hafta say it again."

Tuck reached out and grasped Bobby's thigh gently. "We're here. Right here for ya."

Bobby stared down into his empty mug, watching the reflections of light in the dark-glazed interior as he turned it in his hands. "My childhood wasn't the best. It wasn't the worst—I'm sure it could have been much, much worse. But it wasn't the best."

Odis reached out and took the mug from Bobby's hands, then quietly went to the kitchen. He returned and handed a full mug back to Bobby.

"Dad's kind of a hothead. He never beat on us or anything, but he could be very vocal, and I guess—" Bobby took a gingerly sip. "He mouthed off a lot, so he spent a lot of time 'looking for better jobs'. We moved around a lot because of that."

Tuck kept watching Bobby. "He got fired a lot?"

Bobby nodded. "Never *his* fault, of course."

Odis had to bite his tongue. He didn't like seeing Bobby struggle with this. It made him wish he had thought to grab some weed when they were at the house the other day. That might have helped Bobby relax. Couldn't worry about that now, though. He'd just have to be patient and look supportive.

"Anyway, his name's Ricky. My brother."

Tuck nodded as if all of this made perfect sense. It was a technique he'd learned to help keep witnesses at ease when they had to discuss painful events. Sympathy and obliquely probing questions were his best strengths. "What about other siblings?"

"It was just the four of us until junior high. Then, I never did really know if Mom kicked him out or if he just left, but Dad was gone after that, mostly."

Bobby paused and sipped from his mug. "Ricky's the smart one. Skinny but smart. I knew I'd never be as smart as him, but I had the body and coordination he didn't have, so I kinda concentrated on that. And started baseball."

Tuck nodded. "He's older?"

"By about two and a half years."

"And ya started baseball ta get your dad's approval?" Tuck asked in a leading way.

Bobby scowled. "Not Dad. I—I guess instinctually, I knew he was never gonna be happy with anything, so I didn't try. It was for Ricky. With so much moving around, he was my only friend, and I looked up to him."

"What about your ma?" Tuck asked.

"Oh, she rode on me a bit, but I'm sure she was proud of anything I did, as long as I didn't grow up to be a loudmouth drunk."

"So, it was just you, your mom, and Ricky," Tuck prodded.

"Right. He graduated and got some kind of brainy scholarship and went to college. By then, I was in high school and getting a lot of attention with baseball. So I focused more on that. I knew baseball would have to be *my* ticket."

Tuck nodded. "Where'd Ricky go to college?"

"MIT. That's how we ended up in Boston. Mom wanted to move closer, and since she just had a waitress job at the time, she figured she could do that anywhere."

With another nod, Tuck asked, "So she just moved ya? In the middle of high school?"

"Yeah. I shoulda realized then…." Bobby trailed off before finishing his coffee.

Tuck watched Bobby carefully. As his story got closer and closer to that moment of pain, Bobby's face tightened with more tension, looking more like a cringe.

Odis reached out for the empty mug and asked, "Realized what?"

Bobby clutched the mug and wouldn't let Odis take it. "That *he* was her favorite."

Tuck raised his hand from Bobby's thigh and took hold of the mug. Bobby finally released it. Tuck left and returned a moment later with a full mug, which he handed over.

When Bobby brought the drink up close to his lips, he could smell the alcohol. "What the hell is this?" he asked, staring at Tuck.

"Hot Jack," Tuck said, but Bobby just looked confused. "Coffee with Jack Daniel's."

Bobby looked down at the drink, then sipped it.

Tuck nudged his arm. "Yer in a new high school…," he encouraged.

"Right. New high school. I dated girls, just enough to avoid any rumors, and put all my energy into baseball. And it paid off. Scouts started noticing me."

"That must have been exciting," Tuck said when he saw the brief look of joy on Bobby's face.

"It was. And Mom was so excited when Notre Dame people came to visit. Most of her family's Irish Catholic."

Odis looked surprised. "That's where ya went?"

"No." Bobby shook his head. "Got a scholarship at Boston University, but she was just as happy about that."

Tuck chuckled. "I'll bet," he said with a grin.

"Things got… kinda weird after that."

"Weird?" Odis asked.

"Mom started gushing all over me, which she'd never, ever done before. It made Ricky a bit jealous, I think. Anyway, then she married this guy she's been seeing awhile, Gerry. A real creepy guy. So I tried to avoid them."

Tuck nodded. "What do ya mean by 'creepy'?"

"Still don't really know. Wasn't anything I could ever put my finger on, but the first time we were alone, I got so weirded out by him that I thought my skin was gonna crawl off."

Odis nodded. "So that Gerry guy's why ya didn't wanna go home that first summer?"

"Yeah." Bobby took another sip. "I steered clear of him as much as possible."

Tuck looked over Bobby, feeling perplexed. Usually he had no trouble at all putting together various little pieces of a story and figuring out where it was going, but deducing the ending of Bobby's story eluded him. Who was the principal player? This Gerry guy? The mom? Tuck knew the brother factored into it somehow, but he couldn't see how Ricky fit into this mosaic.

Feeling dumb, Odis looked over at Tuck. He could see the guy's cop gears turning and churning, but they didn't seem to be getting any traction. Tuck was just as confused as he was, which made him feel a little bit better.

Bobby sat quietly, sipping without saying more.

Tuck patted Bobby's leg. "So ya graduated Boston University? What was your degree?"

"Business. Generic business. I didn't have it in me to be a lawyer or anything. I only had a 3.6 grade average."

"Then?" Odis asked, thinking that kind of school record was nothing to sneeze at. "What happened at Boston U.?"

"Well." Bobby drained the mug. "You know I met Nathan that summer. He suggested we go see my mom that weekend, and I could come out and show him off. But I didn't listen." Bobby shook his head. "Looking back, I bet he was trying to change the course of things, but I was too stubborn."

Odis took the mugs this time. After he brought back the refills, Bobby sniffed it and smelled only coffee.

"So," Bobby continued, "on Tuesday, we decided to have breakfast on his porch. We horsed around a little and started making out. We moved it inside to the living room, and things got really hot and heavy on the couch. In our hurry, we didn't close the front door all the way."

Bobby grimaced briefly. "When we heard someone come in the hallway, we didn't have time to scramble and get dressed before he came into the living room." Bobby clutched the mug.

Tuck patted his leg again. "Who came in?"

Hesitantly, Bobby said, "Ricky." He gulped down some of the coffee, but it was still hot, burning his tongue, and he winced. "He—when he saw—Nathan on top of me, he—Ricky went absolutely bat-shit. I mean utterly, insanely crazy."

Tuck gave Bobby a moment to collect himself, then urged the story forward. "What did Ricky do?"

"He went into a rage and started babbling all kinds of shit while he pulled Nate off of me and punched him. When I stood up, he punched me, then screamed something and took off. I pulled on my clothes and tried to follow him, but he was already gone."

Odis put his hand under Bobby's chin and pulled his gaze out of the coffee mug he was clutching so tightly. "What kind of shit did he say?"

"It was, like, babbling mostly. Gerry, he said his name a few times, something about being corrupted, called Nathan a faggot. Not very coherent stuff."

"Okay," Tuck said. "So you tried to follow him, but he'd left. What happened next?"

"I came back in the house and Nathan was waiting for me. He'd already packed up a bag and handed it to me. Then Nate said, 'Go to your mom's. You need to get through this,' before he tried to push me out the door."

Odis frowned. "That's what Nathan said?"

Bobby nodded. "So he knew. He already knew what was gonna happen. I can see that now."

Tuck nodded. "Then what happened?"

"I argued with him. Tried to steer Nate to the kitchen and get some ice or something for the red mark on his cheek that was swelling up and starting to bruise. But he argued back, getting more insistent, and eventually pushed me out the door."

"Okay," Tuck said with a nod. "Then you went to your mom's?"

"No, not right away. I went back to the apartment to get some stuff. I don't even remember what was so fucking important I had to go get."

"Then what?" Tuck asked.

"I drove out to Mom's. She wouldn't open the screen door for me. She wouldn't look me in the eye, either. She told me to take my business elsewhere, like I was the fuckin' Avon Lady or something."

"What did you do then?"

"I tried to talk to her. I begged her to look at me. She started crying. Then Ricky came up behind her and pulled her out of the doorway and slammed the door in my face."

"And after that?" Tuck asked.

"I hung around. I thought maybe once she had time to calm down, we could chat. So I hung around down the street until I saw Ricky leave. And I went back." Bobby took a deep breath. "She still wouldn't open the door. Mom told me Ricky was too disgusted to deal with me. I told her that I'd seen Ricky leave, and it was just me and her. I begged her to let me in. She started crying again and said she wasn't gonna go against Ricky's wishes and closed the door on me."

Odis scowled. "Holy fuckin' shit. How could a mother *do* that?"

Bobby shook his head. "She felt like she had to choose, I guess." His face twisted with grief. "Shit. That fucker Nathan. Why didn't he *tell* me? Be more direct? If I'd gone that weekend or even left right when Ricky did, I might have been able to talk to her before Ricky poisoned her against me."

Tuck wrapped his arm around Bobby's shoulder in a reassuring hug. "You can't beat yourself up over it. You didn't know."

"But *he* did. Fucking bastard Nathan *knew*."

"Stud," Odis said and waited for Bobby to look at him. "We don't have any way of knowing *what* Nathan saw. Maybe, from his side, it just looked like a speed bump or something. Ya can't blame him, or yerself, for any of it."

Nodding in agreement, Tuck said, "It was the actions of Ricky. He's the one responsible."

"I'm responsible too, though. If I hadn't been so careless and stupid. If—"

"Stop it," Odis said sharply. "Those 'what ifs' never go anywhere but Crazytown."

"Right," Tuck agreed. "Did you try to see her again?"

"Not until the funeral. Didn't get to talk to her, though. Gerry saw me first and had his brother throw me out. Damn weasel couldn't even do his own dirty work."

"What funeral?" Tuck asked pointedly, following some strange suspicion.

Bobby clutched the coffee mug so tightly, Odis thought the clay cup was going to shatter in his hands. Bobby finally whispered, "Ricky's."

"When was this?" Tuck asked.

"End of that year."

"How…?" Odis asked.

"Ninety-five-mile-an-hour collision into a highway bridge pylon. Right after Christmas."

"Fuck," Tuck muttered before he caught himself. He pulled his cop face back on. "What did the investigators come up with?"

"Never came right out and said. Report did mention he never braked before he hit the bridge. Minimal alcohol, no drugs. I think it must have been a suicide."

"Why?" Odis asked.

"He'd flunked out that semester, the papers later reported. Maybe he couldn't face the humiliation of it."

Tuck shook his head but didn't say anything. His cop instincts told him that, more likely, poor school performance was just a symptom of a nastier underlying cause, the *real* fuel for the suicide. He looked over at Bobby. "Can you recall anything more specific Ricky said when he was babbling?"

"Does it fucking matter?" Bobby asked as he shook his drooping head.

"Guess not," Tuck said, letting the subject drop.

Odis shrugged at Tuck almost apologetically. He hadn't expected Bobby's past to bring the evening to a screeching halt and leave the atmosphere burdened with such a heavy dankness.

Tuck frowned back. He waffled between weeping or punching somebody. He gave Bobby a squeeze around the shoulder, then stood up and went into the bathroom.

Odis tried to ignore the clattering noises that sounded like plastic bits bouncing around on tile. A minute later, the guys couldn't ignore the shattering noise of something like heavy glass breaking. Odis just smiled weakly at Bobby when he looked up.

Bobby held up his empty mug. "I think I want another one of those Black Jacks."

"Hot Jack," Odis corrected. "I'll get ya one." He claimed the empty mug and went to the kitchen.

Bobby turned to look over the couch at him. "Isn't Jack Daniel's from, like, Kentucky or Tennessee? Don't Texas have its own whiskey?"

"Not really. Distilling laws were pretty restrictive after prohibition. Things have only loosened up recently. So Jack is an honorary Lone-Star whiskey." Odis brought back the full mugs as Tuck left the bathroom.

"What's that about whiskey?" Tuck asked as he stepped into the living room.

Odis glanced over, noticing Tuck didn't have his mug anymore. "He just asked why Texas doesn't have its own whiskey."

Tuck went into the kitchen and started another pot of coffee. "I could give ya a lecture of the history of Texas liquor laws," he yelled over his shoulder. "But I doubt ya really wanna hear all of it."

Bobby shook his head. "Prob'ly not."

Odis chuckled. Tuck stepped to the back of the couch and looked quizzically at Odis. "He said 'prob'ly'," Odis explained. "Our evil plan to turn him into a Texan is working."

Tuck chuckled along.

Bobby smiled weakly. "Guess bein' a Texan is a good as any other."

Tuck bristled in mock surprise. "Ya hear this bullshit, Odie? We're just as good as everybody else?"

"Almost sacrilegious," Odis agreed as he punched Bobby in the arm. "Texas is the only state that was ever its own country first. We're *better* than everybody else."

Bobby chuckled back. "Oh? But ya don't even have yer own whiskey," he teased.

Tuck smiled. "Workin' on it. Got some good contenders, just a matter of who rises up to top dog."

Odis nodded. "That Balcones might."

Tuck scowled as the coffee pot beeped. "Not that blue corn shit. My money's on Garrison Brothers," he said as he went back into the kitchen area.

"*Blue* corn?" Bobby asked.

Odis nodded. "Made with blue corn and cocoa in the mash. Ya didn't even mention Rebecca Creek," Odis yelled at the kitchen.

"That's fer highbrows," Tuck said, shaking his head as he came back to the couch. "Not quite the same thing, so it don't count."

Bobby looked over at Odis and smiled. "Now you've got me curious. What does *blue* corn taste like?"

Odis and Tuck shared a quick gaze. Then they burst into grins. "Taste test!" they yelled out at the same time. Noting Tuck was still dressed in his sweats, Odis stood up. "I'll run to Pearl's and we can settle this."

"Don't get lost," Tuck teased as Odis left the apartment.

"Who's Pearl?" Bobby asked.

"Owner of the liquor store. It's just across the street," Tuck explained before he got up and dug around the kitchenette for his short bourbon glasses.

CHAPTER
Twenty-Seven

AFTER Bobby and Odis downed several sample shots, they failed to reach a consensus. Bobby quickly grew fond of the unusual touches of flavor in the Balcones, but Tuck smirked when he sampled a tiny sip and claimed the mocha hint was just "too damn weird" as he continued to defend the Garrison Brothers. Odis couldn't decide either way. He thought they tasted pretty much the same. Bobby and Tuck both teased him, saying straight boys must not have delicate enough palates to tell the difference.

In a much lighter and tipsier mood, Bobby returned from the bathroom and dropped to the couch between Odis and Tuck. "No more," he said. "Or I'll end up shit-faced."

Tuck reached out and stroked Bobby's jaw. "Yer face never looks like shit."

"Yer right 'bout that," Odis agreed as he gazed over.

"You two," Bobby said with a grin as he patted each guy on the nearest leg.

Odis grinned back. "Us two, what?"

"A couple of horndogs, I think," Bobby said.

"Well," Tuck drawled, "it *has* been two days. And we missed our big date."

"Real big," Odis agreed. "Two whole days ago too."

"Well then," Bobby said and let out a fake sigh. "Somebody better hurry and kiss me." He leaned back into the couch and closed his eyes. He felt the warm and fuzzy kiss on his mouth and sparklers on his cheek. Keeping his eyes closed, Bobby opened his mouth for Odis, who lightly explored with his tongue as the sparklers moved over to his ear.

Odis pulled back and chuckled. Bobby opened his eyes to see him grinning. "Ya taste like whiskey, stud."

"Really?" Tuck asked as he leaned over. He gently planted his lips on Bobby's mouth. His larger tongue probed at Bobby's as he breathed him in through his mouth. The air sent sparkly shivers down Bobby's neck before Tuck pulled away. "Sure do," Tuck agreed with a silly grin.

"Whatever," Bobby said with a smile as he closed his eyes again. He felt someone shift; then a warm presence squatted between his legs, pushing on his knees to widen the gap. He felt the cold smooth plastic of the cast against his neck as Tuck readjusted and rotated Bobby's head toward him slightly.

When he felt hands fumbling with the waistband of his jeans, Bobby reached down and gently took hold of the hands and pulled Odis toward him. "It shouldn't be like this," Bobby said as he opened his eyes and motioned Odis back to the couch between him and Tuck. "We should take care of Odis, since he's not going with us," he said to Tuck.

Tuck nodded. "That's right, he'll be *all* alone. He'll need somethin' to keep him warm 'til we get back."

"Geez." Odis chuckled. "Exaggerate much?" He sat on the couch between them and thumped at Tuck's ear. "It's not like ya guys are abandonin' me in the desert or somethin'."

"Quit complainin'," Tuck said as he leaned in and touched his sparking lips to Odis's. As Odis opened, Tuck stood and scooted around to Odis's left side so he could rest his casted right hand on the back of the couch. Tuck leaned closer into the kiss while Bobby unsnapped Odis's jeans.

Odis pulled back. "I wasn't complainin'," he said as he gazed at Tuck. While reaching out to stroke Tuck's smartly trimmed graying eyebrows, he lifted his butt and Bobby slid the jeans from his hips.

"Henry, over at the Sharpened Shears," Tuck replied in answer to Odis's unspoken question. "He's been doin' me fer over ten years now."

"Humph," Odis replied with a smirk. "And what exactly has this guy been doing?"

As Bobby knelt between Odis's legs, Tuck swatted Odis on the arm and said, "Nothin' like that. Henry's like, a hundred years old, and the nelliest queen ya've ever met."

"Nelly?" Odis asked.

Tuck shook his head with a smirk. "Clueless straight guy," he said while glancing down to Bobby squatted in front of Odis. He looked back at Odis. "Over-the-top effeminate. Like the worst of the stereotype."

"Oh," Odis said while nodding with understanding. "Haven't met him. I didn't think we had any 'nelliest queens' around here."

"Not," Tuck replied. "He's in Jenkins. I've been goin' there ever since I met him. He was at his sister's house when some shit went down years ago."

Bobby reached out and playfully slapped Tuck's knee. "Are we just gonna gossip over hairstylists? Or...?"

Tuck grinned down at Bobby. "Impatient, are we?"

Odis chuckled. "Who's the horndog now?" he teased.

Tuck adjusted his hips, trying to take the pressure off the bruise near his ankle. Moving didn't help much. With a pat on Odis's chest, he asked, "Can we move this to the bed?"

"Sure," Bobby agreed, standing. He reached out and took Odis's hand and pulled the little man to his feet as Tuck also rose.

Trailing behind Tuck, Bobby said, "I don't have my duffel. You got supplies?"

Tuck motioned to the nightstand. "Second drawer," he told Bobby with a grin as he and Odis sat on the edge of the bed.

Bobby opened the drawer and nearly laughed when he saw the array of lubricants, dildos, and other products neatly arranged in intricate columns inside. "Geez, Tuck, ya should go into retail. You'd have the neatest store shelves."

"Shut up," Tuck muttered with a chuckle. "You've been snoopin' my drawers?"

Odis laughed. "We had ta find ya some socks and undies the other day. Bobby said it was like going shopping."

Bobby looked over the items in the drawer. "What's on the menu tonight?" he asked as he retrieved a larger bottle of lube.

Tuck gazed at Odis. "What would ya like, midget?"

Odis scowled. "Don't fuckin' call me that."

Tuck looked wounded. "I'm sorry, Odie, I didn't mean—"

"I know," Odis cut him off. "Just don't like that word. I hate it when yer brother calls ya that too."

"Well," Tuck said with a sigh, "he means it affectionately, even though it started as payback."

"Payback?" Bobby asked.

"Growing up, bein' older, I was bigger and used to tease him with it. When Hawk hit puberty and outgrew me, he started teasing me back with it. Now it's just kinda a thing."

Odis shook his head. "Still don't like it."

"Okay." Tuck leaned down and kissed his forehead. "I won't ever use it again."

With the drawer still open, Bobby glanced over at Odis and went back to the question. "What do you want, Odie?"

"I still haven't—ya know," Odis said with a shrug.

Tuck looked over at Bobby, sharing a worried glance. He knew neither he nor Bobby would be considered "starter" material.

Bobby gave a weak smile, silently saying, *If it's what the man wants,* and turned back to the contents of the drawer.

Tuck looked back at Odis. "Ya sure?"

Odis gave a stiff nod in reply. "Yeah." He sat up straighter. "Ya wanna leave me with something to remember, right?"

Bobby reached into the drawer and got the blue silicone stick arranged with smaller Ben Wa beads. The first bead was smaller than a pea, but each of the ten beads graduated larger in size along the stick to a final bead, about the diameter of a hefty English walnut. Bobby wrapped his hand around the large end and used his arm to shield the rest of the rubbery silicone stick before closing the drawer and going to the bed. "Okay," Bobby said with a warm smile. "Then get the rest of those clothes off."

Tuck reached out and lifted Odis's T-shirt off.

While Odis's head was covered, Bobby quickly removed his own T-shirt and hid the beads inside the wad of jersey cloth before dropping it on the bed next to the bottle of lube. Bobby watched Tuck move Odis farther up the bed as Bobby slipped off his shoes and socks. Bobby slithered out of his jeans as Tuck pulled the boxers down Odis's legs, revealing a half-mast erection that continued to grow.

After directing Odis to turn on his side facing away, Tuck tried to quickly yank off his sweatshirt, but the material grabbed and caught on an exposed part of the Velcro strip on the cast. Bobby leaned forward to help him untangle, then grasped Tuck by the shoulders and pulled him toward the edge of the bed. As Tuck dropped the sweatshirt on the floor, Bobby leaned in next to his ear and whispered, "You ever been with a virgin?"

Tuck shook his head. "At least not that they said," he whispered back. "You?" he asked as he slipped off his sweatpants.

Shaking his head, Bobby whispered, "Guess we'll just hafta go real slow and wing it."

As Tuck nodded, Odis called out, "What's all that whisperin' for?"

Tuck crawled back onto the bed. "Just comin' up with a game plan," he said as he sat above Odis's head.

"Now's not the time for any fuckin' surprises," Odis scolded as he propped himself up on his elbow.

Bobby scooted up behind Odis's butt. "Just relax and trust us. You do trust us, right?"

Odis smirked. "I'm beginnin' to wonder, when ya ask questions like that."

Bobby picked up the T-shirt, adjusting it so that only the first two small beads of the Ben Wa stick were visible. He held it over for Odis to see. "We're gonna start out real small."

Odis eyed the iridescent robin's-egg blue of the beaded stick. "And it won't hurt?" he asked. Now that he had time to think about it and recalled the size of the men beside him, maybe this wasn't such a good idea.

Tuck leaned down but had to readjust when the pressure on his side bruise complained. He kissed Odis with brief sparks. "It didn't hurt when I used the vibrator, did it?"

"No, that was just—weird."

"I promise," Bobby said, "as long as you relax and follow directions, this won't hurt. It might feel kind of awkward and strange sometimes, but it'll be pleasure too."

"Okay," Odis agreed with a nod and lay back down. "I trust you."

While Tuck positioned Odis's knees up toward his stomach, Bobby dropped the T-shirt and applied some lubricant to the end of the stick, keeping it behind Odis's back. He slowly teased Odis's anus with the small end. "Now just relax. Your first instinct will probably be to clamp down and fight it, so just resist that urge. Try to open up to it."

"Okay," Odis said. "Let's do it, then."

Tuck leaned closer and rubbed Odis's neck. "Close your eyes. Just feel it."

Closing his eyes, Odis tried to concentrate on the rubbing sensations near his opening. It did feel nice, much more pleasant than he had expected. When he felt more pressure, Odis relaxed and allowed the bead to penetrate. The tiny bit of sensation as the bead slipped in didn't hurt at all. He tried to appreciate the strangeness.

Tuck moved his hand up to Odis's cheek. "Yer smiling."

"I am?" Odis asked as he looked up.

"Close your eyes," Tuck urged as he rubbed at Odis's forehead.

He felt Bobby move the stick around a little. "Number two," Bobby said as he slid in the second bead. While Odis felt a tiny stretch, he thought he must be more sensitive to the sensation now—he could actually feel every bit of movement as the bead popped onto the other side of the muscular ring. It felt nice.

Bobby moved the stick around inside him a little. "How is it so far?"

"Nice. Weird. Feels like I hafta pass gas."

Tuck chuckled.

Odis was slightly surprised when Bobby reversed direction and slowly pulled the bead out. He felt the stretch of the firm bead. Now that he knew what to expect, he relaxed further, and it seemed to heighten the pleasure even more.

Bobby squirted more lube onto the second and third bead. "Okay, going back in."

Odis kept his eyes closed and concentrated on the feelings of stretch and movement. "It's good, by the way, since ya didn't ask."

Tuck chuckled again. "With that grin on yer face, didn't think I had to ask."

"Oh. Oooh," Odis replied, his tone changing as the third bead entered. This one felt *so* much bigger as his sphincter stretched wider to accommodate it. He opened his eyes in surprise.

"Eyes closed," Tuck said as he rubbed Odis's shoulders again.

The muscle closed, trapping the bead in as Odis took a deep breath. This definitely led to a strange, more "full" sensation. When Bobby wriggled the stick inside, Odis thought he felt the tiniest something as the end of it brushed the interior wall of the colon. The awkwardness of the sensation must have shown on his face, because Bobby asked, "Keep going?"

"Yes," Odis said with a nod. "It's just weird and different."

Reversing direction again, Bobby slowly pulled out the third bead. Odis let out a tiny moan as it stretched his hole and slid out. Odis clamped his jaw closed. He wasn't gonna let himself get carried away like some silly girl. No need to get all vocal over having a piece of rubber stuck up his butt.

Bobby lubed the third and fourth beads, then inserted the stick again.

Odis concentrated on relaxing as the third bead penetrated and stretched again. Another moan slipped out. Bobby wriggled the stick a little. "Four," he announced as he advanced the stick farther in.

This time, Odis felt the stretch again, and it kept stretching to the point that he felt a little tingle in the muscle as the new larger bead moved inside. He clamped his jaw and inhaled, forcing himself to be quiet.

Bobby wriggled the stick a little. "You okay?"

Odis nodded, fighting another moan as the end of the stick brushed the colon's interior wall, and he felt a stronger sensation of something, almost like he had to pee. "Enjoying," he finally managed to say without moaning.

After slathering more lube onto the exposed stick, Bobby wiggled it again and announced, "Five."

Odis worked on relaxing as the bead pushed its way in. This one seemed *so* much bigger, the widening leading to even more of that warm tingle before the muscle closed around the other side of the globe shape. He tried to fight the sound, but another moan escaped.

Tuck glanced over at Bobby. "Just rest a minute," Tuck said as he rubbed Odis's forehead. "Breathe a little."

"I'm okay," Odis said.

Bobby wiggled the stick again. This time, when the tip brushed against the colon wall, the sensation felt even stranger. Not in a bad way, just very different from anything Odis had ever felt before. Bobby rotated the stick more. The pressure of the foreign object on his interior wall was kind of odd. Odis stayed silent. He couldn't think of any words to describe the sensation.

"Ready for another?" Bobby asked.

Odis nodded. "How big *is* this stick?" he asked.

Tuck rubbed his cheek. "A couple more beads, if ya want more."

"Yes. Want more."

"Okay," Bobby said as he slathered lube onto the next bead. "Six."

Odis felt the familiar stretch that continued. The warmth heightened as the larger bead opened the muscle a little more, then the muscle slipped over the end of the globe, and the bead nearly plunged inside. "Oh," Odis moaned unexpectedly at the feeling of having even more inside him.

Bobby paused before wiggling the stick again, watching Odis's face as it squirreled up into a weird expression. "You okay?"

"Yeah," Odis said with a nod. "This. It's just—" Odis still couldn't think of any words to describe it. Bobby maneuvered the beads, and he felt that intense pressure on the front side of his colon that made his dick jump again. "It's—" He felt Tuck lean down and kiss him, fireworks nearly exploding in his gut as Bobby continued.

Odis opened his mouth to Tuck's kiss and tasted the whiskey on his gently probing tongue as he heard Bobby say, "Seven."

As another moan escaped into Tuck's mouth, Odis felt himself open further, those sensations growing more enjoyable with the familiarity. This bead felt even bigger, cranking up the signals from his nerve endings as his hole spread wider to accommodate it. He reflectively pulled his knees up, moving into more of a fetal position as he opened himself to accept it. The bead seemed to slip inside with an audible sound as Odis moaned again. Tuck's kiss grew more fervent at the sounds of Odis's pleasure.

The stick wriggled again inside him, but the sensations inside weren't quite the same, not intense like before. Odis pulled away from Tuck. "I think it's too far in," he said.

"Hurts?" Bobby asked.

"No, just not the same… oomph it had before," Odis tried to explain.

"Prob'ly past the G-spot." Tuck replied. "Ya wanna stop?"

Odis paused, not thinking of a reason to end this. "How many more?" he asked as he turned and glanced over at Bobby.

"Three," Bobby said. "But you've done great for your first time. We can stop if you want."

"No," Odis said. "I wanna go for it all. It's—almost addictive." He let out a strange chuckle.

Tuck grinned down and kissed Odis again as Bobby applied more lube and announced, "Eight."

Odis closed his eyes as the new bead pushed against his hole. This one definitely felt larger, but he relaxed and accepted it, feeling those new sensations as it slowly slid farther inside. With a moan, he pushed down, enjoying the movement as he pulled the bead inside himself. "Fuck," he muttered with another moan. "That's so—"

Bobby added more lube to the stick. "Nine," he said with a grin as pushed the Ben Wa stick forward. He watched Odis, seeing that same look of lost bliss that had covered his face when Bobby gave him the blow job days before.

Odis pushed down. Bobby was moving the stick so slowly, and he wanted that sparkly feeling now. This wider bead brought out even more intensity as it stretched open his hole. "Fuck," he moaned again as the bead, which felt like a golf ball, slipped inside. "Incredible," he managed to say as the residual warmth danced in his sphincter.

"Last one," Bobby said as he started to push.

Odis couldn't wait. He rose on his elbows and pushed down onto the stick. "Fu—" he moaned as his opening stretched even wider, sparking with wild intensity as what felt like a tennis ball opened him up and slipped inside. He nestled back down with his eyes closed, just enjoying the residual pulses and that feeling of fullness from the foreign object inside him. "Shit," he moaned with a wide grin. "If I knew it was like *this*, I'da bought a dildo years ago."

Tuck laughed warmly. "I think we found another bottom."

"Looks that way," Bobby agreed with a chuckle.

Looking down at Odis, then over at Bobby, Tuck couldn't help but grin. This was what sex was supposed to be like. Instead of power games or nervous tension or desperation to get off, it should be sharing and fun. Just like this. Sex, for him, hadn't felt this way in years, probably not since his early twenties, when the world was new and all full of excitement.

Still wearing the silly grin, Tuck gazed over at Bobby. "Think we need a break now. You want some dinner?" He shifted as if he was getting ready to crawl off the bed.

Bobby grinned back. "Hm, need to think on that a minute."

"Hey, boneheads," Odis yelled. "What about me? Still have a stick up my butt."

Tuck and Bobby both laughed. Tuck smiled down at him. "I'm not even gonna take the bait on that one. *Way* too easy."

"Actually," Bobby said when he stopped laughing, "you can do the extraction yourself, Odie. You can either reach back and pull it out, or you could try to expel each bead one at a time and practice some refined muscle control."

"Expel?" Odis asked.

Tuck chuckled again. "Basically, just poop it out."

"Oh," Odis said, feeling utterly stupid when he realized how easy that would be.

"Or," Bobby offered, "I could pull it out for you."

Odis shook his head. "No, let me try *expelling* it myself," he said, thinking "expel" was a much nicer word than "poop." He closed his eyes, relaxed his sphincter, and pushed with his rectal muscles. The bead caused the now familiar stretching and tingling as it emerged past the muscular ring and suddenly popped out. Odis quickly clamped down again before the next bead escaped.

"Keep going," Tuck urged.

Odis did the next few beads the same way, but the warmth lessened each time as the beads reduced in size. He didn't have enough control at the end and the last three beads all expelled at once. "Oops," Odis said in an almost defeated tone.

"That was great," Bobby complimented him. "It takes *a lot* of practice to control the really small ones, so don't feel bad."

Odis sat up and grabbed the stick, actually seeing the beads for the first time. "That's all?" he wondered aloud. "That last one felt like a tennis ball."

Bobby and Tuck laughed. "No," Bobby said. "Lots of sensitive nerves down there make things *feel* bigger than they really are."

"Yeah," Tuck agreed. "If ya did do a tennis ball, it would feel like a watermelon."

Odis stared over at Tuck quizzically. "You did a tennis ball?"

Tuck smiled and shrugged.

Tuck crawled to the end of the bed. "You guys ready for that dinner now?"

"Hey," Odis nearly yelled, "we just got started here, I hope. Don't go runnin' off now." The pleasure he felt from the stick left him itching for more. He wanted the real thing now.

Tuck frowned. "That's not enough?"

"I thought," Odis said with a smirk, "one of you *men* was gonna screw me, but now I'm wonderin'...."

"Hey," Bobby called back defensively.

Tuck bristled. "That's a cheap blow. And *not* the way to get on my good side."

Odis huffed under his breath. "Well, wasn't this just supposed to be a warm-up?"

"Okay," Tuck said with his hands up in defeat. "Decide who ya want."

Odis looked from Tuck to Bobby. "Bobby's smaller. Maybe start with him."

Tuck crawled off the bed and retrieved a small hand towel from the top drawer of the nightstand. He handed the towel to Odis to clean up the Ben Wa stick before continuing to the living room.

Bobby went to the nightstand and checked the toy drawer. "Maybe one more stretching first?"

"Okay," Odis said with a resigned sigh.

Tuck brought back the bottle of Garrison Brothers whiskey and their glasses. He poured a couple of fingers in each glass and handed them around before leaving the bottle on the nightstand. "Liquid courage," he said in a half-assed toast.

Bobby downed his glass and set it on the nightstand before he got one of the larger anal plugs from the drawer. "If you can handle this first, then okay."

Odis eyed the purple silicone plug that started with a small taper but widened to nearly the size of a golf ball at its largest point. "That's not bad," he said, nodding and taking another sip of his glass. "I don't understand why ya guys are bein' so reluctant."

"'Cause," Tuck said as he finished his glass and climbed back onto the bed, "we don't wanna hurt ya, bonehead." He looked over at Bobby. "We'll stop anytime you say. You don't hafta do this to prove something."

Shaking his head, Odis reclined onto his side. "Not tryin' to prove anything. I just want to feel yer dicks in me." He pulled his knees up. "So let's get on with it."

CHAPTER
Twenty-Eight

AFTER being very liberal with the lube, Bobby inserted the end of the anal plug just inside Odis. Odis closed his eyes and enjoyed that sensation of stretching again. As Bobby pushed it in farther, the warmth joined the stretch, almost making Odis sigh in pleasure. More widening led to more intense pulsing. It felt like his sphincter was open to the same point as that last Ben Wa bead, and a tiny moan escaped him.

After a brief hesitation to wriggle the plug a little, Bobby gently pushed it in farther.

Tuck felt another boner growing as he watched Odis. That look of slackened bliss on Odis's face and the tiny little moans he made quickly had Tuck solidly hard and leaking. This scene really turned him on, which surprised Tuck a little. He'd never thought of himself as a voyeur. He reached down and stroked Odis's cheek. "You really like this," he said in an almost teasing tone.

Odis nodded. *This plug feels nice, but it also feels—what?* Odis struggled in his mind for the word. *Inanimate* was the word that finally surfaced. *It feels dead and unyielding.* That thought made Odis even more determined for the feeling of live flesh.

As more spreading continued, the nerve signals intensified further, then changed into something less pleasant. Tuck must have seen something on his face, because Odis heard his voice aimed at Bobby, saying, "Hold on." The plug stopped moving.

Tuck stroked his cheek again. "Hurt?"

"No," Odis told him. "Just kinda—uncomfortable."

"Take a breath," Tuck said.

Odis inhaled, feeling Bobby remove the plug a little, then wriggle it a bit. Odis opened his eyes and looked up at Tuck. "How much more?"

"Almost there," Bobby answered. "A quarter inch more, about."

Tuck gazed down at Odis and stroked his jaw. He didn't bother to ask if Odis wanted to stop, because Tuck saw that look of determination in his brow.

Odis closed his eyes again when the tingles lessened, and nodded. "Okay," he said as he concentrated on relaxing his sphincter.

Bobby squirted a little lube onto the plug, then twirled it around to spread it evenly before pushing in slowly again. Odis felt the stretch and very intense tingles, but they didn't pass the point of pleasure this time. The movement paused, then resumed, opening the sphincter even more and more. If Odis hadn't seen the plug beforehand, he'd have sworn it was as big as a grapefruit. The nerve signals intensified again, growing into a sharp prickly sensation before the plug seemed to suddenly leap forward as his sphincter closed around the end of the bulge.

"Oh my God," Odis said with a moan.

Bobby leaned down and shared a warm kiss with Odis before saying, "Now, see if you can expel it."

Odis relaxed and bore down, but the plug seemed to be firmly planted. He couldn't get it to move.

Seeing the frustration on Odis's face, Tuck leaned down. "It's okay." He looked over to Bobby. "Help him with it."

Bobby took hold of the large, circular flange bottom of the plug and slowly pulled. The plug popped out, leaving Odis feeling suddenly empty. "I want *you* now, stud," Odis told him.

Jacking himself, Bobby stiffened his erection and applied some lube to his cock. "Okay, then you'll get me," he said with a touch of excitement in his voice.

Tuck started to scoot down for a better view, but Odis put his hand on Tuck's thigh. "Don't go anywhere," Odis said before leaning forward and licking the end of Tuck's leaking dick. The precome tasted salty and kind of starchy, making Odis think of potato chips.

Bobby reclined on his side and spooned in behind Odis. He positioned his cock. "You ready?"

Odis nodded as he licked Tuck's dick again. "Oh," he exclaimed with a moan as Bobby's dick stretched its way into him. Just like the anal plug, it kept stretching and spreading to that tingling point. "Lord have mercy," Odis muttered.

Bobby stopped. "Too much?"

"No. Keep going," Odis almost whined. This felt so different from those silicone things. This was Bobby's flesh, which felt so alive. The stretching stopped, but the tingles continued as Bobby entered farther and filled him up.

"Odie, you are *so* tight," Bobby said as he pushed farther in. He hadn't topped in so long, he'd nearly forgotten that feeling of the warm fleshy glove engulfing his cock. Bobby slowly slid forward until he was fully inside.

Odis couldn't believe how incredible this felt. Live flesh, with a heartbeat, buried inside him. When Bobby stopped, he practiced relaxing and tightening his sphincter. "All the way," Odis said.

"Greedy bitch." Bobby chuckled. "I'm in to the balls already," he said, shifting and giving one final nudge up against Odis's butt.

Just from watching Bobby and having Odis lick his prick, Tuck felt near an orgasmic climax. "You guys are *so* fuckin' hot."

"We are?" Odis asked as he leaned forward a bit more and slurped in the head of Tuck's dick.

"Fuck yeah," Tuck muttered.

Odis pulled back from Tuck's dick and tried to glance around at Bobby. "Well?" he asked, wondering why he wasn't moving.

"Give me a minute," Bobby said softly. "Or this is gonna end real fast."

Odis chuckled, feeling Bobby's hug tighten as he did so. "Now ya know how *I* felt the other night."

"Hush," Bobby said. He used only his hips to pull out about an inch and slip back in. "Better?"

"Oh," Odis said under his breath. "Holy fuck, yes."

Odis was too distracted to keep working on Tuck's prick, but strangely, Tuck didn't feel at all neglected. Just watching those pleasured expressions on Odis's face as Bobby impaled him was enough satisfaction. "Gods afire," he muttered.

Feeling Bobby move out again, Odis relaxed. He clamped down his sphincter when Bobby changed direction and slid back in.

"Shit, Odie," Bobby hissed. "So fuckin' tight." A little faster this time, Bobby slid out and back in again.

Bobby's dick inside him felt so wonderful all on its own, but it seemed there was something missing. As Bobby moved again, Odis asked, "What about that G-spot thing?"

"You ready for that?" Bobby asked rhetorically as he adjusted his angle to push his cock farther forward and slid out about four inches. He pushed forward and in, but Odis didn't really respond. Bobby slid out a bit farther and tried again. He knew he found it that time from the strangled moan that escaped Odis's throat.

"Oh fuck," Odis muttered as his dick jumped. It had been at about half-mast, but that little maneuver woke it up.

"Like that?" Bobby asked as he pushed forward again.

"Oh yes."

Tuck scooted down to Odis's hard and pulsing prick and stroked it lightly.

Odis looked down at him. "Don't make me come yet."

Tuck frowned. "Why not?"

"Because you're next, bonehead," Odis said with a chuckle.

Bobby stopped moving. "You want him too?"

Odis nodded.

"Okay, then, slow down, stud," Tuck said as he climbed off the bed. He retrieved something from the toy drawer and returned to the bed. He lubed up a bright-orange anal plug and inserted it into himself.

Odis shook his head. "No, I want *you* to fuck *me*," he told Tuck.

"I get it," Tuck answered. "But while I do that, Bobby can take *me*."

"Oh," Odis muttered as Bobby adjusted the angle again. "Shit," Odis spat in frustration when he realized they would be behind him.

"What?" Bobby asked and stopped moving.

"Nothing, really. I just won't be able to see it. We need some mirrors or somethin' in here."

Tuck chuckled in agreement. "Yeah, that *would* be hot, wouldn't it?"

"If we're changing out, better do it now," Bobby said as he withdrew himself from Odis. He scooted farther over on the bed, making room for Tuck to get between them.

After lubing himself up, Tuck hugged in behind Odis and kissed his ear. "You are so fuckin' hot. I don't think this will take very long." He positioned his prick and entered Odis. He'd been prepared to move slow, but Odis opened up and more than half of him slid in with the first push. "Fuck, Odie," Tuck said with a chuckle. "You *are* a greedy bitch."

Odis chuckled. "Lots of years to make up for, I guess."

Tuck bit his lip as the sphincter around his prick clenched with spasms while Odis laughed. He was already so close to the edge, he could feel his prick start the final swelling before ejaculation. Tuck pushed farther in.

"Oh, holy fuckin' shit," Odis muttered with a moan. Tuck's flesh was even more of a presence than Bobby's. He worked on relaxing, wanting it all.

Tuck pushed all the way in, then brought his knees up behind Odis's, creating a sort of fetal spoon. He reached back and popped the plug from his butt like a cork. He waited while Bobby lubed up and got behind him. Tuck had fantasized about this sort of thing but had never actually experienced it before. He felt himself agreeing with Odis. They definitely needed some mirrors so he could appreciate the full view.

Bobby got behind Tuck and pushed into him. He nearly gasped at the feeling. Odis had been like a warm glove, but Tuck surrounded him like a hot, tight fist. Bobby had to fight a climax just from pushing inside. He gave his all and then hugged behind Tuck.

No man said a word for a moment. They enjoyed the feeling of each other's bodies. Tuck finally asked, "How do we do this?"

Bobby adjusted and scooted back a little. "I guess you'll have to be the one to move, mostly."

Tuck nodded and then slowly pulled out of Odis, moving back onto Bobby as he did so. "Oh shit," he said. He pulled away from Bobby and leaned forward into Odis again. "Oh shit. I can't even describe this," he told them. "But it's not working very well. I don't think either of you is really getting serviced right."

Bobby withdrew. "Then maybe you should take care of Odis. Then I can come back while you're still in him."

"Sound good to you?" Tuck asked into Odis's ear.

"Whatever works," Odis agreed.

Tuck scooted back and adjusted his angle, then drove more firmly into Odis.

Feeling shivers in his groin from the new angle of Tuck's dick, Odis moaned and muttered, "Holy Christ." Tuck's dick felt so different from Bobby's. Another movement and Tuck bumped into his prostate again. Odis felt a strange tingling in his balls as Tuck hit against the gland once more, causing his dick to swell so hard, his head emerged from within its foreskin sheath.

Increasing the pace, Tuck angled more toward the back for some faster thrusts, then moved forward again, hitting at the gland twice in quick succession. The bumps set Odis's groin into climax, and he nearly screamed as Tuck bumped the gland again as his body started pumping the semen forward. It felt as if Odis's orgasm started at his navel and traveled quickly downward inside. His dick jumped again from another prostate poke. "Jesus, I'm fuckin' coming," he managed to squeal out before his dick spurted gobs of ejaculate all over the bedsheets in front of him.

The clenching of Odis's anal sphincter was all Tuck needed. He withdrew himself until only the head of his prick was inside and let the spasms work him into climax. "Fuck, Odie, I'm so clos—"

He suddenly felt Bobby enter him again, that talented prick of his going right for Tuck's G-spot. Bobby slammed his spot three times in quick succession, and Tuck yelled out, "Valhalla!" as he exploded inside of Odis, eliciting huge moans from the little man.

He felt Bobby's prick swell before Bobby moaned out, "Oh shit."

Bobby came, pulsing and throbbing inside Tuck before falling on top of his back. With his own knees weak, Tuck nearly collapsed onto Odis, but he managed to kind of roll sideways a little and fall onto the bed.

The three men lay silently on the bed a few minutes, panting and breathing heavily from their physical efforts. Tuck finally broke the silence. "Can we have some dinner now? I'm still starving."

Odis chuckled as he rolled over. "Geez, Tuck, you blow my mind with the best sex I *have ever* had, and all you want is food?"

"Hey, I've been on that hospital shit they called food for two days. I need some fried chicken."

Bobby nodded as he sat up. "Fried chicken sounds damn good to me. With lots of those home-style french fries."

"And some okra too," Odis added. He glanced over at the sweat glistening on Tuck. "But we need showers first. And we ain't all three gonna fit in yer little excuse for a tub."

"Oh, definitely not," Tuck agreed.

"How about," Odis suggested, "Bobby hop in first, then he can run get the food while we clean up?"

Tuck looked over at Bobby. "You know where it is?"

Bobby crawled off the bed. "Yeah, went for chicken the other day," he said over his shoulder as he headed for the bathroom.

CHAPTER
Twenty-Nine

THE next morning, Tuck and Bobby barely made it to the airport in time for their flight.

They settled into their seats on the left side of the smaller plane. Bobby took the one near the window and Tuck sat by the aisle.

As he stuck his duffel under the chair, Bobby glanced over and noticed Tuck looked a little pale. "You ever flown before?"

Tuck plastered on a fake smile. "Sure, once."

Eyeing him as Tuck tightly clutched the armrest with his left hand and held his casted right hand close to his chest, Bobby asked, "And?"

"I was just a dumb kid. I'm sure the excitement was what made me throw up."

"Wonderful," Bobby muttered sarcastically. "Just once?"

Tuck shook his head. "Twice. Once at takeoff, then again later."

Bobby pried Tuck's hand from the armrest and surrounded it with his fingers. "Look at me, Tuck," he said. "Take a deep breath." He glanced over at the little pocket in the back of the seat ahead of them, relieved when he saw the top of a sickness bag sticking out from behind the magazine. Hopefully they wouldn't need it.

Tuck turned and inhaled sharply.

"Just look right at me. You're getting yourself so worked up, you're gonna blow a gasket or something. Slow deep breath." Bobby took in a breath, watching as Tuck copied him. "Look right in my eyes and tell me a story."

"Story?"

Bobby nodded as he slowly exhaled. "Yes, a story. Tell me about your first day at the academy."

Tuck winced. "Let's not go there right now."

"Okay, okay." Bobby inhaled deeply and Tuck copied him. "Then something happy. Tell me about your first time. You haven't told me that story yet."

"First time?" Tuck asked quizzically. "Oh, you mean sex?"

Bobby nodded as he exhaled.

Tuck relaxed a bit as he also exhaled.

With relief, Bobby watched some color return to Tuck's face.

Tuck glanced around the plane, but none of the other passengers seemed to be paying any attention to them. With a lowered voice, he asked, "You mean, the *first*-first time, or the first *real* time?"

Bobby didn't understand the difference, but he wanted to keep Tuck talking as long as possible. "Tell me both," he said with a warm smile as he reached over and closed the little shade over the window.

"Okay." Tuck nodded as he exhaled slowly. "The *first*-first time, I was thirteen."

Bobby squeezed Tuck's hand to keep his attention as the stewardess stood at the front and began announcing the safety protocols. They felt the plane jolt slightly as it started to move. "Keep those green eyes looking at me and go on," Bobby said with warm encouragement.

Tuck took a few breaths. "I'd seen Wally eyeing me. He was in my class but fourteen. He seemed older and so much more mature...." Tuck took another breath. "Anyway, I invited him along to go dirt biking. We ended up in the woods. And the subject of masturbation came up." Tuck grinned as he remembered. "Before I knew it, we both had our pants open, jacking away. He seemed very hesitant when I touched him, but he still got into the idea. Wally touched me briefly, and I decided to taste him. I bent down and barely had him in mouth when he squealed and pulled away, coming all over me." Tuck frowned.

"What happened after that? Did he reciprocate?" Bobby asked with an encouraging hand squeeze.

"No. He zipped up, hopped on his bike, and took off. He wouldn't even look me in the eye after that."

"Bastard," Bobby replied as the plane rolled farther from the gate. He felt Tuck's grasp tighten. "And what about the other one?"

Tuck smiled wistfully. "Oh, that was the second time I went to Amarillo. I'd barely had enough courage to walk into a gay club the first time I visited. That second time, I actually made it up to the bar and ordered a beer."

"I never imagined you being so unsure," Bobby said as he felt the plane turning onto the runway.

Tuck shook his head. "Wasn't unsure. I knew I was gay, knew what I wanted, but I'd already started the academy and was so worried about being outed."

"So you got a beer. Then what?" Bobby asked when Tuck clenched his hand while the plane began accelerating.

Tuck took a deep breath, gazing into Bobby's eyes and trying to ignore the plane's movements. "I got the beer and kinda scoped the place out. I was kinda cruising this studly guy sitting by the pool table, but he hardly gave me a once-over before ignoring me."

As the plane left the ground, Tuck started going pale. Bobby started massaging Tuck's hand between his palms and asked, "Then what?"

"This skinny guy came over and said hi to me. He was kinda cute, but not the type of guy I would'a chased after. Me and Dale talked over beers for almost two hours, and I kinda warmed up ta him."

Happy to see Tuck looking more composed, Bobby smiled. "See there? Nothing to be nervous about. We're already airborne."

"Yeah, I guess."

"So what happened with Dale?"

"Oh, he asked me if I wanted to leave, so I followed him out to his truck. And we made out there for a while. He was my first kiss, if ya don't count Odie."

"What? You'd *kissed* Odie? When?"

"High school prom. Just a quick peck on the lips, but he was too drunk to really remember it."

"Oh," Bobby said with a chuckle. "I'll hafta rib him about that." He let go of Tuck's hand. "So you and Dale just made out?"

"For a while. Then he invited me to his apartment."

"Did he know? That it was your first time?"

"I didn't tell him at first. But once we got to his place, I started gettin' nervous, and he noticed. So I told him." Tuck hesitated.

"Did he get off on that?"

"No. In fact, he almost kicked me out. He said my first time shouldn't be just a hookup."

"Wow, kind of a gentleman, then."

Tuck nodded. "Yeah. So I told him 'bout my situation and how it kinda limits my opportunities, and managed to reassure him. And we eventually ended up in his bed."

"Then what?"

"I actually met up with him a few more times until he called it off. Said he didn't like the long-distance thing."

"Oh, that sucks."

Tuck nodded. "But he had a point. I wasn't exactly available. I was still fightin' to keep it all on the down-low, and it wasn't really fair to him."

Bobby patted his hand. "You okay now?"

"That was a fuckin' long time ago. And there weren't really any hurt feelings."

"No, I mean about flying."

Tuck wobbled his head. "Oh. Still tryin' not to think about it. But yeah, not nauseous or anything."

"Good."

Tuck settled back into his seat. When the steward came by with the drink cart, both men just got soft drinks. Looking over at Tuck, Bobby commented, "I'm surprised. I figured you would go for some alcohol."

"No, I'm actually good now, I think. You're so calm and easy to talk to. It's part of what I love about you."

Bobby nearly choked on his gulp of soda before breaking into a wide grin. He gazed over at Tuck. "Bastard," he said.

"What?"

"You tell me you love me for the first time while we're in a plane full of people. And I can't even kiss you or anything."

Tuck gazed over at Bobby, then smiled and leaned down. "Fuck it," he said as he kissed Bobby's lips.

Bobby shared the sparking kiss very briefly before pulling back. "Let's not make a scene," he said with a sigh.

"Okay," Tuck agreed as he settled back into his seat. "How long *is* this flight?"

Bobby took his hand. "Quit thinking about it. Just take a nap."

Tuck doubted he could sleep, but he closed his eyes and nestled into the chair. It *had* been a long and pleasantly tiring night. Maybe he could doze for a minute or two.

A BIT later, when Bobby continued feeling the vacuumous pressure in his ears that refused to clear, he pulled out his duffel bag and dug around inside for a pack of gum. While searching, he stumbled across the printout note Odis must have stuck inside. He pulled out the note and the gum.

"What's that?" Tuck asked groggily.

Bobby unfolded the note and handed it to him with a few pieces of the gum. "Nathan's last riddle. The inscription that was to go on the bust he ordered from Odis. We can't make heads or tails of it."

Tuck opened the gum and put it in his mouth before reading over the printout.

turn around the sine, fluff the feathers and freshen the nest
treasure Be un-mined, upon our Early Day of the past

"Well, it has something to do with your bedroom, I would guess."

"How do you get that?" Bobby asked.

"The nest part. It's usually a metaphor for a place to sleep, like a bedroom." Tuck peered carefully over it and then chuckled when he spotted something. He handed the note back to Bobby, saying, "Look at the only capital letters."

Bobby read aloud, "Be Early Day?"

"B-E-D," Tuck said with a nod. "So, definitely your bed."

Chuckling, Bobby shook his head. "God, that seems so obvious now. How did Odie and I miss it?"

"Prob'ly 'cause ya were too focused on the meanings of the words. Didn't actually look at the structure or patterns," Tuck said with a smile.

"Okay, genius," Bobby said with a teasing smile, "what about the rest of it?"

"I'm sure those are clues that'll make sense once we find out whatever it is about the bed. You said this was supposed to go on a bust?"

"Yes. Bastard was gonna have Odie deliver a bust of his own head, with that inscription, in July, for our anniversary."

Tuck crinkled his lips. "Gods, that's kinda—creepy."

"Tell me about it. I'd have been a basket case had it just shown up unannounced." Bobby folded up the paper and put it back in his duffel. "Guess we'll have to wait and see. But definitely need to take a close look at that bed when we get there."

Nodding, Tuck reached over and patted Bobby's hand. "Then we will." He glanced over at the closed window shade. "Can you open that?"

Bobby glanced over at the window, then back at Tuck. "You sure?"

"Yes," Tuck said with a smile. "I'm fine now. I'd like to see."

"Okay," Bobby said with a touch of hesitation in his voice as he reached over and raised the shade.

"Wow," Tuck said as he leaned over and peered out at the crystal-blue sky cluttered with bulbous clouds. "That is so freakin' beautiful."

"It is, isn't it," Bobby agreed as he looked out. He turned back to Tuck. "We've still got a ways to go. Why don't we try and nap for a bit?"

"Sure," Tuck agreed as he settled back.

Bobby nestled in and closed his eyes, hoping the landing would go as smoothly for Tuck as the takeoff had. They both soon dozed.

Later, they landed without incident. Tuck actually slept through it and didn't awaken until the plane decelerated on the runway.

Bobby grinned over at Tuck as his grass-green eyes blinked blearily. "Welcome to Boston."

CHAPTER
Thirty

TUCK gaped as they approached Bobby's house. The guarded gate at the entrance to his neighborhood was impressive enough, but seeing the huge house at the end of the long driveway left him speechless.

"It's not all mine," Bobby told him. "All this and to the east is a park. My part is just the house and half-circle drive."

"Still." Tuck gazed around, wide-eyed. "It's quite a house. Why such a big one?"

"Nate wanted it. At one point, he had plans for lots of kids."

"But you never did? Get kids, I mean?"

"No, he suddenly dropped the idea about ten years ago. Guess he saw they weren't in the future anymore."

Bobby pulled the Prius into the giant garage. After grabbing their bags, Bobby led Tuck into the house. Tuck tried not to stare at the dirt bikes, two other covered vehicles, and plethora of other items on the way to the door.

As they moved through the hall to the living room, Tuck paused to look at the pictures hanging on the wall. He stopped when he saw a framed photo of Bobby and another man, taken a few years before, from the looks of it. The other man's reddish-brown hair and taller build made him freeze. "*That's* Nathan?" he asked while pointing at the photo.

Bobby backed up and looked at the photo. "Yeah. That was taken right before his dad died."

"Shit," Tuck hissed. "*That's* the guy who ran into me."

"*What?*"

"Yep, sure is," Tuck said as he took one last look at the photo, then took his bags to the living room.

"When was this? Where did you see him?" Bobby asked as he dropped his bags by the couch and led Tuck into the kitchen.

"Like I said, he ran into me. Literally."

Bobby retrieved two beers from the refrigerator and motioned for Tuck to sit at the counter bar when he handed one of the bottles to him. "Literally? What do you mean?"

Tuck nodded as he opened his beer. He had to hold the bottle against his chest with the cast and use his free hand to twist the top. The maneuver was almost becoming second nature now. "About… six years ago, I guess." Tuck took a sip.

"And this was in Texas?"

"Yep," Tuck said with a nod. "In Jenkins, actually. I'd just gotten a haircut and came out to find a white Mustang parallel parked *right* in front of me. Barely inches of a gap."

"Damn," Bobby spit out. "He drove his own fuckin' car to Texas? This must have been during the season. I don't remember him *ever* taking a trip like that."

Tuck shrugged. "I got into the SUV and was gonna grab my ticket book. Not that I could have written one—legally, anyway, since it was Jenkins—but I wanted to put a scare into whoever did such a lousy parking job."

Tuck paused and took another sip. Bobby gazed over at him. "Were you in uniform?"

"Think I was." Tuck nodded. "I'd just sat down in the SUV when I felt the jolt. I looked up to see that damn Mustang had backed right into my cruiser. I immediately jumped out to confront that idiot driver."

Bobby chuckled. "And I bet you looked so happy and cheerful too."

Tuck smirked. "Right. I checked and didn't see any damage to either vehicle. It was more of just a bump than actually hitting me. And Nathan got out, all apologetic. I remember those hazel eyes of his, almost yellow-green, the way they glowed as he yammered away with that thick Massachusetts accent, trying to talk his way out of a ticket."

"He could really be a charmer," Bobby said wistfully.

"And I remember he kept touching me on the right forearm. Which I thought, at the time, was pretty damn ballsy. Most people wouldn't dare touch a cop in that kind of situation. I can't think of *anybody* else ballsy enough to ever touch me like that."

"Was kind of a thing for him, touching I mean. Always touching everybody. I'm guessing now, that's part of how his vision worked." Bobby sighed. "So you let him off?"

Tuck chuckled. "Like I said, couldn't have written a ticket anyway, but I gave him a thorough what-for over being so damn careless."

"Then he left?"

"I had to back up first to give him room to maneuver out. But there was something he said before he got back in the Mustang. I'm trying to remember it."

"Oh." Bobby smiled crookedly. "Was it one of those half-baked off-the-wall statements that didn't seem relevant?"

Tuck nodded.

"I got those a lot." Bobby nodded. "Of course, now I know it was his way of trying to clue me in to something he saw, usually a warning or a nudge of some kind."

Tuck leaned back into the chair and closed his eyes. "What in Valhalla was it?" he asked himself aloud as Bobby fetched two more beers.

"Real estate," Tuck nearly yelled out as he sat up again. "He said, 'Take into account all the real estate you've forgotten' as he got in his car."

Bobby smirked. "More cryptic bullshit."

"I guess," Tuck said as he clutched the new bottle to his chest and opened it. "Speaking of cryptic bullshit, maybe we should go check on that bed."

"Yeah, sure," Bobby said. He got up and led the way up the stairs. He paused at the entrance to the master suite, letting Tuck stroll into the room first.

"Wow," Tuck said as he glanced around at the rich furnishings. "Was he a decorator?"

"No," Bobby said as he shook his head and stepped in. "Just landscaping. I'm sure he hired one, though."

Tuck set his beer on the nightstand. "What did that poem say? Something about fluffing the feathers?"

"Shit," Bobby said with a sigh. "It's still downstairs in my duffel. I'll run and get it."

After Bobby left, Tuck pulled the pillows out of the covering spread and gave them a quick examination. Because he couldn't grip them with his casted hand, he had to use his mouth to bite the satiny cases and slip them off the pillows so he could check for any hidden writing.

Bobby returned. "Right. It says, 'fluff the feathers and freshen the nest'."

"Well, it's not the pillows," Tuck said over his shoulder. "Maybe the mattress?"

Going around to the other side, Bobby yanked off the covers and sheets. They didn't see anything on top of the mattress. Bobby lifted his side as Tuck slid the mattress toward him so they could flip it over.

"Wait," Bobby said. "Pull it off."

Tuck grabbed the mattress as best he could with one hand and steered it as Bobby pushed from the other side and forced it to the floor. Tuck could see the plywood square that had caught Bobby's attention in the center of the bed's lower platform-style box frame.

Tuck stepped around to Bobby's side. "What's that?" Tuck asked. "A trap door?"

"Don't know." Bobby kneeled onto the frame and lifted the loose plywood. "Nathan redecorated in here two years ago, while I was on the road," he said while moving the square of plywood then setting it aside on the floor.

Underneath, they found a firesafe door, one of the old-fashioned kinds with a turn knob for the combination. "Well, that fucker." Bobby nearly giggled. "I never knew this was here."

Tuck chuckled. "Now the part about turning makes sense. So the combination must be in the poem too."

"Right," Bobby said, nodding as he read over the note again. "Upon our early day of the past," he read aloud. "Which day?"

Tuck sat on the edge of the box frame and peered over. "You said you were supposed to get this on your anniversary? Try that date."

"Right," Bobby said with a nod, and he turned the dial to seven, then four, and ended on the current year. He pulled at the bar, but it didn't move.

"No," Tuck cut in. "Early day. The year you actually met."

"Right!" Bobby said with enthusiasm as he redialed the numbers using the earlier year. He pulled on the bar, and this time it swung across with a click. He lifted open the safe door, holding his breath in anticipation of what "treasure" they might find.

His excitement soon deflated when all they saw was an eight-by-eleven manila envelope sitting on top of a stack of notebooks. Hundreds of notebooks, from the looks of it.

Tuck started laughing aloud, almost guffawing with throaty barks as he pulled out the envelope.

"This isn't fuckin' funny," Bobby nearly spit.

"Don't you see?" Tuck said as he pulled out the top notebook, with the dates August to October clearly written across the front. "The bust was symbolic. These are his journals. His *mind*." Tuck laughed again. "Even in the poem, he used the homonym 'un-*mined*'."

"Fuck you, Nathan," Bobby growled in frustration.

"Stud," Tuck said in a soothing voice as he started pulling out notebooks, "you wanted some answers. Here they *are*. He prob'ly wrote down everything he ever saw and why he did or didn't do whatever about it."

Bobby looked at the growing stack of books next to Tuck as he retrieved them from the safe. Nathan's choice of documentation material seemed very inconsistent. Some of them were simply written on yellow legal-style pads. Others were done in fancier three-ring binders. Deeper into the stack, others were done in spiral-wired notebooks, and he even saw a few of those bright-blue college composition-style notebooks.

Down at the very bottom, Bobby noticed some bright-red covers. He reached in and yanked out two of the Big Chief primer writing notebooks, dated from when Nathan was only five years old. "Holy shit," Bobby whispered. "He wrote down *everything*," he said with a touch of awe in his voice.

"Sure looks like it," Tuck said with a nod. He held out the manila envelope to Bobby. "This must be his final note."

Bobby wobbled his head without taking the envelope. "Let's take it downstairs. I need another beer."

"Okay," Tuck said. He clutched the envelope to his chest with the cast and grabbed his bottle from the nightstand before following Bobby out of the room.

They settled back at the kitchen counter. Tuck slid the manila envelope over to Bobby.

"No," Bobby said as he shook his head. "*You* read it."

"But, he left it for you," Tuck argued. "*You* should read it."

"Then read it aloud," Bobby said firmly.

Tuck sighed, opened the envelope, and slipped out half a dozen printout pages of words. He cleared his throat. "Hey, lover." Tuck paused and looked up. "You sure you want *me* to read it?"

"Yes," Bobby hissed out, still feeling a bit disappointed at the paltry findings in the safe. "Or I'll throw the fucking thing in the trash."

Tuck cleared his throat and started again. "Hey, lover. I know you've spent the last months utterly pissed at me because of the things I've kept from you. And I know it will be at least a year after finding this note before you can appreciate my final gift. Right now, you probably don't even want to look at them, but eventually you will. New paragraph. I'm not sure when you might see this note. The window of possibility is open from as early as April to as late as August, depending on how things roll out."

Tuck paused to take a sip of beer and nearly spit it out when he silently read ahead to the next line.

"What?" Bobby asked as Tuck took another sip.

"But if Tuck is the one reading this to you, then even though Tuck may disagree as he rubs his cast"—Tuck scowled as he yanked his left hand away from his right arm, pulling his fingers off the Velcro strap he absently fiddled with—"things really have rolled out by the best scenario."

"Bastard," Bobby said.

"New paragraph. I've really hated keeping all this secret from you. So many days, I had to fight not to spill my guts about the aneurism or my visions. But Sharon helped keep me on track. Not so much directly, but the memory of how it changed our relationship back when I had that weak moment and spilled everything to her back in high school kept me steady."

"Stop," Bobby said as he scowled. "High school? I thought he met her in college. Damn liars, the both of them," he spit out. "Will these secrets *ever* fuckin' stop?"

Tuck reached out and took Bobby's hand, offering his support. "I think they're stopping now." Tuck held up the stack of pages as evidence. "He's got a lot more to say."

"Fine," Bobby said with a tone of defeat. "Read on, then."

Tuck gazed over at Bobby, then stuck the pages back in the envelope before pulling Bobby over into the crook of his armpit. "We can do this later."

"Sure," Bobby agreed as he nestled against Tuck's chest and rested his head on the man's shoulder. "Later sounds good."

Tuck hugged him closer, enjoying the feel of Bobby in his arms. "Later," he said with a hard sigh.

Bobby rotated around and looked up at Tuck. "Are you upset with me?"

"Why the hell would I be?" Tuck asked. "It must hurt like a bitch hearin' Nate's words from the grave, so to speak."

"No." Bobby shook his head. "Not that."

"Then what, stud?" Tuck asked in sincere confusion as he gazed down at Bobby.

"I never answered you when you said that on the plane."

Tuck continued looking down in confusion.

"When you said you love me."

"Oh. *That*." Tuck hugged Bobby with a tighter squeeze briefly. "Not upset at all. I hadn't even thought about it 'til ya brought it up. I don't expect ya to feel obligated."

Bobby nestled against Tuck and bit down on a yawn.

Sitting up, Tuck patted his shoulder. "We should get the bed back together and get our bags upstairs. I think you need a nap."

"The bed's fine the way it is. I actually staked out one of the guest bedrooms."

"Okay, then. Let's go upstairs," Tuck said as he leaned Bobby upright and pulled him to his feet.

"Yeah, a nap sounds good," Bobby agreed as he followed Tuck to the living room. They picked up their bags and took them up the stairs. Bobby led Tuck down the hall to the guest room.

After fishing his phone from the duffel bag, Bobby set it on the charger and put the duffel aside. Tuck set his bags on the other side of the bed and started removing his shirt.

"Curtains," Bobby said as he moved over to the window. He pulled the heavy drapes closed.

"Doesn't look like anybody could see in," Tuck said as he gazed out at the expanse of the vacant grassy park before Bobby closed off the view.

"This window's on the east. Sun gets kind of blinding in the morning. I kept forgetting to close the curtains before bed."

Stripped down to nothing but his boxer-briefs, Tuck pulled back the bedcovers and climbed in. As he pulled off his own clothes, Bobby noticed the huge egg-shaped bruise on Tuck's side looked really nasty now, all yellowy and almost green at the edges. It must be feeling better, though— Tuck wasn't moving about as gingerly as he had before. Bobby stripped himself to nothing but socks and slid into the sheets, then scooted over to Tuck.

"I thought ya wanted a nap?" Tuck teased as Bobby pushed into him with his naked body.

"Take off those boxers. We can sleep in a minute."

Without argument, Tuck slid off his underwear and threw it out onto the floor. He hugged up against Bobby, their hardening pricks solid presences pressing up against each other. Bobby leaned forward and kissed Tuck with lips weary and needy. Tuck put his hand behind Bobby's head as he kissed back gently, lending comfort with his passion. Bobby pushed his hips up against Tuck as he moved his hands to Tuck's lower back, carefully avoiding the bruise as he pulled him closer.

Tuck pulled back and lightly rubbed his stubbly cheek against Bobby's. "You feel so nice," he nearly sighed out.

"I was going for more than just *nice*," Bobby said as he pushed his hips into Tuck again, driving his hard cock against the other man's stomach.

"Well, that too," Tuck said. "But we're not gonna get any sleep if ya keep that up."

"Like I said, we can sleep in a minute."

"I'm too tired for anything very involved," Tuck said as he stifled a yawn.

Bobby leaned back far enough to reach the nightstand. He pulled a bottle of lube and a hand towel from the drawer before turning back to Tuck. "Doesn't have to be any more involved than this," Bobby said as he squirted some lube onto his cock and put another squirt on his stomach. He leaned into Tuck again, his cock now gliding smoothly against the other man.

"Oh," Tuck said as he pushed forward, sliding his prick along Bobby's slickened stomach. "Goin' for a quick slip-and-slide." Tuck grinned before kissing Bobby deeply as they moved their hips in an asynchronous rhythm.

The sparks of Tuck's kiss and the firmness of his slippery stomach soon had Bobby close to orgasm. When Tuck changed the angle slightly so that the heads of their cocks bumped into each other with each stroke, the maneuver put Bobby even closer. He could feel Tuck's cock swelling harder and firmer against him as his rhythm slowed. "That's it," Bobby urged as he pulled away from the kiss. "Let me feel it." He pushed himself harder against Tuck.

"You first," Tuck nearly hissed as he held his breath and stopped moving.

Bobby put his hand on Tuck's hip, pulling at it at the same time he drove harder against Tuck. "If that's what you want," Bobby said as he felt Tuck's body stiffen next to him. The head of his cock bumped into Tuck's again, sending a shiver through his balls. "Now," Bobby said before one final stroke drove him over the edge.

"Thank gods," Tuck choked out as he clutched up against Bobby, their pulsing pricks coming all over each other in the fleshy fold of their bodies.

Bobby gazed into Tuck's eyes as they panted and clung to each other. Bobby cleared his throat before whispering, "I *do*, you know." He smirked. "It's almost spooky how fast, but I do love you already."

Tuck smiled warmly. "I thought so," he drawled slowly before leaning in and kissing him.

Bobby rolled his hips out far enough to clean up their slickery mess with the towel. He threw the used cloth toward the nightstand, but he didn't know if it landed there or fell to the floor, and didn't care either way. "Now we can sleep," he said with a lazy grin as he nestled up against Tuck again.

Tuck let out a quick hiss. "Bruise," he explained as he tried to shift under Bobby's grasp.

"Oh, sorry," Bobby replied with a flinch, moving his hand farther down to Tuck's hip.

Tuck hugged him tighter and exhaled a sigh. It didn't take long for the comforting embrace to lull Bobby into sleep.

SOMETIME later, Bobby awakened to an empty room. With the heavy drapes closed, he couldn't tell if it was still daylight or if the full dark of night had arrived. He rolled over to face the nightstand to look at the clock. The LED display showed 8:27 p.m. as the current time.

Bobby continued rolling and got out of bed. He claimed a pair of workout pants from the dresser drawer and pulled them on, then grabbed a T-shirt and slipped into it as he left the room to find Tuck. *Maybe he went down to the kitchen?* He doubted that thought as soon as he saw the light pouring out of the master bedroom doorway at the other end of the hall. Bobby moved down the dim hallway to investigate.

As he stepped in the doorway, Tuck looked up from the floor. Wearing only his boxer-briefs, he was sitting cross-legged, the stack of notebooks arrayed in front of him in a fairly neat semicircle as he held one of the red Big Chief writing pads in his hands. "Hope you don't mind?" Tuck asked.

"Of course not. Somebody should read them, I guess," Bobby said as he walked up and sat on the floor near Tuck.

"These first ones are really sad," Tuck said as he held up the red child's primer. "At five years old, Nate thought he was insane, soon to be put away in the 'hospital with locked doors', as he called it, just like his grandmother."

"Geez," Bobby cursed. "Committed? He never told me any of that."

"Hurts my heart," Tuck replied. "Not only sufferin' those kinds of thoughts, they were compellin' enough to drive him to write it all down. At only *five* years old," he emphasized again with a frown.

"He didn't, did he? Go to an institution, I mean."

"No, looks like he learned to keep his mouth shut about his visions when he realized nobody else saw the world that way. Sounds kind of remarkable to see everybody connected together with different-colored threads." Tuck sighed. "I'm not explainin' it worth a shit. If you read the first one, he goes into great detail about how it all worked," Tuck said as he motioned to the first red notebook at the far left end of the semicircle stack.

"Not today," Bobby answered. "Prob'ly not for a while."

"I can agree with that on this past stuff," Tuck said as he leaned over and took Bobby's hand. "But that envelope. We really should get to that soon, I think."

Bobby shook his head.

"He probably have something important to tell you, with all those pages."

"*You* read it, then," Bobby said. "And you can tell me if there is. Nate already saw you reading it, anyway."

Tuck gazed over at the resolve in Bobby's eyes. "Okay, then."

Bobby stood. "Let's get some dinner. I'm hungry," he said as he left the room.

Tuck put down the red notebook and followed Bobby downstairs to the kitchen. He was surprised to see Bobby go to the phone instead of the fridge.

"Chinese okay?" Bobby asked as he picked up the receiver and punched in three numbers.

Tuck nodded as he sat down at the counter. He opened the manila envelope and pulled out the pages of notes from Nathan.

Bobby spoke with someone at the guard's station and made arrangements for a food delivery while Tuck read through the letter.

He hung up the phone and turned to Tuck, saying, "It'll take about forty-five minutes."

Tuck nodded and kept reading. Scurrying around, Bobby got plates, silverware, and napkins and brought them to the counter as Tuck made it through two more pages.

Bobby started to sit but jumped up again and retrieved two beers from the refrigerator, which he brought back to the counter. He opened both, saving Tuck the trouble.

Tuck finally put down the last page without saying anything.

"Well?" Bobby asked, surprised by how interested he actually felt.

Taking a sip of the beer, Tuck pulled together his thoughts. "First off," he began while looking at Bobby, "what does 'Buzzer' mean?"

Bobby smiled crookedly and laughed. "His nickname for me. He tried calling me hummingbird after we got the tattoos, but it was kinda awkward and never stuck. Then I once remarked when we saw some hummingbirds at the zoo, they made a buzzing kind of sound and didn't really sound like birds. And he started calling me his 'Buzzer' after that."

Tuck nodded in acknowledgement. "You really should read it." Seeing the hard look in Bobby's eyes, Tuck continued, "But I guess I'll give you the main highlights." He picked up the pages and scanned over them again. "Don't hassle Sharon or Ivette; they don't know anything."

"Oh, okay," Bobby said with a smirk. "Hadn't planned on it. Yet, anyway."

"He says you probably won't, but he wants you to at least read the Big Chief notebooks, just for background."

"Maybe," Bobby considered.

Tuck turned to the next page. "If April 3 hadn't happened, something much worse would have. He doesn't come right out and say, but he kinda hints that I might have ended up dead."

Bobby scowled. "Shit. How the *hell*?"

"Carl Travie was a double agent. I guess he couldn't get through to the brothers and warn them about the raid ahead of time, so that's why he was inside the house, trying to warn them. Maybe them trying to shut down the cookers was what caused the explosion."

Bobby shook his head as he looked at the cast. "But if that hadn't happened, you wouldn't have been hurt."

"Not then, no. Nate wrote down that if Travie was confronted later, it would turn into a hostage situation. And even more people would have died."

"Oh. I see."

"He details it all out," Tuck said, offering the pages to Bobby.

"Later," Bobby said dismissively as he waved his hand. "Anything else earth-shattering?"

"Well, he does mention Ricky and some details *I* was suspicious of after hearing your story." Tuck paused until Bobby looked him in the eye. "Gerry abused him."

"What? Abused how?"

"Nate doesn't come right out and say, but I'm suspecting from Ricky's reaction to finding you with Nate... it was sexual abuse."

"*What?*" Bobby shook his head violently. "No fucking way. Ricky had just started college when Gerry showed up. He would have been eighteen by then. It's not like he was some little kid who could be taken advantage of."

"Doesn't matter," Tuck argued. "Someone can be vulnerable to a crafty predator, no matter how old they are."

Bobby shook his head as he sipped at his beer. "I still can't see that."

"Okay. So let me ask, did Ricky have a *better* relationship with your dad?"

"Maybe, for a while."

Tuck nodded. "As I guessed. Then he may have had a desperate craving for that missing father figure, which Gerry, if he's a skilled predator, could easily have exploited."

Bobby softened at that explanation. "Maybe. Why do you keep using the word 'predator'?"

"It's the word Nate used, and he hints Gerry's had several victims besides your brother."

"Fucking bastard," Bobby spit out. "He knew about Gerry this whole fucking time and let him go on to get *more* victims? How *could* he?"

"It's not that simple," Tuck tried to defend Nate. "It's very clear from what little I've read, Nathan saw the world and all its intricacies in a way you and I could probably *never* really understand. But from what I gather, Nate trying to alter things is like pulling on the thread of a sweater. Too hard, or in the wrong place, or at the wrong time, and the whole damn sweater unravels to nothing." Tuck frowned. "Well, that may be a bad analogy. I don't think Nate was a threat to destroying the universe," he said with a smirk. "But it seems trying to change things could often be a delicate matter. He did say Gerry will get caught in June, though. So we'll have to trust Nate's judgment."

"I guess," Bobby conceded when the doorbell rang.

He returned minutes later with bags of Chinese food. "Anything else?" Bobby asked as he pulled out the cartons and arranged them on the counter.

"Oh, Odie's not supposed to read the Arvin book, whatever that is," Tuck said as he grabbed the carton of General Tso's chicken. "The rest is more personal, that you should read yourself."

"Fine. I'll read the damn thing later."

Tuck sampled the chicken, a little surprised by the flavor. The orangey sauce didn't have quite the same sickly-sweet taste he was used to from the Texas chefs. With less sugar, more of the peppery bite came through. "What *is* the Arvin book?" Tuck asked between bites.

"A book that was part of that first scavenger hunt. I think I told you already. *Woke Up in a Strange Place*, the one about the afterlife."

"No." Tuck shook his head. "Don't believe you did. You mentioned something about a scavenger hunt that first car ride but never went into any details."

"Oh." Bobby chewed another bite of his wonton. "Well, it's a good book, won some awards and shit." Bobby picked at the rice on his plate. "After seeing all those shelves in your apartment, I'm guessing you like to read. I should just let you have it to judge for yourself. Unless Nate said I'm not supposed to."

"No, he just said not to let Odis see it."

"Wonder why?" Bobby mused aloud.

"Maybe there's something in it that triggers a bad memory for him? I'll read it and see if I can figure it out."

Bobby nodded. They finished the rest of their meal in quiet contemplation.

CHAPTER
Thirty-One

AFTER eating and cleaning up, Bobby led Tuck downstairs into the den. The book he'd retrieved from the pawnshop still sat on the coffee table where he'd left it. Tuck looked around at all the fancy sound system and video equipment to go with the gigantic TV screen.

"Nathan liked his movies," Bobby explained. "For some reason, he didn't like going to theaters. He seemed so grateful when DVD came out. I think he bought one of the first ones ever built," Bobby chuckled. "Come to think of it, it's like he knew years ahead and was just waiting."

Tuck peeked into the cabinet. Inside he saw the latest in Blu-ray technology, one of the six-disc carousel models. "Impressive."

Bobby just shrugged and sat on the couch, enjoying the view of Tuck's ass in nothing but his boxer-briefs.

Tuck walked over, still glancing around the room. "So what's the game plan? Are you gonna move all this stuff?"

Bobby nodded. "I guess. Most of the equipment's practically brand-new, hardly a year old. I don't remember seeing even so much as a TV at Odie's."

"Well, with mine, we'll have at least two," Tuck thought aloud.

Gazing up, Bobby got a serious look on his face. "So we're really gonna do this? You're gonna give up your apartment?"

Tuck shrugged. "Why? You having second thoughts?"

"No," Bobby admitted as Tuck sat on the couch next to him. "It's.... I guess it's like something Odie said. I got a gift I didn't even know I wanted."

"Yeah." Tuck nodded in agreement. "Seems like that to me too."

Bobby scooted closer to Tuck and rested his head on the man's bare shoulder. "I can't believe how quickly this is all happening, though."

"Too quick?"

"No, just surprising."

Leaning forward, Tuck picked up the book on the coffee table. "This the book?" he asked.

"The very one."

Tuck turned it over and read the back blurb. "Sounds interesting." He set it down on the couch and nestled closer to Bobby.

Fighting back a yawn, Bobby nodded.

"So, what else you taking?"

"Haven't thought that far ahead. With the housing market the way it is, the real estate agent suggested I might get a better price if I sold the place furnished, or at least partly. No reason to drag all this furniture down to Texas, anyway."

"What about all those vehicles in the garage?"

Bobby shrugged. "Sell them, I guess. Was never into the dirt bikes like Nate was. And his Mustang. Unless you want it?"

"Not particularly. Odie might want one of the bikes; he always enjoyed the 'cycles. What's the other car? The one under the other tarp?"

"Oh. The GranCabrio. I actually kinda like that one, but it wouldn't be practical in Texas, I don't think."

"A what?"

"GranCabrio. Maserati." Bobby sat up a little so he wouldn't fall asleep.

"A Maserati? A *real* Maserati?" Tuck gaped.

Bobby shrugged. "Don't think Nathan would have bought a *fake* one for my birthday."

"You rich bitch," Tuck almost squealed. "A fuckin' birthday present?" he teased. "I've never even *seen* one."

"Oh. We can go look at it, if ya want?"

Tuck nearly jumped off the couch. "Any more silly questions?"

"Well, then," Bobby said with a smirk as Tuck pulled him up to his feet, "to the garage, I guess."

Not sure if he was leading or following, Bobby made his way to the garage, Tuck in tow. The fluorescent lights echoed with a slight hum as they blinked to life and illuminated the large space. Bobby moved to the tarped vehicle by the far wall.

"When did you get it?" Tuck asked as he helped Bobby lift the softened cotton fabric.

"Thirty-fifth birthday," he replied as they slid the fabric away from the car, revealing the green color. Bobby had always thought of it as a light forest green, but some other label tried to worm its way forward in Bobby's tired brain.

As he stepped around to the side to gather more fabric, he froze when his eyes fell on the logo emblazoned in the center of the hubcap. "Damn you, Nate," he said. He felt the spasm of hysterical laughter seconds before the sounds escaped his throat.

"What?" Tuck asked as he froze in place. "Don't go all loco on me, I don't have my Taser."

Bobby leaned against the car as the fits of his diaphragm brought tears to his eyes with each barking laugh. "Logo," he finally managed to say.

Tuck glanced over at the scooped shape of the front grill and saw the symbol. "Oh." He looked over at Bobby. "Looks more like a trident than an algiz, but…."

Bobby managed to get his laughing under control. "From what I've been learning, Nathan always went about things deliberately. This *can't* just be a coincidence," he said as he helped Tuck remove the rest of the cover.

"Guess not," Tuck agreed. "What do you think he meant by it?"

Bobby shrugged. "Who knows?"

Tuck looked over the sleek lines of the gorgeous green automobile. He decided this beautiful vehicle should never be referred to as a mere "car." This was a work of art on wheels. "Can I drive it?"

"Sure," Bobby said. "I guess I'm too practical at heart. Never did get a hard-on over it the way Nate did."

Tuck could hardly take his gaze away as Bobby walked over to the wall and grabbed another tarp.

"Might as well see it all," Bobby said, and he uncovered the blue motorcycle.

Tuck glanced over at the bike and then did a double-take as his jaw dropped open. "Is that a fuckin' Timmin's Cycle?"

"Yeah," Bobby said as he looked down at the blue machine. "That name sounds right." Something about that blue nagged at him. That sky blue. And the green car. That grass green.

"You've gotta be shittin' me," Tuck muttered as he approached the motorcycle. "Do you know how rare these are? Each one is individually custom-made, by hand," Tuck cooed as he ran his fingers along the pectoral-like curve of the upper tank. "The guy even had his own reality show for a while."

Bobby looked up into Tuck's eyes as he admired the motorcycle with the car framed behind him. Then that worming thought suddenly burst forth into the light. The car was the same color as Tuck's eyes. He looked over at the bike again. That sky blue was the color of Odis's eyes. "Oh fuck me," he muttered, trying not to laugh again.

"What now?" Tuck asked in an almost exasperated tone.

Bobby pointed over at the car. "Don't you ever look in the mirror?"

Tuck's brow furrowed in puzzlement as he glanced back at the Maserati. "Of course."

"Nothing familiar about that green?" Bobby hinted.

Tuck still looked puzzled.

"Or maybe that blue?" Bobby asked as he pointed to the Timmin's.

"Not really," Tuck said as he shook his head.

"Eyes," Bobby hinted more strongly, but Tuck still didn't seem to get it. "Odie's eyes." He pointed back at the Maserati. "*Your* eyes."

"Oh," Tuck said as the realization and its implications crept over him. "Loki's nuts."

Bobby laughed. "So I guess you can drive *your* car home, but what should we do about Odie's motorcycle?"

Tuck glanced over at the Prius. "You sure ya want that one?"

"I like my car," Bobby said with a firm nod. "Not giving it up."

"Well," Tuck thought aloud, "I suppose we could rent one of those smaller trucks with enough room for the Timmin's Cycle and whatever personal things ya wanna bring. Then get a car dolly and bring the Prius along behind it."

"That could work," Bobby agreed.

Tuck grinned as he glanced around the garage. "So what other treasures ya got hidden away?"

Bobby grinned. "You haven't seen the Blu-ray collection yet. Or the library."

"Fuckin' *library*?" Tuck teased as he followed Bobby back into the house.

Going across the living room to another short hall, Bobby led Tuck to a smaller room. All four walls were lined with neatly arranged bookshelves.

Tuck looked around at the array of books. "Gods, have you read all these?"

"Only about half," Bobby said from the doorway. Tuck looked back and noticed the calendar hanging on the wall next to the door. It displayed January of 2010, which drew Tuck in for a closer look, since it seemed odd they would have such an out-of-date artifact displayed in the room. Then he saw the picture at the top showed Bobby sitting on a dugout bench, his chest shirtless and glistening as he pulled his leg up as if he was preparing to tie his cleat. The angle also showed off his firm ass hidden in the tight baseball pants.

"We did those for the children's hospital every year," Bobby explained with a shrug. "Kind of a fund-raiser thing for them. Nate saved that one because I was the 'cover boy' that year."

"Really nice picture," Tuck complimented as he waggled his eyebrows.

Bobby grinned. "If you like that one, you should see July."

Tuck grinned. "I'll come have a closer look tomorrow," he said as he stepped past Bobby into the hall. "It's getting late. We should call Odie and get to bed."

"Sure," Bobby agreed, taking Tuck's arm, and pulled him farther along to the end of the hall, where it opened up into a glass-enclosed room. "And this is the solarium."

Tuck gaped at the huge solar space. One side was cluttered with weights, machines, and other workout equipment. On the other side, he saw the narrow pool, which seemed to be shaped for swimming laps. Tuck thought it seemed like the kind of space you might find in a fancy hotel.

"To bed," Bobby said as he tugged at his arm again.

Tuck followed him through the house and back up the stairs. "Ya sure you wanna leave all this? Seems like a helluva house to me...."

"I'm sure," Bobby said as they approached the guest room. "I can't look anywhere without seeing Nate."

"Oh. Right."

Bobby went over to the phone and the business card before remembering Odis was probably at Tuck's apartment. "Your number's not on here," he remarked.

Tuck stepped over to the nightstand and grabbed the receiver before dialing his number and handing the phone to Bobby. While Bobby chatted with Odis, Tuck went down the hall to the bathroom.

WHEN he returned a few moments later, Tuck found Bobby already off the phone and undressing. He leaned against the doorframe and watched as Bobby slid off his T-shirt, and enjoyed the slight ripple of the muscles along Bobby's bare back and spine as Bobby bent down and removed his left sock. The man was hot enough to melt the cover of any calendar he posed for, and he didn't even seem to know it.

Bobby quickly yanked around like he sensed an audience. "Hey," he said playfully as he bent down and slipped off his other sock, wriggling his ass a little this time and drawing a smile from Tuck.

Maybe the man *did* know it. "So how's Odie?" Tuck asked, not trying to hide the appreciative happiness growing in his boxers.

"Sounded chipper. They came out and took measurements for the glass and are installing it tomorrow. Said the studio is fine and he spent half the day there, but power's still out." Bobby glanced down at Tuck's bulging boxer-briefs.

"That's promising."

Bobby playfully smiled. "You plan on sleeping in the doorway?"

"No," Tuck said without moving as he fought a grin. He looked down at the jogging pants Bobby still had on. "Maybe I need some enticement."

Looking back at the growing boxer-briefs, Bobby grinned. "Looks like you're pretty enticed already."

"Not totally," Tuck teased. "Still needs more work."

"Yeah." Bobby smirked. "Forgot you're an old man."

Tuck smirked back. "Better be careful what ya say, young'un. I noticed another bedroom across the hall," he said, peering back over his shoulder for emphasis. "I might just end up in there."

Bobby chuckled. "Well, guess we couldn't have that," he said as he walked up. "Wouldn't be very neighborly for me to make ya sleep alone."

"Not the least neighborly at all," Tuck agreed, trying to keep a firm face.

Bobby held Tuck's gaze as he stepped closer and reached out both hands, using his fingertips to ever so lightly tease along the pectoral lines under Tuck's nipples. The excited little inhaling sound Tuck made sent a shiver through Bobby. "Have I ever told you what a great chest you have?"

"Once. Or twice. I think," Tuck replied with rapid breaths as Bobby teased his fingers around his nipples and across the top of the muscles to his armpits. As he felt Bobby gently explore, Tuck held his gaze. "Is that all ya like? My chest?"

"Top three, or maybe top five," Bobby said as he looked into Tuck's eyes. "Somewhere on the list."

"And what else? Is on this list?" Tuck asked as he relaxed further back against the doorframe, bringing his head a little closer to Bobby's eye level.

"Your eyes," Bobby said as he peered into them and glided his hands back to the front of Tuck's chest. "Your ass, those little dimples in your buttcheeks."

Tuck reached out and brushed his hands down Bobby's sides all the way down to his hips. "And what about my prick?"

"Way too big to be called a prick," Bobby said as he brought his hands together and lightly slid his fingers down the center of Tuck's abs. "That word always makes me think of a needle."

"No," Tuck said nearly in a hiss as Bobby's hands slid farther down. "Not a needle."

Still holding Tuck's gaze, Bobby spread his hands and moved them under the waistband of his boxer-briefs, carefully avoiding the pubic area. "It's a very ample cock," Bobby said without touching it.

"Would ya like? To feel how ample?" Tuck asked with ragged breaths as Bobby's hands teased down his thighs inside his boxers.

"I would."

Tuck slid his hands inside Bobby's jogging pants and lightly massaged his glutes. "I'd like to show you."

"Just need to be slow. I haven't ever bottomed anyone quite your size."

Still holding Bobby's gaze, Tuck leaned forward and kissed him with tenderness and warmth. "I'll give you whatever you need," he breathed into Bobby's ear.

Holding firmly to Tuck's hips, Bobby pulled him toward the bed while sharing another kiss. When he neared the edge, Bobby slid his hands over Tuck's legs, pushing the boxer-briefs down to his knees as Tuck worked the sweatpants past his butt. Each man took over removing the rest of his clothes. Bobby sat on the edge of the bed, using only his tongue to tease at the swelling and protruding head of Tuck's cock, pushing the foreskin further back.

"Oh, stud," Tuck moaned as he grinned at Bobby. "You make me want you right now."

After a teasing nibble at the tip of Tuck's very ready member, Bobby grabbed the lube off the nightstand and slid back onto the bed. He pulled up his knees and used his own lubed fingers to open and loosen himself.

"Gods, you don't know how hot a sight that is," Tuck told him as he kneeled onto the bed.

"Not trying to be hot," Bobby said as Tuck took the lube from his hand.

Tuck chuckled. "Ya don't hafta *try* at all," Tuck complimented with a gentle coo as his larger fingers took over the job of preparing Bobby's sphincter before he slathered up his swollen prick.

As Tuck lined up and pushed his cock in, Bobby tried not to wince. "You're so damn big," he said with a relaxing exhale.

Tuck pulled back. "Ya don't hafta prove anything."

"Don't stop," Bobby nearly begged with another deep breath. "I'm just commenting."

After lining up again, Tuck pushed inside and paused before sliding farther and submerging the whole head of his cock within Bobby. He hesitated when Bobby took another deep breath.

Bobby lifted his feet and started to wrap them around Tuck's waist just below his ribs before he remembered the Easter-egg bruise. He lifted his right leg further, nestling back into the bed as he placed his right ankle over Tuck's shoulder.

"Limber," Tuck commented as he leaned forward and slowly pushed himself deeper into Bobby.

"You don't have to be *that* slow," Bobby urged as he pulled Tuck closer with his feet and brought his ass up to meet Tuck.

Tuck slid his knees forward and, with a quicker thrust, buried himself the rest of the way into Bobby.

Looking into Tuck's eyes, Bobby panted as he grinned. "That's more like it."

Putting his hand on Bobby's shoulder, Tuck tried to lean down enough for a kiss, but the pangs from his bruised side made him stop short. Bobby curled his neck up enough for their noses to brush together.

"Sorry, I can't get close enough to kiss you," Tuck said.

Bobby smiled as he nestled back. Just feeling Tuck so amply inside him was more than enough. "I'll pretend like you are, then. Giving me one of those sparking kisses."

Tuck pulled back and slid forward calmly and carefully a few times while watching Bobby's eyes. Bobby put his hands on Tuck's thighs and rubbed firmly, urging him on. Surprised at himself, Tuck already felt near the edge. Tuck asked, "How much do you need?" as he slid back in at a higher angle, searching for the sweet spot.

"Oh shit," Bobby whispered when Tuck found it on his next stroke. "Not much."

Angling down for two harder and longer thrusts, Tuck brought himself closer, then pushed back up for Bobby's spot again. A fervent moan and the sparkle in Bobby's eyes let Tuck know his aim was true. He watched Bobby's face as he alternated his longer and shorter strokes, working himself and Bobby closer. He saw the veins in Bobby's neck start pulsing as his eyes began glazing over.

"Oh, now," Bobby nearly begged. "I'm—"

Tuck punched at the sweet spot twice as he wrapped his hand around Bobby's cock, but he had to let go when he couldn't brace himself properly on his casted arm. He tried to reposition, but his orgasm wouldn't wait and overwhelmed him with little warning. "Oh fuck," he choked out as his cock swelled and his body stiffened, his spewing spasms squirting inside Bobby, one after another. His back muscles loosened and turned to jelly, tumbling him forward and almost collapsing him on top of Bobby.

"Shit, Tuck. Oh God," Bobby hissed out as he jacked himself one quick stroke and came, gushing all over his own stomach.

Tuck managed to roll them sideways instead of squishing on top of Bobby as he continued pulsing inside of him. "Shit," he whispered again.

Bobby rolled onto his back without dislodging Tuck's still swollen cock. "Damn, Tuck," Bobby muttered between panting breaths as Tuck's cock spasmed again.

"Sorry," Tuck replied meekly. "I was having a little trouble with the cast," he said as he shifted on the bed to get a more comfortable angle.

"Shut up," Bobby teased. "Not talking about that. Do you always come like that?"

Tuck withdrew his softening self and scooted up next to Bobby's side. "Like what?"

"Like—shit," Bobby whispered. "I've never *felt* somebody come like that before. I swear, you got twice as big. And the pulsing. Like a frantic heart beating."

"I guess not," Tuck said with a silly sideways grin. "At least, nobody ever said such a thing." Tuck gazed at Bobby. "Must all be *your* fault, sexy stud."

Bobby leaned over and kissed him with such electric depth Tuck felt like he might come again. Tuck pulled back. "I hope it was okay for you, that I wasn't too clumsy."

"Clumsy?" Bobby asked. "I didn't notice *anything* like that," Bobby chuckled as he scooted off the bed to find a towel. "If that's you being clumsy, bring it on."

CHAPTER
Thirty-Two

TUCK awoke the next morning alone in bed. At least, he assumed it was morning. He stretched out with a yawn, feeling so rested, like he'd slept for twelve hours. Maybe it was afternoon, he thought with a grin.

Thinking about the solarium and all that workout equipment, he climbed out of bed and retrieved some clean jogging shorts and a sleeveless T-shirt from his suitcase. After pulling on the clothes and his grubby high-tops, he headed downstairs in search of Bobby.

Rounding the corner of the kitchen, Tuck found Bobby sitting at the counter bar, reading Nathan's note as he ate his breakfast. It looked like he was on the last page, so Tuck hung back to give him time to finish. When Bobby set down the papers, Tuck strolled into the kitchen. "Mornin', stud."

"Morning," Bobby replied with a smirk. "You didn't tell me about the attic," he said as he got up and went to the freezer. "Frozen waffles okay?"

"Oh," Tuck apologized, "fergot to mention it. Waffles would be great." Tuck sat at the counter. "You sleep well?"

Bobby's grin was all the answer he needed. "Just got up a few minutes ago. It's almost noon already." Bobby popped the waffles into the toaster and got a plate and mug of coffee for Tuck as they warmed up. "Wonder what surprise Nate has now?"

Tuck shook his head before sipping at the coffee. "With Nathan? Who knows?"

"Guess we'll have to go look in a minute," Bobby said as the toaster popped.

Tuck just grinned, watching Bobby as he fished the finished waffles out of the toaster with a fork and brought the plate over to the counter.

Bobby smiled at the silly expression on Tuck's face. "What?"

"Oh, still tryin' to wrap my head around all this. That it's real."

Bobby nodded in confirming silence as he cleaned up his dishes and watched Tuck eat.

"Yer starin' at me," Tuck said as he took his last bite.

"Sorry," Bobby said with a smile. "Guess you're just worth looking at." He took Tuck's empty plate and put it in the dishwasher. "Let's go check the attic before I lose my nerve."

"Okay," Tuck replied. He followed Bobby back upstairs and down the hallway. At the end of the hall, Bobby opened a door Tuck had thought might be a closet, but inside was a half flight of stairs that led over the garage area. He stepped inside as Bobby turned on some fluorescent lights.

At the top, they found a half dozen tall, neat stacks of folded moving boxes, a few cases of rolls of the clear wrapping tape, and two of those handheld tape gun dispensers next to a box of Sharpie markers.

Bobby chuckled. "No excuses, huh, Nate," he said out into the attic space. He turned back to Tuck with a smirk. "Guess he wants us to pack."

Tuck chuckled along. "Seems that'a way." He looked over at Bobby. "Anything else ya want to do today?"

"Guess not," Bobby replied as he picked up the top case of tape and the two dispensers. "Grab some boxes. Might as well start in the library."

After grabbing as large a stack as he could carry and the box of markers, Tuck followed Bobby back downstairs to the library. While Bobby folded up a box and taped the bottom closed, Tuck looked around at the shelves. "Did you want to take *all* of these books?"

Bobby looked around. "Hm, probably not, I guess. But we should pack all of them up," he said as he taped another box. "Should prob'ly make a few categories, gay and non-gay, for donating somewhere, and the ones to take to Texas."

"Okay," Tuck agreed with a nod.

After unfolding and taping up another box, Bobby went to the shelves. "I'll go through and pull out the ones I definitely want to take, and you do the same. Then we can sort the rest as we go," he said as he pulled out some DIY home improvement books and put them into a box.

The guys worked most of the afternoon, building stacks of sealed and labeled boxes, but after glancing around, Tuck surmised they were barely half done with the room.

Noticing the look on Tuck's face, Bobby said, "I guess this is gonna take a few days."

"Reckon so," Tuck agreed.

THEY spent the next three days in a kind of routine, working out in the mornings, packing in the afternoon and evening, then relaxing a bit before bed. On Friday, Bobby took some time in the afternoon when the Realtor dropped by to hash out details to set up an open-house style viewing for Sunday.

About ten on Saturday morning, Bobby got a call from the guard station as they finished a free-weight session. After a brief exchange over the phone, Bobby hung up and turned to Tuck. "Better get dressed," Bobby told him as he headed to the stairs. "Sharon's dropping by."

A few minutes later, Bobby answered the doorbell. "Shar," he called out warmly.

"Don't give me that." She pouted as she entered the living room and saw the stacks of boxes. "Asshole. Didn't even tell me you were packing already," Sharon scolded as she hugged him warmly. She glanced up and saw Tuck on the stairs. "And who's this handsome fellow?" She gazed up with her charming smile.

"This is Tuck from Texas," Bobby said. "He's helping me move."

"Pleased to meet ya," Tuck said as he walked down and offered his left hand for a shake.

Sharon tried not to stare at the cast. "So you're the *other* one." She scoured Tuck with her eyes before turning to Bobby. "I still think this whole three-way thing is weird, but at least he's a keeper."

"Well, thanks," Bobby said sarcastically. "At least I got your approval."

Tuck chuckled. "And yer just like he described," Tuck said as Sharon shook his hand.

"Meaning?"

"He might have mentioned ya were feisty, with a quick tongue."

Sharon glared at Bobby but soon smiled. "Don't believe a thing he says. Now, where's those journals of Nathan's you told me about?"

"Oh." Bobby mocked being wounded. "I see how it is," he said as he led Sharon down to the den. "Don't care about me at all."

"Hush. We can get caught up over lunch. I wanna read those first ones you were talking about."

Tuck tagged along behind them as they went down the stairs to the den. Bobby took Sharon to the untaped box with Nathan's first set of journals. "The red ones," Bobby told her as he turned to Tuck.

Smiling, Tuck said, "Looks like ya got yer hands full. Why don't I go get the car checked out, like we talked about, and leave ya two to gab."

"Okay," Bobby agreed. "Maserati keys are on the hooks right by the fridge. Did you want to bring back some lunch?"

Tuck shook his head. He also had some other plans but didn't want to fill Bobby in on that yet. "Better just scratch yerselves something up. Don't know how long it'll take and all."

"Sure," Bobby said. He gave Tuck a quick kiss. "There's another cell phone in the far-right kitchen drawer. Take it in case you get lost or something."

"Will do. See you later," Tuck called out before heading back up the stairs.

Bobby sat on the couch next to Sharon as she read through the first journal.

"Shit," Sharon nearly spit out. "The poor kid. God, to be thinking this way at such a young age."

"I know," Bobby agreed as Sharon continued reading.

HOURS later, Tuck returned to find Bobby alone, sorting through the kitchen cabinets.

"Hey, stud."

Bobby glanced over. "Hope the car's okay. It took a damn long time," he said a little harshly.

"Sorry," Tuck said as he went to the refrigerator. "You want a beer?"

Bobby shook his head. "Well?"

"Car's fine, I just got caught up drivin' around, I guess." Tuck leaned against the counter but had to shift positions when he noticed how sore his hip felt. "It wasn't *that* long, was it?"

"No, but you didn't get a chance to meet Sharon."

"I met her," Tuck argued. "And thought ya guys might want some alone time. I kinda wanted a few minutes of my own too."

"Sure, I guess," Bobby replied in a flat tone.

"Not that I'm tryin' to say I regret it or anything, but we have been pretty much in each other's faces since Tuesday."

"Oh," Bobby replied. "Where'd you go? Besides the mechanic?"

"Just around," Tuck said with a shrug before sipping at his beer.

"*Around?*" Bobby repeated as he stiffened. "Around where?"

"Why are ya bein' like this?"

"Like *what*? I'm not the one being evasive," Bobby spit out.

Tuck pushed away from the cabinet. "Can't a man have a few minutes of his own?"

"Not when he's keeping secrets," Bobby said. "I had a lifetime's worth of fucking secrets with Nathan. Don't need any more from you."

"Fine," Tuck said as he set his beer on the counter. With his left hand, he undid the top button of his jeans and started undoing the fly buttons.

"What the fuck?" Bobby yelled. "Put your pants back on."

"Shut up and look," Tuck said as he pulled down the elastic of his underwear over his right hip, showing the fresh bandage. "I was gonna show ya later but didn't know ya was gonna get all squirrelly on me."

Bobby stepped forward and looked at the bandage as Tuck peeled away the tape enough to show the new reddened marks inside his sheriff's star tattoo. He could plainly see the new algiz rune tattoo centered within the star. "Oh," Bobby said meekly. "I didn't know."

Tuck smirked as he retaped the bandage and fastened his pants again. "Yer birthdays are gonna be a real bitch if ya keep bein' so damn suspicious."

"Sorry," Bobby said as he helped Tuck with the buttons.

Tuck put his hand under Bobby's chin and pulled his face up to look at him. "And what was this all about? Ya don't trust me?"

"Of course I do, I just—like I said, Nathan's burned me out on secrets."

"Okay," Tuck said with a nod. "Maybe ya should work on that." Tuck leaned down and kissed Bobby's forehead. "And what did ya think I did?"

Bobby shrugged. "I don't know. But you have to admit, with the way you're... built, and that accent of yours, you're a gay man's wet dream."

Tuck laughed. "I don't walk around with my dick hangin' out of my pants, so most guys don't have a clue as to how I'm 'built'. And I'm *very* satisfied with what I already have. I'm not lookin'."

"Okay," Bobby agreed with a sigh. "I'm sorry. I didn't mean to freak out on you."

"I know. We can work on that."

Bobby hugged Tuck close. "I guess I am just a little—protective."

Tuck chuckled. "Possessive, I think is more like it."

Bobby looked down to Tuck's hip. "Isn't that on the wrong side? I mean, where you wear your holster? Shouldn't it be on the left?"

"Yeah, suppose so, but it's such a habit now," Tuck agreed with a head nod. "My Dad never did like the idea of me bein' a south-paw. When I's growing up, I had a toy gun set and he made me wear the holster on my right, hoping I'd use my right hand to draw the gun, I reckon. Never did though. I flipped the holster around so the butt of the gun was in the front and kept using my left hand." Tuck chuckled. "Drove them nuts at the academy too. Always got bad marks for drawing across my body."

"You don't ever talk about your dad much," Bobby commented.

"Not much to say. He wasn't a bad guy, just one of those stoic men that didn't really show emotion. He was never the same after mom got sick, and after she passed, he kinda pulled in and drank himself to death."

Bobby gave him a quick squeeze before pulling away.

Tuck glanced around at the open cabinets and the items on the counters. "I've had enough of this damn packing. What say we knock off for the night, and maybe ya show me off around town, since it's Saturday."

"Sure. But we at least need to make everything presentable first," Bobby said as he went and started putting items back in the cabinets. "We have that open-house thing tomorrow."

"Ya got it, stud," Tuck agreed as he pitched in to help.

Tuck was beginning to think they'd never finish, as the packing process dragged on another week and a half, but Bobby finally declared the job done when the Realtor called with the sale offer. It was much less than the original asking price. After only a token effort at dickering, Bobby took the offer.

By the time they got a truck packed and ready to leave Boston, Odis was already in Atlanta, preparing for his art show. The news altered their plans. Tuck and Bobby decided to drive down to Atlanta first and surprise Odis at his opening.

The clock in the Maserati showed 6:45 p.m. as Tuck followed the rental truck into the parking lot just down the street of the downtown Atlanta gallery. Tuck got out and ran over to the truck. "This thing starts at seven, right?"

"Right," Bobby said as he leaned down from the open-doored cab of the rental truck. "Won't be any time to find a hotel or anything first."

Tuck raised his arm and sniffed at his pit. "Shit, and I think the both of us could use a shower first."

Bobby looked down at the rumpled jeans and the wrinkly T-shirt clinging to Tuck's frame. "We can at least find someplace to change," Bobby said as he reached back into the cab and grabbed his duffel bag. "Guess that'll hafta do." He locked up the cab and followed Tuck to his car. "Did you tell Odie we were coming?"

"Nah, told him we wouldn't be leaving 'til May," Tuck replied as he got his own bag from the trunk of the Maserati.

"He should be surprised, then." Bobby had looked up this area of Atlanta on Internet maps the night before, so he led the way around the corner and down the sidewalk to the gallery. Just inside the door, they found a restroom to use.

Tuck walked up to the mirrors to check his hair after changing. "How's this?" he asked Bobby, ruffling through his hair with his fingers.

Bobby smiled. The new black jeans Tuck had put on still had that crisp, creased look to them, so they almost looked like slacks. And he wore his green Navajo-print shirt to show off his eyes. "Yummy enough to eat," Bobby teased. "Just wish we'd had enough time to get tuxedos or something."

Tuck nodded in agreement. "Never been to one of these opening things. Have you?"

"Opening for an art gallery once. The whole thing was so hoity-toity, I didn't hang around," Bobby said as he watched himself in the mirror and played with the collar of his polo-style shirt, trying to get it centered.

"Quit fussin', ya look fine," Tuck told him. "We should get on out there, I guess."

"Let's do it, then," Bobby agreed as he followed Tuck out the door and back into the foyer area. They followed the signs pointing upstairs to an open loft space. Once at the top of the stairs, they had to squeeze and nearly fight their way through the crowd to get around the corner.

Tuck smirked as they navigated the throng. "Wow, are they all here just 'cause it's a show, or do they *know* Odie's work?"

"Who can say?" Bobby replied. "Does seem like a huge crowd, though."

They managed to get around the corner of the landing and into the open loft show space. Bobby froze when he saw the plaque on the easel stand by the doorway advertising the name of the show:

Balls In Flight
Sculpture work of Odis Vorleik.

Tuck gave him a suspicious look. "*Balls*? In flight?"

"Don't ask me," Bobby whispered in a worried tone. "Did you ever see any of the pieces?"

With a headshake, Tuck replied in a hushed voice, "No. I sure as hell hope he didn't go all homo…." He trailed off as he led Bobby forward by the arm. "Better find out, I guess."

Holding each other's arms, the two made their way forward into the cavernous space buzzing with the noise of many conversations. They noticed the large curtain toward the back, maybe shielding another work for a big reveal later.

Bobby relaxed when he saw the first piece near the door, a work about a foot tall of an oversized baseball, surrounded by clumps of tall grass, with a hummingbird perched atop it. The whimsical work immediately brought to mind thoughts of summer. "Ah. The show's named for baseballs and hummingbirds."

"Hm," Tuck teased with a smile as he gazed down at Bobby, "wonder what inspired that?"

Bobby gave his arm a firm squeeze. "Hush."

Both men froze when they saw the little placard advertising a price, with at least one too many zeros in it. "Holy shit," they echoed at nearly the same time.

Shaking his head in disbelief, Bobby whispered, "You think it's worth *that* much?"

Tuck shrugged. "Don't ask me. I'm used to shopping at Walmart."

They made their way along the wall to the next piece. This one depicted a baseball bat with a gun holster stuck on the handle end.

Grinning over at Tuck, Bobby squeezed his arm. "Looks like I'm not the only inspiration," he teased back.

They passed by more of the sculpture works, each seemingly inspired by some aspect of Bobby or Tuck, as they made their way to the giant curtain in central back area.

"You see him anywhere?" Bobby asked, craning his neck to try to peer through the crowd.

"Not yet," Tuck replied, gazing around from his taller vantage. Movement that looked like a short blond-haired man near the curtain grabbed his attention. "Over there," he said as he led Bobby toward the back.

They found Odis bouncing around all agitated and saying something to an older woman. "I don't wanna be here all night. Let's do it now."

The other woman frowned at Odis. "But it's not scheduled until nine, honey. Lots of patrons won't even show up any sooner."

"What am I gonna do 'til then?" Odis nearly whined.

Tuck stepped up and cleared his throat. "We having a problem?" he asked in his strong cop voice.

The woman glanced up, looking surprised and flustered. "No, sir," she replied.

Bobby's heart swelled in his chest when he saw that huge grin beaming from Odis's face.

"Bonehead!" Odis cheered as he rushed forward and hugged him. "And stud!" he yelled as he reached out an arm and pulled Bobby into the hug. "What the hell? Thought you'ns still in Boston?"

Tuck noticed the woman used her opportunity to slip away.

Bobby grinned back, leaning down almost close enough to kiss him before he caught himself and stopped. "We couldn't miss your big night. Wanted to surprise you."

"Well, it worked," Odis said while squeezing the guys and beaming that huge grin again.

Tuck pulled back a little but kept his hand on Odis's shoulder. "And what was that argument all about?"

Odis shook his head. "Just a disagreement. I wanna do the reveal now, so I don't hafta hang around."

Bobby frowned. "But aren't you supposed to mingle?"

"Been doin' that for three hours already. I'm tired."

Tuck patted his shoulder. "I thought it didn't start 'til seven?"

"Not officially, but some of 'em started showing up at four. Seems another Vorleik show is a bigger deal than I thought. Some guy even came all the way down from Toronto just for this."

"No shit?" Bobby asked, wide-eyed. "We noticed the price tags look pretty healthy."

Odis smirked. "I *know*, right? And that's after I talked 'em down a bit."

"So," Tuck asked as he motioned to the curtain, "what's back there?"

Odis grinned. "I'm not tellin'. My boys will just hafta wait like everybody else." He glanced down at their empty hands. "Ya didn't find the buffet yet?"

Bobby shook his head. "No. Wanted to find you first."

"Well, then," Odis said as he led them toward a larger crowd in the corner, "libations await."

As they made their way to the back, the throng seemed to part open a bit when they saw Odis coming. He smiled and mostly shrugged off the greetings from the other patrons while stepping up to the table. "Have some grub," he told his boys before turning to shake hands with an older gentleman.

"Odie V?" A strong feminine voice sang out from the corner of the crowd.

Odis sort of froze in place, looking toward the source of the voice. Tuck clutched at Bobby's arm and quietly hissed, "Shit, I hope that ain't Tina."

"Odie V?" the voice called out again.

Odis smiled widely when he recognized someone in the crowd and stepped in her direction. "Is that you, Marigold?"

Marigold reached back and grabbed at someone. "Told ya. He's right here by the food." She stepped closer to Odis and pulled him into a warm hug. "About time ya did another show."

Odis gave her an air kiss. "Is that Rustler and Moonbeam I see over there too?"

"Sure is," she said, waving back at them again.

"So great ya showed up," Odis said as he led her to the table. "There's some guys I want ya to meet."

Odis stepped up between Tuck and Bobby, putting an arm around each man's waist. "Boys, this here's Marigold Sunflower. This is Tuck and Bobby."

Tuck reached out his hand. "Pleasure to meet you."

"Hello," Bobby said with a smile.

Marigold turned back and waved Rustler over again before smiling at Odis. "I'm guessing yer not with Tina anymore?"

"Nope. She made her leave of me four years ago."

Rustler and Moonbeam finally made it through the crowd. Marigold turned to them with a grin. "I think Odie has big news for us."

Rustler stared over at the men, focusing a moment on Bobby. "Bobby Lane?" he finally asked.

THE sextet ate and chatted warmly for over an hour. Tuck was surprised to learn the Sunflowers had just celebrated their eighteenth anniversary. The news left him feeling hopeful that three-ways *could* work in the long run.

The older woman Odis had been conversing with earlier, whom Odis introduced as Harriet, the gallery owner, pulled Odis aside. "It's almost nine."

Odis followed her to the platform next to the curtain. She gave a signal to kill the music. As the room hushed and eyes turned their way, she said, "Now for a few words from our artist, Odis Vorleik."

He stepped forward to a quiet spattering of applause. "Thank ya all for coming out here tonight. It's been a while since I had a show, and nice to see ya haven't forgotten me."

Another spattering of applause made Odis pause. "I'm sure you've noticed from the other pieces a bit of a theme running through the works. Well, no need to drag this out," Odis said as he reached for the curtain button. "I present to you the central piece, *Cleats in Clay*." Odis pushed the button, and the curtain parted in the middle and slid quickly open.

The patrons in the room let out a hushed coo as they took in the phenomenal work that stood nearly five feet high. The piece's tall central column was fashioned from a nearly transparent blue acrylic, giving the illusion of a jet of water flowing forth from a garden spigot resting at the top. At the bottom of the column, the acrylic beaded and bounced like water as it splashed over a pair of cleats, a dirt-smudged baseball, and a sheriff's star badge, fashioned from white clay and coated with a shimmery glaze that looked nearly gold. While the background was stunning in its own right, the most spectacular part of the work was the three large hummingbirds that played and flirted around the column of water, seemingly floating in midair amidst sparkles of bursting pink fireworks that defied gravity.

Marigold finally broke the silence of the room, first whispering out, "Fantabulous." Then, she said a bit louder, "You have *so* outdone yerself, Odie V."

Bobby still couldn't find words. Every area of the huge sculpture his eyes landed on bore some small token of him, or Tuck, or Odis. The molded monument to the three of them was beautiful beyond his describing. He glanced down at the placard, wondering how many zeros were in *this* work's price tag, only to find the words "No Sale" displayed.

Tuck noticed Bobby's stare, then glanced down at the placard. He stepped over to the platform and quietly asked Odis, "No Sale? Why not?"

"Bonehead," Odis leaned over and whispered. "I made it for you two."

Tuck glanced over and saw Bobby shaking his head violently. Bobby spoke up. "Odie, that's too fucking beautiful for us to just drag it home and throw it in a closet. It needs to be someplace where people can see it and appreciate it."

Odis looked over at Tuck, nodding in agreement. "Okay, then." He went over to Harriet and told her to put a price on it. She scurried away, then returned a few moments later and changed the placard.

As Bobby stared at the incredibly large number, Odis stepped up. "I've had more than enough. Let's say bye to the Sunflowers and y'all can follow me to my hotel."

"Sounds good to me," Tuck agreed as Bobby nodded.

CHAPTER
Thirty-Three

THIRTY minutes later, they made it inside Odis's hotel room. Before the door had even clicked closed, Odis stripped off the jacket and frantically worked the buttons to get his shirt off as he kicked away his shoes. Shirt finally removed, he ran over and stretched out on the king-size bed. "Get over here."

Bobby and Tuck both chuckled. "Somebody in a hurry?" Tuck asked.

"I just wanna feel your hands on me," Odis said. "So get over here."

As Bobby walked up to the bed, he saw the new splash of color on Odis's chest, just over his left nipple. He stepped closer and saw the new tattoo of a yellow six-pointed sheriff's star with a red algiz rune in the center. "A tat?"

Tuck noticed it too. "Ya got inked?" Tuck laughed when he got close enough to make out the work.

"Why's that funny?" Odis asked.

Tuck undid his pants and opened them enough to reveal his right hip. His new algiz rune in his sheriff's star was done in black ink, but the tattoos looked nearly identical otherwise.

Tuck sat on the bed and rubbed his large hand over Odis's bare chest. Odis smiled. "I did think about a hummingbird but was afraid I'd be disappointed if it weren't as good as Bobby's."

While Tuck leaned down and locked lips with Odis for a gentle kiss, Bobby unbuttoned his polo shirt and slipped it over his head. He kneeled down on the bed close enough for Odis to see the new ink on his own chest, a small six-pointed star with an algiz rune. His new star was much simpler and positioned in front of his hummingbird, looking almost like a flower the bird was feeding on.

"Oh cool," Odis said when he pulled back from Tuck.

"I guess we all think alike," Bobby said before moving in to kiss Odis while Tuck pulled off his shirt.

"Loki's nuts," Odis said with a sigh as he reached up and pulled the men down next to him on either side. "I *really* missed you guys."

"Oh," Bobby teased. "How much?"

"About ten pieces' worth," Odis said with a grin. Tuck and Bobby both gazed back, looking puzzled. "I was only supposed to do five pieces for the show tonight, but keeping myself distracted in the studio while you's gone, I came up with fifteen sculptures."

"Wow." Tuck kissed him slowly on the lips. "Busy little bee, huh?"

Odis chuckled. "I even got into your toy drawer too."

Bobby grinned. "Why am I not surprised."

"It's not the same, though," Odis said as he slid his hands down to the men's crotches to fondle their growing erections. "Ain't nothin' like the real thing."

"I thought you's tired," Tuck teased as he ran his hand along Odis's stomach.

"Not too tired for my boys," Odis replied with a twinkle in his eyes.

Bobby reached down and unclasped Odis's slacks before zipping down the fly. "*Boys*, huh? Last time you said we were big men."

Odis pulled Bobby down into a warm and fuzzy kiss to shut him up as Tuck worked his hand into his open slacks and fondled his swelling dick. Odis felt Tuck's strong hands pulling down his boxers; then a hot and moist mouth surrounded his dick, bringing it to full attention.

"Oh shit," Odis hissed out as he pulled back from Bobby. "That ain't your hand."

"Just let us say hello," Bobby scolded before he smothered Odis in another kiss. Odis squirmed underneath him as Tuck worked his hot mouth up and down on Odis's swelling dick.

Odis squirmed again and tried to pull away as his orgasm drew closer, but Bobby held him pinned with his kiss and firm hands rubbing across his chest. Tuck slowed his movements but applied a bit more suction, drawing the orgasm from Odis.

As he came, the little man bucked, and Bobby released his mouth. Odis whispered, "Oh fuck," as he panted and his body shivered, releasing weeks of sexual tension into Tuck's mouth. Tuck greedily suctioned and swallowed.

With a grin, Tuck crawled up to the head of the bed as Odis continued to pant and spasm.

Sounding almost hurt, Odis asked, "Why'd ya do that? Make me come so soon?"

"Too tired for any big-assed thing," Tuck told him. "But it seemed like you needed it," he said with a crooked smile as he gazed over at Odis.

Bobby nodded. "We'll have plenty of time to catch up tomorrow," he added as he undid his jeans and worked his way out of the denim before throwing them to the floor. He started to hug in to Odis until he saw Tuck sitting up and struggling with his cowboy boots. Bobby jumped up and ran around the bed to help while Odis also undressed. Tuck was soon naked to his boxer-briefs.

Bobby crawled into the middle of the king-size bed and rolled to his left side. "Over here, Odis," he said as he patted the bed in front of him. Tuck spooned in against Bobby's back, resting the fiberglass cast across his hip as Odis turned out the lights. Bobby wrapped his arm around Odis when he crawled in front of him. Bobby heard Tuck yawn as he patted Odis's chest.

As the three of them settled in, it dawned on Bobby that he'd forgotten to tell Odis about the Timmin's Cycle. *Well*, he thought with a yawn, *it can wait until tomorrow. Or even until we get home.* A grin spread across his face when he realized his own thought. Texas, and these men, felt like home now. Another yawn pulled him toward sleep as he hugged against Odis and nestled into Tuck. It felt so nice to have a home again.

APPENDIX

Letter from Nathan found in safe by Bobby and Tuck on April 6:

Hey Lover,

I know you have spent the last months utterly pissed at me because of the things I've kept from you. And I know it will be at least a year after finding this note before you can appreciate my final gift. Right now, you probably don't even want to look at them, but eventually you will.

I'm not sure when you might see this note. The window of possibility is open from as early as April to as late as August, depending on how things roll out.

But, if Tuck is the one reading this to you, then even though Tuck may disagree as he rubs his cast, things really have rolled out by the best scenario.

I've really hated keeping all this secret from you. So many days, I had to fight not to spill my guts about the aneurism or my visions. But Sharon helped keep me on track. Not so much directly, but the memory of how it changed our relationship back when I had that weak moment and spilled everything to her back in high school kept me steady.

Right now, you're probably craving answers. Most of those answers will be buried somewhere in my journals. (Yes, I know, *another* fucking secret, I bet you're thinking)

Please don't blame Sharon or Ivette, they don't deserve it, and know very little, actually. So leave the poor girls alone.

Just as background, you should read the first three red notebooks before looking at any others. Most of the time, you don't, though. I only see Tuck, Odis, and sometimes Sharon reading those. But I wish you would.

If this is April or May as you read it (or should I say, as Tuck reads it ☺ that seems to happen in most early scenarios), I know your biggest bone of contention is how I could allow April 3 to happen. I know that will have been a horrible day for you, but you'll have to trust me. Maybe after you read some of the past journals and you see some of my past decisions and consequences, you'll be more willing to put faith in me. But April 3 *had* to happen. Any attempt to forestall or avoid it leads to a much worse disaster because of the gears already in motion.

I guess I need to back up a little on that explanation. When I took my little road trip in August (Tuck: July-August of six years ago, in the yellow three-ring binder is where to find details about our little "accident"... I know you're anxious to read about it), I confirmed then how integral Tuck was to a life with you and Odis. Dammit, I'm getting sidetracked. I'll have to get back to those two later.

Anyway, on my road trip in August, I ran into a squirrelly dude, Carl Travie, at the gas station on my way out of town. When I touched his arm, I saw all the details of April. As Tuck would put it, there's a fox in the henhouse of the Sheriff's Department. Carl is actually a cousin of the Thursons who set himself up to be their "inside man" with the law enforcement office. If April 3 doesn't happen, later evidence will surface of Carl's duplicity, leading to May 7, a *very* bad day. Trying to confront Carl results in a hostage situation that spirals out of control and leads to five deaths, one of them very close to home.

Also, if the fire doesn't happen on April 3, a much worse one will spark on May 14, with strong winds blowing from the west, as they tend to do in the summer months, and parts of the town will succumb. The charred ground seems to keep that one from starting.

So please trust me. April 3 *is* the best scenario.

Okay, I'm sure by now thoughts of Ricky have crossed your mind. Especially if you've already had your little heart-to-heart with Tuck (I only see Odis there about half the time). Anyway, your suspicions are right. I did see it coming. But like so many of these other situations, we were caught up in gears already in motion. Nothing you did could have prevented that outcome. The details might have been slightly different, but it seems Ricky was destined to take his own life.

By the time we met on June 3, Ricky's psyche was already damaged beyond repair. Gerry gets sole blame for that. His manipulations and abuse left Ricky so battered and broken, Ricky couldn't see any other way out.

And don't worry, it will all catch up with Gerry in June. His latest victim won't be as scarred, cajoled, or intimidated as the others, and he gets the word out about Gerry's predatory truth.

Once Gerry is no longer at the house, you will have an opportunity to mend some bridges with your mother. But don't expect too much. Gerry has been feeding her bullshit for the last twenty-five years, leaving her saturated with poison. I'm sorry it won't result in more. Try not to set yourself up to get hurt again.

Okay, back to Odis and Tuck.

I've never in my life seen a bigger mess than those two. They're like star-crossed lovers five times over. Even Shakespeare would have thrown up his hands at dealing with them.

So, you're probably wondering how all this even came about. Well, from the second I walked into that Key West gallery and saw Odis, I had an image of you two (Odis and Bobby, in case Tuck is reading this) along with that stupid rune stuck in my head. That rune plagued me and nagged at me like an evil spirit. After talking to Odis, I also saw Tuck. It took some time for me to realize the rune was speaking of unity between the three of you.

But the whole thing was such a complicated quagmire. I did my best to set things up for you to meet Odis first and provide some hints to guide you along the way (by the way, hope you enjoyed the Arvin book, I found it strangely comforting. Don't let Odis read it, though; just trust me on that).

I can only hope things work out. I still see a 5 percent chance that you meet Tuck first, which will complicate matters a bit, but it should still be workable.

If things take one of those twists and you don't find this until July or August, your concerns will be of a much different variety. I can only say, I tried to deal with Mother as best I could, and trying to get you away from the business is for your own sake. I don't see anything but misery ahead for you if you stay in Boston. You *have* to get your ass out of here. If Texas is screwed (and don't give up on it too soon, Odis is stubborn but not stupid, and Gertie can be a strong ally), then look to Denver. Follow that lawyer kid's lead to Colorado.

Well, I guess this is it. I've always kept my promise to look out for you, and I still am, by steering you in the best possible direction after I'm gone.

I wish I was there to give my Buzzer a warm hug when I say thank you. I sincerely mean that. Thank you for letting me have a more or less normal life, and I will always love you with all that my heart has to give.

You never failed to leave me the space I needed, to be who I needed to be. Don't ever forget to do that. Your future lovers will need it as much as I did.

Hugs and Kisses Forever,
Nathan Ichabod Price
P.S.: I left you something in the attic.

JACKSON CORDD first attempted writing in junior high, when he put together an eight-page comic book. His lack of drawing skills doomed the work to failure, though. In high school, he learned to rely on the words alone and placed third in a regional short story contest his senior year. (He still feels he didn't get first place only because of the homoerotic elements).

To get a steady paycheck, he works in the software industry writing and proofreading programs and manuals, but he returns to weaving the tales of his hunky fantasy men at night.

Visit Jackson on Facebook: https://www.facebook.com/profile.php?id=100003616877972.

Also from JACKSON CORDD

DUANTA BEADS

JACKSON CORDD

Romance from DREAMSPINNER PRESS